# Kn
# Knock

# BOOKS BY CHRIS MERRITT

# Knock Knock

## Chris Merritt

bookouture

Published by Bookouture in 2020

An imprint of Storyfire Ltd.
Carmelite House
50 Victoria Embankment
London EC4Y 0DZ

www.bookouture.com

ISBN: 978-1-83888-0-200
eBook ISBN: 978-1-83888-0-194

*For my Irish Nan, who loved to tell a story.*

# PART ONE

# CHAPTER ONE

If she'd known it was to be her last night alive, he wondered, how would she have spent it? Gossiping in an overpriced bar with her friends and dancing until the early hours? Or hooking up with one of those square-jawed randoms she seemed to collect on Tinder? Perhaps she'd get sentimental, gathering her relatives privately for a solemn, tearful goodbye. Knowing her, though, his guess was hosting an obscenely expensive, self-aggrandising charity bash with champagne and fireworks. She certainly wouldn't have chosen to sit alone like this, tapping away her final hours at a computer.

Standing in darkness opposite her house, he watched her through the porthole window in her garden wall. She was sitting at her desk in the study, totally absorbed in her own world, oblivious to his observation. If only she knew what he had planned for her.

His memory of the last one was still sharp and fresh, setting his skin tingling and his heart racing as he recalled it. The whore's initial reluctance to play his little game by slipping the ring on to her finger. Her frown of discomfort shifting to full-blown terror as she realised what was happening. The panic as her windpipe closed and the oxygen in her lungs started to run out. Then the light in her eyes fading as her brain slowly shut down. He'd never felt so potent.

He had all that to look forward to again tonight. Except that, this time, it'd be so much more meaningful. Like the rest of her kind, this one was promiscuous, duplicitous, treacherous. She had to pay for what she'd done to him. For what they were doing to men everywhere. This would be another step towards restoring the natural order of humanity: man dominating woman. And it was just the beginning. There were many more of those steps to come, with little chance of anyone being able to stop him. He'd arranged it too carefully.

People called him a 'planner' as though it was a bad thing, rolling their eyes and switching off whenever he started to go into the details of stuff. Well, they'll want to know all about his *planning* once her body is discovered. He guessed that'd be some time tomorrow. Then the media feeding frenzy would start, scavengers picking over her carcass while the public gobbled up their news coverage like swarming locusts. He couldn't wait.

There was one individual out there that he particularly wanted to take notice. The man who'd guided him gently along the rocky road, shepherded him through the storm, helped him rebuild. His protector, his advisor, his mentor. And when He heard about this, He'd understand what was going on. He'd be pleased, because this is exactly what He wanted.

Through the window pane, he saw her shrug off her fluffy dressing gown without taking her eyes from the screen. Underneath were those blue silk pyjamas she loved. They were his favourite too. Despite loathing her and everything she represented, he could admire the way those pyjamas shimmered and slid against her skin for hours. But it was time to act, now.

Dipping a hand into his coat pocket, he extracted the little black box. Carefully, he prised it open and made a final check that he had the ring ready. Satisfied, he tucked it back into his jacket, picked up the rest of his gear and crossed the road towards her front gate. Reaching out with a gloved hand, he pressed his fingertips to the wrought iron and felt it yield. The gate opened silently.

She should've put a lock on it.

# CHAPTER TWO

Detective Inspector Dan Lockhart glanced at his watch as he marched up the path towards the Victorian red-brick building that housed the South-West London Trauma Clinic. The large Suunto display on his wrist read '07:55'. Five minutes early. Spot on. And he knew they'd start on time; his therapist, Dr Green, had been ready at 8 a.m. sharp every one of the last ten Tuesday mornings. Americans were punctual like that, they didn't waste your time. He could do the hour's session, jump back in the car and be at work in Putney by 9.15 if he was lucky. Nice one. Reaching the large wooden front door, he saw that it was off the latch. That was unusual. He listened and, over the antiquated heating that rumbled like a tractor engine, thought he could hear Dr Green's deep, soft voice coming from the reception in calm, hushed tones. He gave the door a cautious push and it swung open soundlessly.

Then he froze.

Lexi Green was facing him from the other side of the large waiting area, her hands raised, palms open. Shielded behind her were two more clinic staff: another psychologist who Lockhart knew was called Dr Edwards, and the administrator, Maureen. All three of them were staring at the man in front of Green. He was an older guy – maybe sixty – with thin grey hair combed across a bald patch that gleamed under the strip lighting. About five ten, twelve stone. He wore a tracksuit and his right arm was extended towards Green. Lockhart crept over the threshold and sideways to get a better view. The guy was holding out a 12-inch black-handled kitchen knife. It was raised, shaking slightly, the tip of its massive blade so close to Green's neck that Lockhart saw it catch briefly on the skin of her throat. Her eyes flicked to him in a split-second of recognition, but she returned her attention immediately to the man threatening her.

'None of you move!' barked the guy. 'No alarms, yeah?'

Was he a criminal off the street? A drug user looking for a fix? Or a patient who'd wandered in from one of the hospital's secure psychiatric wards, his aggression simply the result of anxiety and disorientation? Lockhart couldn't tell. And right now, it didn't really matter. The most important thing was the knife about an inch away from Green's throat.

'It's OK,' she responded gently. 'It's all right.'

Lockhart was absolutely still. The guy hadn't heard him come in over the noise of the heating. He slowed his breathing, feeling in his trouser pocket for the Leatherman multi-tool he always carried, with its own blade tucked away. Just in case. He scanned the room: another exit to Green's left through the reception, a lampstand he could use as a weapon, a fire alarm on the far wall. None of it accessible without giving himself away. Slowly, carefully, he eased the door to behind him.

He'd have to deal with this situation here and now.

One option was to try a 999 call from his coat pocket, knowing that if he subsequently pressed 5-5 on the keypad without saying anything, a police car would be dispatched to his location straight away. Could he be sure of hitting '5' twice on the touchscreen, though? It wasn't like in the old days with actual buttons you could feel... and it would take too long. Second option was to stealth his way up behind the guy and tackle him, controlling the knife and allowing Green to push the alarm and get out. But that was risky. The third option would be to create a distraction, and hope that—

'Delivery!'

The door behind him flew open and Lockhart instinctively dodged as the heavy wood came at him. The knifeman looked over his shoulder towards the postal worker in the doorway; each as startled as the other. Lockhart knew this was the moment. The knife was six strides away, he reckoned.

Lockhart had taken three before there was a blur of movement. Green's hand shot out and grabbed her assailant's wrist, turning it as her other hand swept across, breaking his grip and pulling the handle towards her. The whole sequence took less than a second and by the time Lockhart reached them, Green was holding the knife. She was breathing heavily, but she was in control. She took a swift step away as Lockhart closed in on the guy, pulling his arm behind his back and bending his wrist up. But without his weapon, the attacker's energy seemed to be gone and after a few seconds' struggle, he stopped resisting and Lockhart manoeuvred him to the wall. He glanced across at Green and nodded. She nodded back, still clutching the knife.

'I'll call security,' said Maureen. 'That's the second time this month.'

⁎

Lexi Green was still shaking slightly as she plucked Dan Lockhart's file off her desk and took her seat opposite him.

'You sure you're OK?' he asked.

'Usually people don't come here to ask me that,' she replied, forcing a brief smile, aware that the humour was probably the result of her nerves. The adrenalin dump after the flight-or-fight reaction. Was it better to call off the session? No, she reasoned; Dan was here, she was unharmed. Security had escorted the knife-wielding patient back to his locked ward. Everyone was OK. Oh, and there was the money she didn't particularly want to lose: £80 for the hour. She cleared her throat. 'Seriously, I'm fine.'

'It's just… you've had a knife to your neck. Most people don't, you know,' he shrugged, 'start their morning like that.'

'Actually, there's like five hundred assaults a year on staff in this hospital. Guess it was my lucky day.' She knew police officers were attacked by members of the public far more frequently – eleven times every day across the capital, in fact – but there was always a physical threat in the National Health Service, too. That was the reality of the NHS.

'It's totally blunt,' she said as an afterthought, opening the manila file and taking out the notes from their last session. 'That knife. He got it from our kitchen. It can barely cut bread.'

'Still could've hurt.'

'I know.' She picked up her Montblanc ballpoint pen and clicked the top a few times. Stared at it as a memory stirred of the person who'd given it to her. Someone she'd lost, but whom she'd always love. She shook her head. 'We need to stop wedging the doors open, anyone can come in. Thank God there were no other clients in the waiting room.'

He pressed his lips together, nodded. 'Yeah. This clinic's meant to fix trauma, not cause it, right?'

Dan met her gaze, a mischievous look on his face. She wanted to laugh, but their conversation had already strayed a little too far and she needed to bring it back inside the boundaries. So, she settled for a non-committal: 'Hm.'

Breaking eye contact to check her notes, Lexi clicked her pen a bunch more times; she knew it was a kind of nervous tic. When she raised her eyes again, Dan was glaring at the pen.

'By the way,' he said, reaching into his jacket pocket and producing a smartphone which he placed on the low table between them, 'I'm on call at the minute. Well, sort of. Technically our team's "in frame", meaning there's a spreadsheet somewhere that claims we haven't got enough work to do. So, I've got to keep this on today. Sorry.'

Lexi made a note: *In frame.* It was always useful to know a client's expressions from their profession, community, family. A person's choice of words often held the key to what was going on in their mind. She was aware that Dan's job had the potential for trauma exposure every day: he was a detective in a murder squad, or Major Investigation Team, as he'd told her it was officially called. Ordinarily, she'd suggest he took a break from the MIT while their treatment proceeded, but as there was no let-up in the demand for his expertise, that wasn't practicable. They'd have to treat his trauma while he worked. Besides, she knew he hadn't told the Met that he was having these sessions.

'No problem,' she said. 'OK, let's make a start, then. How's the past week been, generally?'

'Let's see.' He blew out his cheeks and exhaled slowly. 'More of the same.' He closed his eyes briefly, and when he opened them again she saw his gaze flit from window to door and back, his fingers drumming on the chair's armrests. She jotted: *Hypervigilance?* Dan Lockhart had a complex presentation of trauma. He'd referred himself to her as a private client, after the successful recovery of an old friend from his military days. Bob's post-traumatic stress disorder was from his combat experiences in Iraq; his PTSD flashbacks were triggered in London years later by oncoming car headlights, and Lexi had treated him at the clinic. Bob knew Dan was having a hard time, and suggested he try some therapy. Understandably, Dan didn't want to wait a year on the NHS list. So, as a public servant she offered him a discounted rate; he agreed, and they started the following week, choosing an 8 a.m. slot before her regular NHS caseload started at nine.

Lexi remembered when he'd first walked into her consulting room: the short, neat hair, straight back, broad shoulders, long wiry limbs, North Face jacket and polished shoes with double-knotted laces. A face that was more soulful than handsome, yet alert, like a foxhound. Her immediate reaction at their first meeting had been that this was a man she could trust, who'd be there for her if she ever needed him. Somehow, Dan just made her feel safe. But Lexi's job was to help *him*, so she'd had to push down the desire to be enveloped, to draw on that sense of safety he exuded.

Dan reminded her so much of a younger version of her own dad that it was uncanny, even a little weird, given that she found herself kind of attracted to him. Freud would've had something to say about that, for sure. Because of those similarities, she'd have guessed Dan's background even if she didn't know he'd worked with Bob: *you can take the boy out of the military...* Same as her father; even once he'd left the US Air Force, he continued to live like he was still in it, from the way he answered the phone to the way he pressed his pants.

Although that first assessment with Dan had been ten weeks ago, her professional formulation of his problems was still evolving. It'd taken a long time for him to open up to her. She got the impression he wasn't a guy with a wide circle of friends, nor did he give out his trust easily. He spent part of the first few sessions asking about the forensic psychology books on her shelves until she gently steered them back to what was going on for him. But once he began to disclose, there was a whole lot to unpack.

Dan had seen friends blown up by roadside bombs and witnessed body parts strewn around a helicopter crash site. He'd performed emergency first aid under fire, twice, and had a soldier die in his arms while he tried to resuscitate him. That was worse than most people could imagine in a lifetime. There was more there, she knew it. Things he'd done. And yet, that wasn't the stuff he wanted to fix.

The main problem he reported was coming to terms with the loss of his wife, Jess. *That* was the complex part. One day, while he was on a tour of duty in Afghanistan, ten years ago, Jess hadn't picked up for their usual weekly phone call. His subsequent attempts to message her had also met with silence.

The day after, Dan had asked his mum to go to their apartment and check on her. And that was where the mystery started. The door was unlocked, but his wife wasn't at home. No note, no word, nothing. Just gone.

The police had investigated, of course, but they hadn't found anything. There were no witnesses who'd seen her leaving the flat, no cameras capturing her journey away from it. Dan had told Lexi about the various theories that'd been proposed by the Met: an accident, where she'd fallen into the nearby Thames and been washed out to sea; an abduction, though there appeared to be no motive for that; and – the explanation favoured by Jess's family – that she'd had a 'breakdown' of some sort and run away. For Dan, those options either meant that Jess was dead, that someone was stopping her from coming back, or that she'd chosen not to come back. He wouldn't accept any of those possibilities; Lexi guessed it was probably because each was too painful for him to bear. She had pushed him, a little, on what he thought had happened, but he simply said he didn't know. If he did have a theory of his own, she knew he'd share it when he was ready.

Lexi hypothesised that Dan might have PTSD from the moment his mum told him his wife was missing. It'd be uncommon, but possible. Equally, she thought he might also have something she'd been reading about, called Prolonged Grief Disorder – a relatively new diagnosis that was less about trauma, more about longing and bereavement. And that was a big thing for Dan: he didn't believe his wife was dead, despite her family thinking otherwise. One of Lexi's theories was that this belief could be stopping him from processing his loss, keeping him in a kind of suspended animation, a relationship limbo of painful emotions he had difficulty expressing. It was her task to help him do that.

She watched him, his eyes closed once more, aware that he hadn't spoken for a whole minute. He wasn't asleep, but he was definitely someplace else.

'Dan?'

'Yeah.' He blinked and sat up.

'What was going through your mind just now?'

'I…' He wiped a hand over his face. 'I was thinking how she—'

His phone rang. They both looked at the screen. It said *DCI Porter*.

'I have to get this,' he said. 'Sorry.'

'Sure.' She clicked her pen and sat back, reading over her notes again.

'Boss,' said Dan, snapping right back into work mode. Then he said 'yup' and 'uh-huh' a few times. 'SIO?'

She looked up at his change of tone, and noted: *SIO*.

'Yes, sir. I've done the course,' said Dan. He swallowed, then said, 'I'll be there,' and rang off. His foot was tapping on the carpet.

'SIO?' she asked casually, before catching herself. 'I'm sorry, that's none of my—'

'Senior Investigating Officer,' he replied. 'Normally on a suspected murder you'd have a detective chief inspector down there, but the boss is tied up so…' He glanced back at the phone. 'It'll be my first time.'

'How do you feel about that?'

His jaw clenched. 'I'd better go.'

# CHAPTER THREE

Lockhart parked his ancient Land Rover Defender behind the group of police vehicles that had already massed at the address in Battersea, just across the water from Chelsea. He counted four white area cars with their yellow-and-blue panelling, driven here by the 'lids', the uniformed officers. He could see a couple of them cordoning off the perimeter of the scene with tape and another standing sentry outside the property. Three unmarked vehicles: a grey coroner's van, the scene of crime officers' white van, and a saloon car that he guessed belonged to his lot, the MIT 'suits', here too. Most likely the Homicide Assessment Team who would've been first on the scene, since the body was discovered outside of regular working hours. The cars effectively blocked off the narrow private road that wound south from the River Thames.

The building was small – an old gatehouse, perhaps – but it was detached and overlooked the river; that alone was enough for a seven-figure price tag. It was set back among trees behind a high wall whose brickwork was half-covered with the dense foliage of creepers. The place had privacy, certainly. But in London, that also meant vulnerability.

At the SOCOs white van, he donned the obligatory paper suit, plastic overshoes and blue nitrile gloves before signing in with the Crime Scene Manager. He checked the list above his own name. As expected, he was the first to arrive from Putney's MIT 8; others would be here soon. A detective sergeant called Patrick Connelly had arrived forty-five minutes ago – probably the on-call guy – but he couldn't spot a pathologist listed. He'd have to rely on his own medical knowledge for now. The CSM radioed inside to let them know Lockhart was coming in.

Approaching the gate that was flanked by two more uniformed officers, he noted there was no lock on it, just an iron latch. That allowed anyone off the private road to walk right up to the front door without challenge and, more worryingly, with minimal chance of observation. Lockhart turned three-sixty, looking up at street lamps and the nearest buildings in search of a camera, but he couldn't find one. There was a stat about the average Londoner being caught on CCTV three hundred times a day. But that average masked the real numbers, which varied from zero to a thousand depending on where you went and what you did in the capital.

The front door was open, and Lockhart could see two figures in hooded white suits talking in the hallway. Before entering, he paused to look at the frame, handle and locks. No immediate evidence of damage. Had the victim let her killer in? *Victim.* He didn't even have her name yet.

'DI Lockhart?'

He glanced up and nodded as the man approached. 'That's me.'

'DS Connelly, Lewisham.' He extended a hand and Lockhart shook it. 'So, yous're taking over here?' The guy's Irish accent was as thick as his grey eyebrows. 'It's a bad one, sir, I don't mind telling you,' he added with a grimace before Lockhart could reply. 'Hope you've a strong stomach on you this morning. Come on and I'll show you.'

'She had a bob or two, then,' observed Lockhart as he took in the designer furniture and modern art in the large living room that opened out to their left. 'Any sign of burglary?'

'Hard to be sure, but not that we can see.'

They proceeded down a broad hallway and stopped outside another room. The door obscured his view of its interior, but the part he could see looked like a home office. More SOCOs were at work inside. One had a camera with a flash unit that popped off every few seconds, throwing light bursts over the walls and ceiling. The effect reminded Lockhart of a thunderstorm. He couldn't yet see what the photographer was pointing his lens at. But he could guess.

'Cleaner found her this morning,' said Connelly. 'He's got keys. Seems he came in as usual and, well…'

'Where's he now?'

'Giving a statement up the road at Lavender Hill station. They're trying to get an interpreter for the fella, he's Brazilian. English wasn't up to much, unfortunately. But I didn't need to speak Portuguese to see it'd scared the shite out of him.'

'Right.' Lockhart knew he couldn't rule anything out at this stage. The cleaner's statement about finding the body would be crucial, particularly if there weren't any other witnesses. He just hoped the guy hadn't disturbed the scene too much. And he needed to keep an open mind; there were many cases where the perpetrator was the one who reported the crime. Without signs of forced entry, it suggested someone the victim knew, maybe someone who could let themselves into the property. Right now, his suspect strategy was a blank slate. Normally, it was down to a more senior officer to make those calls. This time, it was on him. 'Let's have a look then.'

'Aye, she's on the far side here.' Connelly led the way.

As Lockhart rounded the door his heart thumped, and the adrenalin coursed out from his gut. A split-second later the image from the summer registered in his mind.

A near-identical scene on the opposite side of London.

A hotel room.

A victim he'd known personally.

He tried to compose himself. 'Er, do we have a name yet?'

'The owner of the house is listed as Natasha Mayston. Same name's on the MBA certificate on the wall, there. Looks from the photos in the lounge next door and a quick search on Google like it's her.'

Lockhart could understand why his Irish colleague couldn't be more definitive. Natasha Mayston was seated in a high-backed executive chair that had been pushed up against the wall, her torso strapped to its leather upholstery with a thin cable that looked like washing line. Her head was bowed, long blonde hair drawn back in a loose ponytail from which many strands had escaped, presumably as she fought for her life. She was barefoot and wore blue silk pyjamas. Her ankles were pinned to the chair's rolling feet with crude plastic ties. Similar restraints held her wrists at the chrome armrests. The skin around those ties bore signs of Natasha's frantic, failed attempts to free herself. Leaning closer, Lockhart noticed a small amount of dried blood near the base of her left ring finger, where he'd expected to find it. Other than these few superficial marks there were no obvious external injuries on the body. But, even in the absence of those signs, he'd known her cause of death as soon as he'd seen her. He'd call it through to the duty pathologist to confirm, but he imagined that would be a formality.

He bent down level with her face, noticing the red spots on her cheeks that showed where her veins had burst beneath the skin. Her parted lips were a blueish colour and the tip of her tongue protruded, thick and dark. Her eyes were open; one was completely bloodshot.

'Have you got a spatula?' he asked a SOCO. She went over to a large case and produced a thin plastic packet which she handed to Lockhart. He tore it open and, kneeling down, inserted it gently into Natasha's mouth. He could feel the rigor mortis on her jaw and carefully depressed her tongue, craning his neck to see better. 'Can I get a torch beam here, please?'

As the Maglite illuminated the inside of her mouth, Lockhart caught the glint he'd expected. Her tongue was swollen but, just visible behind it, a smooth metallic surface reflected the torchlight back at him. 'She's been choked to death,' he announced. 'Probably by a steel ball.'

'How d'you know that, sir?' said Connelly.

'Because Natasha isn't this guy's first victim.'

# CHAPTER FOUR

Lockhart rapped his knuckles on the door and peered through the window of DCI Marcus Porter's office. Porter was on the phone but, glancing up, he beckoned Lockhart in. The room was on the corner of Jubilee House, four floors up, with a double aspect that offered its occupants a partial view of the river between other buildings. Nice in the summer, but on this dull autumn morning the water was somewhere between grey and brown; a colour he wasn't sure even had a name. *Thames*, maybe.

Lockhart had been in Putney for only two months – having transferred from Hackney's MIT across town – so the boss's impressiveness still struck him each time he stepped into the office. Porter was physically imposing: a six-foot-three, muscular man of Afro-Caribbean heritage who'd played a year's semi-pro rugby before committing to his police training. His career had progressed apace and, with some big operations under his belt and strategic moves around the Met's different commands, he'd made DCI shortly after his fortieth birthday – one of the youngest in the force at that rank. Porter was fond of saying that it wasn't bad for the son of a bus driver who'd grown up on a housing estate in Croydon and left school at sixteen. Lockhart agreed.

Now forty-five, nine years Lockhart's senior, he was tipped for even greater things. The only question was whether those great things would be in the Met. Rumour had it that he was being courted by politicians on the left and right, both at city and national level. What that meant for Lockhart was that Porter always had one eye on the media, his choices heavily influenced by public reactions. Though that was an unavoidable fact of modern policing, Lockhart did sometimes wonder whose interests that media focus best served.

Taking a seat, he scanned the familiar items adorning the wall to his left: a Commissioner's Commendation, a relaxed photograph with the Mayor of London and, most significantly, Porter being awarded the rare Queen's Police Medal. By the Queen. No one in the MIT knew exactly what he'd been given it for. There was talk of undercover operations, hush-hush stuff, and Porter's smiling refusal to confirm or deny anything – even after a few beers – only fuelled the speculation.

His boss ended the call and put the phone down. 'Dan. Where are we?'

Lockhart summarised the scene in Battersea, while Porter listened and nodded, his eyes narrowing at the mention of the metal ball which appeared to have been pushed into Natasha's throat.

'So, what's your initial suspect strategy?' asked Porter.

'Actually, sir,' Lockhart coughed into his fist, 'I think it's a serial offender.'

'Go on.' Porter already sounded sceptical.

'Back in July a sex worker named Kim Hardy was found dead in one of those cheap hotels on Romford Road, east London. You know the kind of place: cash only, no names, no cameras. Identical MO. Metal ball, plastic ties, the lot.' He blinked. 'I knew her. She was a witness in one of my cases.'

Porter paused for a moment as if summoning a memory. 'MIT 12 in Newham caught the guy that did that, though. He's on remand now.'

'They caught *a* guy. Damon Pagett.'

'You don't think it was him?'

Lockhart snorted. 'No, sir, I don't. He was a paying client of Kim's, but he has a borderline learning disability.'

'And that means he couldn't kill someone?'

'I think anyone's got the capacity to kill.' Lockhart tried to ignore an image that'd just flashed into his mind of swirling sand, a memory of stifling heat and shouting. 'But the degree of planning was beyond him. In my view,' he added. 'And I don't think it was a sex game gone wrong, either.'

'Well, the jury will decide that when it comes to trial.'

Lockhart could feel his frustration growing. 'Natasha Mayston was murdered in exactly the same way as Kim Hardy.'

Porter sat back and folded his hands. 'Copycat? Once stuff's out there in the press, any old lunatic can read about it and do the same thing.'

'That's the point, sir. Not everything was in the press. Restraints, chair, choking, yes. But the metal ball wasn't mentioned, and neither were the ring finger injuries.'

Porter shrugged. 'Maybe those details were leaked.'

'Maybe. Or maybe there's one guy who murdered both women and who's still out there, probably planning his next attack on a stranger.'

'Hm.'

'I'd like to speak to Pagett in prison, sir.'

'Not going to happen.'

'But if I can just sit down with him and—'

The DCI held up a hand to stop Lockhart. Then he shifted in his seat and sighed. 'Look, Dan, I know what it's like. Every detective wants a serial killer case in their career, the evil guy who preys on strangers. But almost none of us gets one. You know why?'

Lockhart took a deep breath. 'Because they're rare.'

'*Very* rare, thankfully. Decades of stats don't lie. Most people are likely to be killed by—'

'Someone they know.'

Porter looked momentarily affronted by the interruption, but his expression softened into something approaching an indulgent smile. 'Right. So, I suggest you prioritise her partner, if she's got one, her exes, colleagues, circle of friends. Keep an open mind about family, too. Have they been informed yet?'

'We've traced her parents' address in Harrogate. Family Liaison Officer from North Yorkshire Police is going round there any minute to break the bad news.'

'OK. Once that's done, let's organise a media briefing here. We can appeal for witnesses, ask members of the public to come forward. I don't want anything about a serial killer in there though, understand? The last thing we need is every woman in London panicking, when the most likely explanation is that Natasha Mayston was killed in a crime of passion.'

'This was no crime of passion, sir.' Lockhart could hear the slight growl in his voice. 'The guy sourced the kit to murder her and brought it with him. That's as premeditated as it gets.'

Porter stayed irritatingly calm. 'You said yourself that there was no sign of forced entry. So, it was probably someone she felt comfortable letting into her house. Agreed?'

'Yes.' Lockhart did believe that, but it wasn't incompatible with a serial offender. The question was what linked Natasha and Kim: two women at opposite ends of London's social spectrum. And not just what linked them. *Who* linked them? He suspected it wasn't the guy with an IQ of 75 who was in prison last night when Natasha choked to death. Though Newham MIT, who'd arrested him for Kim's murder, would be the last people to admit that.

Porter raised himself up in the chair. 'Right, so, you've got your actions, then?' It was a statement more than a question.

Lockhart had learned in the military that if you wanted to challenge authority, you needed to pick the right time and place. And that wasn't here or now. He needed more evidence in support of his theory. He stood to leave. 'I'd better go and get things started, sir.'

# CHAPTER FIVE

As half of MIT 8 assembled around the portable whiteboards that'd been brought together in the open-plan office, Lockhart realised that this was the first time he'd led the briefing on a murder case as SIO. He had ten detectives, three civilians and two uniformed officers under his command, with one aim: find the person responsible for killing Natasha Mayston. The same individual he believed – despite Porter's reservations – had murdered Kim Hardy. Although the group represented just half of the MIT, it was the best they could do with available staffing, and more resource than he'd seen allocated to some homicides. Chairs were dragged across the old carpet tiles, a dozen mugs of tea were handed out off a tray, notebooks were opened. After a couple of minutes, silence settled and fifteen pairs of eyes turned to him.

'Right, for those of you that don't know, the body of a woman, who we presume to be Natasha Mayston, was discovered this morning at her home in Battersea. She'd been strapped to a chair and choked, most likely with a metal ball.' Lockhart paused, aware of murmurs among the group, then opened his file and extracted a photograph from the crime scene that he'd printed off. He pinned it to the whiteboard with small magnets. It wasn't pleasant, but he knew that such raw images could be a powerful boost to team motivation. He pinned another picture up alongside it, this one a head-and-shoulders portrait from Natasha's company website. It was professionally shot and showed a smiling, confident young woman in a crisp white shirt and dark suit jacket. Seeing the victim in life and death was usually all that a murder squad needed to remind them why they were there.

'The cleaner who found her says it's Natasha,' he continued. 'We're hoping North Yorkshire Police can get an additional ID from her parents up there with the photos, tough as that's going to be for them so soon after receiving the news. And we should get full confirmation tomorrow at the post-mortem. For now, though, we've no reason to suspect it's anyone else. Natasha is registered as the owner and occupant of the property where she was found, and she matches the general physical appearance of the person in photographs around the house as well as images on the web of Natasha Mayston.'

Establishing the victim's identity was one of the first actions in any inquiry, and it wasn't always a given. He'd seen detectives go in completely the wrong direction because of assumptions they'd made about who the dead person was. Here, though, he felt confident.

'So, in terms of victim strategy, we need to find out about Natasha's life. Luce, I know you've only had about five minutes to look into that, but do you want to tell us what you've found?' He invited Lucy Berry to step up and moved aside for her, perching on the nearest table.

In her early thirties, Berry was a few years younger than Lockhart, a civilian analyst and working mum completely devoted to her young family – except between the hours of 9 a.m. and 5 p.m. when she was mostly devoted to data. Lockhart knew the team teased her for being a neat-freak, but a bit of OCD was a strength when it came to analysis. If there was a pattern or an abnormality in the numbers, she'd find it.

Berry cleared her throat and studied her pad of paper. She glanced at Lockhart, who nodded his encouragement, then she tugged at the sleeves of her jumper and looked at her notes again. He knew she preferred to be in the background, but right now they needed her centre stage.

'Um, OK, so…' She ran a hand through her bob-cut and read from the page without making eye contact with anyone. 'Natasha Mayston was thirty-three, and she was CEO of a small investment company called Atalanta. They specialise in funding start-ups of all kinds, provided they're led by women. She'd studied economics and management at Exeter College, Oxford University.' Berry's voice was quiet, and Lockhart noticed several colleagues leaning forward to hear better. 'Um, she founded Atalanta two and a half years ago and she's the sole director listed on Companies House. Prior to that she'd worked as a management consultant for KPMG, according to LinkedIn. She was quite active with women's charities, too. I haven't got much about her personal life, yet, but she tweeted at 6 p.m. yesterday about a funding event she'd been to earlier in the day.'

'Gives us the start of our window for time of death, then,' offered Lockhart.

'Mm-hm.' Berry flipped the page in her notebook. 'Oh, and there's a photo online from last year of her with a guy. It was the only public image of Natasha that I could find on Facebook. Looks like a friend tagged her and the man together while they were skiing in Switzerland. I haven't got the picture printed yet, but the two of them are arm-in-arm. Could be a boyfriend.'

'Does he have a name?'

'He's tagged as Hugh Chadwick. But I haven't had time to look at him online. Sorry.'

'Don't worry, I'd say you've done pretty well for five minutes' research.' There were a few chuckles around the group and Berry blushed, allowing herself a smile. She might not be the world's most natural public speaker, but her grasp of detail was second to none.

'Thanks, Luce.' Lockhart stood again. 'I'd like you to keep digging, find out anything else you can about her. Other relationships, more on her education, work, interests, social media, the lot. Let's see what's on her mobile, too. Call records, content download off her smartphone. Her killer crossed paths with her, some way or other.' Berry nodded and retreated to her chair. 'That brings us to suspect strategy. Clearly, we need to take a look at this Chadwick guy, the boyfriend. Max, can I leave that with you? And any close friends we can identify.'

'Guv.' Detective Sergeant Maxine Smith – known as Max – didn't need to say any more; Lockhart knew it'd get done. Smith was old school, a Londoner born and bred. She'd grafted her way to detective, then up to sergeant, over a twenty-year career in the Met. Hers was a journey that few thought she could make. When she'd joined in the late nineties, police forces were still exempt from legislation on equal opportunities for people with disabilities. But she refused to be put off, training hard and proving her case that a person with only two fingers and a thumb on her left hand could do everything an officer with five digits could, including handcuffing a resisting suspect. Not only did she do the job better than most of her peers, she'd also managed to raise a son during her time in the Met, for several years as a single parent. Now he was grown up, Smith did as much overtime as anyone else in the MIT. She was the embodiment of grit: exactly the kind of person you needed on a tough case.

'Some of you might also be aware,' resumed Lockhart, 'that this murder bears striking similarities to the death of Kim Hardy in east London last July. The detail about choking on a metal ball wasn't ever disclosed to the press, so if this is a different guy, that's one hell of a coincidence. And you know what I say about coincidences.'

'You don't like them, boss.' The words were spoken through a wad of chewing gum. It was just a matter of time before their speaker chipped in. Detective Constable Mohammed Khan – or Mo to everyone on the team – was, like Lockhart, new to the MIT. But unlike Lockhart, he was new to the role of detective, too. And despite his low boredom threshold, the excitement of that hadn't worn off yet for him. Lockhart gave it another year or two, at most, but he couldn't fault Khan's enthusiasm. He reminded him a bit of himself when he was 'army barmy' back in the day. The main management problem, as Lockhart saw it, was keeping Khan's energy focussed on his work and his ego in check. He felt for Mr and Mrs Khan; though their son was twenty-six he still lived at home with them in a state of perpetual frustration, desperate to cut the apron strings. And with Khan preferring nightclubs and motorbikes to mosques and marriage, Lockhart knew the tension in their family ran both ways.

'Right, Mo.' Lockhart nodded at him and Khan flashed a grin. 'The only problem with a serial attacker theory is that Newham MIT have a suspect on remand for Kim's murder. Damon Pagett. We know she was a sex worker and Pagett was one of her clients. I had my reservations about him to start with, but this pretty much seals it. Our colleagues over the water aren't going to be happy, but I reckon they've got the wrong guy. What we need are their paper files on Kim's murder. Any volunteers to ask nicely for them?'

A couple of detective constables raised their hands.

'Cheers guys, I'll call their DCI after this and we'll drive over there together early afternoon.'

Khan raised his hand and spoke at the same time. 'Boss, what about the witness strategy?'

Lockhart pressed his lips together and glanced across to the whiteboards. In the column marked 'Witnesses' there was a single word:

*Cleaner.*

'We don't really have one yet,' he replied. 'That's why I need you guys,' he indicated the uniformed officers at the back as well as three other detectives, 'to go door to door around Natasha's house. See what CCTV there is, too. Didn't look like much in the immediate vicinity, but there must be something. This is London.'

Lockhart ran through a few more actions, noting names and tasks on the whiteboards. Once he'd given everyone something to chase down, he put the cap back on the marker pen and turned back to his team.

'And one last thing,' he said, surveying them. 'Worst-case scenario is that this guy's attacking strangers. If that's right, then he's probably not going to stop at two women.' He let that sink in for a moment, then clapped his hands. 'All right, let's go.'

# CHAPTER SIX

As the underground train rattled east, Maxine Smith hunched over in her seat and took a massive bite of the cheap tuna sandwich she'd grabbed at Waterloo railway station. Cramming in a tasteless lunch on the move like this wasn't going to win her any beauty contests, or help her digestion, but she didn't care about that. Like most police, she'd learned not to be precious about what she ate or where she ate it, and she knew the importance of keeping fuelled during the long, full-on days at the start of a murder investigation. Opposite her, Khan was busy inhaling a protein bar whose wrapper bore the words 'muscle mass'.

'Don't see why we had to take the tube,' he huffed.

She smirked; his intonation a reminder of her son as a petulant teenager. She knew Khan would've loved nothing more than to arrive in one of London's financial centres with sirens wailing and, if it were possible, guns blazing. She might agree with him on the latter part, depending on which bankers you were talking about.

'You know why, Mo,' she replied through a mouthful of sandwich. 'Usual story – not enough cars.'

'Yeah, but we're on one of the main gigs, here.' He jerked a thumb in their direction of travel. 'The boyfriend.'

'Hence the boss sending a couple of legends.' She stuffed the rest of the sandwich in, chewed hard and brushed crumbs off her trousers. Khan chuckled and hauled himself to his feet as the train slid into Canary Wharf station.

At the top of a towering escalator, they emerged into a water-front world of steel and glass: temples to the financial gods. Gods who clearly enjoyed a drink, to judge by the number of bars at street level. The looming skyscrapers of Canada Square appeared to bend as Smith stared up at them. Walking to the address, she and Khan had to sidestep a couple of tall, thirty-something men who were laughing so hard they were oblivious to anyone else. For a second or two, she felt a tremor of intimidation grow. This wasn't her world: men in suits, laddish banter, casual misogyny and hard boozing. But she emitted a small snort when she realised that could've been a description of the Met. The only difference was that these guys had nicer suits. And nicer buildings, she noted, entering the spacious lobby of the tower that was home to Capital Assets, Ltd., the firm that employed Hugh Chadwick.

Smith only gave the company name to the security guards, which sufficed for them. She hadn't called ahead either, gambling slightly on the fact that Chadwick would be in his office. The element of surprise could be crucial when dealing with a 'person of interest'. At this moment, Smith didn't know if they'd find a fragile, bereaved partner or their prime suspect, but she had to plan for both scenarios. If Chadwick was involved in Natasha's death, then turning up unannounced gave him no chance to destroy evidence or arrange an alibi. But they had to tread carefully; as much as the doorstepping tactic could trip up the guilty, it could also traumatise the innocent.

A receptionist with a mask of make-up sat behind a polished granite desk. She looked from Smith's face to her cleft hand and back again. 'Can I help you?'

Smith flipped open her warrant card, holding it out to the receptionist with her 'different' hand, as she called it, so the young woman could get a better look. 'I'm DS Smith and this is DC Khan. We'd like to speak to Hugh Chadwick at Capital Assets, please.'

'Do you have an appointment?' She arched a pair of thick black eyebrows whose ends were perfectly squared off.

'No.' Khan smiled. 'But it's an important personal matter. He'll want to hear what we have to say.'

There was no faulting his charm. Smith watched as the receptionist hesitated, glanced across at another young woman next to her, then clicked her mouse and scrolled. She called a number and, after a brief and half-whispered conversation, replaced the receiver. 'Fourteenth floor. You can take the lift.' She gestured to a pair of chrome doors set between marble cladding across the lobby. 'Mr Chadwick will see you up there.'

Smith noticed Khan's gaze lingering on the receptionist. 'Come on, then, DC Khan.' The use of his rank and surname was all the reprimand needed.

The lift doors had barely glided open at the fourteenth floor when the hand shot out in Smith's direction. She automatically took it; a hand no bigger than her own, its skin soft and delicate.

'Hugh Chadwick.'

The man in front of her was average height and build, clean-shaven, with side-parted ginger hair that rose in a small quiff. He wore a collared shirt with silk tie, and suit trousers with no belt: tailored. His slim watch was circled in gold that matched his cufflinks and a signet ring.

Smith stepped out of the lift mid-handshake, momentarily wrong-footed. Chadwick had sought to pre-empt them, perhaps even keep them out of his office and away from his colleagues, if he could. Such was the risk of white-collar crime – she never liked that phrase – in these places that reputations could be seriously dented by an ill-timed encounter with the boys and girls in blue.

He lowered his voice. 'May I ask what this is about?' His accent bore every hallmark of a private education.

Smith took in the smoked-glass walls of the office behind him, the few people milling about. It was time to establish control of the encounter. She introduced herself and Khan, again flashing the warrant card; its authority usually added weight. 'Is there somewhere more private we can talk, please, Mr Chadwick?' She paused a beat. 'It's about Natasha Mayston.' Smith watched his face as she said the name. His eyes narrowed, lips compressing slightly. Then his expression lightened.

'What's Tashy done now, eh?' He was smiling, but Smith could see the effort behind it. She didn't reply. 'Right, you'd better come through then,' he said, eventually. 'We can talk in my office.'

As they passed a small reception desk, Chadwick stopped briefly, leaning across and muttering something to the woman seated behind it. The only word Smith was able to catch was *lawyer*. Chadwick shoved his hands casually into his pockets as he walked, but his shoulders were tense.

'Nice watch,' remarked Khan as Chadwick offered them chairs in his room. The view from the window was spectacular but Smith tried not to be distracted by it.

'This,' he replied, turning his wrist one way then the other. 'Yeah, it's a Patek.'

'No way! That's sick.' Khan stared at the item whose brand name meant nothing to Smith. *Boys with toys.*

Chadwick sat down behind his desk. 'It was a gift from Tashy, actually, a couple of years back. So, what's this about?'

Smith took the lead. 'Are you in a relationship with Natasha Mayston?'

The asset manager snorted. 'Was.'

She let the silence grow. Khan knew better than to break it.

'We were together for six years,' added Chadwick after a few seconds. 'Got engaged about this time last year.'

'What happened?'

'She broke it off.' There was no mistaking the bitterness of his tone. 'In February.'

*Motive.*

'Why?' Smith always favoured the direct approach.

'I don't think that's any of your business,' he retorted. 'Now, what's this about?' Chadwick leant forward, and Smith realised that his own chair was elevated over his guests; a classic power move.

'Mr Chadwick, I'm sorry to have to tell you that Natasha Mayston is dead.' She let the words hang briefly. 'And we're currently treating her death as suspicious.'

'Dead? Tashy's *dead*? But, my god, this is awful.' His mouth stayed half-open and he looked from Smith to Khan and back again, before he rotated his chair and his gaze drifted out of the window. Smith saw his Adam's apple bob in profile as he swallowed. 'How did she die?'

'I'm afraid we can't give any details about that, yet,' said Khan.

'Was she… murdered?' He was still looking out over the city below.

'Her death was in very suspicious circumstances, but a post-mortem will give us more information.' Khan delivered the practised line evenly. They had to be extremely careful, especially early in a murder inquiry, with how much information was revealed. Occasionally, lead investigators would even hold some details back from members of their own team depending on their sensitivity.

Chadwick put a hand to his mouth. 'Tashy.'

Watching carefully, Smith gave him a moment to process the news before she spoke again. 'I'm sorry to have to ask you this, Mr Chadwick, but can you tell us where you were last night, please?'

He spun his chair towards her. 'You think I *murdered* her? What the f—' He caught hold of himself.

'It's just a routine question, in the circumstances.'

'Am I suspected of anything here? I mean, do I need a lawyer?' One hand reached towards his phone.

'That's up to you,' replied Smith. 'If you'd like a lawyer we can arrange a voluntary interview at our office.' She glanced at her own watch for effect. 'But we're based in Putney, so it'll need some time to get there and back. And we wouldn't want to take you away from your team, or your markets.'

Chadwick nodded silently, retracting the manicured hand that hovered over the desk phone. He gave a deep breath. 'I was here until around seven thirty, then out with a client.'

'Which client?'

'That's confidential.'

Smith was getting mildly irritated. 'OK. Where were you, then?'

'Duck and Waffle.' He waved a hand vaguely. 'From around eight till ten thirty.'

Next to her, Khan took out a notebook and wrote a few words. 'And what about after that?'

He pursed his lips before replying. 'We went to a club.'

This was like getting blood out of a stone. 'Which club was that?'

Chadwick tidied something on his desk without making eye contact.

'Which club, please?'

'Look, I didn't – the clients wanted to go there.' He leant back in the chair. 'White Rhino.'

'The strip bar?' offered Khan.

'Gentleman's club,' corrected Chadwick.

'Strip bar,' stated Smith. 'And what time did you leave White Rhino?'

The asset manager shrugged. 'I don't know, around one, maybe. I got an Uber back to my flat in Chelsea.'

Right across the water from Natasha's house, thought Smith. *Opportunity.*

'Were you alone?' asked Khan.

'Yes.'

'And can anyone verify that?' Smith kept her tone light, but the severity of its implication was clear.

'The Uber bloke.' He wafted a hand in Khan's direction; the micro-behaviour didn't go unnoticed to Smith. 'He'll remember me. It'll be on my app. He dropped me at my front door.' He wagged a finger, the hint of a smile forming. 'Even better – there's a camera in the reception of my apartment block, as well as 24-hour porters. The chap behind the desk will've seen me come back. And I didn't go out again until I came here this morning.' It seemed that in less than a minute, Chadwick had gone from devastated to cocky. Smith didn't know what to make of it.

'Well, DS Khan will look into all that, if you don't mind, Mr Chadwick.'

'Of course not.' He smiled briefly at Khan who grinned back, probably at the prospect of a free trip to White Rhino.

'And in the meantime,' Smith took out her card, 'give me a call if you think of anything else that might be relevant. And probably best not to go too far away from London, in case we need to speak to you again.'

Chadwick pulled a face of contempt. 'But I've got to fly to Zurich tomorrow.'

'I'd suggest one of your colleagues goes instead,' replied Smith. The balance had tipped as far as she was concerned: *Person of interest*. 'We'll see ourselves out. Can I trouble you for one of your cards, please?' She reached across and plucked one off the edge of his desk. 'Thanks very much for your time, Mr Chadwick.'


'So, what did you think?' asked Smith as they walked back to the underground station.

'Pretty sweet.' Khan nodded a few times. 'You could see half of London from his office. And I bet he drives a badman car, too.'

'Don't be a dick, Mo.'

'All right. I reckon he hates her. She dumped him. But he had to look upset when we said she'd died, because that's the done thing, right?'

'Agreed.'

'Thought his alibi sounded solid, though. And I've no problem checking it later. You?'

Smith glanced down at her hand. She'd spent forty-odd years proving that making assumptions about anyone was a mug's game.

'I'm not sure yet,' she said quietly as they boarded the down escalator and London's underground swallowed them up.

# CHAPTER SEVEN

Lexi Green brought her feet back down to earth. She'd been in the handstand position, the heels of her sneakers propping her up against the wall. Her arms were tired and shaky, but she felt pretty good. After a day that'd started with a knife to her throat, followed by nine hours of trauma therapy sitting on her butt, she needed to do something active and distracting. And there weren't many better options for that than the CrossFit gym.

The simple brick building was tucked away at the end of a residential road, just up from the flat she shared with her friends in Tooting, and not far from the hospital where she worked. Despite living in a huge city, Lexi sometimes wondered if her whole life could take place just in the small triangle formed by those three spots. She couldn't work out if that was kind of sad or kind of cool.

Gazing up through the skylight into the dark, starless fall night as she took a rest, she felt grateful for the warm and well-lit gym. For the pumping music she could feel pulsing through her. For the human company of those training around her. For the reassuring presence of the cute dog chilling in its basket in the corner. She'd be lying if she said she hadn't looked over her shoulder at least once on the walk here, with Dan's words about a suspected murder echoing in her head. She'd checked the news online when she had got back from work. A young woman killed in her own home, a couple miles away in Battersea. Was that his case? The guy who did it must still be out there… *Come on, Lexi.*

She needed to focus on the here and now; tough as the exercise was, it wasn't traumatic like everything else seemed to be.

Tonight, she'd already done some rope climbs and toes-to-bar – two exercises she couldn't do at all when she first started training – and she felt a little glow of pride in how far she'd come. But there was still a long way to go; for her, the Holy Grail was a handstand walk. When she'd seen Erica, the South African coach, walk the length of the gym on her hands like it was nothing, Lexi knew she had to train until she could do it too. That was a year ago, though, and despite practising regularly, she couldn't crack it yet. She could hold the handstand for thirty seconds, but take away the support of the wall and her body crumpled to the rubber mats.

She glanced across at a woman doing overhead squats with a loaded bar, and did a double-take when she realised the woman was pregnant. Jeez, that was hardcore, especially in her condition… Lexi realised her hand had unconsciously drifted to her own stomach. To a choice she'd made in her senior year at college to terminate the life that'd been growing inside her. A decision that'd led to the end of her long-term relationship. But she knew that the abortion had only been the trigger for her leaving the US. The foundations of her desire to escape had been laid a year earlier by the death of her kid brother Shep.

While she was at college, majoring in psychology and having a blast, Shep had drifted into depression and drugs back home. He attended high school less and less until, one day, he was found dead in an abandoned house where local users went to get high. According to his autopsy, he'd overdosed. Lexi couldn't forgive herself; she and Shep had been so close and, as the older one, she'd been like a protector to him. They were inseparable growing up – each other's rock in the storm of constant displacement as her father moved them across the Atlantic and around the US with his job in the Air Force.

The news of Shep's overdose had been totally unexpected. And it'd hit her hard. Today, she still felt that there was something more she could've done for him at the time, before he OD'd, maybe even before he'd gotten addicted. She should've been there for him, but she'd been too busy thinking about herself. Once he was gone, though, there was nothing more Lexi could do. Her way of coping had been to spend every day helping other people deal with their traumas. But had she dealt with her own?

'Ach, Lexi! Stop daydreaming and get into that handstand.' Erica's distinctive accent carried over the music. How did some South Africans manage to sound both friendly and terrifying at the same time?

She took a breath and, with trembling arms, kicked back up into the wall.

\*

Dan Lockhart cracked open a cold can of Stella Artois, dropped into the sofa and gulped down big mouthfuls of the strong, sweet-tasting lager. He didn't have time for that craft beer nonsense, just give him a Stella any day. The hipster mob might turn their noses up at it for not having enough fancy hops or whatever, but Lockhart didn't care. Stella was 'ally', as they used to say in the military: proper, quality. A beer with its own style. Shame it'd picked up the nickname 'wife beater' somewhere along the way. The phrase angered Lockhart, because any scumbag who laid a finger on his wife – or any woman for that matter – deserved prison time.

*His wife.*

Jess.

Who should be here with him. In the tiny flat they'd bought together in a mansion block just behind Hammersmith flyover. It was all they could afford back then, barely scraping the cash together from two salaries plus savings inherited after their grandparents had passed away. And that was before house prices went crazy. A boxlike apartment where you could hear traffic and trains almost twenty-four hours a day, but it was theirs. Definitely not enough space for the family they were planning to start. They'd both wanted kids, especially her.

Jess.

He'd kept their home just how it looked when she left, preserving it like some kind of time capsule, ready for the day she came back. The only exception to that was the section of living room wall he was staring at now. Anything on Jess went up there: potential sightings marked on a map, photographs of her, missing persons leads he'd followed that'd gone cold. It all went on the wall. People would make fun of him if they saw it, call him obsessive or whatever. But that didn't bother Lockhart. The only person who ever came round here was his mum. And she was the only other person who thought Jess was still alive. He took another massive swig of Stella.

Jess.

His gaze drifted from the wall towards the front door as he recalled their final conversation. They'd stood, there, in the hallway. Him with his kitbag already over one shoulder, ready to head back to his barracks and on to Afghanistan. Jess leaning against the wall, hand on hip. They'd argued playfully about where to take the holiday when he came back for his mid-tour R & R. She'd wanted somewhere hot – the Canary Islands, maybe – while he'd pushed for a colder spot to give himself a break from the scorching desert sun. Neither one had convinced the other and, smiling and shaking their heads, they'd agreed to sort it out on the phone. But they never did.

Jess.

It was amazing he hadn't been thinking about her when he came home just now. Probably the result of the new case; a different kind of stress to occupy his mind. It'd been a long old day and there'd be more of the same tomorrow. His mind had been whirring away ever since he got the call from Porter this morning and had to leg it out of the session with Green.

Green.

Damn, he thought, drinking more beer. He'd missed out on his therapy. He didn't want to sack that off, not when he was starting to make progress. Green wasn't like the head doctors he'd seen in the army years back, all quick appointments and box-ticking. She and Lockhart actually *talked*. More accurately, *he* talked, and she listened without judging him or making him think he was nuts. It was as if he could tell her anything and she'd understand.

Lockhart liked being with her, in a way he couldn't quite explain. It made him feel a bit guilty, as if he'd somehow betrayed Jess. And, yet, his wife would want him to keep seeing Green; it was doing him good. He'd call her tomorrow and rearrange their session. Perhaps she could even shed some light on these two, apparently related, murders. He needed all the help he could get.

Right now, Lockhart was in the dark as to what connected Kim Hardy, a meth-addicted sex worker, and Natasha Mayston, a high-flying businesswoman and philanthropist. Kim's rough streets and dingy hotels on the east side of town couldn't have been more different from Natasha's million-pound riverside house on its private road to the west. Yet they both ended up choked to death by metal balls.

One thing was for sure. Newham MIT weren't going to offer up any explanations. He'd gone to see them this afternoon and been shown the case notes. As far as they were concerned, they had their man: Damon Pagett, the client of Kim's who barely had the IQ to understand the charges levelled against him by the prosecutor. Apparently, Pagett had visited her on the evening of her death. His DNA was on her body, her clothes and in the hotel room where she died. Newham MIT called that a 'slam dunk'.

Despite DCI Porter's earlier rejection of his idea, Lockhart had asked Newham's lead detective, DCI Flynn, if he could meet Pagett in prison. Flynn had flatly refused, simply asking him: *Who else could've killed Kim?* One of Flynn's team had followed this up with the observation: *It was written all over Pagett's face in the interviews.* Questioning their suspect's guilt was basically the same as saying their work was a pile of shit. Lockhart wasn't swayed by their certainty – and not just because Natasha had died while Pagett was on remand in prison. It was also because there were other, more likely, explanations.

Kim had been a witness for one of Lockhart's cases against a guy accused of murder for a street stabbing. That provided more than enough motive to want her out of the way, although how the suspect could've known her identity was a mystery he hadn't worked out at the time. Now there was a new possibility: that Kim and Natasha were both victims of the same serial murderer. A cold, calculating bastard who was full of hate. Lockhart was sure he'd kill again; the cold ones usually did. He closed his eyes and tried to marshal the evidence, but his brain was too tired and all he could see in his mind's eye were the two murder scenes. Two dead women tied to chairs. And a new image from somewhere in his imagination: his wife, tied to a chair…

Lockhart felt a rage start to bubble somewhere inside him. He drained the rest of the can, crushed it in his hand, and threw it at the opposite wall. It bounced off and clattered onto the floor. Then he got up to fetch another from the kitchen. He hadn't even taken off his jacket or shoes.

# CHAPTER EIGHT

So, they've found her. He hadn't expected it would take long. Not with someone like her, someone so active and busy and sociable and well-connected. He felt a shiver of excitement ripple through him as he munched his cereal, drank his tea and watched the morning news. Press conference footage from yesterday was being replayed behind big, urgent headlines in red and white.

LONDON: WOMAN'S BODY
DISCOVERED IN HER HOME

Then some shots of her house by the river. He smiled to himself. Imagined all the people who'd be watching. The thought of it made his chest swell, as if his body was being pumped up, as if he'd grown six inches.

Back in the studio, a chubby woman wearing too much make-up was talking about what a wonderful person she'd been. How tirelessly she'd worked to empower women in business. *Empower.* The cliché almost made him choke on his cornflakes. How ironic would that be? Fatty was going on about how she'd redefined the economic landscape for women. How generously she'd donated to women's charities and backed their fundraising events, as if she was some kind of fucking saint. The hagiography made him physically sick. And it was just plain wrong. Those were alternative facts, as some of his brothers across the pond might say.

The truth about that bitch was that she'd been given all the money she'd started with. She hadn't paid a penny for her outrageously expensive education. That'd all been bankrolled by – guess who? A man. Her father, specifically. Men had given her the job at KPMG that launched her career. And then her father had just handed her the cash to start her own business. He was certain that her old man helped her buy that beautiful home of hers, too. Pity for her that a man didn't set up the security system for it; that might have kept him out. He shook his head, chuckling. It was pathetic, this obese commentator eulogising about her financial acumen, when the entire system she operated within was built and run by men.

She'd deserved to die. There was no doubt of that in his mind. And her death restored some equilibrium to the world. But while this was probably the most exciting breakfast he'd ever had – watching the live coverage on her murder – he could already sense the buzz starting to fade. The feeling of killing someone up close like that – intimate killing, they called it in the military – was the greatest power you could have over another human being. Power was something denied to him by *her*, by all of them. Soon, the pleasure would be gone, replaced by his old friend, desolation. He knew he'd start to crave that intoxicating feeling again, just as he had the time before. Action was the only way to banish that desolation. All of which meant one thing.

It was time to move on to the next one.

Another offering to Him.

He already knew who it would be.

*

'Lex! Have you seen my Converse?'

Lexi stopped scrolling through Instagram on her iPhone and looked up. Her flatmate, Sarah, was standing in the kitchen doorway. Though she wasn't much above five feet tall, her frizzy hair almost filled the frame. She'd inherited her incredible hair from her Jamaican mother, her lack of height from her white English father. The sense of justice and equality that made her choose to be a social worker was the product of being raised by both of them in a tough part of south London.

Lexi swallowed a mouthful of oatmeal and pointed her spoon over Sarah's shoulder. 'Think I saw them in the bathroom.'

'What, the actual bathroom, or the toilet?' Sarah grinned.

'Piss off,' replied Lexi, using one of her favourite British expressions.

Sarah's wide smile evaporated. 'You seen the news?'

'What news?' The question was disingenuous, given that Lexi hadn't thought about much else since yesterday evening. Her brainless use of Instagram had been nothing more than an attempt to distract herself from it.

'About the murdered woman.' Sarah gripped the lintel. 'They found her in her own home.'

'Yeah, I saw.' So much for taking her mind off it. 'It's horrible.'

'I know, it's like, the scariest thing ever.' Sarah knocked on the frame. 'Let's keep the door locked, yeah? I don't want some psycho coming in here tonight, OK? Or any other night for that matter.'

'Psycho?' The deep Scottish voice preceded Liam's appearance behind Sarah. 'I've told you both not to date any psychos. But will you listen? No.' He placed his hands on Sarah's shoulders and manoeuvred past her into the kitchen. 'Morning, hen,' he nodded at Lexi. He wore skinny dark chinos and his bare torso was all smooth, lean muscle. It wasn't a bad sight to start the day, though she knew the appreciation wasn't reciprocated.

'Hey, Liam.' Lexi spooned some more oatmeal into her mouth.

'I was just talking about that murder.' Sarah waited for a reaction from Liam. 'In Battersea. The woman?' She blinked and held out her palms. 'Come on!'

'You serious? Oh my god. When?' Liam's mouth remained open.

'Probably two nights ago,' mumbled Lexi.

'Christ. Poor lass. How'd she die?'

'They haven't said yet.' Sarah put her hands on her hips. 'But I reckon—'

The doorbell rang. The three of them turned to the front door, its frosted panes revealing a dark shape in outline.

'I'll see who it is,' said Liam, shuffling past Sarah. He opened the door with a flourish. The postman stood behind it: a balding middle-aged man with red fleece tight over his belly. A postal sack was over his shoulder and he held out a wad of letters like an offering. Lexi smirked at the evident discomfort on his face at being greeted by a hot, half-naked young man.

Liam took the letters. 'Thanks, pal.'

The postman muttered something and craned his neck to see past Liam into their kitchen.

'All right, then,' said Liam cheerfully, closing the door slowly in his face. 'Have a good day.' He returned to the kitchen and tossed the letters on the table. Three of them, all normal sized.

Lexi frowned. 'Why didn't he just post those envelopes through the letterbox?'

Liam rolled his eyes. 'Isn't it obvious? The guy fancies the pants off you, Lexi.'

'Er, what about me?' Sarah swept her hands down the length of her body. She had great curves.

'Aye, you too, Sarah. You're both gorgeous. How could any sane man who liked women not think that? The pair of you are almost enough to turn my head.' He winked and went over to the fridge.

Lexi spun the envelopes and felt her heart sink. All three were addressed to her. One carried the logo of the utility company that supplied their gas. Another was from her bank; given the date, it was probably her credit card statement. And the third, as if to add insult to injury, looked like the offer of a loan – yet another company that'd gotten her name and address from somewhere. Was there no damn privacy in the world anymore? The bills were badly timed, too. Money was tight for all three of them and, with Dan taking on this new murder case where he was SIO, he wasn't likely to be coming to see her for a while. Which meant £80 a week less for her to pay those debts. Dammit.

Almost immediately, she caught herself. How selfish was that? A woman not much older than her had lost her life yesterday – no, not *lost*, had it *taken* from her – and yet she was sat here complaining about a few hundred pounds. That was stupid. *She* was being stupid. Get some perspective, she told herself. She stirred the oatmeal, staring into it.

Maybe it wasn't just the money. She had to acknowledge that she wanted to see Dan again. Every training course and manual taught you to be neutral as a therapist, but Lexi couldn't deny that she – same as pretty much every other clinical psychologist – liked some clients more than others. Dan came across as physically tough and mentally solid, but she knew he was emotionally vulnerable. And she wanted to help him heal, to help him get better and move on with his life. She tried to imagine what effect investigating this murder would be having on him, and wished there was something she could do. As she interrogated that desire more closely, she wondered if it, too, was selfish. Did she think that by helping Dan deal with his loss, she'd somehow deal with her own?

# CHAPTER NINE

Lockhart had first seen a dead body when he was just eighteen. Not long after signing up in the army, he'd been on night patrol at his barracks and discovered the corpse of a fellow private who'd shot himself. He still saw the image of that young lad today, as clearly as if it'd happened last week. And no matter how many more bodies he encountered, whether in war during his military service or in London as a homicide detective, he never became accustomed to the dead.

Perhaps it was because all those bodies were people whose lives had ended prematurely, without warning or preparation for death. Whatever the reason, Lockhart was ultimately glad of his inability to become used to a corpse. It kept him aware that the lifeless body was *some*body, an individual with – in most cases – family, friends, loves and losses. A person for whom he needed to get justice. And, now, standing in the post-mortem room of Westminster Mortuary, looking at the violated body of Natasha Mayston, that sense was stronger than ever.

Dr Mary Volz had already completed her examination before Lockhart entered the brightly lit room, his shoes squeaking slightly on its linoleum floor. It wasn't essential for him to attend a post-mortem, but in this case, he wanted to. Though they still had leads to pursue, anything that Volz could tell him about Natasha's death might be crucial to their early investigation.

Volz was one of the most experienced Home Office Registered Forensic Pathologists currently working in London. She normally performed two post-mortems per week, with the rest of her time spent writing their lengthy reports. Lockhart hoped to shortcut that process by hearing her observations directly and, if possible, taking any material away with him for immediate testing. If there was evidence on or in Natasha's body, there was no one he trusted more than Mary Volz to find it.

'Morning, Dan.' Volz spoke from behind a surgical mask, looking up at him as he crossed to where Natasha lay on a stainless-steel table. She was covered with a sheet, but Lockhart could see the final stitches in her torso where Volz would have opened the skin to remove her internal organs. The pathologist wore a plastic apron over scrubs, and her grey hair was held tightly in a bun on top of her head. Her pale blue eyes were watery, as if she were holding back tears.

'Mary.' Lockhart compressed his lips into a flat line and returned his gaze to Natasha. 'Thank you for doing this so quickly.'

Volz removed her mask. 'Anything to help.' She paused before continuing. 'Most of my post-mortems are routine investigations with some leeway in timing, but when it's a suspected murder, I clear my diary.'

'Appreciate it.'

'So. Natasha died from choking. As you noted in the crime scene report, there was a metal ball wedged in her throat.' Volz went over to a side bench and retrieved a clear plastic bag. She held it up for Lockhart to see: the silver sphere was about two inches in diameter, its smooth surface mottled with blood. 'That was what killed her. Her airway was completely cut off, starving her brain of oxygen. It would have taken her less than a couple of minutes to die. But those minutes would've been the most terrifying moments of her life.'

'She was alive when it happened, then?' asked Lockhart, though he knew what the answer would be.

'Yes, the swelling in her throat around the ball shows that her body was reacting to its insertion. I can't imagine what she went through. She would've been fully conscious until the last seconds.' Volz exhaled slowly and put the ball down before returning to the table where Natasha lay. 'Right, well, what else can I tell you? Her precise cause of death was asphyxia from mechanical choking. That's choking caused by an object obstructing the airway, rather than manual choking with hands around the neck. Most adults who die from mechanical choking tend to be drug addicts, alcoholics, or people with neurological conditions, like epilepsy.'

Lockhart thought back to his field medic training course in the military. 'People who might lose control over their epiglottis.'

'That's right. But, in an adult without any of those conditions, it's extremely rare. And as a murder method, it's... almost unheard of. I had to look it up, in fact, and there were only two documented cases I could find. One in a Japanese prison, the other on a farm in India.'

'But you think it was murder?' He didn't doubt it, but he wanted to hear Volz's reasoning. When they caught the perpetrator, evidence of intent to kill could make the difference between a murder charge and manslaughter. That was the difference between a life sentence – potentially without parole – and only seven years before the guy was back out on the streets.

'In my opinion, yes, her attacker was trying to kill her. There are two reasons for that conclusion.' She folded down the sheet to expose Natasha's stomach, revealing blotchy purple areas of lividity above her hips. Lockhart knew they were indicative of her cause of death: low oxygen in her blood.

Volz pointed to two small puncture wounds about four inches apart. 'I'd guess that these marks were caused by a Taser or similar device. You see how they're quite close together? That indicates she was shot at close range, then an electrical charge applied to immobilise her. Her restraint wasn't consensual.'

Lockhart nodded silently. He was imagining Natasha's shock as she was tasered. Had she let her attacker into her home? 'And the second reason?'

'Her efforts to stay alive while restrained. You'll already have seen the cuts at her wrists and ankles where she tried to break free from those ghastly plastic ties. Then there are the marks around her face.' Gently, Volz drew lines away from Natasha's lips, back towards her ears and jaw. 'Her mouth was probably forced open with a strong dental gag – metal, I'd say – which allowed her attacker to push the ball into her mouth and, ultimately, down her throat.'

Lockhart suspected as much. He made a mental note to check for similarities in Kim Hardy's post-mortem. He hoped it'd been performed as thoroughly as Volz's work for Natasha.

'There's some sign of recent damage to her teeth as well, most likely as she bit down on the gag to try to dislodge it.' Volz shook her head briefly. 'Restraint, immobilisation, and a tool to keep the victim's mouth open. That's about the only way it'd be possible to mechanically choke a strong, healthy adult like Natasha. This was no BDSM game gone wrong,' she added. 'In case you were wondering.'

'I didn't think it was.'

'There's more. Apart from the tasering, her attacker also tried to choke her once but failed. When I weighed her stomach, it was unusually heavy, so I looked inside and found this.' Volz returned to the bench and collected another plastic bag, also containing a metal ball. It was visibly smaller than the first one she'd shown him but was mostly covered in dark fluid. 'Somehow, she'd managed to swallow this. But, unfortunately for her, the attacker was prepared, and seems to have attempted it again with a second, larger ball. That second ball was wedged so tightly into her throat, she would've required surgery to get it out.'

'Jesus.' Lockhart couldn't contain his reaction. He didn't need Lexi Green there to tell him that this level of organisation was cold-blooded. Bringing a set of equipment to the victim's house, talking his way in somehow, then determinedly murdering her against all her efforts to resist. 'So, she was fighting to stay alive.'

'Yes, she was. Not even the most extreme sex game would involve that.'

He blinked, nodded. 'What about her time of death?'

Volz frowned. 'I'd estimate mid to late evening the night before she was found. She had a partially digested meal in her stomach, along with that ball. So, she'd probably eaten around two to three hours before she was killed. You may have some other data on when she ate but, based on her stomach contents plus observations from the crime scene on rigor and algor mortis – that's body temperature – I'd say she died some time between 8 p.m. and midnight. Can't be more precise than that, I'm afraid.'

'That sounds about right. Can I take the two balls as evidence?'

'Yes, I'll get you to sign for them.' The comment reinforced Lockhart's respect for Volz; she knew the importance of maintaining continuity in the evidential chain. 'And there's one more thing, although I don't know how significant it is.'

'OK.'

Volz carefully lifted Natasha's left arm and, holding her wrist in one hand, displayed her fingers. 'There's slight bruising and two small lacerations on her left ring finger.'

'Yeah, I saw that at the scene.' He'd been wondering about the significance of those marks.

'Was she married?'

'Not that we know of,' replied Lockhart. 'She'd been engaged but wasn't at the time of her death.'

'Well, it looks to me as if a ring has been torn off her finger with enough force to leave a mark. It's nothing compared to the other torture she endured, but I thought you should know.'

'Thanks. Anything else?'

'Not for the moment. I'll get you my report as quickly as possible.'

'Sure.' He was still staring at the ring finger. 'Right, I'd better get back and brief all this in.' He signed for the metal balls, collected the two bags and began walking towards the door.

'Dan.'

He turned. Volz fixed him with a stare, her jaw tight.

'Catch this man,' she said.

Lockhart glanced again at Natasha's face. He thought of Kim Hardy, too. And he knew he wouldn't stop until he'd found the guy who'd done this.

Whatever it took.

# CHAPTER TEN

At 2 p.m., members of MIT 8 assembled around the collection of whiteboards, which had grown since yesterday. Already seated, Maxine Smith allowed herself a wry smile: if it wasn't possible to double the number of staff on a murder case, you could always double the number of whiteboards. It was an indicator of effort and activity, but experience taught her that didn't automatically translate into progress. She'd have to wait to hear the briefing before she could make that judgement. Experience had also shown that the time taken for everyone else to faff about with chairs and notebooks and tea was exactly long enough to wolf down a banana. She finished chewing and reached for her coffee. Sugar and caffeine: the two key fuels of policework.

Smith noticed that one of the new whiteboards was headed 'Operation Norton'. She knew the name would be drawn from a list of British villages and would've been assigned to their investigation, rather than being Lockhart's choice or anyone else on the team's. It wasn't a bad name – at least you could spell it easily and say it clearly over the phone. She'd known cases where documents had gone missing because of a silent k or a double s in the op name, taken from some funny little place in the middle of nowhere.

Lockhart stepped to the front and clapped his hands. Immediately, everyone stopped talking and sat up straight. Maybe it was a military thing, maybe his height, maybe just natural, but whatever it was, Lockhart had it: command. Smith didn't know her boss all that well yet; he kept himself to himself. He wore a wedding ring, but she didn't know anything about his partner or whether he had a family. But what she did know, she liked. And that was his ability to be clear and set a direction. Where that direction would lead them here, though, was anyone's guess. This was no easy case and she didn't envy Lockhart his position in charge.

'OK,' he began. 'Good work so far, everyone. Let's pull it together now and see where we are. Starting off with a victim update. I'll go first.'

Lockhart outlined the main results of the post-mortem this morning. Smith felt her stomach move at the thought of the metal balls, the Taser… this killer was a sick bastard, no mistake. Who knew what the hell was going on inside the guy's head? The bit about the ring finger injury was interesting, though, given their encounter with Hugh Chadwick yesterday.

Next up to brief the team was Lucy Berry. She began by saying that they were still waiting for the mobile phone company to supply Natasha's call records but, other than her broken-off engagement to Chadwick, there was nothing that stood out from her personal life in terms of her being at risk.

'Um, we know that Natasha did a lot of charity work,' continued Berry, 'so, it's possible she might've made some enemies through that. A pro-life organisation criticised her last year for donating money to an abortion clinic. And there were some vague online threats made against her back in April, after she publicly supported a campaign to stop female genital mutilation and breast ironing in the UK. But no indication that she was at risk of violence. And no reason for those threats to be acted on now, months after they were originally made.'

Berry read off her notes, virtually hiding behind the pad. Smith wanted to tell her to sod what anyone else thought and just shout out what she had to say; more often than not, her material was the most important source of leads for their team. Smith had learned that, if you wanted people to take notice, you had to make noise. Especially as a woman with a disability.

Now it was her turn. She stood to face the group and spoke from memory.

'Right, suspect strategy. Yesterday, Mo and I went to see Natasha's ex-fiancé, Hugh Chadwick. He's got a possible motive because Natasha dumped him in February this year. He claimed an alibi of being in a restaurant, followed by a strip club. Mo?'

Khan nodded. 'I went to both places this morning. Just got back.' He stifled a grin and there were a couple of murmurings from behind him. Someone gave a low whistle. 'Whatever,' he said over his shoulder. 'Jealous. None of the dancers were there, anyway.'

'Mo,' Lockhart leant forward, his expression serious, 'does it check out?'

'Yeah. He's on camera at the restaurant, then the club, arriving and leaving roughly at the times he said. Haven't checked his Uber trip, yet. Or his apartment block camera through the concierge. That's on the list this afternoon. But I don't reckon it's him. He's already outside the time of death window when he leaves the club.'

Khan was entitled to his opinion, although Smith suspected he was giving Chadwick the benefit of the doubt because he was impressed with the asset manager's lifestyle. She was undecided on his guilt.

'The time of death's an estimate, Mo. As far as I'm concerned, guv,' she said to Lockhart, 'he's still a person of interest.'

'I agree,' replied her boss. 'Though there's not enough grounds for an arrest yet. We'll see what Mo digs up from his apartment cameras. You spoke to Natasha's friend this morning, right, Max?'

'Yes. Ellie Wood. Thirty-two-year-old university mate of Natasha's. She reckoned Chadwick went crazy after Natasha broke off their engagement. Proper raging. But Wood had known him as long as he'd been going out with Natasha, and she didn't think he was capable of murder, for what that's worth. Too soft, she said. He was never violent, not that Natasha ever mentioned, anyway. She did tell me, however, that the reason Natasha dumped him was because she found out he'd slept with a sex worker.' This was met with a few whispers from her colleagues, and she noticed Lockhart's head tilt up.

'Apparently Chadwick had started going to the strip clubs as part of his *job*,' she continued, unable to keep the scorn out of her voice. 'Entertaining clients. But then he couldn't stay away. There's a spectrum of services in those places, and some of the dancers there will offer full sex inside the club if the bloke pays enough.'

A DC started to make a joke about his wages, but Lockhart cut him off.

'So, Chadwick visited sex workers?'

'Yeah.' Smith knew where he was going. 'You're thinking opportunity for Kim Hardy's murder, too?'

'Yup.' Lockhart scribbled a note on his pad. 'Max, see if you can get him to volunteer what he was up to on the night Kim died, please. Mr Chadwick is one wrong answer away from an arrest.'

'Will do, guv. But, other than Chadwick, who she didn't think was responsible, Wood wasn't aware of any specific person that would've wanted to do this. As far as she knew, Natasha didn't have any stalkers or unwanted attention.'

'She must've crossed paths with her attacker somewhere,' said Lockhart. 'The guy was prepared. He didn't randomly turn up at the house hoping there'd be a lone woman there. He targeted her.'

'Right, guv. Wood said she met a lot of men through work, and it's clear she had a high public profile. People could've seen her online, or at some kind of business event… and Wood said she was pretty active on Tinder, too. I passed that on to Luce.'

'I'm putting together the information request on her account,' offered Berry. 'It'll take a long time to come back, but we should be able to see who she was messaging.'

'So, she was out there on the hook-up scene, then.' Khan folded his arms and tipped his chair back on two legs. 'Always a risk, right?'

'Funny how no one ever says that about men who are prolific daters,' observed Smith. Before she could take Khan to task any more, Lockhart stepped in and distributed follow-up actions, including tracing the purchases of items reckoned to have been used in Natasha's murder. When he started talking about the dark web, too, a little voice in Smith's head was already saying *long shot*.

That inner voice got louder as one of the DCs summarised the results of their door-to-door inquiries around where Natasha lived: sod all. Her house was too far away for even the closest neighbours to hear or see anything. And the cleaner had a rock-solid alibi, apparently, working a second job in a Brazilian restaurant in Soho until 1 a.m. on the night of Natasha's death. Smith sensed the mood dropping, an air of disappointment settling over the team as everyone realised that no one else had a decent lead.

As Lockhart gave out the day's final actions, people started to close their notebooks and wriggle in their seats. Then a small voice came from the back of the group.

'Dan?' It was Lucy Berry.

'Wait.' Lockhart extended a hand towards the officers who'd started to get up. 'Yes, Luce?'

'Erm, well, I was just thinking, you know, about the motive for this murder.' She glanced around uncertainly, gauging others' reactions before deciding to continue. 'So, on a previous case, where it was stranger violence, we got a psychologist in. They looked at the case notes and gave us some really useful ideas. I know they're expensive but I... I just thought it might help. That's all.' Her voice tailed off towards the end.

'Like it did on the cat killer case, you mean?' One of the DCs folded his arms and barked a laugh which several others echoed. Someone muttered the phrase 'mumbo jumbo'.

Smith knew what the DC was referring to: a string of incidents in south London where cats were murdered, sometimes eviscerated or decapitated, and deposited on their owners' doorsteps. The National Crime Agency supplied a forensic profiler, who came up with an elaborate story about the cats representing women, and the killer being a misogynistic man with complex sexual issues who was likely to escalate to preying on humans if he wasn't caught soon. It sounded good, until CCTV was found showing that the killer was just a fox. The whole business confirmed Smith's belief that psychology was a load of rubbish. All that was needed was the application of common sense to the available facts. So, her opinion of Lockhart took a nose dive when he replied:

'No, I think that's a great idea, Luce.' He wagged a finger, and Smith noticed Berry blushing. 'In fact,' added Lockhart, 'I know just the person.'

# CHAPTER ELEVEN

Lexi was catching up on paperwork in her office. There wasn't much opportunity to do that within regular hours, so every psychologist understood the importance of using DNA – Did Not Attend – time to keep on top of admin whenever a client didn't show up. She had session notes to enter onto the computer system, two requests for interpreters to write, a referral to employment support and, if she got through all that, there was some clinic data on recovery to be analysed. A DNA was basically bonus time; without it, she'd have to do unpaid overtime to get everything done. It sucked, but that was the NHS. And that was why she needed the private work.

There was a knock at the door. Dr Rob Edwards stood in the doorway, holding two steaming mugs of tea, his eyes sparkling behind clear-rimmed glasses. Rob was a grade above her, but there was no real hierarchy between them; more often than not, he made the drinks.

'Here you go, Lexi.' He extended one of the teas to her. 'Three sugars, right?'

She couldn't avoid the reflex look of horror before he cracked a grin. 'Just kidding. Your body's a temple and all that. It's a Julie Andrews.'

She stared at him blankly.

Rob rolled his eyes. 'White, none.'

'*Sound of Music*,' she replied, taking the mug. 'A white nun.'

'Yeah. One of my military clients told me that.'

'You know what? Right now, I could use the sugar.' She pointed her Montblanc pen at the screen. 'I'm writing up Andrea's notes. It's complicated.'

Rob scratched his beard. 'Is he using again?'

'He says not, but I think he is. He was a little spacey in our last session.'

'Mm. You taken it to supervision?'

'I will.' Lexi hadn't shared with anyone else why Andrea mattered so much to her. It was because the young Italian man totally reminded her of Shep. When she looked at Andrea, it was almost as though she was sat there with her brother. Almost as though he was still alive, and she could pretend that she hadn't failed him. It was stupid, she knew, but Andrea was more than a client. He was Shep. And helping him was a way of healing that wound in her, or at least trying. Psychologists were supposed to reflect with supervisors on their personal reactions to cases and clients. But Lexi had kept this all private. She defended it to herself with a vague idea that it wasn't relevant to Andrea's treatment, which she knew was a lie.

'So, how many more sessions have you got with him?'

Lexi was trying to think of a clinical reason to say 'lots' when her desk phone rang. She recognised the number and her heart leapt a little, for which she immediately felt ridiculous. 'I'm sorry, Rob, I have to get this,' she said, reaching for the phone.

'Sure. See you later, then? A few of us are going to the pub after work, and I definitely owe you a drink after yesterday when the guy—'

'Dan, hey,' she said, giving Rob a thumbs up before pointing to the phone. He got her message – which was about as subtle as a Fourth of July parade – and left. 'How are you?'

'Bit stressed,' he replied. She imagined that was an understatement. He didn't ask how she was. 'Listen, I'd like your opinion on my new homicide case. I know you've got experience with forensic work, so I thought maybe you could help us?'

'O-K,' Lexi drew the word out, cautious. There was a brief silence as she tried to work out when she might have time. And how much time it would take. She wanted to help, but...

'We can pay you,' he added.

'Oh, no, it's not about that,' she replied hastily. 'I just—'

'Seriously, we've got a budget. It's not loads, but it should cover a few hours. If you can do us a discount?'

'Well, um, sure,' she said, instantly feeling guilty for taking money on a murder case. Maybe she wouldn't ask for payment. Then she remembered the letters that'd arrived that morning.

'Nice one. Can you come to the office when you finish tonight? I'll let you read some of the stuff, then you can tell me what you reckon.'

'OK.' The word was quicker this time.

'Jubilee House on Putney High Street. Just go to the front desk and ask for me.'

'OK.' She wasn't sure what else to say.

'Cheers.' He hung up.

She hadn't asked what kind of help he wanted.

*

Lockhart knew he'd need to work late, again, not least because Dr Green was coming over to the MIT base that evening. So, with as many actions in progress as possible, he felt no qualms about taking his first break of the day: an hour away to visit his mum.

Iris Lockhart still lived in the flat where he'd grown up, although she was there alone, now. Lockhart's dad, Tom, had passed away five years earlier from a heart attack. He'd died in their living room, drinking beer in his favourite chair, watching his beloved Arsenal football team play on TV. Though he missed his old man, Lockhart couldn't help but smile at the thought that it was exactly how Dad would've wanted to go. Whether his life could've been saved if he'd got help sooner was another matter.

Lockhart had made the short drive east from Putney and was striding up the concrete steps to the third floor. The lift was perpetually broken, and he knew it took his mum a lot longer to get up and down, especially now she used a stick to walk. But there was no way she'd ever move. 'I'm part of the furniture, love,' she'd say, tutting and dismissing his suggestions of relocating with a wave of her hand.

The small apartment was crammed into a block on an estate in Bermondsey, with the noise of trains, traffic and city life a constant backdrop. Lockhart wouldn't have wanted to bring up here the children he and Jess had planned. Nothing against the place – it was his home for eighteen years – but breathing exhaust fumes all day and having nowhere to run around probably wasn't the healthiest start in life. And the estate wasn't as safe as when he'd grown up there in the eighties and nineties. Today, it seemed like every young man carried a knife, and he guessed there was at least one flat in the block that was a trap house full of street drugs ready for distribution to local addicts. His mum hadn't come to any harm, but that didn't stop him worrying about her.

As he approached the familiar red front door off the walkway, the aroma of frying meat wafted towards him, and he began to salivate. He'd called ahead, and Mum had insisted on making a quick tea 'to keep him going'. Bacon, sausages, eggs – he wasn't going to say no. He noticed that the door was off the latch and shook his head as he pushed it open.

'I told you to keep the door closed, Mum,' he called down the little hallway to the back of the flat.

'Daniel!' she exclaimed. Mum was the only person who called him that.

As he moved through into the tiny kitchen, she gave the pan a final couple of jabs with a slice and turned to him. He wrapped her in a big hug, bending down and planting a kiss on her cheek.

Holding her, he could feel the bones of her back; she was frail, but sharp as a pin and mentally as strong as anyone he'd ever met.

She waved the slice towards the cooker. 'Tea's ready.'

'You didn't have to.'

'Nonsense.' She prodded him in the chest. 'You need to keep your strength up.'

Lockhart hadn't realised how hungry he was until he started eating. It tasted great: a plateful of greasy, home-cooked comfort. As he tucked in, he told her about his sessions with Dr Green, and a bit about the new case he was working on; sparing her the details she wouldn't already have seen on the news. She told him about visiting a friend of hers who Lockhart had known growing up, and about how another local shop had gone out of business. Sometimes, he wished he could stay here in this kitchen, just eating and talking with Mum. And pretend that all the shit that went on outside didn't happen. But he knew that was an illusion.

She waited until Lockhart had mopped up the last of his egg yolk with toast before asking the question she always asked at some point during his visits:

'So, anything new on Jess?'

He sighed. 'No, Mum. Not really.'

'Not really?' She frowned. 'There is something, then?'

'Maybe. No. I don't know.' He lined up the knife and fork on the side of the plate. 'There's a missing persons website I came across last month. I posted a picture of her up there, thinking, you know, what harm can it do? Anyway, some guy came back to say he'd seen a woman who looked like her around Dagenham way. About a year ago. I don't know if he's yanking my chain, though.'

'Did you put it up on your wall?'

'Course.'

She sniffed. 'Dagenham. That's a dodgy area if ever there was one. Druggies, hookers—'

'Sex workers, Mum.'

'Sex workers, then. What would she be doing round there?'

'No bloody idea. Probably not even her.'

'You gonna go have a look?'

'Yeah, I mean… it's worth a trip, when I get a minute. I'll ask about.'

She linked her hand with his. Her knuckles were swollen with arthritis. 'Don't get your hopes up, love.'

'I know.'

Apart from Lockhart, his mum was probably the only other person in the world who believed Jess could still be found, though technically her file remained open at the Missing Persons Bureau. Even her own family had given up on her; the easier option compared to living without an answer. He didn't hold it against them, even though he knew they partly blamed him for her disappearance.

Jess's parents and brother favoured the idea that she'd had a mental breakdown and gone off somewhere. They thought Lockhart should've been around to support her through her regular 'ups and downs', as they called them, instead of flying off to war zones and leaving her alone to worry about him. *That's what marriage is about*, her dad had said. Lockhart disagreed. Jess knew he loved being a soldier and she wouldn't have wanted him to quit the army just so he could keep an eye on her. She was resilient and independent and could look after herself. To him, marriage was about what he'd been doing for the past ten years: never giving up on his wife. Not even when the Met stopped actively investigating her disappearance. *Till death do us part.* That was the vow he'd made, same as his parents had done. And he meant to keep it, just as they had.

'I love you, Daniel,' said his mum spontaneously. 'Don't ever forget that.'

'Love you too.' He gave her hand a gentle squeeze. Then he glanced at his watch. 'Better get back to work.'

# CHAPTER TWELVE

Lexi hesitated after she'd walked through the tinted-glass doors of Jubilee House. Despite working in the same general part of town, she'd never been here before. She hadn't visited a police station for a while, but she'd been to enough of them to know that this place didn't look like one. That's because it wasn't a police *station*, she told herself. It was an office block; there were no suspects or detainees here. A security guard directed her across to the reception desk where a guy without uniform sat at a computer.

'Can I help you?' he asked as she approached. She recognised the practised tone of voice: neither welcoming nor hostile, just neutral.

'Hey,' she said, tucking a loose strand of hair behind her ear. 'Uh, I'm here to see Detective Inspector Dan Lockhart.' It sounded odd giving his rank; to her, he was just Dan. She fished in her bag for her NHS pass. 'I'm Lexi Green.' The pass read Dr Alexis Green, but she disliked calling herself doctor because it created an immediate power imbalance. Sometimes, though, that was necessary, depending on the situation; the title got people's attention. Most people automatically attributed authority to doctors, whether they had it or not.

'Take a seat, please, and I'll tell him you're here.'

She was walking over to the row of chairs – identical to those in her clinic – when she heard the door open behind her, admitting a blast of October night air that made the tiny hairs on the nape of her neck stand up.

'Lexi.'

She turned. Dan was wearing the same suit he had on yesterday. She couldn't swear to it, but it looked like the same shirt, too. She took in the lines of his face, the dark bags under his eyes; maybe he'd been awake all night, perhaps he'd not even been home to change. It was weird seeing him outside of the clinic and she suddenly felt unsure of herself in his domain. Maybe that was how everyone who came for therapy at the hospital felt around her. She hoped not.

He gave her a grim smile as he crossed to meet her.

'Thanks for dropping by.'

'Pleasure. So, how can I help?'

He jerked a thumb towards a set of double doors. 'Follow me.'

She'd been sitting in the small, empty meeting room alone for nearly ten minutes when the door burst open. Dan dropped two manila files on the table in front of her. He separated them and arranged them side by side.

'Natasha Mayston,' he said, tapping the first. 'And Kim Hardy. Both murdered. Kim three months ago, Natasha two nights ago. You probably saw the news…'

'Uh-huh.' Her heart was beating a little faster.

'Both died from asphyxiation by mechanical choking. They'd each had a metal ball wedged in their throats.'

'Oh my god,' she blurted, before she could get a hold of herself.

'Yeah, I know.' He met her eyes briefly. 'Both were restrained in chairs with plastic ties. Both seem to have been immobilised with Tasers before they were choked. Both had small injuries to their left ring fingers. Both around thirty years old.'

She didn't reply. She was already picturing their bodies. And her morbid sense of curiosity was telling her to open the files.

'But there were differences too,' he continued. 'The two women were found across town from one another. Natasha was in her million-pound house by the river in Battersea, Kim was in a cheap hotel room in east London. And we've found no people or places that connect them.' He ran a hand around the back of his open collar. 'To be honest, they're about as different as you could get. Natasha was a successful independent businesswoman who ran her own investment firm and owned her home. Kim was a sex worker with a meth addiction and no fixed abode.'

She waited for him to say more.

'We have a number of leads we're following up,' he added, without much conviction. 'But what we want to know is whether there's anything you think of when you read this stuff. Victim profile, suspect profile. Anything… psychological. You know, that we might've missed. I just want to make sure we've covered all the bases.'

She swallowed. 'Sure.'

'I can't put everything in those folders, you understand, but all the main stuff's there. How long do you need?'

She wanted to say that she hadn't a damn clue about any of it and could she please go home. But she took a breath, looked at the two files: young women, about her age. In the city that was the closest thing she had to a hometown. The money didn't seem so important any more.

'I'm guessing you think it's a serial offender?' she asked.

He nodded once. 'My boss thinks it could be a copycat, but the detail about the metal ball was never made public. So, my view is, yes, it's the same guy.'

'Do you think he's going to kill again?'

'We have to work on that basis,' he replied. 'Right now, because there's nothing linking the victims, it looks like stranger violence. And those guys usually don't stop until they're caught.'

She opened both files and ran a thumb up the wad of papers in each. 'Couple hours OK to start?'

He checked his watch. 'I'll come find you at nine, then. Get reception to call up if you finish earlier. And, goes without saying, but don't photograph any of it and don't remove anything from the files. Security will do a bag search on the way out.'

'Sure.' She could understand his caution, but she'd already signed a bunch of papers that threatened her with jail time if she stole any material or passed details to anyone outside of Dan's team.

'Have you eaten? Can pick you up a sandwich or something from the canteen.'

'No, I'm good.' Her stomach was hollow, and she instantly regretted turning down the offer of food. However bad it might be, it couldn't be worse than a hospital cafeteria. Whether she'd have any appetite once she started reading, though, was another matter.

'OK.' Dan stood and left as quickly as he'd entered. He was so different to how he was in the clinic room. Gone was the tentative patient. Here, he was in control. There was something special, she thought, about him choosing to let her see his vulnerable side. She imagined not too many people saw that. Maybe no one else. Maybe not even his mom.

Lexi slid the Kim Hardy file in front of her, its cover still shut. Most of her work with the police had been victim and offender risk assessments, mental state examinations and cognitive testing for stuff like IQ or impulsive behaviour. She hadn't told Dan that she'd never written an offender profile before. Then again, he hadn't asked. She had that feeling from the start of her therapy training all over again; conscious incompetence, they called it. Imposter syndrome. When you have enough self-awareness to know that you don't know what you're doing. Should she have said something? Had she not wanted to put him off hiring her? Underneath her good intentions, was she really just thinking about money? Or was it something else… did she want to impress Dan? Lexi wasn't sure. She glanced at the door, half-expecting one of her training therapists to step in and tell her that the exercise was over, or hoping her clinical supervisor would enter and guide her through it.

She closed her eyes for a few seconds before opening them again.

Then she turned the cover on the Kim Hardy file and started reading.

*

It'd been Lockhart's idea to get out of the office, and the pub by the river was ideal. Being a weeknight, it was only half-full, and they'd easily snagged a quiet corner table. He placed the bottle of pale ale in front of Lexi Green, briefly mesmerised by the elaborate artwork on its label. It was from a brewery he'd never heard of, in a gentrified part of south-east London that, a few years ago, even his mum would've been scared to live in. He took a long pull on his pint of Stella before climbing on to the bar stool opposite her.

Lockhart realised that, to anyone observing them, it might've looked like they were on a date. He immediately thought of Jess and felt suddenly guilty. But this was work, he reassured himself. That's all it was.

'Your burger's on the way,' he said. 'Extra cheese, as requested. And sweet potato fries.'

'Thanks.'

'So,' he leant in, 'any thoughts? I mean, you can write a report in slower time, obviously. Just wanted to know if there was anything immediate.'

'Um,' she spun the bottle with her fingertips. 'OK, so, apart from the fact they were both young women, I agree, nothing else connects them. That suggests two possibilities. Either the perpetrator is attacking total strangers—'

'Or?'

'Or he chose Kim as kind of a test run,' she grimaced after the phrase, 'before targeting Natasha. She was the higher-status individual, and she was killed after Kim. Maybe Natasha was the intended victim and your offender is a highly organised psychopath who'd kill someone just to practise killing. And, now that Natasha's dead, that's the end of it.'

'Could be.' He nodded, took a sip of beer. 'Some people in our team mentioned that "test-run" theory. They like the ex-fiancé for it, and apparently, he's visited sex workers before. Although his alibi looks good, so I'm not getting too fixed on him.'

'If it was him, though,' countered Green, 'that might explain those little scratches on Natasha's ring finger. And Kim's, if he was rehearsing the murder or whatever.'

'Hm.' Lockhart drank some more lager and felt it wash away a bit of the tension in his body.

'Or maybe it's not about Natasha's broken engagement at all,' continued Green. 'And that's just a coincidence.'

'Go on.'

'So, I'm thinking, if it's stranger violence, then perhaps the ring has some special value for him. Like, it's symbolic.'

The idea had briefly occurred to Lockhart, but he hadn't got any further than that.

Green took a swig of beer. 'You know if you get an oversized ring, you can fix it in place with these, like, little springs?'

He shook his head. 'Nope.'

'Maybe that's what caused the cuts on their fingers.'

Lockhart thought in silence for a moment. 'You said "symbolic". How?'

'OK, well, what does a ring on the third finger represent?' She glanced down at his left hand.

'Marriage,' he said quietly, before taking a gulp of beer. 'Commitment.'

'Right. The ancient Egyptians believed that finger had a vein in it that went straight to the heart. So, it probably started as a romantic thing to wear a ring on it. But for some guys today, it's possession. Ownership.'

'Really?'

'Yeah.' She gave him a rueful smile. 'The woman as property, her identity subsumed into the man's. People have written about it. So, taken with all the evidence of restraint, you're probably looking at a guy who likes to control, to own. To possess. Which makes me think he's somebody who's experienced a trauma. He's probably lost something... Maybe he's lost a woman.'

'Like the ex-fiancé?'

'Sure, except you said his alibi checks out.'

'A man who's lost something,' he repeated.

'I mean, it's just my opinion. And I realise it's not exactly specific.'

As SIO, it was his call to bring in a psychologist. Green was the obvious choice: she was on the chartered list, was police-vetted, had forensic experience and didn't charge half as much as the shrinks from the NCA. More than any of that, she was one of the few people he trusted. But he was starting to wonder how he'd justify the additional cost of Green to DCI Porter when the result of her analysis was that they should be looking for someone who'd lost something. And he could already hear the mockery at the morning briefing if he asked his team to go out and find that person. His frustration started to grow.

'I'm sorry,' she said, as if reading his thoughts, 'there's not much to go on with only two data points.' She spread her hands in apology. 'Jeez, listen to me, *data points*. They're two women who've died.'

'Let's hope there aren't any more data points for you, eh?' Lockhart drained the rest of his pint. He was wrong to think Green would wave a magic wand and solve it for them. And yet, there was something in what she'd said. A layer of meaning beyond what he or any of his team had seen. That glimpse gave him the same feeling as when he'd first met Green. He'd seen it in her eyes, and he was sure she'd recognised it in him, although it was almost gone. It was something he'd needed then as much as he needed it now.

Hope.

# CHAPTER THIRTEEN

There were few signs of life at the nondescript suburban house as Sophie Wright walked up the path to its front door. She'd parked her car in the next street and looked behind her a couple of times to make sure no one had followed her. In her line of work, you had to be careful. Giving away this address could be extremely costly to quite a number of women, and she wasn't talking financially.

The only clue as to the building's purpose were its twin security features: the frosted glass on every window facing the street, and the two small hemispherical cameras peeking out from under the roof tiles on each side. She rang the buzzer and turned to scan the street one more time: nobody there. The sound of shuffling footsteps from inside the house was followed by a pause – no doubt as the spyhole was checked – and then two bolts slid back before a lock turned. The door opened six inches, but it was still on a chain. A pale face with large, red eyes regarded her warily.

Sophie held up her ID card. 'Is Maggie in? I'm her lawyer.'

Two minutes later she was seated on the single wooden chair in a small, sparsely furnished bedroom, her client perched on the bed opposite her.

'How're you doing, Maggie?'

'All right, s'pose.' Her client picked at her nails, one foot tapping on the old, worn carpet.

Poor Maggie looked anything but all right. Sophie knew what she'd been through at the hands of her ex-partner and, tomorrow, she would have to face him in the family court. Getting out of her relationship was an incredible act of bravery and yet, here she was, effectively still a prisoner. Well, Sophie intended to do something about that.

'I know you're probably a bit nervous about tomorrow,' she offered, extracting a couple of files from her briefcase.

'Damn right, I am.' Maggie's body tensed. 'That bastard's going to humiliate me in front of everyone.'

Sophie had seen that situation often enough in court and was determined not to let it happen to Maggie. As a legal aid barrister, she'd lost count of the number of times she'd acted for a female victim while their male abuser represented himself, criticising and ridiculing his ex-partner across the courtroom. Sophie's clients were often made to feel unreliable, unstable, untrustworthy. *How could she remember, your honour? She drinks. She's always been forgetful.* And so on. Sophie had heard every excuse and experienced almost as many personal insults as her clients. The whole system was skewed in favour of the man. It made her blood boil. And that was before the security issues of abusers following their victims home from court to places like this, women's refuges hidden away in quiet parts of town.

But it was precisely these challenges and struggles that gave Sophie her sense of motivation. She earned a fraction of what other barristers made doing corporate cases, but that didn't matter. She was fighting. Standing up for women who'd been beaten down for so long they didn't believe they could stand up on their own any more. And when she won, sometimes even getting an abuser sent to prison in a criminal trial for assault or rape, the satisfaction was better than anything else in her profession. When you got the law to work for the vulnerable person and the aggressor was punished, there was nothing like a custodial sentence to take the swagger out of an abusive man. From then on, he'd be the one looking over his shoulder. Sophie knew what happened in prison to men who beat women.

'I'll make sure he doesn't do that,' she said confidently. 'We know what our arguments are, and I think we've got a really strong case for you getting sole custody.'

Maggie's head dropped. 'Even if I win, I'll have to move, won't I? He knows where me mum's house is.'

'If we win, there'll be a restraining order on him. He won't be able to come within half a mile of you.'

'Yeah, but he's got friends, hasn't he? Some evil pieces of shit who'd do a job for him.' She put her head in her hands. 'I don't even want to think about it.'

'Then let's not. That won't help us right now,' said Sophie firmly. 'Let's focus on the facts we've got and go over them one more time.' She laid a hand on the files.

'It's all right for you,' replied Maggie, her voice catching, 'you don't have to deal with any of this. You don't know what it's like!' Then the tension seemed to drain from her body and she began to shudder silent tears, her face creasing.

It wasn't the time or place to disclose that Sophie *did* know what it was like. That the seemingly nice, middle-class home where she'd grown up, in a picture-postcard village, was a pit of abuse from her father towards her mother. People around them must've suspected, but no one talked about it. When Sophie was old enough to know what was going on, she didn't know who to talk to. To this day she berated herself for that inaction; she should've done something. But nobody seemed to think that wealthy, educated people could perpetrate or experience abuse, as though it was something that only happened in working class families, to women like Maggie.

In these moments of raw emotion, Sophie had to stop being a barrister and just be a human. She put down the folder and stood up. Then she crossed to the bed, sat next to Maggie, and put her arm around her.

*

It was going to be deeply satisfying to kill this bitch. Like the last one, she thinks she's a bloody saint, too. Visiting those refuges, going to court to help the weak and the oppressed. She couldn't be more wrong. She wasn't helping anybody. All she was doing was distorting the natural operation of market forces. He'd read about that online, discussed it in the forums. But the message hadn't truly sunk in until He – the Guru – had written about it. Of course, His book and Twitter and anything else 'official' was in his real name, as a professor of social sciences. But in the chatrooms, he was simply the Guru. And that was where he put the most interesting stuff. The true knowledge.

The Guru understood economics and he'd explained it on the web forum like this: women's worth is conferred by their attractiveness. They each have what's called a sexual market value. And, these days, they can choose who they want to have sex with. Even the ugliest woman can have sex any time she wants because women control the supply of sex and men will always demand it. So, what do the guys do? Get an expensive haircut and a nice shirt and stand around in bars waiting for a woman to choose them? Opt out and sit at home, jacking off all day to free porn? Pay for it with a hooker? Or choose a different path: control by violence.

Evolution made it such that men naturally control the supply of violence, the Guru said: we're bigger, stronger, more aggressive. And when we want something, we go out and get it – that's what our biology intended. So, if we want sex, but women won't give it to us, then we can use violence. It could be a random rape, or – better yet – controlling a woman in a relationship.

Reading that was like someone flicking on a light in a dark room. Violence was a market force, too, and it was something men could bring to the marketplace of sex; a service they could supply whenever it was required. The Guru had even posted a graph online to show how it worked. One guy had written a supportive message beneath it: we needed 'to see rape from the man's perspective', and he was right. Someone else had listed and categorised ways to control a woman, under the headings: physical, emotional, financial. That was all useful, but he had bigger plans.

This barrister was a distortion of the market, because she was reducing men's control in relationships. That was unacceptable. He'd asked the Guru what should be done about a distortion to the market. The Guru had replied that, according to neoclassical economic theory, a market distortion should be removed to allow the 'invisible hand' to operate freely. So, that was what he needed to do.

Remove the distortion.

He'd sit tight until she came out of the refuge and follow her home. Much as he'd love to do it tonight, he'd be patient. Check and double-check the details: her living arrangements, her working patterns, routes to and from her house, security features on her property, the configuration of nearby CCTV and its dead spots. He could hardly wait.

In the meantime, though, he'd have to settle for a simpler act in the fight. When he got back, he'd post the refuge's address online. He thought of the respect he'd receive from the brothers for doing that and felt a frisson of excitement.

The buzz was returning.

# PART TWO

# CHAPTER FOURTEEN

Lockhart had to admit he was struggling. It was four days since Natasha Mayston's body had been discovered and Operation Norton was going nowhere.

They'd practically eliminated Natasha's ex-fiancé, Hugh Chadwick, from their inquiries, after his alibi checked out from the moment he left his office to the hour he returned to his flat, each movement caught on camera. Not to mention his alibi for the time of Kim Hardy's death three months ago, too. He'd been entertaining a delegation of Chinese investors in the upmarket district of Mayfair, almost ten miles away from the cheap hotel in east London where Kim was murdered. It was too far back to get the CCTV footage from Mayfair, but Khan had checked the restaurant booking and even emailed the Chinese visitors to confirm. As much as some of his team wanted it to be Chadwick, there was no evidence to support his involvement. And he'd been their only person of interest.

Nothing they'd found in Natasha's private or professional life indicated that she had enemies; no family members desperate enough to cut her out of an inheritance, no business rivals vying for control of her firm or assets. She hadn't been sexually assaulted or robbed, which suggested that her attacker's goal was murder rather than her death being the unintended consequence of another crime. The killer had set out to choke her, but why? And there was still nothing linking her to Kim. Operation Norton hadn't made a single arrest and people were starting to notice.

They'd long passed the crucial first forty-eight hours for a homicide investigation. And Natasha's death had all but vanished from the headlines, their early media appeal producing nothing but crank calls whose follow-up had drained half of his team's working hours.

Now, they were relying on Berry to find something in the data. They had Natasha's mobile phone records and were combing through them, checking the subscriber details of each person she'd called or been called by in the past three months. That painstaking work had swallowed up the other half of his team, querying the various databases which the Met could access, as well as requesting details from mobile phone service providers. The dating app, Tinder, hadn't released her contacts, yet, and as for the big social media companies, he might as well forget it. They took data from you 24/7, often without permission. But God forbid you want something back from them, even on a murder case... Last but not least, tracing the purchases of items used in the murders hadn't produced anything so far – there were simply too many potential suppliers to work through.

Lockhart sensed what his team was feeling: that their investigation had run out of energy and ideas. With no clear victim profile and no obvious suspects, they were almost totally in the dark. DCI Porter had already shifted his attention to other matters, and he'd even authorised attendance at a training course for one of Lockhart's team. Both of those actions indicated that he expected no outcome from the case. Lockhart wondered if Porter had held that view right from the start. Was that why he'd put Lockhart in charge, to hang the inevitable failure on him?

Pretty soon, people would begin to question his strategy as SIO. His only hope came from the prospect that Lexi Green could shed some light on the case. She was coming in today during her lunch break to brief her report to the team. Lockhart felt an impending sense of dread; if her material didn't move their investigation forward, then not only would his leadership and decision-making be criticised further, but his relationship with Green would be damaged, too. And he didn't want either of those things to happen.

His phone pinged with the arrival of a text. Lockhart saw that it was from Green, saying she'd just got off the bus and sorry that she was a little late, but she'd be at Jubilee House in two minutes. He texted back to say he'd meet her by reception.

Lockhart refreshed the screen on his webpage one last time. As expected, no one had posted anything further about his wife on the missing persons forum. No corroboration of the Dagenham sighting, and the guy who'd posted it hadn't been active in almost a week. He closed the browser window and set off downstairs to meet Green.

⁎

Lexi could feel her pulse racing. As the Major Investigation Team slowly gathered around her, she got a little stab of adrenalin somewhere in her belly. She'd turned down Dan's suggestion of coffee; that would only make her anxiety even worse. No way did she want to stand up in front of all these detectives with her heart going a hundred miles per hour while sweat circles spread around her armpits. Oh God, she was sweating already... But she needed to get a hold of herself. This wasn't about her, it was about Natasha Mayston and Kim Hardy. And finding the guy who killed them.

'Hey, Dan, can I get a little space on the board to write, please?'

'No probs. Mo, can you help clear an area up there for Dr Green?'

'For sure.' A young Asian man rose from his front-row chair and approached the whiteboards. He clearly spent as much time in the gym as he did in front of the mirror. His aftershave was strong. And he was standing awfully close to her.

'I'm Mo,' he said, offering his hand.

'Lexi,' she replied, shaking it. He held on a little too long.

'So, you're a psychologist?' He arched an eyebrow.

'Uh, yeah.' She didn't need this right now. She wanted to look over her formulation, rehearse her lines.

'All right,' he persisted. 'So, what am I thinking, then?' From the way he was looking at her she could make a pretty decent guess.

'Lemme see.' Lexi feigned a moment of concentration. 'OK. You're wondering what stuff to move so I can use the board.'

He took the hint, and, with a few laboured sighs, began clearing space behind her. She caught Dan's eye and they shared a brief smile. When Mo was done, she thanked him and set about writing up her key points.

Next thing she knew, Dan was clapping his hands and calling for attention. As the silence settled her adrenalin shot right back up again. Her fingers and toes were tingling, and she could see the tremor in the notepad she was holding.

'Listen up everyone,' he began, 'for the uninitiated, Dr Lexi Green is a clinical psychologist with forensic experience who's had access to the case files for Operation Norton, as well as Kim Hardy's murder, which is not officially part of Norton.' He glanced sideways at her. 'We've worked together before.' He didn't give any more details. 'Lexi, over to you.'

'Thanks Dan, er, DI… Dan.' There were a couple of sniggers as she stumbled over what to call him. She tucked some loose locks of hair behind her ears and tried to compose herself. They were all staring at her.

'So, modelling these two crimes as the work of one serial offender,' she started, 'we can use the Five Ps Formulation to help profile the—'

'Where are you from?'

The question came from a middle-aged guy in a suit near the back. He held his hand up as if it excused his interruption.

'Andy, just let Dr Green—'

'No, it's OK, really.' She extended a palm towards Dan. 'I probably should've given you all some background before I started talking about the case.' Lexi hated these moments where her accent immediately marked her out as different. When she had to explain herself to the other Brits, despite holding one of their passports.

'Well, my dad's American, but I was born here. My mom's British. I grew up in the US, in a whole bunch of places, and came back here five years ago to train as a clinical psychologist. Now, I work in the NHS at a clinic in Tooting.' She avoided the temptation to add: *does anyone have a problem with that?*

The guy in the suit just nodded.

'Have I seen you on *CSI*?' said another, unleashing a barrage of laughs.

Lexi felt her face flush red. Her hands were getting clammy.

'All right,' boomed Dan. 'That's enough! The next person who interrupts Dr Green before she's finished giving us her profile is going to find themselves cataloguing public tip-offs for a week.'

A hush descended, and she returned to the board, realising only then that her writing was probably too small for them to read at the back.

'OK, so, like I said, the Five Ps Formulation. That's a way of trying to understand behaviour, in this case, our offender's actions. The first P is Presenting, that is, what's going on right now? We believe our perpetrator has murdered two women by choking them on balls.'

There was a snort from somewhere in the group, and Lexi glanced up to see a chubby man biting his knuckle. Jeez, who the hell were these guys in Dan's team? They had all the maturity of high school kids. No, make that junior high.

'That's a very unusual act,' she continued, 'because it combines a lot of anger and rage with a whole lot of control. This guy is very controlled, he's precise, he's organised, and he's smart. He doesn't lash out, punch, kick or stab. He chokes young women. That brings me on to the second P: Predisposing.' She indicated it on the board. 'What in this guy's background would make him able to do this? He probably has high levels of dark personality traits like psychopathy and narcissism. You couldn't deliver that degree of suffering to another human being in such a deliberate way without the ability to switch off your empathy towards them. Which gives us a second clue: he hates women. Our offender probably has longstanding negative beliefs about women, most likely formed much earlier in life, maybe at home. We can't say what exactly he hates, because we don't know what connects Natasha and Kim. Maybe it's sex, maybe it's something about money.' She drew an arrow from Predisposing to Presenting.

She scanned their faces. A tough-looking woman at the front had her arms folded with obvious hostility. Lexi noticed she only had two fingers on one hand, and inwardly chastised herself for staring a fraction too long. She had the full attention of that guy Mo, but he seemed more interested in her body than her formulation on the board. And the rest of them looked either bored or confused. Apart from Dan, the only one who seemed to be following was a woman with a bob-cut hairstyle who sat in the middle. She wore a jumper and looked a little older than Lexi. Her frequent note-taking showed she was paying attention.

'Third P: Precipitating. What made him do this now? My guess is that he experienced some kind of triggering event, possibly a trauma, quite recently.' She outlined her theory about the ring and its symbolism of possession and loss, maybe of a woman, most likely a romantic relationship. There were a few coughs and some fidgeting in the group. Even Dan looked uncomfortable and Lexi realised he was probably thinking about his wife. She made a mental note to check with him afterwards that he was OK. For now, though, she had to keep going.

'Right, ah, where are we? Yeah, fourth P: Perpetuating. What's keeping his behaviour going? Well, obviously we hope he isn't planning any further attacks. But Dan says that we need to assume he is, and I agree. If he's continuing, it's because the act of killing only temporarily meets his need for... whatever purpose it serves.' She paused. 'And we don't know what that is yet. It could be restoring his ego after a traumatic event like being abandoned.'

Dammit. The profile had sounded good when she'd rehearsed it. But, met with this wall of indifference, Lexi found herself losing confidence. She thought the formulation was on point, given the lack of available information. But the expressions of the MIT detectives suggested they thought otherwise.

'OK, final P: Protective. That sounds a little strange, but it's important. Why isn't this guy choking a woman every night? An obvious reason is that he's careful. He doesn't leave a lot of forensic traces.'

'*Any* forensic traces,' added Dan, shaking his head. 'That we could find.'

'Right, so that's one reason. He plans, he's kind of a perfectionist, he likes to be in control. He takes his time. Another reason could be that, deep down, he has some doubts about what he's doing. That's more of a feeling for me, though.' She saw a few eyebrows lifting. 'There's a whole lot of documented evidence that even the most prolific and psychopathic serial killers have a flip side. That they question at times why they're doing it. That they look in the mirror and hate themselves, if they can bear to look in the mirror. Quite a number even tried to kill themselves at some point during their activity.' She looked at the whiteboard and back to the group. Someone stifled a yawn.

'In terms of profile,' she added, 'I'd say we're looking at a male, aged twenty to fifty, with above average intelligence. He probably works in a professional or skilled manual job. He probably lives alone or has access to another private place and, if he's sourcing all his… equipment over the internet, then he's computer savvy and most likely spends a good deal of time online.'

'Sounds like you, Andy,' quipped one of the detectives. 'Apart from the bit about above average intelligence, obviously.' This was met with a ripple of laughter.

'OK,' she concluded, trying to remain upbeat. 'Any questions?'

She'd expected nothing, but fifteen hands shot up. Virtually everyone in the room. And at least half of the people they belonged to were smirking.

Dan pointed to the tough-looking woman at the front. 'Yes, Max?'

'Thank you, Dr Green. I wonder, can you actually give us anything practical to follow up?'

'I, um, well…' Lexi met the woman's challenging gaze. Suddenly she was unnerved again. 'Ah, OK, just gimme a moment.' She looked at her notes and then back to the whiteboard.

She couldn't think of a single thing to say.

# CHAPTER FIFTEEN

The Elegance Hotel on Romford Road was anything but what its name aspired to. Maxine Smith recognised it from the photographs in Kim Hardy's file; this was the place where her body was found three and a half months ago. Smith took in the exterior: it was a large, detached house built between the wars, which had obviously been converted into a budget hotel some time in the nineties, to judge by the faded signage out front. In addition to some of the cheapest rooms in London, the Elegance offered currency exchange and money transfer services. Presumably, those facilities were aimed at itinerant foreign traders, although Smith knew that a large proportion of the cash that changed hands here was between sex workers and their clients. The hotel had a one-star average rating on Google and wasn't even listed on *Booking.com*. Its cream paintwork was filthy and flaking and, in the grey semi-darkness of late October, Smith could hardly think of a more depressing place.

It was two weeks since Natasha's murder and, though no one had said it out loud, they had no decent leads on her killer. Ten days ago, a young psychologist had come in and spouted a load of long words at them. The male officers in the MIT seemed happy enough to look at her, but when Smith listened, she heard nothing of substance. Nothing that could be followed up with feet on the ground, eyes on physical evidence or conversations with people who knew something worth knowing about this case. It was a serious error of judgement on Lockhart's part to use their miniscule budget for that profile; Smith knew how much those shrinks charged the police. And, obviously, it'd got them nowhere. That was why she'd come here.

In the absence of anything else to work through, Smith believed that a visit to the crime scene always had the potential to offer something new. If nothing else, you were in the place where it actually happened. You might see something that others had missed the first time. Particularly if those others were a bunch of lazy so-and-sos at Newham MIT, led by the arrogant DCI Flynn, who were convinced they had their man. Despite her reservations over Lockhart's faith in the psychobabble, Smith agreed with him that their killer was a serial offender and therefore not likely to be Damon Pagett, the man arrested and charged with Kim's murder before Natasha had been killed. But Smith understood the politics of policework; she'd messaged her colleagues in Newham to say she was visiting the hotel because she was working on a copycat theory. They didn't seem to care either way and told her to crack on.

The cramped lobby smelled of damp and there was no one behind the desk. Smith rang the little bell at the counter. No one came. After thirty seconds, she started shouting. Another thirty seconds later, a small man appeared through a side door. He was about Smith's age, but his skin was sallow and greyed, most likely from years of hard smoking. Thin, lank hair was plastered to each side of a centre parting in a style that Smith guessed pre-dated the hotel's opening.

'Can I 'elp you?' His accent was a nasal, high-pitched Cockney.

Smith showed her warrant card and explained her interest in the place. 'How long do you keep your CCTV footage?' she asked.

The man laughed through his nose. 'We ain't got none, love.'

'You don't have any CCTV?'

'If my guests ain't got no need for it, then neither 'ave I.' He gave her a gap-toothed smile.

'What about the guest book?' she asked. 'You must register the people who stay here. That's law.'

'Course I do.' He reached under the counter and produced a ledger.

She flicked through, aware that the man was staring at her cleft hand with obvious revulsion. Screw him. Scanning the names, she knew this was a dead end too. *John Smith, Mickey Mouse, James Bond.* All men. And all bullshit. She found the date of Kim's death. More aliases and deliberately illegible names were written, with only Damon Pagett printing his name clearly and truthfully. Hardly the actions of someone about to commit a murder. It was too much to hope that Hugh Chadwick would've signed in here. Still, she photographed the page. She asked the man about the night of Kim's death, but he said he couldn't really remember anything unusual or anyone other than Pagett coming in with her. Newham MIT would've made sure he knew what to say, probably in exchange for not probing too far into his other clientele.

Smith knew exactly the kind of operation this greasy little sod was running. A few years ago, some of her colleagues had busted one of these squalid shit-holes after intel suggested the place was just a brothel masquerading as a hotel. Sniffer dogs had found a hundred thousand pounds in cash, stuffed into biscuit tins in the manager's bedroom. It'd been seized as proceeds of crime and the manager arrested, which was a massive result. Nevertheless, Smith couldn't help but think of that money as thousands of sexual encounters, many of which were probably conducted under duress or to buy substances. The desire to stand up for those women was the real reason why she'd come here.

Smith couldn't bear the thought that Kim's death hadn't been properly investigated because she was a sex worker and a meth addict. That it'd somehow been deemed her own fault because of her risky lifestyle. While some women chose to be sex workers, a lot of those who worked on the street defaulted to it as their only way to pay for a drug habit. Desperation led them to accept potentially dangerous clients without even the questionable protection of a pimp or madam. Smith knew how many serial killers had preyed on sex workers precisely because of that vulnerability.

Of course, there was London's most notorious murderer, Jack the Ripper, who remained unidentified to this day. There were also more recent cases, like Peter Sutcliffe – dubbed the Yorkshire Ripper – where police had discounted the testimony of sex workers he'd previously assaulted as unreliable. Or the lesser-known but equally chilling Saeed Hanayi, the Spider Killer, in Mashhad, in Iran. Hanayi was a married father-of-three who took sex workers back to his house before strangling them with their own hijabs. Some religious conservatives had defended his actions, even praising him for performing a public service and 'cleaning up' the streets. The list went on. But, wherever sex workers were murder victims, harsh moral judgements about those women were never far behind.

For Smith, it didn't matter if you were a billionaire aristocrat or a homeless addict without a penny to your name. They all deserved the same justice, especially in a huge and impersonal city like London, where money was the main measure of a person's power.

'Can I take a look at the room Damon Pagett used that night?'

The guy made a show of checking his watch. 'Fine, I'll take you up there.'

Smith didn't expect it to yield anything, but she wasn't leaving this place without turning over a few more stones. Even if every single one had nothing underneath it. That was the way she worked cases: good, old-fashioned graft. It was the only way she knew.

And she didn't give up easily.

*

Sophie Wright was working late at home. She often needed to do that on weeknights, particularly when she had a trial starting. And her current case was important. Her client, a woman in an abusive relationship, had decided to pack her bags one day and leave her partner. The mistake she made was waiting for him to come home from work to tell him personally. He'd flown into a rage, grabbing her ponytail in one hand and marching her into the kitchen where he'd gone straight for the knife block. She'd lost a huge chunk of her hair breaking away from his grip before running and locking herself in the bathroom.

The guy had tried to break down the door, telling her which parts of her body he was going to cut. Terrified, she'd jumped from the first-floor bathroom window to a patio below, fracturing both ankles and a wrist. Despite her injuries, she'd managed to hide in a neighbour's garden, shivering until dawn when she dragged herself to the nearest police station, making the journey on her hands and knees when the pain of walking became intolerable. Tomorrow was the day of reckoning: the man who'd attacked and threatened her would be in the dock, charged with grievous bodily harm. Sophie hadn't been able to convince the Crown Prosecution Service to go for attempted murder, but she hoped the abuser would still get a substantial prison sentence. She was ready for a fight.

Sophie had worked solidly since returning from her barrister's chambers, barely pausing to eat a green curry she'd had the local Thai place deliver. There were just a few more points of planning to go through before it was time to put away the files and take a hot, relaxing shower ahead of a good night's sleep. She was so focussed on her case notes that the doorbell made her start. It was nearly 10 p.m. Who'd be calling round at this time? Her neighbour, maybe, with some trivial point about managing the recycling bins again? It rang once more. Whoever it was, they'd well and truly broken her concentration now. She got up and padded down her hallway towards the front door. She pressed the intercom.

'Hello?'

'Delivery. Net-a-Porter, for number 16.' The soft male voice had the rolled r of somewhere Mediterranean. 'Just needs a signature.'

Had she ordered something online? She didn't think so... but she might've lost track, what with her workload recently. Sometimes her sister, Isobel, who lived in Singapore, got stuff delivered here to save on postage costs. Then there was the odd surprise from Mum and Dad, sent directly. And the neighbours always put each other down to receive packages if they were away. Could be any of the above. She opened the door.

A man in an open jacket and courier's uniform stood there.

He was holding a cardboard box.

He looked familiar.

# CHAPTER SIXTEEN

One advantage of Putney's MIT being based in an office rather than a police station was that they could use the nearest pubs. While officers across London tried to calculate the minimum distance from their station required to obtain booze without running into local suspects, Lockhart and his team could leave Jubilee House and take their pick of riverside pubs on the doorstep. Not that you could enjoy the river view much in the darkness of an October night, mind.

Lockhart carried the tray of drinks over to the set of three tables his team had commandeered and shoved together to make one large, increasingly rowdy group. He distributed lagers, gin and tonics, and white wine to vocal appreciation. The round wasn't cheap, but as SIO he was obliged to get it and, given their lack of results on Op Norton, he felt it was the least he could do for the troops' morale. It was turning into a classic 'Big Thursday', a favourite Met tactic to ensure that your hangover was spent on company time during the Friday before the weekend rest days he'd rostered for all of them except himself. At least he had the day off tomorrow before working Saturday and Sunday.

Smith was telling a story they'd all heard before from her beat days about how she once managed to trick both a teenage detainee and a duty nurse into thinking her fingers had been cut off during a stop-and-search in which she'd uncovered a large-bladed knife clasped between the teenager's buttocks. Khan was crying with laughter, while Berry was prompting Smith for extra details. Lockhart sipped his Stella – the fourth this evening, or was it fifth? – and forced a smile. He knew he should be getting into it, sharing stories of his own and building rapport with his team. He was only two and a half months into joining MIT 8 and he feared his reputation had already been dented by his decision-making in the past fortnight. He needed to win them over. But something held him back.

He used to love getting on the beers in a big group. But over the years, he'd changed. First, with his military surveillance training. There were only so many times you could have situational awareness drilled into you before it put you in a near-constant state of alert; knowing exactly where you were, checking doors and windows, risk-assessing the strangers around you. That made you wary of drinking a skinful in public. And, secondly, after his wife Jess went missing.

He and Jess had met in a pub: the local boozer on the estate where Lockhart had grown up. He'd been nineteen, she was seventeen. He was back from barracks catching up with old mates, she'd been out for the birthday of a friend Lockhart vaguely knew. Jess had approached him first; later saying that she'd done so because she thought he was 'fit', but staying because she felt a calmness talking to him that she liked, even needed in her life. Jess was sparky and funny, making him laugh so often his face was aching by the end of their conversation. Listening to her, he forgot all his stress. And he fancied her, of course. They started dating and that was that. It'd all begun in a pub. Now, somehow, it didn't feel right to be out having a laugh without Jess. Not when he could be doing something to find her.

So, instead, he'd shifted to solo drinking more often, mainly cans of Stella in the relative safety of their tiny flat late at night. That seemed to numb his pain in a way that going out didn't achieve. These days, even when he was drinking with others, he still felt alone. He wondered what Lexi Green would say about that.

Thinking of her reminded him that he'd meant to text. They'd barely been in touch since her briefing. It hadn't gone well… and he felt a bit guilty about the ruthless grilling his team had given her for an awkward half hour until she'd needed to get back to the clinic. But he still believed that there was something in what she'd said. Certainly, there was no one in his team – himself included – who could interpret the mind like she could. Maybe it was just a case of giving her the right material to work with. He wanted to discuss the case again with her. And he should probably set up some more appointments for himself with her, too.

Lockhart excused himself and took his pint outside. He wandered across to the river wall opposite the pub and stared out at the black expanse of Thames water, glinting now and then as it ebbed and flowed under a crescent moon. It was late, and he should probably wait till morning. But something made him want to contact her now. To know there was at least one person in this city, other than his mum, who would listen to him. Who understood him.

He took out his phone and texted Green.

*

Lexi Green was losing herself in the music. The bar was rammed and sweaty, but she and her flatmates had established a space and were proceeding to own the dancefloor. She'd drunk a little too much, but this had been her first proper night out since the train wreck of her briefing for Dan's team and, well, she deserved to party.

It wasn't the greatest idea to go out on a Thursday night when she had a full day of therapy tomorrow, but you couldn't get the free entry and two-for-one offers on Friday or Saturday nights. There was an unspoken agreement between her, Sarah and Liam that, when every penny counted, those deals made the difference between going out and staying in. And she was painfully aware of her bank balance now that she was unlikely to be doing any more work for Dan. Yet, with a few drinks, some good music and her friends, it was surprisingly easy to forget about those problems. Her phone vibrated in her back pocket with a message, but that could wait. Right now, she was in the moment.

Sarah and Liam were in a dance-off to an Afro Swing track, its thumping bass making Lexi's whole body vibrate. As they aped each other's moves with increasing difficulty, a small crowd gathered, whooping, whistling and cheering them on. Lexi took a deep drink from her beer bottle and felt her shoulders and hips starting to move with the beat. She closed her eyes, enjoying a few seconds of nothing but sound and movement. When she opened them again, she noticed a guy was holding his phone up in her direction. Immediately, she snapped out of her fun zone.

'What the fuck?!' she yelled at him, stepping nearer and batting away his phone. 'What're you doing?'

'Huh?' He pretended not to understand. What a dick.

'You were filming me,' she shouted, feeling the anger rise inside her.

'No, I wasn't.' He shrugged.

'You were!' she protested.

'Sorry, it's just, you're hot.' He grinned. 'Where are you from?'

Jeez, not again. 'Delete that video,' she ordered him.

'There is no video.'

'Bullshit.'

He was holding the phone loosely at his waist. Without thinking, she brought her beer bottle down hard on it, knocking it to the floor. Before he could bend down to pick it up, she'd smashed a three-inch stiletto heel through the screen.

'Whoops,' she said.

'You stupid bitch!' he cried, shoving her backwards. Sarah caught her and then Liam was in front of her, shielding her from the guy and raising his hands in a non-confrontational defensive stance. Liam was tall and well-muscled, but the guy's friends were getting involved now and pushing him. Before she knew it, the bouncers were in the mix and Sarah was marching her out of the door and into the freezing night, with Liam right behind them, clutching their jackets.

'I swear that lad was gonna hit you, Lex,' said Liam, his breath quick.

Lexi looked back over her shoulder towards the bar as they walked away. 'He was filming me on his phone.'

'Well, he'll need a new one now,' Liam chuckled.

'Ugh!' Sarah pulled a face. 'What a creep. I swear that happens all the time. Next thing you know it's posted on social media or some website for pervs.'

Lexi threw her hands up. 'Where do these losers get off thinking it's cool to do that?'

'They see it online and it makes them want to try it.' Sarah took Lexi's arm and linked her own through it. 'Forget it, Lex. Come on, let's go somewhere else.'

Despite the encouragement, Lexi had lost her enthusiasm and felt suddenly drained. 'Maybe I should go back. You guys carry on.'

Sarah squeezed her arm. 'Nah, it's all good. I've had enough for one night anyway.'

'Aye, me too.' Liam took her other arm and the three of them walked together. They were still arguing about who'd won the dance-off as they went into the underground station. But Lexi was thinking about Sarah's words: *They see it online and it makes them want to try it.* Even through the alcohol, an idea was starting to form.

# CHAPTER SEVENTEEN

Sophie Wright's eyelids flickered as she opened her eyes. Light flooded in, but her vision was blurry. She was sitting upright in one of her kitchen chairs. Her body felt rigid, her muscles heavy. What happened? She must've been unconscious, but she didn't know how long she'd been out for. The last thing she remembered was opening the door to the courier and... oh God. There was something in her mouth, something *on* her mouth.

Her jaws had been forced wide apart as if she were at the dentist and, as she tried to bite down and close them, she felt the horrible grinding of metal on her teeth. Whatever it was wouldn't budge. Blinking and straining her eyeballs downwards, she could just make out some silver bars protruding on either side of her face. Shifting her lips and tongue made no difference; the bars were pulled right inside her mouth by thick straps that she could now feel snaking around her head, tight against her jawbone and the back of her neck. What the fuck was going on? Her heart was thumping against her ribcage.

Instinctively, she tried to reach up to get the metal away from her face. That was when she realised she couldn't move her wrists... or her ankles. All four limbs were bound tightly to the arms and legs of her kitchen chair with solid white plastic ties. As she wriggled, she could feel a cable below her chest, too, pinning her torso to the chair back. She pulled hard at them all, tensing her muscles, but the only result was a sharp pressure across her skin, her ribs and on the bones of her joints.

The agony was followed by confusion as she noticed a ring on the third finger of her left hand. It wasn't her ring. Why the hell was there a ring on her finger? Frantic, she glanced around but there was no one there. Then she remembered the news about the woman who'd been attacked in her home in Battersea two weeks ago. Hadn't she been tied to a chair like this?

Oh God.

Small rattling, clinking noises came from the hallway. Sophie's next instinct was to scream. She sucked in a lungful of air and braced herself.

'HEL—'

She hadn't even got the single word out when her whole body became engulfed in pain, her limbs shuddering as it felt as if her insides were going to erupt through her skin. Her cry turned into a muted, mangled, meaningless sound. Then, as abruptly as it had started the pain stopped and she was left taking hard, shallow breaths, her eyes moist with tears she couldn't control. She craned her neck forward and, below her breasts, saw two wires trailing from her stomach. She followed their path to the ground, along the tiles and out of the kitchen door. A pair of shoes appeared in the doorway and her gaze travelled upwards as she tried to make sense of what she was seeing. The courier stood there, holding one of those Taser guns, the wires attached to its muzzle. OK, that explained the paralysing jolt she'd just been given. But who the fuck was this guy?

'Don't make another sound if you want to live,' he said, looking down at her, his face momentarily expressionless. Then he cocked his head, as if listening, and, apparently satisfied that she hadn't successfully raised the alarm, he stepped closer to her. Was it worth another shout? Her neighbour would probably be home…

'I mean it,' he added softly, as if he could tell what she was thinking. He pursed his lips and held the Taser barrel against them to reinforce the message.

She nodded, blinking rapidly and trying to focus on his face. There was something familiar about him, but she didn't know what it was or where she'd seen him before. Was he someone she'd convicted or beaten in court? An abuser with a vendetta who'd tracked her down? Who would do this? She racked her memory. But another part of her brain was telling her that the who or why didn't matter now.

Her mind raced from cursing her own stupidity at opening the door to a stranger to the thought that she was about to be raped. Oh God. Was he going to rape her mouth? Was that what the gag was for? She started to think about sexually transmitted diseases… surely, he'd use a condom to avoid leaving evidence? Please, let him use a condom. Please.

She felt a blast of adrenalin course around her abdomen, driving her to action, but she was trapped. Her only chance was to do what he said. She'd heard stories of women who'd tried to fight back during a rape or a home invasion robbery. Many had ended up in hospital with stab wounds or broken bones or brain injuries. In some cases, they'd simply ended up dead. Was that what happened to the woman in Battersea?

The man approached her, so close she could smell his sweat now. He tucked the Taser into his trousers at the back and reached deep into his pockets as if checking for something. Panic rose up through her chest, a feeling of nausea in its wake. She tried to say, 'please', but with the metal against her teeth, it was just a strange noise. A tiny burst of urine came out and she felt warm dampness spread through her pants and into the crotch of her jeans.

He took his hands out of his pockets. In one was a thick spanner with a circular end. In the other, he held a smooth, silver sphere about the size of a golf ball. She searched his expression for a trace of compassion or mercy. But there was nothing, except perhaps a hint of pleasure.

The memory of where she'd encountered him popped into her head. Immediately after this she realised why he wasn't bothering to hide his face.

It was because he was going to kill her.

# CHAPTER EIGHTEEN

Nothing cured a hangover better than a swim in freezing cold river water. Lockhart had parked his Defender by the towpath a couple of miles down the road from his flat in Hammersmith, then swum upstream for half a mile towards Barnes Bridge – his open-water distance marker – before turning back for the easier downriver return leg. The late morning autumn air was biting, and even with an extra-thick wetsuit and cap on, Lockhart could feel his body working hard to stay warm as the Thames drained all sensation from his hands and feet. Getting in had been like a slap in the face, particularly after six pints of Stella the previous night. But, once he'd overcome the shock and got his heart rate under control, he'd settled into a steady rhythm of crawl. Now, half an hour later, he was almost back to his car.

People who knew he did this every week often asked him why he swam in the Thames rather than an indoor, heated pool. Or even in an unheated lido – one of London's massive Victorian-era outdoor baths – if he insisted on the masochism of cold water. Maybe there was something about the sense of self-punishment that appealed to him, in a weird way. Best not discuss that with Lexi Green. But there was more: the Thames had been the lifeblood of London for centuries and, as a Londoner, Lockhart felt a strong connection to the river. It wasn't clean – in fact, it'd once been declared biologically dead in the 1950s – but it was swimmable. And ploughing through its murky waters, against the tide and in all weathers, somehow fitted his role in the city. That didn't stop his mum telling him he was mad for doing it.

Lockhart heaved himself out on to the jetty and stood up, dripping wet. He took off his goggles and cap, the breeze already icy against his exposed skin. He crossed to his car and slid underneath the vehicle on his back, extracting the car key from where he'd secured it with a wingnut to a bolt he'd screwed into a metal plate. Popping the back of the Land Rover, he poured himself a steaming cup of tea from the Thermos flask alongside his towel. He spat out the remnants of Thames water in his mouth and gulped down the tea. It was hot and sweet, and he could feel it gliding down into his stomach, warming him up. He poured a second cup and instinctively tapped his phone. There were three missed calls from DCI Porter. Shit.

The warmth began to seep away as he processed the significance of this. Multiple calls from Porter on Lockhart's day off when their team was neither on call nor in frame. No, no, no. It couldn't be… He called Porter straight back without even checking the voicemail. His boss answered on the first ring.

'Dan. Where've you been?' Porter's tone was admonishing.

'Sorry, sir, I was swimming. I'd rostered a day off for myself today, because—'

'There's another body,' stated the DCI. 'Like Natasha Mayston.'

'Like, as in…'

'Killed in the same way, it seems. And in her home, again.'

Lockhart swallowed, felt his face tightening. 'Right.'

Porter's news was grim vindication of Lockhart's theories about the case. He was already berating himself for not catching this guy two weeks ago.

'The victim appears to be a barrister called Sophie Wright. Her flat's in Wood Green,' said Porter, matter-of-factly. 'MIT 6 were in frame, but once the initial crime scene features were recorded, someone noticed the similarity to Natasha's death and called me.' He sounded detached, like he was thinking about something else as he spoke.

'Do you want me to get up there, sir?'

'Yeah, yeah.' Porter cleared his throat. 'I've made you SIO, again.'

'OK.'

'If it *is* the same, bring it under Operation Norton.'

'Will do.'

'I'll text you the address now. Come see me when you're back in Putney.' Porter put the phone down.

Lockhart stood holding his mobile. He was still dripping from the river, wet hair plastered to his head. As the wind picked up, shaking the tree branches and whipping his wetsuit, he realised he was shivering.

SIO. His case, his responsibility. He wasn't going to make the same mistake as last time by waiting nearly two days. This time, he wanted her in from the start. He flicked through the contact list on his phone and dialled Lexi Green's number.

*

He stood in front of the wide toilet mirror and stared at his reflection. There was nothing in his face that gave a clue as to what'd happened last night. No scratches, no marks. And no visible emotions either. That was good. Inside, though, his stomach felt knotted. Was that… anxiety? He'd not slept last night – he'd been too excited – but he had to come in to work today, otherwise it would've looked odd. People might've noticed and, in time, someone would start totting up the coincidences. So, he'd drunk espressos – too many of them – to keep him going and now he felt kind of jittery.

Reaching into his pocket, he extracted a sheet of pills, popped two out of the foil, and washed them down with a slug of water from the bathroom tap. Immediately he began to feel calmer. He knew beta blockers couldn't work that fast, so part of their effect must be psychosomatic. But he'd taken them too late; the anxiety had already spread to his mind, turning to worry. What if he'd left a trace? What if someone had seen him? What if, what if... Last night had been more balls-out than the previous two; he was pretty sure there'd been a neighbour in the flat above when he'd done it. Initially, it'd given him a feeling of superiority, invincibility, even. But that'd ebbed away and doubts now chased each other around his head. He needed to think his way out of it and get back to work, try to look normal.

Taking in his whole body in the mirror, he moved his hand across to his groin, cupping his cock and balls. He began to massage them slowly. He swallowed and took a deep breath, casting eyes over his own chest, shoulders and arms. Focussing on his body in this way, and as the beta blockers began to take effect, a sense of calmness returned. He massaged himself harder, allowing his eyes to close with the soothing motion of his hand.

Then the door flew open and a colleague walked in. His hand shot from his crotch to the tap in front of him and he started washing his hands, bending over the sink and avoiding eye contact. As he lathered soap on his palms, his heart palpitating, he was aware of the man walking behind him. He heard the zip of flies followed by the splashing flow of piss against the urinal and the soft exhalation of relief.

The guy hadn't said anything. But maybe that was just the unspoken rule of the men's toilets. Had he seen? Surely not; the door opened towards him and he'd hit the tap immediately.

The whole sequence disgusted him. He shouldn't be feeling like this. He should be feeling like the most powerful man on the planet. It wasn't good enough. If he wanted to finish this and be immortalised – canonised as a saint, even – he'd need to step up his game. That's what the Guru would expect from His most devoted follower. There was a plan and he needed to stick to it.

Three more sluts were going to get what they deserved.

Time to move on to the next one.

# CHAPTER NINETEEN

Smith had arrived well before the start of the short-notice team briefing to be sure of a front row seat. This was turning into the biggest and perhaps the most serious case of her career, and she didn't want to miss a thing. She knew she'd have a role to play, that to catch a serial offender this careful would require her particular style of hard-grafting, diligent policework. And she was ready for the task.

She noticed that there was less faffing about from her colleagues this time and guessed that was the result of both the terrible discovery earlier that day and the presence of DCI Marcus Porter in their office. Lockhart stood to one side while Porter took centre stage. Their boss was a big, powerfully built man. Even without his senior rank, he'd command attention. The smooth brown skin of his freshly shaved head shone under the ceiling lights, which gave a blueish cast to the dark smudges under his eyes. Smith understood that tiredness; if she thought Lockhart's job was stressful, you could triple it or more for what Porter dealt with every day.

'Listen up. You should all be aware by now that Operation Norton has been expanded today to cover the investigation into the death of another young woman,' began Porter, his deep voice filling the open-plan office. 'On the available evidence, we're presuming her to be Sophie Wright, a thirty-two-year-old barrister. She was found just before midday today at her home in Wood Green. Though her flat is being treated as a live crime scene and the SOCOs are investigating as we speak, there's already enough to suggest that she was murdered in the same way as Natasha Mayston.'

'And Kim Hardy,' added Lockhart.

Porter turned and acknowledged the intervention with a small grunt. 'Sophie's and Natasha's deaths are therefore being treated as linked incidents with a sole perpetrator presumed responsible,' he continued. 'I will be convening a press conference after close of play today to make a public appeal, and we'll be joined by Sophie's parents who have been visited by our Family Liaison Officer.' He paused, checked his watch. 'They should be on their way into London now. DI Lockhart is going to meet them for a formal identification of the body from crime scene images. Dan.'

'Thank you, sir.' Lockhart stepped forward. 'What we know so far is that Sophie Wright was due in court today to represent a client in a case of alleged domestic abuse. When she failed to appear, her client called her office and eventually got through to a colleague. After another hour of nobody being able to contact her, and with sufficient time elapsed that they were confident it wasn't just transport problems, a junior clerk was dispatched from the chambers to Sophie's house to check on her. Apparently, they'd set up protocols for such an event after an older barrister died at home from heart failure a couple of years ago.' Lockhart spoke without notes and, like Porter, Smith couldn't help but respect his handle on the material and authoritative delivery. 'Sophie kept a spare house key in her office and the clerk took that, just in case. She let herself in and found the woman we presume to be Sophie dead in her kitchen. The MO of her apparent murder is described as identical to that of Natasha Mayston and,' he glanced at Porter, 'Kim Hardy.'

Smith could feel the anger welling inside her. Who did this bastard think he was, getting into women's homes and choking them to death? He was one hell of a coward, that much was clear. As her hands tightened around her notebook and pen, she realised that the rage wasn't useful. She needed to channel it into work: relentless, careful, dispassionate work. That was what got convictions. But right now, all she wanted to do was find the fucker before he got to any more women and choke him herself. The way Smith felt, she reckoned she could strangle him with her 'different' hand alone. She snapped out of that fantasy as Lockhart invited Lucy Berry to speak.

'OK, um, Sophie Wright was a barrister who specialised in defending victims of domestic abuse and gender-based violence,' said Berry, reading from her notes as usual. 'She'd only been practising for seven years but she seemed to have had quite a lot of success in that time. The website of her chambers lists a number of key cases she'd won. So, ah, I can circulate those as needed. That's it so far. Sorry.'

'Thanks, Luce,' said Lockhart. 'Right, in terms of suspect strategy, then, the first thing we need to do is clear Hugh Chadwick, again. He was our key person of interest for Natasha's murder. Mo, can I leave that to you?'

'All over it, boss.' Khan was clearly keyed up: eyes wide, both feet tapping, his jaw working a piece of gum. It wasn't a million miles from how Smith felt, but experience had taught her the benefit of slowing down. That way, you were less likely to miss something.

'Max.' Lockhart turned to her. 'Can you speak to Luce and get the full list of cases that Sophie worked, then go through them one by one? Take Andy, Priya and Sam to help you.' He turned to Porter. 'We could use some extra pairs of hands, sir.'

Porter nodded once. 'I'll see what we can do.'

'We need to know who she's had convicted,' continued Lockhart. 'Basically, anybody who'd have a motive for revenge against her. Some of those guys will still be inside, I'd imagine. So, prioritise anyone who's just come out of prison. Check any ongoing cases, too.'

'Will do,' replied Smith.

'OK, next up, we—'

'Er, sorry, guv.' Smith hated interrupting him, but she had to know her efforts were going to be focussed in the right place. 'It's just, you know, unless one of these guys that Sophie convicted also knew Natasha Mayston – which seems unlikely – isn't it looking more like stranger violence?'

Lockhart compressed his lips into a line and thought for a moment before responding. 'Thanks, Max. Yup, a stranger will be one of our suspect strategies. The problem is that we have no known offenders with a history of mechanical choking using the equipment this guy has. Luce trawled the databases for assaults where the attacker stuffed something into his victims' mouths, didn't you?' He raised his eyebrows, inviting Berry to chip in. Smith turned in time to see Berry going bright red as the room shifted its attention to her.

'Er, yeah, I did.' She flipped a few pages back in her notebook. 'But, um, yeah, that's it. They were all either sex crimes or robberies. So, it didn't seem to fit the profile of our guy, who did neither of those things. And there's never been a homicide by mechanical choking in this country before. Until Kim, I guess.'

'Right.' Lockhart folded his arms. His eyes flicked to Porter. 'We've got to keep our options open at this stage.'

Smith sensed the lack of substance here. 'So, what do we think is the overlap between the two – three – women who this guy's murdered? As I see it, they were all isolated, killed indoors, two in their own homes where they lived alone, all about the same age.'

'Go on, Max,' urged Lockhart.

'Well, we think Kim Hardy went voluntarily to the hotel room where she was murdered. Natasha and probably Sophie both opened the door to this guy. He's someone who people trust, who can knock on a door and get them to open up. Who can do that?' She numbered off the jobs on both hands. 'Gas man, postman, charity collector,' she paused. 'Police officer. Sorry, but it has to be said.' There were some murmurs behind her, but she kept going. 'TV licensing person, courier, takeaway delivery guy. All strangers who we feel comfortable opening our doors to. Maybe he's one of them or he's posing as them.'

Porter held up a palm. 'I see what you're saying, DS Smith, but that's a hell of a wide range. Think about how many of those people are moving around London, all day, every day. And that's if we assume he's not impersonating one of them and has a different occupational background altogether.'

Smith had been so focussed on her train of thought, she'd almost forgotten Porter was there. She hadn't expected to be shot down by him. 'True, sir, but—'

'Er, that's good thinking, Max,' interjected Lockhart, treading carefully. Smith knew that he wouldn't want to undermine the big man in front of their whole team. 'Let's pay special attention to people or vehicles of those types in the local CCTV footage, and when we go door to door. Sophie's flat was in a much denser area of housing than Natasha's and we might get lucky if someone heard or saw something. Maybe they wouldn't have thought it relevant at the time, but it could be our guy.'

'What about dating?' blurted Khan. 'I mean, if that's how he's finding the victims. Natasha Mayston was big on Tinder, so we should probably check that for Sophie and maybe some other apps, too. Bumble, Badoo, whatever. And that other one that works by how close you are to the person.' Smith expected some jokes about Khan's dating habits, but none came.

'Nice idea, Mo,' replied Lockhart. 'Luce, can you action that? In the meantime, I'm going to bring Dr Green back. We can't ignore the psychological angles of this case.'

'That's your call, Dan.' Porter thrust his hands into his pockets. 'Just keep the budget in mind, OK?'

'Sir.' Lockhart distributed some more actions, but Smith found herself losing concentration. Green? She couldn't believe it. The team had comprehensively shut her down when she hit them with all her psycho-nonsense last time. However much Lockhart had paid her for that crap, it hadn't got them anywhere. Now he wanted to get her in again. Why? Smith tried to make sense of it. Was it a kind of jobs-for-the-boys thing, or more than that? She thought she'd sensed something beyond a professional relationship between Lockhart and Green when the shrink came into the office – was he shagging her on the side? He didn't seem the type, but she knew how common infidelity was in this job, the unfortunate product of high stress and after-hours binge drinking. There were stories of SIOs misallocating resources to personal contacts with thin justifications and minimal results. That kind of leadership belonged back in the bad old days of police corruption. And it wasn't going to help them catch this choking maniac.

Smith tried to keep her reactions to herself. But, for the first time, she found herself questioning Lockhart's judgement.

# CHAPTER TWENTY

Lockhart crossed the lobby of Jubilee House to the small waiting area where a couple sat in silence. He guessed they were in their early sixties. The woman had one arm around the man, who clutched a small white handkerchief in both hands. There was no doubt who they were.

'Mr and Mrs Wright.' Lockhart spoke gently. They nodded, the man's eyes red-rimmed and shiny with tears. 'I'm Detective Inspector Dan Lockhart.'

'I'm Megan and this is my husband, Peter,' replied the woman. 'He's Sophie's step-father.' Her jaw clenched, perhaps with the effort of containing her shock. They would only have been notified a few hours ago and the unexpected news would still be completely raw.

'Thank you so much for coming.' Lockhart shook hands briefly with them. 'I understand this must be very difficult for you.'

In these situations, he needed every ounce of empathy he could muster. Nobody in MIT 8 doubted that the woman who'd been found earlier that day was Sophie Wright, but a formal ID was still required to be certain. For a police officer, conducting the identification of a body was one of the toughest tasks in the job; perhaps second only to the so-called 'death knock' to deliver the message cold; that job usually fell to the Family Liaison Officer, or FLO. But for the next of kin, making the ID was sometimes worse than receiving the initial news. Lockhart had an idea how Peter and Megan Wright would be feeling. He'd personally identified the bodies of two men in his military unit back in Afghanistan; briefly he wondered if he'd ever need to identify his wife… Now wasn't the time to dwell on that possibility.

'If you'd like to come with me, please, we have a room just down the corridor.' He gestured towards a set of double doors and waited for them to stand.

Inside the meeting room, Lockhart invited them to sit and offered them glasses of water. He took a chair at ninety degrees to the Wrights and placed a manila folder on the table. Sophie's parents could've opted to view these photographs in their local police station in Hampshire, but they wanted to join the press conference in Putney this evening. As hard as it was for the deceased's family to appear in front of the media so soon, having them alongside the detectives leading the investigation was a powerful combination for rallying public support.

'I'm sure the news from our Family Liaison Officer will have come as a tremendous shock to you both,' he said. 'And I know this is going to be hard, but we have to be one hundred per cent sure that the person we found is Sophie.'

'We're ready,' said Megan, squeezing Peter's hand. 'The Family Liaison person told us what would happen here.'

'OK. So, I'm going to show you some images and I'd like you to tell me if you believe they show your daughter. You can take as much time as you need, and if you'd like a moment to prepare—'

'No, thank you, Inspector.' Megan took a deep breath. 'Let's just see the photographs.'

Lockhart had already edited the set of digital files sent by the scene of crime officers. He'd selected and cropped pictures that showed Sophie's face as well as her hands, avoiding signs of the torture she'd endured in the final moments of her life. He opened the folder and extracted the first print-out, rotating it towards Sophie's parents. Almost immediately, Megan's hand flew to her mouth.

'Dear God,' whispered Peter. They were his first words since meeting Lockhart. Then his face crumpled, his lips drawn wide and eyes screwed shut. At first, his tears were silent, then he began to shudder and wail, shoulders hunched. Megan exhaled, blinked and drew him into an embrace. Lockhart knew that the ID was positive. He also knew that everyone who'd encountered death dealt with it in his or her personal way, so the best thing he could do for now was to sit quietly and let Peter and Megan Wright process the sight of their daughter like this in their own time. After a minute or more, Megan spoke.

'It's her. It's our Sophie.' She pulled her husband closer, holding him tighter, and Lockhart felt a terrible sense of intrusion into their grief. But he was also here to do a job that he hoped, ultimately, would get justice for the Wrights as well as for this killer's other victims and their loved ones.

'I'm sorry to have to ask,' he spoke quietly but clearly, 'are there any distinguishing features that make you certain that it's Sophie?'

Peter buried his head in Megan's shoulder and continued to sob as she stroked his thick grey hair. She composed herself and, with her other hand, pointed to the image. 'She got that little scar on the side of her nose from chickenpox when she was twelve. And you can see a mole just below her hairline, there.' Megan bit her lip and nodded. 'That's her.'

Those were the details Lockhart was looking for; there was no need to show them any further images. 'Thank you.'

Lockhart returned the image to the file and placed it to one side. He gave them a moment before he spoke again.

'I know this must seem very sudden, but while we're all here, together, do you mind if I ask you both a couple of additional questions?'

Megan's hand balled into a fist and she met his gaze. 'Whatever you need to do to find the person who did this to our daughter.'

Her bravery was incredible. From what he'd heard of Sophie's work, he imagined that she'd inherited that spirit from her mum.

'Rest assured,' he said, 'we will do everything we can to catch her killer.' Witnessing their pain first-hand like this, his conviction to see this case through couldn't have been stronger.

'Was Sophie dating anyone that you knew of, or did she have a boyfriend? Perhaps even a fiancé?'

Megan glanced at Peter before shaking her head. Peter wiped his eyes on the handkerchief and blew his nose. Lockhart could see that he was trembling. 'Not that she told us about,' replied Megan. 'I don't know about dating, but she hadn't had a boyfriend in a while. She was so focussed on her work.' Her voice caught in the final sentence, and Lockhart wondered if he'd already pushed too far. 'And she certainly wasn't engaged. We'd only seen her two weeks ago. Why do you ask that?'

Lockhart cleared his throat. 'There was some evidence of an injury to the ring finger of her left hand, which may have been caused by a ring being forcibly pushed on or pulled off. But...' he hesitated, 'we're not making that public for the time being.'

'Right.'

'And can you think of anyone else who might've wanted to hurt Sophie?'

'You mean apart from all those vile men she had sent to prison or barred from seeing the women and children they'd abused?' Megan barked a dry laugh and, again, Lockhart thought he'd said too much. 'No,' resumed Megan. 'Apart from them, no. Sophie was a wonderful, kind soul.'

Lockhart closed his notebook. 'I'm so sorry for your loss, Mr and Mrs Wright.' The words sounded clichéd, but he didn't know what else to say. Losing someone who had so much life left to live was tragic. It was the sort of thing that could tear you apart. He knew that more than most.

Suddenly, Peter sat up straight and gripped Megan's arm. 'Hang on. There was that one man who said he wanted to kill her. Do you remember, darling? Sophie didn't take it too seriously, mind. But he was a nasty piece of work. He'd tried to murder his own wife, Sophie reckoned. Put that thing in her mouth to keep her quiet, didn't he?'

'Yes, that's right,' said Megan. 'What was his name?'

Peter pinched his temples. 'Oh…'

Lockhart's mind was racing. It hadn't occurred to him that their perpetrator might have attempted a homicide by mechanical choking without actually killing his victim. Such an incident might not even have been recorded if the victim never went to the police at the time. Lockhart tried to supress his instinct to jump on this instantly. 'If we get you a list of names to look at, do you think you could identify the one she mentioned?'

Megan lifted her chin and blinked. 'Yes,' she said confidently. Lockhart recognised the determination in her expression.

# CHAPTER TWENTY-ONE

Lexi was used to the feeling of not belonging, but she hadn't been prepared for it this evening. After receiving Dan's voicemail during her afternoon clinic, she'd hustled through a Friday rush hour after work and arrived in Putney just in time for the press conference. But, having got there, she wasn't sure where she was supposed to be.

She didn't belong in the assembled audience with the media, among the journalists with their microphones, voice recorders and cameras. And she certainly didn't belong on stage with Dan, his boss and the parents of Sophie Wright. So, she'd settled for a spot to one side with some of Dan's team whom she recognised from her disastrous briefing a couple of weeks ago. They were friendly enough, but probably as surprised to see her as she was to be there. She hadn't expected another invitation to consult for the MIT but, in his message, Dan had said that they needed her input now more than ever. He believed she could help them crack this case. The question was whether she believed that too.

Lexi stood, her notebook and Montblanc pen in hand, ready to take down anything useful from the media briefing. But she had to admit that having something in her hands had the added benefit of making her feel less awkward about being here, once more the imposter. Lexi caught her self-focus and the guilt spiked; this wasn't about her. It was about the victim, her family, and the investigation to find out who'd done this – and might well do it again.

Looking up to the tables on the small stage where Peter and Megan Wright sat, she could only imagine how they would be feeling. Since Sophie was found at midday today, there had barely even been time for them to register the trauma of what'd happened. Now, they sat blinking at the camera flashes. Sophie's mom, Megan, had her arm around Sophie's dad, who seemed ready to break down. They were probably still in denial that this had happened to them, to their daughter. You hear about tragedy all the time in the paper and online, but it always seems like something that happens to other people. You never think it'll happen to you. You think you're immune.

When Shep died, it'd been mid-semester in Lexi's junior year at college and she was on campus in Princeton. One of the Dean's assistants had come into her class, taken her out and broken the news to her. She'd had literally no idea what to do; the whole thing had seemed unreal, like some terrible prank. Even the phone call to her parents, just minutes later, had been like a dream, a nightmare, where you think you'll wake up and realise that it was all in your unconscious mind. She could still picture those moments now, hear those conversations.

It'd taken more than a week, back home with Mom and Dad, before she accepted the idea that Shep wasn't going to be around any more. She thought about him all the time. And she treasured this beautiful pen he'd given her for her twenty-first birthday; she knew he'd saved hard to buy it. She'd been writing with it when they came in to tell her he'd died. Carrying it with her today was like carrying the memory of Shep. That was something she never wanted to let go.

She snapped back to the room as Dan's boss introduced himself as DCI Marcus Porter and began to speak. He was a huge guy of African heritage and – in contrast to Dan's charcoal suit and dark tie – he wore full dress uniform. He spoke slowly and carefully as he outlined what'd happened to Sophie, his voice resonant.

Apart from listing mechanical choking as the cause of death, the details given were pretty minimal; Lexi understood the need for that while each forensic aspect was investigated.

'We are treating Sophie's tragic death as suspicious. We not only believe it to be murder, but we also consider it to be closely linked to the murder of Natasha Mayston two weeks ago in Battersea. These linked offences could well be the work of a single individual.' Marcus Porter scanned the crowd. Though no one tried to interrupt him, there was a buzz among the reporters and Lexi noticed several of them taking out their phones and texting.

'We would like to appeal to anybody who may have heard or seen anything suspicious last night in the area where Sophie lived, on Moselle Avenue in Wood Green, to come forward and talk to us about it,' he resumed. 'It might be something small that you believed to be insignificant – such as a person who you didn't recognise, or some unusual behaviour.'

He handed over to Dan who gave a short briefing on Natasha's death and listed some ways the public could get in contact if they had information, including an anonymous tip line. One of the detectives standing next to her whispered something about 'floodgates' and 'nutters', shaking his head. There was no mention of Kim Hardy; Lexi knew they believed the same guy had killed her too. She thought about those poor women – all three of them around her age – and wondered if it could've been her or one of her friends. Where had this guy met or seen the women he'd attacked?

Dan announced that, prior to Sophie's parents reading a statement, he and Marcus would take a few questions. Hands shot up and one guy asked if they were dealing with a serial killer. Dan repeated his boss's line about linked offences but didn't use the term. Another reporter wanted to know if they'd made any arrests. Dan glanced at the DCI, then said no, they hadn't, and reiterated the request for assistance from the public.

Another question followed: did they have any suspects? Dan said they couldn't comment on that. How was this serial killer targeting his victims? Should all young women in London be scared? Dan advised everyone to be vigilant, particularly with letting people who they didn't know inside their house, but Marcus added that there was no reason for Londoners to be afraid and that they were doing everything possible to apprehend the person responsible. Dan seemed poised to move on to the parents' statement when a woman from the media pack spoke.

'What can you say about the mindset or the mental state of this killer? Are you seeking input from experts to profile the individual?'

Lexi's heart started to beat a little faster.

Porter linked his fingers and nodded. 'You can mention that, Dan.'

Dan flicked his eyes to Lexi and back to the reporter. 'As is standard practice with a major investigation, we are involving a range of allied professionals.' He paused. 'Including a chartered clinical psychologist with forensic experience.'

Without warning, he gestured towards her at the side. Cameras swung in her direction and flashes popped before she was able to react. Even Sophie's parents were looking at her. A couple of reporters started speaking, asking questions, demanding her name. How had they known she was the psychologist? Was it an assumption because she was the only woman in the small group from Lockhart's team? Then she realised: she was still wearing the distinctive blue-and-white NHS lanyard around her neck. She'd left the clinic so fast she hadn't taken it off. Dammit. She covered it with her notebook and wished she could cover her face, too. She wanted to hide behind one of the detectives, to get the hell out of there, to curse Dan for ambushing her like this. But it was too late.

Marcus's voice got the media's attention once more and he introduced Peter and Megan Wright to make their statement. As the cameras returned to the stage, Lexi retreated to the back and slipped away, desperate to find someplace to go with no reporters. Stealing the limelight from bereaved parents was not the part she wanted to play in this case.

# CHAPTER TWENTY-TWO

Beta blockers and espresso were a bad combination. It was late, and most of the country would be asleep, but he couldn't rest. The anxiety was still there, in his body and mind, but the disgust he felt at his shameful performance in the men's toilet earlier had developed into something he recognised all too well. A feeling even more familiar than emptiness, because he'd felt it for a lifetime.

Self-loathing.

He needed to fix this, otherwise he couldn't move forward. And he knew exactly where to go for help.

Grabbing his laptop and waking it, he fired up the special web browser and typed the address of one of his favourite sites: *manosphe.re*. The place where brothers came to exchange news and support. He logged in with his alias, 'Priapus', and entered the members-only chatroom. As predicted, it hadn't taken long after the news broke today: seven of the top ten active chat threads were about the murders. *Now that's what I call choking,* ran the title of one. *Death by cock-blocking*, proclaimed another. He was tempted by *Balls deep* but chose the heading *London murders: a new hero rises* and clicked into it. He couldn't believe his eyes.

Joy and jubilation were unusual on the forum; normally its threads were full of bad news and legitimate, heartfelt complaints about the many flaws of women, or female humanoid organisms – FMOs – as a lot of the guys liked to call them. But these comments were celebratory, ecstatic.

*Make this dude a saint now* one brother called BlackPillll97 had commented, bullet-pointing what the slut barrister had done for a living. This alone had received over two hundred likes. BlackPillll97's posts were always on the money.

*About time someone struck back* offered a further comment from a guy using the handle BloodCel. Nice. But it was the next comment and its reactions that caught his eye and made his chest swell.

*All hail the Throat Ripper*

This was incredible. Members had picked up on the nickname and were already reusing it below the original post. The thought of the Throat Ripper trending gave him a shiver of delight. The thought that *he* was the Throat Ripper. Wow. He read all the way to the end of the thread where comments were still being added in real time as he watched. He could follow this all night long, but he had to check social media, too. He typed the handle he'd typed a thousand times… and, yes! Sure enough, there it was on Twitter. Just half an hour ago, the Guru had posted. The Master. His heart leapt when he saw what He'd written:

> *Not condoning any violence against women but all men have to ask: when have We had enough?*

The reactions were crazy: triple-digit comments, retweets and likes. This was almost as enjoyable as the act itself. Almost.

Opening a further tab for the national news, he was slightly disappointed to see that he wasn't the main headline, but he was still on the home page: top ten articles. He clicked into the link entitled:

## POLICE APPEAL TO PUBLIC ON
## LONDON 'SERIAL' MURDERS

The writing was terrible, as he'd expect from a left-liberal shit-rag like this, but they had a video of the press conference, at least. He hadn't had a proper chance to watch it yet. He hit play and made it full screen, virtually salivating.

First up was the police intro and descriptions. Despite the press pushing them on the term 'serial killer', neither of them used the phrase. They were hedging their bets with the words 'linked incidents'. Well, if there were any questions about the Throat Ripper being a serial killer, pretty soon there'd be no doubt.

Then the camera panned across the room and zoomed on a gaggle of three stiff-looking guys in suits. And his heart skipped a beat. There she was, in front of the suits, tipping her head down. She looked awkward as hell, trying to cover up her ID card with a notebook. That was unusual; normally women liked to flaunt everything they'd got at the first sign of a camera. They were just programmed that way. But he knew this one was shy. He liked that more. And when she glanced up to the journos, there was something in her expression that he found indescribably fascinating. He knew he would never be with a woman like her. Not in a conventional sense, anyway. The caveat brought a smile to his lips.

He clicked back thirty seconds and watched again. She was wearing her hospital ID pass. Even better. Maybe she could psychologise him, he thought, snorting a laugh. He paused the video at the moment where she looked up.

Then he reached a trembling hand out to the screen and stroked her face as gently as he could, his fingertips kissing the image. His other hand was between his thighs.

# CHAPTER TWENTY-THREE

Lexi's skin tingled as the hot water cascaded over it, washing off the sweat and warming her up. The morning had felt almost as cold as the New Jersey winters of her college years, her face stinging as she ran around Tooting Common. A few other joggers and dog walkers had sacrificed the Saturday morning lie-in for what the Brits cheerfully called 'fresh air', though in London she wondered exactly how fresh it was. But the struggle was worth it.

The run had gotten her muscles working and even taken her mind off the murders a little. Now, enveloped in clouds of steam, she felt great. The citrus tang of her shampoo as she lathered it into her hair was delicious. It made her think of whipping up a smoothie for breakfast... maybe served with scrambled eggs on buttered toast. She was starving but there was a certain pleasure in waiting; breakfast didn't need to be rushed on the weekends and she'd see if Sarah and Liam wanted to join her. She'd heard reggae music drifting from Sarah's room just now, but Liam hadn't stirred, if he'd come home at all.

Once she was done, Lexi shut off the water and stepped out to dry herself. The towel had been on the radiator and it was warm and soft on her body. She wrapped it around her hair, twisting the end, and looked around for her bathrobe. But it wasn't there. Shoot, she'd forgotten to bring it in. Lexi hesitated. It was only a few paces to her room. What the hell, she should just go for it. Opening the door, she stepped out just as Liam's bedroom door swung open and he emerged, wearing only a pair of Calvin

Klein boxer shorts. Lexi froze, then ripped the towel off her head and hugged it to her front, just covering her breasts and crotch.

'Jeez, Liam. Don't jump out like that!'

'Aye, might say the same to you, hen.' He grinned, sweeping a hand through his tousled bed-hair and rubbing his eyes. They stood there for a couple seconds, looking at one another. Her first instinct had been to run back inside the bathroom, but she hadn't done that. She took in his eight-pack abs, his hairless pecs and the thick veins that ran down his biceps. The boxer shorts were tight and didn't leave much room for imagination. Or anything else for that matter. God, he was hot.

'I didn't think you were home,' she said, somewhat defensively. 'I mean, I didn't hear you come in last night.'

'That's cos I'm quiet as a wee church mouse.' His voice was an octave lower than usual. That was often the sign of a good night. 'Don't even know what time I got back.'

'You look like you haven't slept,' she said.

'Thanks a lot.' He pulled a face of mock outrage.

'Sorry. So, how was your date? You meet the man of your dreams?'

He gave a wry smile. 'You know I never kiss and tell, Lex.'

'Yeah you do! All the time.'

'Aye, whatever.' He moved towards her, turning sideways to pass her in the narrow corridor of the landing outside their bedrooms. For a moment, their bodies were a foot apart and she could smell him; a potent combination of sleep, sweat and last night's cologne. This was the closest she'd been to a half-naked man in a while, and she couldn't deny feeling just a little turned on. But he wasn't interested, she reminded herself. He probably didn't even care that she was almost naked.

'Hey.' She wanted to point a finger but couldn't let go of the towel. So, she settled for cocking her head. 'You're not getting out of it that easily, mister.'

'It's doctor, thanks very much.'

'Smartass. I want details later, OK?'

'Maybe.' He flapped a dismissive hand then turned back to her in the bathroom doorway. 'Anyway, I know what you were up to last night. Saw you on the telly!'

'Telly?'

'Aye, the news. The press conference.'

She reddened. 'I wasn't even meant to be—'

'You looked good,' he insisted, straight-faced. 'Very professional.'

Lexi didn't know if he was joking.

'It's awesome you're helping the police on that,' he added.

She was starting to get a little cold now. 'You know what? I'd be happy if I can just consult for them without being in the newspaper.'

'Well, like it or not, you've got some fans, now. Check social media.'

Lexi groaned. 'That is so not what I am about.' She was going to protest further when her phone rang from inside her bedroom.

'You'd better get that,' said Liam. 'Might be your policeman. He's a handsome fella, in a sort of rough way.' He winked and ambled into the bathroom.

Lexi padded into her room and looked at the phone. Briefly, she thought about not answering. Then she picked up.

'Hey, Dan.' She held the phone between her ear and shoulder as she pulled on her bathrobe.

'Morning, Lexi. First of all, sorry again about yesterday. Didn't mean to put you on the spot.'

'Well, you did,' she replied firmly. 'And it wasn't cool. That press conference was not about me.'

'I know. It was a stupid thing to have done.'

She let the silence hang between them.

'It won't happen again,' he added. 'Promise.'

'Good.' She took a breath, felt herself calm down a little. 'Look, I'm not interested in being some kind of media personality. I just want to help the case. That's all.'

'Understood.' He paused a beat. 'Speaking of which, I'm heading up to Tottenham now for Sophie Wright's post-mortem.'

'Tottenham?' Lexi had never been there but knew the name; it was a tough neighbourhood most famous for its soccer team.

'Yeah,' replied Dan. 'It's at Haringey Mortuary.'

'Of course. She lived in Wood Green.'

'I know it's the other side of London, and it's the weekend, but any chance you could make it? I can clear it with the pathologist for you to come. You might see something we'd miss.'

Lexi doubted that. Even though it was an hour or more on the subway, she'd do it. But after last night, she needed to know one thing. 'Will Sophie's parents be there?'

'Yup, they're planning to attend.'

She considered this. 'Uh, in that case, I'll stay back. Sorry, I just… I don't wanna intrude, you know?'

'You sure?'

'It's such a private thing. It's part of their grieving, and after the press conference…'

'I get it.' He sighed. 'OK, how about you come to Putney this afternoon, we'll get a coffee and I'll brief you on the PM. See if it gives you any ideas for us to follow up.'

'I can do that.'

'I'll call you when I'm on my way back from Tottenham. Probably around threeish.'

'All right.' There was a scuff of shoes from the street outside, followed by the snap of the letterbox. Lexi crossed to the window.

'Cheers, Lexi. Take care,' Dan said, and rang off.

She looked down to see the postman standing outside their front door. He was staring up at her, his domed belly protruding as he leant back. Ugh. She shivered and pulled the curtain back across.

*

Though he was miles away in a different part of the city, and he'd never been there before, Lockhart had noticed a distinct feeling of déjà vu as he'd entered Haringey Mortuary. The similarity of the building to the one in Westminster, from its brick-and-stone exterior to its steel-and-linoleum examination room. The presence of Dr Volz, who'd answered Lockhart's call yesterday and given up her Saturday to conduct Sophie Wright's post-mortem. And, most significantly, the body of Sophie. Laid out on the table, mostly covered by a white sheet, she looked just like Natasha had two weeks ago. A young woman whose life had been brutally stolen from her.

When he arrived, Sophie's parents had been inside the mortuary, which was below ground. He knew from talking to them yesterday at Jubilee House, following the press conference, that they planned to come today. Neither Peter nor Megan looked like they'd got any rest last night. But Lockhart understood their desire to be there, to see Sophie, and he admired their resilience. They'd even thanked him for making the journey across town. Of course, he didn't need to attend; he'd chosen to. As SIO, the responsibility for finding the perpetrator lay at his door. Responsibility to get justice for Natasha and Sophie. And to protect anyone else this guy might attack. Being here enabled him to keep that in mind, to ensure the victims and their loved ones stayed front and centre. That human aspect was crucial to energise the investigation, particularly when they'd made so little progress.

The Wrights had left the examination room after viewing Sophie's body and meeting Dr Volz. They'd gone back up to the lodge, leaving Lockhart and Volz alone, underground, with Sophie. Volz had begun the post-mortem with her customary precision and care, talking Lockhart through it as she went. He was glad that Sophie was in safe hands.

'The injuries are almost identical,' explained Volz. 'Bruising and cuts at the wrists and ankles, and to the ribcage in line with her solar plexus, most likely as she struggled against her restraints. Small but significant bruises and lacerations to the left ring finger. Evidence of a dental gag applied around the mouth and, of course, the metal ball wedged in her throat. Two small puncture wounds in her stomach, again, most likely from a Taser.' Volz's choice of words was professional, but Lockhart detected the emotion in her voice: sadness, with an edge of anger. He felt that too.

As she worked, it was hard for Lockhart not to feel deflated. The post-mortem was conclusive on cause of death and the killer's method, including details not released after Natasha's death a fortnight ago. They could be confident it was the same perpetrator and that, as Green had suggested, he was organised, meticulous, cold and full of rage. He clearly had a kitbag that he brought to the victim's home; that might help them profile any suspicious individuals from local CCTV footage. But everything Volz had found so far was merely confirmation of what they had already known from Natasha's post-mortem; none of it had the potential to advance their investigation.

'I'm going to remove the ball,' Volz told him, adjusting the flexible lighting rig and turning up the LEDs to illuminate the inside of Sophie's mouth. Their efforts to trace the chrome steel balls had come to nothing so far. There was no manufacturer's mark and his team had found literally hundreds of sellers online who produced metal spheres ranging from a millimetre to a metre in diameter. Their uses varied from machine parts to garden decorations to catering and, of course, the famous Baoding meditation balls used in Chinese medicine. Lockhart had brought evidence bags to take the ball away, but he didn't expect—

'Dan.' Volz spoke through her surgical mask, bent over Sophie's body and peering into her mouth.

'What is it?' he asked.

'There's something here.'

# CHAPTER TWENTY-FOUR

A stone's throw from the docks at Woolwich, Smith brought the car to a stop and looked up through the windscreen. Even craning her neck, she couldn't see the top of the twenty-storey tower block.

'Is this the address?' she asked. A passenger jet roared into view overhead, huge and low, reminding her that the runway of London City airport was right behind them on this stretch of the Thames. Not the most peaceful place to live.

Next to her, in the passenger seat, Khan checked his notebook. 'Westland House,' he raised his voice to be heard over the aircraft. 'That's the one.'

She took a breath, still gripping the steering wheel. 'Right, then.'

Khan clenched his fist. 'Let's go and see if this bastard's home.'

Smith agreed with the sentiment but knew they needed to put the opinions inevitably formed by their preliminary work to one side. 'Whatever you might think of this guy, try not to let it influence your questions or your judgement. Dean Waters is a person of interest in Operation Norton, and no more than that for now.'

'Come on, Max! Don't tell me you wouldn't like to dash him off the balcony way up there and watch him go splat on the ground.'

The thought had occurred to her that such an act would probably make the world a better place, but she shook her head. 'Just stick to the plan, OK?'

Khan grinned. 'You got it.'

Dean Waters had been identified by Sophie Wright's parents as the man who'd threatened to kill her after his conviction. Sophie had landed him a two-year prison sentence for defrauding his ex-wife, Carrie, out of nearly twenty thousand pounds, which she'd inherited when her mother had passed away. He'd done a year inside before being released to serve the second half of his sentence in the community. He was six months into his year 'on licence' and was apparently living a normal life, albeit with the blight of a criminal record. Smith admired what Sophie had done to get him convicted; a painstaking financial investigation that proved beyond doubt he'd stolen the money and attempted to hide it elsewhere. But that was about the only thing she had been able to prove. If Carrie was telling the truth, fraud was the tip of the iceberg for Dean Waters.

Carrie had catalogued a series of abusive acts he'd carried out over the course of their two-year marriage: controlling her day-to-day finances, making her stay in the house, stopping her seeing her family. He slapped her regularly, even when she obeyed his commands, but never hard enough to leave a lasting mark. One incident, though, stood out above all the others.

Three years ago, Waters had begun shouting at Carrie in the bathroom one evening. When she tried to stand up for herself and argue back, he picked up a large tube of toothpaste and pushed it so far into her mouth that she'd gagged and felt it go down her throat. He'd then pinched her nostrils, leaving her unable to breathe properly. Carrie had recalled her skin starting to go blue before he'd eventually let go and she'd vomited over the floor. For added insult, he'd made her clean up her sick. She'd been too scared to tell anyone at the time. But there was no evidence beyond her testimony. The assault hadn't even made it to court; Sophie had focussed her prosecution on his traceable financial theft. The two-year fraud sentence wasn't enough, but at least it had got Waters out of Carrie's life, enabling her to move away and start again.

Smith's personal theory was that their killer was targeting strangers with no more in common than their sex and broad age range. But if there was even the slightest chance that Dean Waters was responsible, Smith was determined to probe as thoroughly as she could. She just had to keep calm, stay objective.

After a long lift journey, Smith and Khan emerged onto a high walkway and were immediately buffeted by a strong, gusting wind. Seagulls wheeled and screeched below them. They knocked on the door of flat 52. No answer. They knocked again, harder, and heard shuffling footsteps. The door opened to reveal Dean Waters. All five foot seven of him. Smith recognised him immediately from his police mugshot. Waters's face was gaunt, the skin pale and dry, making him look older than his thirty-nine years. His close-cropped hair had receded high up his forehead. He wore a sweatshirt and jeans, both liberally stained with white paint and black oil. There was a large flathead screwdriver in his hand.

'Yes?'

'Good morning.' Smith held up her warrant card and tried for businesslike. 'Dean Waters?'

'Er, yeah.' He sounded defensive already.

'I'm Detective Sergeant Maxine Smith and this is Detective Constable Mohammed Khan.' She glanced sideways. Khan had raised himself up to his full height and puffed out his chest in a show of intimidation. That wasn't going to help them.

'What's this about?' Waters looked from her to Khan and back.

'We'd just like to ask you a few questions, please, Mr Waters.'

'About what, exactly?'

Smith watched him closely. 'The death of Sophie Wright. We're hoping you can help with our inquiries.'

'Who?'

'Can we come in, please?' Smith forced herself to smile. 'It'd be easier to talk in private.'

'I'm busy.'

'The other option is for you to come into the station for a voluntary interview,' said Khan.

Waters didn't respond. He just tapped the screwdriver against his leg, pursing his lips.

'You've still got six months of your licence, haven't you, Mr Waters?' Smith didn't need him to confirm that. 'We can always call your parole officer and tell them about you declining to assist us.'

Waters would know that'd be a black mark against him. He narrowed his eyes. 'Do I need a lawyer?'

'That's up to you,' replied Smith. 'We can arrange for a lawyer if you come in for questioning. Or we can just get it out of the way now and let you enjoy your weekend, sir.'

Waters remained in the doorway. He looked over his shoulder. Smith followed his gaze down a cramped hallway to a kitchen. On its table, she could see a laptop and a scattering of tools.

'Fine.' He planted a hand on the door jamb. 'I'll answer your questions, but you're not coming in.'

The wind continued to whip and batter them. Smith thrust her hands into her pockets, hunching her shoulders against the cold. They didn't have enough to justify entering his premises without consent, and there weren't yet reasonable grounds to arrest him. This would have to do. 'Were you involved in a court case approximately eighteen months ago where Sophie Wright was the prosecuting barrister?'

Waters's nostrils flared. 'If that's who my ex employed.'

'It was. Did you threaten to kill Ms Wright after the court case resulted in your conviction for fraud?'

He snorted. 'No.'

'Prior to her death, she alleges that you did.'

'He said, she said.' Waters turned to Khan. 'Always the way, isn't it, mate?'

'What?'

'I'd just got a prison sentence,' continued Waters, shrugging, 'who knows what I told her.'

'Two nights ago,' said Smith, 'Sophie Wright was murdered in her home. You might've seen it on the news. She was choked to death.'

'I don't watch the news.' Waters smirked. 'Too depressing.'

Smith decided to change tack. 'Did you once attempt to choke your ex-wife with a tube of toothpaste?'

Waters's face registered shock, but he recovered quickly. 'I didn't try… look, we were messing around in the bathroom one day. I was joking, and she overreacted, that's all. It wasn't like she said. You know she was a drinker?' He tutted in disapproval. 'The booze did all sorts to her memory.'

It was surprising that he'd admitted the incident occurred, even if he was playing down its severity and his ex-wife's recollection of it.

'Where were you two nights ago, Mr Waters, between the hours of 8 p.m. and 2 a.m.?'

'Here,' he replied instantly. 'I'm working a bit from home. I do funny hours depending on the job.'

'What do you do for work?'

His jaw tightened, limbs tensing. Smith knew the signs of a person holding back anger.

'I fix things.' He held up the screwdriver. 'Electrical things. Toasters, radios, TVs. Got trained while I was inside. I've always liked systems, technical stuff.' There was the hint of a smile before his expression darkened. 'I used to be the manager of a mobile phone shop. I earned thirty grand a year. Now I do shifts at the appliances superstore on Old Kent Road and some odd jobs working in the flat, here. It's all I can get.'

Karma is a bitch, thought Smith. He was lucky to be working at all; only around a quarter of ex-cons managed to get a job on release. She had no sympathy for his loss of status. But the important thing was his alibi.

'Can anyone verify your presence here two nights ago?'

He flapped his arms. 'Nope.'

'No one?'

'Er, I might've gone to the pub down there at some point,' he jabbed the screwdriver towards the ground. 'The Joiner's Arms. I normally have a pint there. Just one.'

'Alone?'

'Yeah.'

Khan made a note. 'And what time would that've been?' he asked.

'Dunno,' Waters shrugged. 'Nine, ten.'

'How long did you stay there?'

'Hour or so. At five quid a pint, I make it last, these days.'

'We'll check that with the staff in the pub.'

Waters turned the screwdriver over in his hand. 'OK.'

'What about the nights of October seventh and July third this year?'

'Same, probably. Here, then in the pub for an hour or two, then back up.'

The alibi could be checked, at least, but Smith knew that the further they went back, the less chance there was of confirmation.

'Is that all you do, then?' Khan was frowning.

'Pretty much. I'm not allowed to do a lot else, on licence.'

Should've considered that before you stole twenty grand off your wife, thought Smith.

'Except on Sundays,' added Waters. 'I go to church.'

'Church?'

'Yeah.' He gave a lopsided smile. 'I'm trying to be a saint.'

'Are you taking the piss?' Khan leaned forward.

'No, mate,' said Waters, shrinking slightly. 'I'm a believer, now.'

Smith had expected to feel angry confronting Dean Waters. Instead, despite his horrible crimes she almost felt a kind of grudging pity for him. His life was pathetic, lonely and dull. Waters was marooned in a bleak, windswept tower block, under the flight path of an airport, with a record that would stop him getting a better job for years to come. Was that motive enough to kill Sophie Wright? And what about Natasha Mayston and Kim Hardy?

Waters would remain a person of interest in Op Norton, but right now there wasn't much more to be gained from talking to him. Smith knew one thing, though. As a convicted criminal his biodata would be on file. That meant that if any fingerprints or DNA were recovered from Sophie Wright's home or body, they could automatically be compared with his. Dean Waters had claimed he was at home on the nights in question; it gave Smith some comfort to know they might not have to take his word for it. They thanked him and left.

As they took the lift back down, a thought occurred to Smith. 'You know something, Mo?'

Khan was checking his reflection in the cracked elevator mirror, smoothing his eyebrows. 'What's that?'

'At no point in that conversation did he deny doing it.'

# CHAPTER TWENTY-FIVE

Lexi held the large takeaway coffee in both hands as they walked by the river. The day had warmed up a little, but she was grateful for the heat of the cup. It'd been Dan's idea to get outdoors; on a Saturday afternoon, the cafés of Putney were too crowded to discuss the case, and he wanted a break from the MIT office. That was fine by her, given the attitude most of his team seemed to have towards her psychology input. Luckily, he'd forewarned her, so she'd dressed in a down jacket and woolly hat, with leggings under her jeans and thick hiking socks inside her Doc Martens.

The sky was clear, the air crisp, and the last coppery leaves clung to the trees lining the riverbank. They strolled together, watching the water ebb and flow. Lexi was again aware of how safe she felt with this tall, broad-shouldered, capable man beside her. For a moment, she imagined they were a couple passing a carefree weekend together, then dismissed the thought instantly. Dan had invited her here to talk about profiling a murderer.

They passed a row of boathouses and paused while a crew of well-built oarswomen crossed in front of them, carrying their boat overhead down the embankment slipway to the water's edge.

'Tide's rising,' observed Dan, looking past the rowers to the brick wall on the far side. 'Few more hours and it'll be up to that line near the top.'

'You know,' said Lexi, 'there's some folklore about the connection between low tide and death.'

'Is that right?'

'Yeah, a whole bunch of people wrote about it. Greeks, Romans, Shakespeare, Dickens.'

Lockhart grunted. 'Well, we should be safe for now, at least.'

'Does it ever flood?' she asked.

'Sometimes,' he replied, still gazing out. 'Even with the barrier downriver. Happened here about three years ago, load of cars got washed away.'

'Jeez.'

'Yeah, right.' He glanced back to her as they resumed their progress. 'That's London for you. Even the river can do you over if you're not careful.'

Lexi laughed, but she knew the joke hid a deeper truth for Dan. He was someone whose trust was hard-won and given only to certain people in his life: his mom, his wife, a handful of military friends, a few Met colleagues and now, it seemed, her. She wanted to repay that faith by assisting with his work and by helping him heal and move on from the trauma of losing his wife. But was her motivation for that completely altruistic?

'How was the post-mortem?' she asked, trying to bring her mind back to the case.

'Same as Natasha's, more or less.' He swigged his coffee and exhaled a cloud of steam. 'Identical injuries and cause of death.' He filled her in on details of the examination by a pathologist called Mary Volz. Lexi mentally added her to the list of people Dan trusted. You could still count them on two hands.

'Was it hard? I mean, to see her like that?'

'Yeah.' Dan looked as if he was about to elaborate, but instead he just cleared his throat. 'Yeah, it was.'

Lexi wondered if she should ask more about his feelings. This wasn't a therapy session, but she wanted to make sure Dan was OK. Before she could formulate a question, he spoke again.

'We might have a lead, though.'

'Yeah?'

He nodded. 'Dr Volz found some hairs inside Sophie's mouth. They were soaked with saliva and blood, but you could tell straight away that they were too short and thick to belong to Sophie.'

'Her attacker?'

'Most likely. They're going to the lab for testing, DNA profiling. There might be more of the hairs in her flat, the SOCOs are still processing it. Or on her clothing. Either way, looks like the guy might've left some evidence this time.'

'So, you're making progress, huh? What with the cell phone, too.' After the press conference yesterday evening, Dan explained how they'd been able to use Sophie's finger to unlock her smartphone, once he'd made sure her parents were OK with it. Lexi was both grossed out and amazed by that; she didn't know it was even possible. Apparently, it didn't work on every phone, and it depended how long the person had been dead. With Sophie, they'd lucked out.

'Let's see what it actually gives us. But you have to hope.' He turned his head to her as they walked, and their eyes met briefly before he shifted his gaze back to the path. 'Lucy's been leading the data exploitation today, comparing it to the phone records we got for Natasha.'

Yesterday evening, Lexi had been able to put the name of Lucy Berry, the MIT's analyst, to the face of the woman who'd been paying attention during her psychology briefing. It was good to have one ally in the team, besides Dan.

Lexi sipped her coffee. 'What about the metal balls?'

'Nothing distinctive that we've found, yet. But when Dr Volz got the one in Sophie's throat out, it did have a couple of small marks on the surface. Scratches, maybe from something pressing on it. In both cases, the balls were wedged in hard and deep.' Dan held his index and middle fingers out, turned them over. 'So, unless this guy has really long, mega-strong fingers, he's probably using some sort of tool to push them in.'

'Tool…' Lexi recalled an expression she'd accidentally used in her briefing. *Choking on balls.*

'Yeah, you know, cos he could get more force if—'

'That's it!' She stopped.

He spun to face her. 'What?'

'Phallic power. Of course. That's what I think this is about.' She grinned triumphantly, holding a palm up in one of those isn't-it-obvious gestures.

But Dan was just frowning. 'Phallic, as in…'

'Cocks.'

'Right.'

'And balls,' she added. Her smile was maybe a little inappropriate, but she couldn't help it. This felt like a breakthrough.

'All right,' he inclined his head. 'Explain it to me then, Doctor.'

'OK. So, the penis is often a symbol of power. Any society where men are in charge, you find that representation. Across time and cultures, from the Stone Age through ancient Egypt and right up to us, today. Architecture, sculpture, painting, industry, whatever. This guy is overpowering women, he's restraining them, and then he's making them choke on balls that he pushes into their mouths with some type of long, hard rod. It's phallic.'

'You're saying it's a sexual motivation?'

'Maybe that's part of it. But I think it's more than that. For him, it's about power over them. The power of his masculinity.' She took a sip of coffee, thinking. 'Or his lack of it. The killer is missing something. He lacks power. Maybe he's impotent. Maybe a woman took his masculinity away, somehow. Whatever caused it, he's using these murders as a way to prove his power and superiority over women. And whether it's deliberate or unconscious, his signature is an embodiment of male genitalia as a weapon, penetrating a female victim. It's sexual, but it's not about sex.'

Dan gave a tiny shake of his head. 'OK, now I'm confused.'

'We know that he's not sexually assaulting these women. So, what's his motivation? I think it's about superiority and inferiority.' She shrugged. 'Alfred Adler.'

'Who?'

'Adler. He was a psychoanalyst around the same time as Sigmund Freud. They were buddies, but they kinda went separate ways over their theories of human motivation. Freud thought it was all about sex, Adler thought it was power. He took the philosopher Nietzsche's idea that we all have a basic drive for power and developed the psychology of it. Adler said that when we don't get what we want – love, respect, food, whatever – we get frustrated. We become aware of our limitations in the world, our inferiority to others. One response to that awareness of our own weakness is to get aggressive, to use aggression to reassert ourselves or compensate.'

Dan took a long drink of coffee. His eyes moved around like he was processing the ideas. 'So, the killer's compensating for some sort of weakness.'

'It's a possible explanation of what he's doing. Men are conditioned by society to aspire towards an ideal of strength, capability and mastery. When they fall short of that, some develop an inferiority complex – basically a set of emotional problems around their lack of power. And one response is to re-cast yourself at the centre of the universe, omnipotent. That's the superiority complex.'

'Like a delusion?'

'Kind of. Probably more like a narcissistic thing, though – it's all about how great he is, though the reality is he's most likely a total douchebag.'

Dan arched his eyebrows. 'That's one way of describing a serial murderer.'

'OK, then. A loser. And the ring finger injuries could fit with that if marriage, ownership, possession or whatever is part of his power fantasy, or the cause of his loss. I'm betting he blames women for the things that've gone wrong in his life, for his weaknesses. He's made it a male-female thing. He hates women and he's dominating them and killing them to restore his ego.'

'Hm.'

He didn't seem that sold on the idea. 'It's just one theory,' she added.

'No, I mean, it makes sense. It's just…'

'What?'

'Well, how's he choosing his victims, then? What connects them?'

Lexi sighed. 'I haven't figured that out, yet. Maybe it's that they're strong women who help other women. Natasha funded female-led start-ups. Sophie defended female victims of abuse.'

'And Kim Hardy?'

'Yeah.' Lexi's excitement was fading. 'I mean, there is a feminist theory that sex workers are empowered—'

'Kim wasn't one of them, though,' he interjected. 'It wasn't her choice to do what she did. She was feeding a meth habit.'

'Sure.'

They walked on in silence for a moment. Lexi wanted to know more about the victims; she needed to profile them, too. And she wanted to know what was inspiring the killer.

'I think there's gonna be something about what this guy's doing online,' she said, eventually.

'You think he's finding victims on the web? Like DC Khan's internet dating idea?'

'Could be… but I'm thinking more, like, if you hate women, where do you go to talk about it today? The web, right?'

Dan pursed his lips. 'Bit vague, isn't it?'

'Not necessarily. There's like a whole anti-feminist thing going on with some websites. Misogynist chatrooms, forums. I read about it.' She felt her enthusiasm returning. 'Maybe I should take a look at some of them?'

'I don't know. Sounds like it could be a lot of work for not very much result. We've wasted a ton of time on web-based stuff in the past. You know what my team and I want – concrete leads.'

'This is concrete,' she protested. 'A website is a real thing. So are the people that use them, most of the time.'

Dan blew out his cheeks. 'But… there are too many of them. People using aliases, sites hosted overseas where we have no ability to trace or interrogate the data. Dead ends. And this guy's careful, right? He's not going to be on there, bragging about what he's done or confessing, is he?'

'Probably not.'

He drained his coffee and slung it into the nearby garbage can harder than was necessary. 'And it won't tell us who his next victim's going to be.'

Lexi could understand his frustration, but she was determined not to be put off; her theory was worth following up. 'I can check out some of the sites and see what's going on.'

'Sorry, I just haven't got the budget to pay you for that many hours working on this.' He stopped and hooked his thumb the way they came. 'I should get back to the office.'

'I'll do it for free,' she blurted.

Dan narrowed his eyes. 'Free?'

'Yeah.' She remembered the bills, the rent, the credit card statement. It was kind of a rash offer to make and she hadn't really thought it through. But this was more important than her personal finances. 'I'm serious.'

He shrugged. 'Well, if you're sure… Just be careful, OK? There are some arseholes and weirdos out there.'

'There are assholes and weirdos everywhere.'

As they returned to Jubilee House, Lexi fought back her disappointment. She wanted to help Dan and his investigation, but she felt as if all she'd done was confuse things. What good was her profiling, her use of psychological theory? She might understand the killer's motivation a little better, but it wasn't bringing them any closer to catching the guy. Dan hadn't really bought into her idea of investigating online. And now she'd committed to working for free. *Way to go, Lexi.*

His ringtone interrupted her self-criticism. He snatched the phone out of his jacket pocket.

'Yeah?' He listened, nodding as his eyebrows rose and a smile crept up his face. 'All right. Nice one, Luce. I'm on my way back now, I'll see you in a bit.' He rang off and pocketed the phone.

'That sounded exciting,' she said. 'Was it Lucy Berry?'

'Yup. And she's found a phone number that's been in contact with both Natasha and Sophie.' Dan beamed at her and picked up his walking pace to a stride. 'That's what I call concrete.'

# CHAPTER TWENTY-SIX

Back in the MIT office, Lockhart had wasted no time. A quick search by Berry had found that the mobile phone number linked to both Natasha and Sophie was associated with a Mr Will Jacobson. The number was listed next to his name on the website of the Olivier Room, a small theatre space that was part of London's vast Southbank Centre. Berry had made a quick, slightly nervous, call to the number with a spurious enquiry about the evening's event. She confirmed it was Jacobson who'd answered – given that he was the theatre manager, there was nothing unusual about her query. Lockhart didn't want their interest exposed at this stage; all he wanted to know was whether the number was active, whether Jacobson was on the other end of it, and whether both phone and owner were located at the theatre. There was no one free to accompany him so, with Berry's confirmation, he set out alone to speak to Jacobson.

The Southbank Centre had a riverside terrace bar that was one of the best summer drinking spots in London. But, other than that, the place wasn't Lockhart's idea of a Saturday night out. The arts complex housed theatres, concert halls, exhibition spaces and a cinema showing the kind of films that won awards at festivals he didn't go to. Lockhart wasn't really interested in any of that. Give him a Jason Bourne movie and a can of Stella and he'd be entertained. Cultural stuff that required interpretation and thought wasn't his thing. His day job demanded enough of that.

As he approached, Lockhart felt dwarfed by the centre's huge modern buildings that dominated this stretch of the Thames.

Looking across the water, he spotted the towering stone of Cleopatra's Needle, standing opposite on the Victoria Embankment. The 3,500-year-old obelisk had a twin in Central Park, New York City. He knew what Lexi Green would say about those monuments. After her explanation of phallic power that afternoon, Lockhart saw it in a whole new light. Maybe that kind of imagery *was* everywhere; he just hadn't been paying attention. Still, he wasn't completely convinced by her theory; it was interesting, but so far there was nothing solid to back it up. A telephone number, on the other hand, *was* solid.

Inside the main building, Lockhart found the Olivier Room. There was a buzz of activity around the doors as theatregoers milled about with drinks. Lockhart guessed a show was starting soon. He manoeuvred to the front and held his warrant card up for a young woman who was checking tickets with a handheld scanner. Her black T-shirt was knotted at the front to expose a slim, caramel-coloured midriff.

'I'm Detective Inspector Dan Lockhart, Metropolitan Police. I'd like to speak to Will Jacobson.'

The woman looked momentarily panicked, then plucked a walkie-talkie from her back pocket. 'Yannis, you there?'

The device chirped and crackled. 'Yeah, it's me.'

'Um, there's a police officer here to see Will. D'you know where he is?'

'He's not in the office, but I'll give him a call. The police guy can wait in here.'

'Cool.' She replaced the walkie-talkie and ran a hand through her hair. 'Sorry, it's crazy tonight. Will's probably dashing around like a mad thing. Curtain's going up in twenty minutes and we're sold out.' She nodded to the double doors behind her and grinned. '*The Vagina Monologues*. You seen it?'

'No.'

Her eyes widened. 'Oh my god, you *so* should. It's incredible.'

'I'll take your word for it. Where's the office, then?'

She pointed along a corridor behind the bar and angled her fingers. 'Down there, second on the left.'

'Cheers.'

Moments later, Lockhart knocked on the door.

'Hello, come in.'

He pushed it open and entered a cramped, chaotic, poorly lit room. The surfaces were littered with papers, flyers, wads of tickets and newspapers. Computers, monitors, laptops and a few more walkie-talkies were spread over the desks, and what free space there might've been was occupied by mugs and glasses, most of which seemed to be half-finished. Documents were stuck to the walls between framed posters of shows. Apart from the posters, it was as if someone had squeezed the entire contents of the MIT office into a space the size of a single bedroom.

To one side sat a small, dark-haired man, his narrow shoulders hunched over a keyboard. The skin of his face and forearms had the ghostly pallor of someone who doesn't spend much time outside. His hair was thinning, a circle of near-baldness centred on his crown. He was typing with one hand and texting with the other, peering alternately between computer screen and smartphone through thick, clear-rimmed glasses. Lockhart introduced himself as the guy checked the mobile once more.

'Mr Jacobson?' he asked.

'I'm Yannis Dimitriou,' replied the guy. He held up the phone. 'Will's on his way. What's it about?'

'I'll wait until Mr Jacobson arrives before I explain.' Lockhart thrust his hands into his pockets, glanced around the office as Dimitriou resumed his typing. 'You guys are pretty busy, by the look of it.'

'We don't sleep,' said Dimitriou, giving an awkward laugh that seemed to come from his nose. 'It's a full house again, this evening. Every night this week. I'm not normally here this late, but there's always issues with tickets, payments, seating, you know?'

Lockhart didn't know. He cast around for a spare bit of desk to perch on, then gave up and carried on standing. 'So, what's your job?' He kept his tone casual.

'Technical genius.' The little man grinned, gesturing to the computers. 'I run the booking system, the website, social media accounts, audio and video recording of events. All of it, basically.'

Lockhart detected the traces of an accent. 'Dimitriou. You originally from Greece, then?'

'Cyprus.'

'Nice,' said Lockhart. 'I've spent a bit of time there.'

'Holiday?' enquired Dimitriou.

'Military.'

'Ah. Tough guy.'

'Eh?'

Before Lockhart could work out whether Dimitriou was serious, the door flew open and a breathless man entered clutching a stack of programmes. A sideways fringe covered most of his forehead, topping an aquiline nose which bisected a pair of rosy cheeks. He wore a beige roll-neck sweater over brown pleated trousers which were turned up to the ankle above a pair of white canvas plimsolls. Lockhart was the last person to ask about fashion, but he suspected this was it right now.

'You're from the police?' The guy sounded agitated already.

'Detective Inspector Dan Lockhart, Met Police.' He flashed the warrant card. 'Will Jacobson?'

'Yes.' He swallowed, still holding tight to the programmes. 'What's going on, officer? Why are you here?'

'I'm hoping you can help with our inquiries.'

'Right.' Jacobson glanced around the room and, failing to find a better spot, dumped the stack of programmes on his chair. He glanced at his watch. 'It's curtain up at seven.'

Lockhart checked his own watch. Sixteen minutes. 'Shouldn't take long,' he said.

'OK, well, how can I help?'

'We're investigating the murders of two young women. Natasha Mayston, just over two weeks ago, and Sophie Wright, two nights ago.' He didn't mention Kim Hardy, for now.

Jacobson shook his head. 'What's that got to do with us?'

'Your mobile phone number was in contact with both of their numbers,' stated Lockhart, watching Jacobson closely.

'*My* mobile?' Jacobson looked horrified. 'But I've never…'

'The one ending zero, seven, four, six,' added Lockhart.

The theatre manager let out a huge breath and his body visibly relaxed. 'Thank God for that.' He glanced at Dimitriou, who carried on typing. Lockhart had no problem with the techy being there. Sometimes it was useful to have a second person hear the conversation, though none of this was under caution. Not yet, anyway.

'You seem quite pleased, Mr Jacobson.'

'Well, no, I'm not *pleased*, of course, you understand. I saw those murders on the news. Shocking. I'm just… you see, that mobile isn't mine. It's the theatre's.'

'You mean it's like a work phone?' Lockhart had the first hints of a sinking feeling.

'Yes, it's the office mobile. We put it on the website for queries about the shows, ticketing, that sort of thing. It's quite useful for us to send mass texts as well, when we need to. You know, if there's a cancellation or something.'

'It has your name next to it on the contact page.'

'Oh, that's because it's me who carries it, most of the time. But Yannis here uses it too, as well as front of house staff, sometimes.'

Lockhart bit back his frustration. 'So, how many people have access to it?'

'About five or six of us. We probably get about a hundred calls a day.'

'Every bloody day,' added Dimitriou, without looking up from his screen.

This was starting to sound like a dead end. The theatre mobile number might as well have been the talking clock. But Lockhart wasn't quite ready to leave. A thought had occurred to him.

'Natasha and Sophie called this phone around two weeks apart in July. Is it possible they came to the same show, here?'

Jacobson pursed his lips. 'It's possible.' His brow creased and his limbs tensed. 'You think that could be connected to their deaths? That maybe the murderer came here? Christ!'

Lockhart held out both hands. 'Calm down, Mr Jacobson. No one's saying that. We just have to follow up every possible lead in a case like this, and your mobile phone number connects the two women whose murders we believe to be linked events.' He was careful not to use the term 'serial killer'. 'We're required to check what the nature of that contact was.'

'Of course. God. Yannis, can you pull up our guest lists, please?'

'Now?'

'Yes, now!' Jacobson raised his voice. Lockhart was glad he didn't work for the guy; his panic threshold was pretty low.

Dimitriou typed, clicked, scrolled and clicked some more. Lockhart waited. Then Dimitriou mumbled something and leant back in his chair. 'Sophie Wright is on our guestlist for a talk organised by the WOW Foundation.'

'That's Women of the World,' added Jacobson. 'Was it the Feminist Futures lecture?'

'Yeah,' replied Dimitriou. 'July seventeenth this year.' Lockhart noted it down while the techy interrogated their system further. Thirty seconds passed before he stopped typing and held up his hands. 'But Natasha Mayston isn't on here.'

Lockhart folded his arms. 'So, why do you think she called the number?'

'Dunno,' shrugged Jacobson. 'Casual enquiry, maybe?'

'She probably rang up about something she was interested in, found out we were fully booked, and went somewhere else,' offered Dimitriou. 'It happens all the time.'

'Natasha Mayston also received a call from the number on the same day.'

'Most likely a call-back,' said Dimitriou. 'If she couldn't get through or whoever picked up couldn't deal with her specific issue.'

'Did either of you speak to Natasha Mayston or Sophie Wright?'

Dimitriou looked at Jacobson, as if seeking guidance. The manager's expression was slightly pained. 'Most of the time, we don't even know who we're talking to. They ask their questions, we answer, they hang up. One or two people want to chat, a couple like to abuse us, but generally, no one introduces themselves. Sorry, I don't recall either of them.'

'Me neither,' added Dimitriou.

With around a hundred calls a day, every day, the chances were that neither Jacobson nor Dimitriou would remember a conversation three or four months ago. Even if they could, it was unlikely to be relevant. Lockhart had to admit it: the mobile number wasn't going to get Operation Norton anywhere. He wanted to put his fist through the nearest computer screen.

'All right, thanks for your time.' He proffered a card to Jacobson. 'If you think of anything that might be useful, give me a call.'

'OK, will do.'

Lockhart began to leave but turned in the doorway. 'One other thing. Are you guys on any dating apps?'

'No,' replied Dimitriou quietly.

'Me?' Jacobson placed a forefinger on his own chest.

'Yeah.'

'Bit personal, isn't it?'

Lockhart didn't reply. He just waited.

'Well, er, yes, actually. Tinder. I've just come out of a big relationship and I'm getting back out there, you know?'

Lockhart *didn't* know; in fact, he was actively avoiding the idea of 'getting back out there'. He swung the door open. 'Thanks. I'll let you get back to work.'

As he marched back down the corridor, a long bell sounded. The noise made him freeze, shooting a burst of adrenalin through his stomach. Was that a fire alarm? It was loud and urgent enough, but no one else seemed to be reacting. He marched over to the young woman who was checking tickets for a line of guests. 'What was the bell?' he demanded.

'The five-minute call,' she said with a smile, as her scanner bleeped over a barcode on a phone screen and she waved a couple inside. 'Means the show's about to start.'

'Right. Cheers.' Lockhart tried to hide his embarrassment at not knowing that. He wasn't someone who went to the theatre.

Leaving the Southbank Centre, Lockhart had to admit he was on edge. His reaction to the bell was exactly the kind of thing Lexi Green had been helping him with in their sessions. *Hypervigilance*, she called it. Clearly, he needed some more therapy with her.

But that'd have to wait. Right now, he just needed something to go his way on this case.

Anything.

# CHAPTER TWENTY-SEVEN

He was back online again. It'd only been a day since his last foray onto the *manosphe.re* website, but he couldn't resist it. He had to see what his brothers were saying about the Throat Ripper. Sure enough, the threads had grown since yesterday, new ones had sprouted, and he was gratified to see the nickname being used more widely now. Word was getting around, people were talking. And what they were saying made him want to touch himself: *Legend. Hero. True incel. A gentleman.* The praise was ubiquitous, the approval unanimous. It was only a matter of time before the Throat Ripper went viral.

Tumescent with pride, he took screen grabs of the most popular threads for posterity. He didn't want this to stop, but that was the problem with the manosphere. Sooner or later, an enemy found the site, inveigled their way through the defences and exposed the content. Then, predictably, the host server would be obliged to shut it down. Even with internet providers in shitty little countries that didn't give a damn about human rights, the whining feminists got their way, eventually. But it was only ever temporary. The brothers would always rise again, phoenixlike, creating a new site and bonding once more. That was the thing about truth: it always found a way to get out, however much you tried to supress it. That's what the femoids and their male slaves didn't realise.

Apart from the growth in messages, two things stood out for him on the chat forum. One was the speculation over the Throat

Ripper's identity. Stories abounded: he was young, he was old; he was a Londoner, he came from outside the city; he was a homeless guy off the radar, he was a rich, bored dude like Christian Bale in *American Psycho* – only smaller and uglier. Someone even claimed to know him, but that wasn't true – he hadn't told a soul. Not yet. He enjoyed the debate, the rumour, and most of all the satisfaction that he was the only person in the world who knew the real name of the Throat Ripper. That was fun.

The second thing was what made his heart palpitate.

The brothers were demanding to know when the Throat Ripper would strike again. When would the third bitch be choked? And who would she be? Some guys were offering odds and taking bets on it with each other. He could feel the pressure starting to grow inside his chest. He'd have to do it again, soon. He took a deep breath. Nice and calm. Yes, he would do it, as he'd planned. And maybe the next death would properly get His attention; the Guru hadn't posted anything further about it on Twitter, and that was more than a little depressing, after all His earlier encouragement. But he had to press on.

There was a plan, of course – that was how he rolled. And once he'd made a plan, he didn't like to change it. But after seeing the American's cameo at the press conference last night, he might have to make an exception. He'd taken a look at her Instagram feed earlier. His verdict: poor. There was barely enough material for a teenage boy with a fertile imagination to wank over. A video clip from CrossFit, a photo of her kissing a dog, a group selfie in a bar. A snap where she was pointing inanely at some street art on a wall. And that was about it. Her social media was a disappointment, a two-dimensional version of the person he knew she was. But that was OK.

Real life was so much better.

✳

Lexi felt a flutter of anticipation as she fired up a private browsing window on her laptop and searched for 'Meninist chat forum'. As a clinical psychologist, she was trained to be a 'scientist-practitioner', meaning she always tried to work on the basis of data. Testing ideas and finding out the results for herself. And she needed to see whether there was any evidence for her theory about the online influences of this killer. As a human being – and a woman – she just wanted to see what the hell was out there. What was being said about women by men who hated them. She didn't have to look hard. Pretty soon, her scientific detachment was out of the window and she was as angry as the douchebags whose posts she was reading.

It turned out that men who hate women hate a lot of other stuff too. Left-liberal politics, gay men, foreigners. She surfed the upper layers of 'Alt-Lite' posts, feeling progressively more furious as she trawled through message boards loaded with Islamophobia and rants about social welfare. There was plenty of misogyny in there, too – denial of the gender pay gap, evolutionary biology as proof of the superiority of men, a critique of equal opportunities. She read a post entitled: *Ten reasons you should never trust a woman*. At number one, it proclaimed: *She will always cheat on you. Always.* And these were the moderates, the ones without the swastika tattoos and Hitler salutes. It was disgusting, depressing, and scary as hell.

Following links in some of the more vitriolic threads, she found herself on websites where men were posting links to their favourite porn videos. Lexi knew that watching porn was pretty normal these days; she enjoyed a video now and again as a warm up to using her vibrator. But her tastes were pretty standard. Clicking through to a couple of the streaming sites these guys were recommending to each other, though, she felt physically sick. Women hooded, ball-gagged, trussed up, slapped around and made to swallow cocks, their faces damp with tears and streaked with mascara. She had to stop watching.

Despite her revulsion, Lexi was confident that the killer was somewhere in this milieu. Her psychological profile of him suggested a high level of congruence with this subculture of dominance and power over anything that wasn't straight, white, wage-earning and male. Meninism, the manosphere, the Alt-Lite, whatever you wanted to call it. But she knew there was a deeper layer, one that might yield even more significant clues to the killer's inspiration and, maybe, his identity. That was the world of the incel: so-called involuntary celibates. Reading about these guys, Lexi started to feel as though she was getting somewhere.

She'd been going for nearly two hours when she found a chat thread entitled:

*Why the Throat Ripper is the best serial killer London's ever seen.*

Was this what they were calling him? She clicked to open the thread and a message popped up:

*This content is invite-only!*

Dammit. How was she going to get in there?

The knock at her bedroom door startled her and, without waiting for an invitation, Sarah burst in, followed closely by Liam. Instinctively, she shut the laptop.

'Hey, whatcha doin'?' Sarah jumped on to Lexi's bed and gave her a knowing smile. 'Are you on a dating site, young lady? Come on, tell us…' Sarah prodded her in the ribs and Lexi winced, giggled, and hugged the laptop close as protection when Sarah began tickling her.

'I'm working!' she replied with a squeal.

Liam was leaning against the wall. He flicked his eyes to the laptop, clearly suspicious. 'Working? What work are you doing?'

'Research.'

'Research?' He pulled a face of disgust. 'It's Saturday night, hen. We're staging an intervention.'

'Exactly.' Sarah relented on her tickling assault. 'Let's get out there and do something.'

Lexi put the laptop to one side. She'd come back to it later. 'I haven't got any money,' she complained.

'Neither have we. But when's that stopped us?' Sarah zhuzhed up her hair, making it even bigger, then spread her hands, grinning. 'We can still go out.'

Liam held up his phone. 'The Bedford's got a stand-up comedy night. Work-in-progress stuff. It's only five quid to get in. Starts in half an hour.'

The pub up the road in Balham was an institution; its comedy and live music nights were legendary in south London. She was tempted.

'I don't know, guys. I'm kinda tired.' She was also kind of depressed after her reading, but they didn't need to know that.

'Do it, do it, do it!' chanted Sarah.

Liam joined in the chorus as it rose in volume.

Sarah took Lexi's hands and dragged her up off the bed as Liam tapped on his phone and some beats started playing. Lexi recognised the song instantly: 'Run Up' by Major Lazer. That was her jam. She couldn't help but dance as Sarah grabbed her by the waist and they started to move together.

Maybe a night out was exactly what she needed.

# CHAPTER TWENTY-EIGHT

At ten o'clock on a Monday morning, the jewellery stores of Hatton Garden were just opening their shutters for the week. Situated north-west of the 'square mile' – the City of London's old-money financial hub – the stretch of shops and vaults was the centre of the UK's diamond industry. People even travelled here from abroad to haggle over stones with Hatton Garden dealers. Despite living in London her entire life, Smith had never visited before. But it was the most obvious place to start if you were following up on a ring used in two murders. Make that three murders. They could've come yesterday but only half of the shops would've been open and, if they were going to go door to door, Smith wanted to do it thoroughly. That was her investigative style, and it'd worked for the first twenty years of her career. No need to change that now.

'You know this street?' she asked Khan as they stood at a crossroads lined with boutiques whose window displays sparkled and shimmered under spotlights.

'Nope.' Khan scratched the neat stubble on his chin. 'Bit out of my price range, innit? You?'

'Same. But I researched it before we came.'

'And?'

'Named after Sir Christopher Hatton. Queen Elizabeth nicked the land off some bishop and gave it to him around 1570.'

'Sucks for the bishop. What'd Hatton done to earn that?'

'Apparently the queen took a liking to him,' said Smith. 'Tall, good-looking, a great dancer—'

'Sounds just like me.' Khan grinned. He shoved his hands in his pockets. ''S'about the only way I'd get hold of a diamond. Maybe if I went to the clubs where Meghan Markle's hanging out.'

'She's married.'

'I know.'

'To Prince Harry.'

'I know. Just sayin', I might catch her eye, then—'

'OK, let's start at the bottom and work up.' Smith gestured to the far end of the road and they began walking down. She held up her left hand and rotated it. 'Even though the ring finger's one that I *have* got, no one's bought me anything to go on it. Never had one off my son's dad – we weren't engaged. And I told my current fella that I'm probably not the marrying type anyway.'

Khan chuckled. 'I'm trying to tell my parents the same thing. They keep offering to pair me up with some nice girl from Pakistan who I've never even met.'

'Sounds tricky.'

'No shit.' Khan paused at one display and Smith watched him scanning the engagement rings, his eyes widening at the numbers next to them. The stones glittered against their black velvet backdrop.

'Anyway,' resumed Smith, 'I told my boyfriend he could still buy me a diamond if he wants, but he hasn't taken the hint. Maybe I need to be even less subtle…'

'Well, he'd better have some cash in his wallet if he comes here.' Khan pointed to a collection of diamond engagement rings whose prices were shown on little tags. They started at two thousand pounds for a stone you'd need a magnifying glass to see and quickly entered the 'unaffordable' category for a rock that looked about normal size. 'You'd have to be on DCI Porter's salary to afford one of these,' he said.

'Well, salary and a ring didn't do Porter much good.'

'Really?' Khan turned to her. 'Why's that?'

'You don't know? His wife left him.'

'How did I not hear that? When?'

Smith pursed her lips. 'Start of this year, I think.'

'Huh. Maybe that explains why he's been in such a bad mood recently.'

'He's got a lot on his plate.' She scanned the street. 'All right. You take this side, I'll take that side, and we work our way up.'

'Looking for anybody that modifies rings with two-pin spring inserts,' confirmed Khan. 'And, specifically, who did so in the few months prior to Kim Hardy's murder.'

'That's the one.'

The post-mortems of Kim, Natasha and Sophie had all shown small injuries to their left ring fingers. Apparently, Lockhart's friend, Dr Green, had 'interpreted' those injuries as having some deep psychological meaning for the killer. As far as Smith was concerned, that was unknowable. The thing they could work with, however, was Green's idea that small springs designed to keep an oversized ring in place may have been the cause of the cuts. Smith had to give her some credit for spotting that, at least.

An hour later, they reconvened halfway up the street.

'Got anything?' asked Smith.

Khan took out his notebook and flipped a page. 'Most of the places don't modify the jewellery themselves. They just sell the stuff. A spring-grip insert is most likely to be added to an antique ring, they say. If it was a new ring, they'd just advise the customer to have the metal resized.'

'Same story down my side.'

'And for modifications like springs and inserts,' continued Khan, 'one name came up three times. Michael Litman. He's got a basement workshop off one of these side streets.'

Smith nodded. 'Two of my jewellers mentioned him too. I think we should go and see what Mr Litman can tell us.'

Khan pocketed his notebook. 'Let's do it.'


Smith waited for the lock to click as the buzzer sounded before she yanked the heavy door open. Since there was no functioning light-bulb above them, she and Khan had to feel their way down the stairs from street level to Michael Litman's workshop. The interior wasn't much better lit, either. Filing cabinets lined one wall, workbenches the other, with a couple of tables in the middle. Various clamps, stands and tools were strewn about, desk lamps casting pools of light over the baize surfaces. There was one man in the room. Even seated, Smith could tell that he was short and overweight. As they entered, he removed a pair of magnifying eyeglasses and stood, not without some effort. He wore a white collared shirt and dark trousers, a kippah pinned to the crown of his short, tightly curled hair.

'Michael Litman?'

'Yes.' He massaged the small of his back with both hands, groaning.

Smith held up her warrant card and introduced herself and Khan.

Litman looked scared half to death. 'How may I be of assistance, officers?'

'We'd just like to ask you a few questions, sir, about modifying rings.'

'Everything I do is completely above board.'

'Yes, Mr Litman, I'm sure it is. We have a murder case where we believe a victim was assaulted with a ring.' Smith described

the injuries and produced a photograph. She handed it to Litman
and he studied it under a lamp. He was visibly horrified.

'Murder?'

'Yes, sir.' She avoided saying exactly which murder, or that there
were three with identical wounds. They had to keep that information under wraps for now, and the ring finger scratches weren't
public knowledge. 'What can you tell us about those injuries?'

'Well,' Litman sniffed, 'they could've been caused by springs,
if the ring was being pushed on or pulled off hard. But it'd be
very unusual for them to break the skin… Let me show you.' He
scanned the workshop, then went over to a bench and ran his
finger along some plastic tubs stacked on a shelf before extracting
one. He popped the lid off it and rummaged inside.

'Here,' he said, holding up a tiny piece of curved metal with
two rounded edges roughly a centimetre apart. 'This is a two-pin
spring adjuster on an insert. The beads aren't sharp, as you can see.'

'Could you sharpen them?' asked Khan. 'I mean, to improve
the grip or something?'

'Possibly, with the right tools… but it's not something I've ever
done. There'd be no need for it, and it'd be much less comfortable
to wear.'

Smith stepped closer and inspected the box of inserts. 'How
often do you do ring adjustments?'

'About, oh, anywhere from five to ten times a day. A lot of the
retailers around here bring them to me.'

'What about spring inserts?'

'Ah, that's rarer. Maybe a couple per week. When the client
doesn't want the metal altered in the ring.'

'Because it's antique?'

'Usually that's the reason, yes. Or if it has sentimental value.'

'Like a family heirloom?'

'Mm.' Litman nodded. 'Say it belonged to a grandmother or
something.'

Smith stepped back from the materials and looked squarely at him. 'Do you recall doing a job like that earlier this year? Maybe around May or June time. A spring insert, with two pins.'

Litman blinked. 'I did a few, yes.'

'Do you keep a record of customer names?'

'I'm afraid not, officer. Some want receipts. Mostly, I'm paid in cash and that's it.'

'Do you have any CCTV?' asked Khan. Smith knew that was a long shot; it was a way back.

'No.' Litman picked at his nails. 'There are plenty of cameras in the streets around here, though.'

Smith tried to stifle her frustration. But it wasn't game over just yet. 'If we were to show you some photographs, would you be able to say if the person had come here and asked for a two-pin spring insert?'

'I'll try. My eyesight's not the best at distance, but… well, I'd certainly take a look. I know most of my clients because they're retailers. Individual customers are less frequent, so I might remember them.'

'Thank you, Mr Litman.' Smith handed over her card. 'We'll be in touch.'

She'd check with Lockhart, but she wanted to return to show the jeweller photographs of Hugh Chadwick and Dean Waters, each submerged within a six-pack of mugshots. Neither Chadwick nor Waters was definitively in the clear, yet. Khan's research had shown that Chadwick had no alibi for Sophie Wright's death. And Waters was seen in the pub on the nights of both Natasha's and Sophie's deaths, but earlier than he'd claimed, meaning there was a big window of his night where no one could vouch for him. They still had a lot of work to do. Before the journey back to Putney, though, Smith needed to top up her twin fuel sources: caffeine and sugar.

Smith blinked in the daylight as they emerged back at street level. 'Come on, Mo,' she said, pointing in the direction of Leather

Lane. 'There's a decent-looking café round the corner that we passed on the way in. My treat.'

Khan's eyes lit up. 'Sweet.' He cast a final glance towards the boutiques as they set off in search of coffee and cakes. 'At least there's some things around here we can afford.'

# CHAPTER TWENTY-NINE

By mid-afternoon, the hospital car park had thinned out and Lockhart had no problem finding a space. He slung the vehicle's Met police log book across the dashboard to avoid getting a ticket and headed up the path to the red-brick clinic building where Lexi Green worked. He hadn't had therapy with her for three weeks and it felt a bit strange coming here as a professional rather than a patient. But Green wanted to speak face to face and told him she had a free hour at 3 p.m. between sessions. She'd only said over the phone that she had 'news'.

Lockhart appreciated her 'comms-sec' – communications security – awareness but hoped the trip wouldn't turn out to be a waste of time. It was worth it, he told himself. Chadwick and Waters were still people of interest, Jacobson at a pinch. But their forensic investigations hadn't yet identified new, clear suspects, and he needed any lead he could get.

He had to acknowledge, too, that he wanted to see Green in person. Over the ten weeks of their therapy, she'd come to represent a source of safety and reassurance in his life that was second only to his mum, now that his wife wasn't around. Did that make him disloyal to Jess? Lockhart didn't know. It was almost a cliché to start feeling something for your therapist… but surely that wasn't happening to him. Maybe it was just because he'd opened up to Green in their treatment sessions. Best not think about it too much, he concluded, pressing the bell at the entrance.

Maureen buzzed him in through the main door, and again into the back corridor which contained Green's consulting room. He was pleased that they seemed to have tightened up on locking doors since that patient had got in and put a kitchen knife to Green's throat. Her door was open and, as he reached the doorway, she spun her chair to him and smiled. Her hair hung in a loose ponytail and she wore a thick navy sweater, black jeans and Doc Martens. The room was chilly and there was a portable heater pulled up next to her at the desk.

'Hey, Dan, come in. Sorry it's freezing in here; the old building takes a while to warm up.'

'Don't worry about it. You wanted to talk?' He realised how abrupt that sounded and cleared his throat. 'I mean, I don't want to take up too much of your time,' he added, closing the door behind him.

'No problem. Same here, I know how busy you are.' She switched off her monitor, closed a manila file of notes, and wheeled her chair across to grab a backpack leaning against the wall. She extracted a laptop and opened it. 'I wanted to show you what I've found. Any developments on your side?' she asked as she fired up the machine.

'Sod all so far,' he replied, dropping into an armchair opposite her. It was where he usually sat in his therapy sessions. His body felt suddenly heavy. 'We've got a few technical investigations in progress. Hair sample's gone to the lab for testing this morning, but that could take a few days for a result. We should get DNA and, if we're lucky, the guy will already be on the system for something else.' That was a long shot and he knew it; this killer was careful. But you never knew. 'You have to hope,' he said, catching her eye. If there was one thing he could rely on Lexi Green for, it was that: hope.

'Sure, you do. Always.'

'As for the rest of it, it's basically a massive exercise in data crunching. Porter's squared away a couple of bodies on secondment to help with that. But unless one of our persons of interest pops up having ordered some metal balls or been on a date with one of the victims, we're in the dark until all of those inquiries converge on an individual we can identify. I can just about deal with the endless paperwork. But my budget's not going to last for ever, with extra staff and overtime.'

'That's tough,' she acknowledged.

'Do you know how many online retailers there are of dental gags?'

'Uh, nope.'

'Over two hundred, and that's just on the surface web, in the UK. It's not so much needle in a haystack, it's a needle in a bloody barn full of needles.'

Green compressed her lips and nodded. 'Hey, at least you've got Lucy Berry running that side of things. She seems to know what she's doing.'

'True.' Lockhart cracked his knuckles.

'What about CCTV?' she asked.

'We've got a couple of DCs trawling through local stuff and trying to rule out the obvious people captured in the footage. Takeaway delivery drivers and stuff. But the killer seems to have chosen his target premises very carefully. They're quiet residential roads with no cameras on the exits. He's smart. And technically very savvy.' He slumped in the armchair. 'To be honest, Lexi, it's driving me nuts.'

She studied him, her eyes wide with concern. 'That sounds like it's really hard.'

'Yeah.' He was about to start telling her how he'd been having more nightmares, how he'd been longing for his wife more than usual, and how he'd felt the urge to drink more. But he reminded himself why he was here. 'All right, then, what've you got?'

She hesitated, then tapped a computer key and glanced at the screen. She clicked the trackpad a few times. 'OK, so, based on what we were saying about male power and men who hate women, I took a look at some websites and chatrooms.' She shuffled her chair closer to him, rotating the laptop. 'This one's hosted in Russia, but it's run by Australians. These guys—'

There was a knock at the door.

'Lexi? You busy?' came the voice from the corridor.

Lockhart recognised it as her colleague, Dr Edwards.

'Oh, shit,' she whispered, glancing at her watch. 'Sorry about this,' she told Lockhart quietly before raising her voice. 'Come in, Rob.'

The door opened slowly, and Edwards nudged it wider with his hip, bending his body to protect two steaming cups of tea. He stopped when he saw Lockhart.

'Oh, hello.' Then he turned to Green. 'Sorry, Lexi, I didn't realise you guys were in a session.'

'We're not,' she replied, turning her chair to hide the screen from Edwards.

Her colleague stood there, glancing from her to Lockhart and back, his face twisted in confusion. 'O-K,' he said slowly. 'Er, we're supposed to have peer supervision now, remember?'

'I'm so sorry, Rob.' Lexi pulled a face of regret. 'This just came up last minute and I forgot to tell you. My bad.'

Edwards looked down at Lockhart. 'Don't you normally come here on Tuesdays?'

'Yeah,' he replied. 'But we're discussing an investigation.'

'Can we do the peer supervision another time, please?' asked Lexi.

'Story of my life,' mumbled Edwards. He seemed physically deflated by Lockhart's presence. 'Well, um, I made you some tea, Lexi.' He proffered one of the mugs. 'White, none. Julie Andrews.' He gave a little laugh.

Lockhart knew that was military slang, but no way was this guy army. He must've got the term off a soldier he was treating.

'Thanks so much, Rob,' said Lexi, taking the mug and immediately putting it to one side. 'That's really sweet of you. Dan, would you like a drink?'

'Yeah, I'd love a brew.' Lockhart rubbed his hands together. 'Tea, white, one, please.'

The silence hung for a moment.

'Well, um, in that case, would you like this one?' Edwards held out the second mug awkwardly. He'd clearly made it for himself, but Lockhart needed the morale boost. He wasn't going to say no.

'Cheers.' He accepted the tea with a nod. 'Appreciate it.'

'Right, then.' Edwards stood there for a moment, gazing at Green's laptop. 'I'll leave you to it. Just shout if you need something, I'll be next door.' He dipped his head at Green before leaving, and Lockhart caught the unspoken message: *if the nutter here tries anything*. Remembering how Edwards had hidden behind Green when the knifeman broke into the clinic three weeks ago, he supressed a smirk.

After Edwards had departed and shut the door, Green showed Lockhart the laptop screen. He read the chat thread she'd screen-grabbed about the Throat Ripper. To say the participants were excited about the murders would be an understatement.

Green extracted a pen from her pocket, where she always kept it: the fancy black one she wrote with during their sessions. Montblanc. Lockhart had seen them on sale at airports; they cost a bomb. Very solid, though, top quality. She tapped the screen with it. 'That's his nickname, Throat Ripper. And these links,' she tapped again, 'take you to a deep web page which is invitation only.'

'Thank God the media hasn't found this yet,' he said, blowing on his tea.

'Probably a matter of time. It took me a little effort, but not much. You know how I was talking about phallic power and stuff on Saturday?'

'How could I forget?'

'Well, I think the killer is one of these guys,' she said. 'I think he's an incel.'

'A what?'

'Incel. Involuntary celibate.'

Lockhart had never heard the term. 'Which is?…'

'OK, so, it basically started out in the nineties as an online lonely-hearts club. A Canadian woman set up the first website as a place where anyone who'd experienced romantic failures and disappointments could go to share their stories.'

'Sounds innocent enough. What happened?'

Green twirled the pen in her fingers. 'The movement got taken over pretty quickly by guys who believed the empowerment of women had come at personal cost to them. They complained that because they weren't tall, hot, rich, good at sports, played in bands or whatever, women weren't interested in them.'

He sipped his tea. 'They reckoned looks, money and talent were all women wanted?'

'Yeah. Apparently, we don't care about personality or sense of humour or intellect.'

'Is that true?' He raised his eyebrows.

She grinned. 'I'm not even answering that. Anyway, I'd say their way of thinking is a sure-fire recipe for inferiority complexes and, potentially, aggressive responses. Remember Adler's theory?'

'Course. So, there's hate speech? Threats?'

'You bet. But it's not all talk. Three mass murders in North America have been carried out by incels in the past few years. All victims were female.'

'Serious?'

She nodded. 'California, 2014. Then Toronto and Florida in 2018.'

'Jesus.' The whole business was news to Lockhart. He clearly had some catching up to do.

'The killers became known as "saints" in the incel community,' continued Green. 'They're basically worshipped as heroes, freedom fighters standing up for men.'

He glanced at her laptop screen again, at the chatroom thread. 'So, you think the Throat Ripper's an incel?'

She spread her hands as if his question was rhetorical. 'Think about it. You guys have much stricter gun laws here, so if there was an incel who wanted to attack women, he probably can't attempt a shooting. Instead, he chooses another MO. Serial murder.' She slapped the pen emphatically on the desk and looked at him expectantly.

He took a big slurp of tea. 'This is really useful background, Lexi.'

'Background?' She sounded upset. 'This is *it*, Dan. I'm telling you.' She jabbed a finger at the laptop. 'This is where you'll find this guy. The profile fits.'

'It's interesting, no question.'

'Interesting?' Her voice had risen in pitch and volume. 'Jeez.'

'Look, it's great work and thanks to you we have a pretty good understanding of who we're probably dealing with here. But what we don't have is any proof that one of these website warriors is connected to the so-called Throat Ripper or knows who he is. Never mind him actually being in this chatroom. There isn't enough actionable detail in anything those blokes have said in their conversation. Don't get me wrong, they're weird guys and this is hate speech. But we've got to prioritise where we put our resources, and DCI Porter is already telling me not to waste too much time online.'

She shot him a look of pure irritation. 'This isn't wasted time. There's a private chat linked to that page. If I can get in there, I think we'll be one step closer to the guy.'

'Maybe.'

'OK, well, I'm going to keep looking at this.' She thrust a hand towards the screen, her body tense. 'When I find him, I'll let you know.'

'Good luck,' said Lockhart.

'And I'm going to be working on this every night, now, because you know what? I think he's going to kill another woman pretty damn soon.'

Lockhart might've been sceptical of her online investigation, but he had to admit he agreed with her prediction. He drained his tea and stood to leave. He was even more frustrated than she was. But, like the rest of his emotions, he just tried not to show it.

# CHAPTER THIRTY

Elena Fernandez yawned, rubbed her eyes and leant back in her office chair. She linked her fingers and stretched her arms above her head. It'd been another long day, much like the one before it, and the one before that. The Lebanese meze takeaway she'd had delivered to work was some compensation, especially the falafel. But she wondered how much longer she could keep going like this. Elena couldn't even remember the last time she'd had a day off. It was important stuff she was doing; she had to keep herself motivated with that thought. *Vamos.* She was making a difference.

The women's rights charity which Elena had founded two years ago – Hermanas – had some amazing projects up and running. She and her team of two assistants ran the little organisation out of a one-room office they'd set up in a closed-down shop unit on a massive, noisy road that connected Deptford and Greenwich in south-east London. She dreamt of somewhere more central that'd make it easier to lobby government… but this was *real*. It was in the community. And, more importantly, it was all they could afford.

The finances were getting tighter every month and the money from her mother's will wasn't going to last for ever. Mama would've been proud of what she'd done with it so far, though. Elena sighed as she felt a pang of absence. Her mother had died in a car accident in Spain while Elena was studying for her master's degree here, at SOAS. Since Mama had been the only real family she'd had, Elena decided to carry on living in London. Over time, the pain of her death had faded into the background, particularly once Elena graduated and started channelling her energy into Hermanas. Work had saved her: being productive and having a sense of meaning had lifted her out of the bereavement, keeping its emptiness at bay. But work never seemed to end, and tonight was no exception. She'd just finished a monitoring report for one of her funders, but she couldn't allow herself to cycle home just yet. She still had about fifty pages' worth of documents to read before a meeting tomorrow. And that wasn't even for a Hermanas project – it was for her other job.

It'd seemed like a good idea at the time to run for local council. She'd campaigned as an independent candidate on a pledge of ensuring access to healthcare for every woman in Greenwich. But it was only once she'd overcome the surprise of being elected that she'd realised quite how much work the role would involve. Quite how many meetings with men twice her age who wore grey suits and squinted at her because she still had a strong Spanish accent when she spoke English. Quite how difficult it was to actually change anything. And how she'd have to do all of it without getting paid. What was that American phrase? *A sucker for punishment.* Yeah, that was her.

And, yet, there were still so many initiatives she wanted to start. She had ideas for a programme with local schools on body autonomy, a stigma reduction plan to help migrant women access psychological therapy, and a back-to-work enablement scheme for mothers who'd been doing full-time childcare. Elena had enthusiasm in bucketloads, but what she needed was focus. And time. And money, of course. Maybe they should run another fundraising drive. They'd had some real success earlier in the year, catching the eye of a wealthy female investor called Natasha Mayston, who'd donated several thousand pounds.

Elena couldn't believe it when she read that Natasha had been murdered in her own home about three weeks ago. It made her grateful that she lived with four flatmates. The house-share was mainly a way to save on rent but, after another woman had been killed in her home last week, it now felt like the safest option for living in London. Perhaps there was a project they could run to support female victims of crime? Women needed more protection, both in prevention and prosecution of crimes.

Last year, for example, police forces nationwide introduced a policy to investigate rape cases only if the victim signed a digital waiver to give the police unrestricted access to everything on their mobile phones. That was typical of the system; making life even harder for the victims of sexual assaults. It was so unfair! But Hermanas had lobbied against that and been successful in getting the Met to amend the waiver criteria. Elena had caused them a lot of trouble and disruption, but she didn't care – she was doing the right thing.

However, she wondered if her activism had backfired after there was a break-in at the Hermanas office back in the spring. The police seemed to remember Elena and hadn't cared at all about investigating the burglary. They'd lost laptops, video equipment and other stuff they didn't have the funds to replace. But all the police did was scold them like naughty schoolgirls for not having any security cameras or alarms. Elena didn't bother explaining that they couldn't afford to have them fitted. They couldn't even afford heating, she thought, pulling her Peruvian shawl tighter around herself. At least by working late she might deter some potential burglars; they'd see the lights and move on to easier targets. Besides, she had to confess it wasn't *all* work this evening.

Recently, she'd found herself a little distracted by the dating app on her phone. She'd only installed it and signed up last month. Her flatmates had been teasing her about working all the time and told her it'd be good for her to meet a guy, even if it was just something casual. One of them had also hinted that, at thirty-three, she didn't have 'loads' of time left if she wanted a baby. As if that was what life was really all about. *Muchas gracias, perra.* Apparently, having a child after thirty-five was referred to as geriatric pregnancy. She'd bet it was a man who came up with that term. Anyway, she wasn't obsessed with the idea of kids – she had enough on with the charity and the local council. Maybe her friends were right, though; she should go out more… especially now she'd found someone worth going out with.

A cute guy had contacted her on the app last week and they'd exchanged a few messages. He seemed funny and cool and hadn't immediately felt the need to send her a 'dick pic'; those were three big positives. His last message, an hour ago, had invited her for a drink at the pub some time. Elena picked up her phone and tapped into the dating app. She flicked through the guy's photos one more time. He was definitely cute. Maybe it wouldn't hurt to finish work an hour early one day.

She popped the last falafel into her mouth, hit 'reply' on his message, and began typing.

*

He'd tried so hard not to be like his father. But, ultimately, as with most other things in his life, he'd failed. One of his earliest memories was walking into the kitchen to find his father grabbing his mother by the hair. Father wasn't a big man, but Mother was even smaller, slightly built and, by nature, submissive. When Father chose to control Mother physically, there was nothing she could do about it. No way could she fight back, even if she dared.

In that early memory – he must've been about six or seven years old – he recalled the acrid smell of burnt toast and Father demanding to know why his toast was burnt. All Mother did was to keep saying *sorry* and *please* as Father got angrier and angrier. Then, quite suddenly, he calmed down. It was as if a line had been crossed and a decision had been made. He took Mother's left hand, removed her rings, and placed her fingers in the toaster slot. Then Father pressed the lever down and held her hand in there as she began to scream. *Watch and learn, son*, Father had told him. He remembered a tiny wisp of smoke curling up from the toaster and a new, different smell that made him feel a bit sick. Then Father had let her go and Mother rushed to the sink, running the cold tap over her hand and crying silently. She'd worn gloves for a long time after that whenever she went out.

Over the next few years he'd witnessed so many more of those incidents that he'd lost count. Not once had it occurred to him to tell anyone. That was just… normal. It was only when he got to about thirteen or fourteen that he'd decided that he didn't like it, that what Father was doing to Mother was wrong. But still, he was too weak to tell anyone, too scared of the backhand slap he knew he'd catch if he tried to stop Father. So, instead, he internalised it. A psychologist might say he identified with his mother, the victim. Eventually, they'd been released from the tyranny when Father had suffered a massive, fatal stroke. Unbelievably, after everything she'd been through, Mother had called for an ambulance. But the bastard had already died by the time they got him to hospital.

Since that time, he'd been determined to have a normal romantic relationship. Not to be aggressive or violent or abusive. To be attentive and caring and thoughtful. He'd tried so hard. And he'd been *so* close. But then she'd let him down, and it was worse than he ever could've imagined. Finally, he understood why Father needed to keep Mother under such close control. He appreciated why Father had done those things. Now, you could say, he was following in his old man's footsteps.

There was a professor called Plomin who reckoned that almost everything we do is programmed by our genes. If violence was in Father's genes then, clearly, it was in his genes too. He could've tried all he liked. Sooner or later, that violence would've come out; it just needed the right trigger. It'd been released spectacularly three times already. And he knew it was only a matter of days before it erupted again, now that he'd turned his attention to her.

He watched her pull some multicoloured ethnic wrap around her shoulders. She was obviously one of those 'cold' women with poor circulation who always wanted to turn the heating up. And she seemed to like falafel, too. She twisted a lock of dark hair around her finger and sniffed it; he wondered if she knew how often she did that. He was getting to know her quite well. It was important to know someone well, he thought, when you were about to become very intimate with them.

He couldn't wait to meet her.

# PART THREE

# CHAPTER THIRTY-ONE

Lockhart parked his old Defender on a quiet side road, cut the engine and scanned his surroundings. Brick and pebbledash suburban terraces with small windows, concrete everywhere and barely a tree in sight. It wasn't high-threat, but it wasn't particularly welcoming either. He was at the north end of Heathway, the main road that sliced through this forgotten district of east London.

Dagenham had been a thriving centre of car manufacturing and housing development in the thirties. But by the sixties it was already in decline as the plants shut down and moved abroad. Today, it was synonymous with poverty and crime, and waves of immigration from Eastern Europe, south Asia and Africa that'd given rise to knee-jerk racism and a fractured community. A couple of years ago it'd even been voted Britain's worst place to live – by its own residents.

Lockhart couldn't imagine what the hell Jess would be doing here, if she was here at all. But that's what the anonymous guy had posted on the missing persons website: he'd seen someone who looked like her around Dagenham Heathway. Lockhart knew it was a long shot, but if there was even the slightest possibility of a lead on Jess then it was worth a try. Not to follow up would mean that he'd abandoned hope of ever finding her, and he wasn't about to do that.

This was the first chance he'd had to come here after seeing the comment in response to his post about Jess on the website, nearly a month ago. His team had been working flat out on Operation

Norton, but they had little to show for their effort and Lockhart knew they were tired and losing belief. It was now mid-November, two weeks on from Sophie Wright's murder, and DCI Porter had cancelled overtime to save money. Their work had slowed down, focussing on two key lines of inquiry.

The first was forensics from Sophie's flat. The hairs in her mouth had turned out to be from an animal rather than a person – meaning they were probably clothing fibres – and didn't contain human DNA. After some cross-referencing with a lab in the US, they'd been identified as coyote fur. But that could still be investigated; coyote-hair clothing wasn't common and, since Sophie didn't appear to own any, their garment of origin probably belonged to her killer. During the later stages of crime scene processing, DNA from another person had been found on her clothes, but it wasn't a match with anyone on the system. The forensics lab at King's College London was doing further analysis to see what it could tell them about the person who deposited it.

The second area was tracing purchases of dental gags in the UK. They'd turned up more than three thousand sales in the past five years from over two hundred sellers and were now working through the list one by one to eliminate each buyer as a suspect. The purchasers fell into two distinct categories: dentists, and couples who liked tying each other up. The team were now taking bets on which group would outnumber the other by the time they were finished. That provided some laughs amid the ongoing threat of failure that'd hung over him since his appointment as SIO. Lockhart couldn't believe how well the killer had covered his tracks. It was hard not to feel despondent at their lack of results, their inability to anticipate the next move. And he was sure this guy wasn't finished at three victims. He didn't need Green's profile to tell him that.

In Lockhart's experience, homicide usually fell into two categories. The majority were 'hot': one-off, impulsive acts of violence, typically sparked by alcohol or drug-fuelled altercations where death may not have been the intended outcome. Such cases were often downgraded to manslaughter, the perpetrator frequently remorseful and unlikely to repeat his or her act. And the unplanned nature of the attack usually meant crime scenes loaded with evidence and a very high chance of catching those involved. The rest – thankfully, a minority – belonged to the other type.

These were the 'cold' murders: calculated acts with preparation, targeting and cleaning up. The perpetrators were generally psychopaths at some level. Green would know more about how those individuals functioned but, for Lockhart, they were simply the harder ones to catch. They often preyed on strangers, rarely left obvious evidence behind and showed little to no remorse for their crimes. And, once they'd started, the cold ones usually didn't stop until they were caught. Lockhart was confident that the man whom the media were now calling 'the Throat Ripper' was in the second group. That strongly suggested he wasn't done; it was 'when' rather than 'if' he'd find another victim. Tonight, however, there was no more that Lockhart could do on Op Norton.

He reached into his jacket pocket, took out the most recent photograph he had of Jess and studied it. It was ten years old. Would she look like this now? Or had the man from the website just seen a woman who resembled his wife in her early twenties? He took in Jess's large, bright blue eyes, the skin crinkled at their corners. Her broad smile and the dimples in her cheeks. When she was in that kind of mood, she'd be the one taking him out to do stuff, to gigs or bars or anywhere else that had as much energy as her. On days when she was feeling lower, he'd be the one encouraging her to come out, to go for a walk together in the park or by the river, eat ice cream – whatever the weather – and forget about the daily grind. Either way, it wouldn't be long before they were both grinning and laughing about something.

Lockhart shut his eyes briefly, recalling the moment he'd kissed her goodbye on the doorstep of their flat, before slinging his kitbag over his shoulder and going to Afghanistan. That was the last time he'd ever seen her. Taking a final look at her picture, he planted a small kiss on it. Then he got out of his car and, with his breath clouding in the night air, set off down the road to find out whether anyone had seen her. Dagenham Heathway was almost two miles long. But he'd walk up and down it all night if he had to.

*

Standard operating procedures, protocols, rules, regulations. Whatever you wanted to call them, Smith knew that what she was doing was probably violating one or more of them. She hadn't been left with much choice, she told herself, after DCI Porter canned the overtime on Op Norton and decreed that the DNA from Sophie Wright's flat was the only real lead worth pursuing. The sample recovered from Sophie's clothing wasn't on record, which meant it didn't belong to Dean Waters. Therefore, he was no longer a person of interest. That wasn't an opinion Smith shared, but you didn't last twenty years in the Met by openly opposing the top brass. Instead, you found ways around them.

That was why she was sitting alone in her car outside Westland House, on her own time, watching the entrance to the tower block where Waters lived. During a cold night in the middle of November, she'd rather have been at home, obviously. Snuggled on the sofa with her fella, a nice glass of wine and a film, forgetting about murder cases until the morning. Maybe it was her copper's nose, as the expression went, that told her something wasn't right about Dean Waters. Deliberately or otherwise, he'd given incorrect timings for his visits to the local pub that provided his alibi. He'd been accused of violent, abusive behaviour towards a woman, including choking her on an object. He'd threatened to kill Sophie Wright after his conviction, and he was released before sex worker Kim Hardy was murdered. And, call her a cynic, but Smith didn't buy the religious faith he'd suddenly found in prison. Waters was still a person of interest to her.

As surveillance jobs went, though, it wasn't too bad. Yes, it was chilly and the planes in and out of City Airport flew so low overhead they made the car vibrate. But she had a flask of strong tea, a packet of chocolate digestive biscuits and Adele belting out some classics through one earphone. She was halfway through 'Set Fire to the Rain' when the front door of Westland House swung open and the diminutive figure of Dean Waters exited, crash helmet in one hand and a carrier bag in the other. He strode over to a moped parked opposite and dropped the bag into a large top box on the back before strapping his helmet on. Was he working as a delivery rider, too? He'd omitted to mention that when they asked him about his job. Smith recalled their profile of the killer: someone you'd open your door to.

Waters straddled the bike, fired up its engine, and was off. Smith yanked the earphone out and set her mobile to Google Maps. Then she pulled out and began following him.

*

Elena Fernandez was about ready to go home. Her bicycle, propped against the office wall across from her desk, was calling to her. The twenty-minute ride back to her house in East Dulwich would be cold at this time of night, sure, but she was dreaming of the hot bath she could take when she got in. So long as none of her housemates were in the shared bathroom, Elena could set the water running, drop in some of that incredible cypress and sea fennel bath gel, let the foam pile up and then strip off and slide in. She could almost feel the tension dropping from her muscles at the thought of that. She'd definitely earned it today.

This afternoon, she'd given a presentation to Greenwich Clinical Commissioning Group – the board of doctors and directors who chose how money for healthcare was spent in the borough – on underserved female populations locally. She'd lobbied for women with postnatal depression and birth-related post-traumatic stress disorder to be prioritised in psychology services. She'd argued for teenage girls at risk of coercion by gangs to be identified in schools and youth centres before they were sexually or criminally exploited. And she'd pushed for older women who'd lost partners and friends to have better access to bereavement services, including home visits. The doctors had listened and pledged to consider all her proposals. It was a great start – and a beautiful overlap between the work of Hermanas and her role as a local councillor.

The glow she'd felt afterwards had lasted into the evening, barely diminished by the paperwork she'd needed to catch up on. Her assistants had gone home at 6 p.m., as usual, leaving Elena to push on into the night. She promised herself that she'd finish at 10 p.m., and it was quarter to ten now. She'd wrap up a couple more emails to some charities in Latin America she wanted to reach out to; since they were five hours behind, it made sense to contact them while their working day was still going – that way she might have a reply by morning.

She'd just started composing the first message in Spanish when the door buzzer went, startling her. Who would it be at this hour? She considered ignoring it; more than once in the past, a local alcoholic man had asked if he could come in and sleep there. She sympathised, but it wasn't Hermanas's job to offer a bed to the homeless. Besides, they didn't have any beds. The buzzer went again. Elena sighed, got up and crossed to the door. Behind the frosted glass was the blurred silhouette of a person holding what looked like a box.

'Yes?' she called out.

'Delivery,' replied a man's voice. What was he bringing here at night? Her takeaway sushi had already been delivered an hour ago, unless there'd been a mix up on the app. She tried to think if they'd ordered anything… 'Amazon,' he added. *Amazon?* Had one of her assistants bought some stationery or books or something? Elena knew these gigging couriers worked all hours and only got paid for completed jobs. She didn't want the guy to miss out.

'Who's it for?' she asked, one hand on the latch.

'Hermanas,' came the response. What accent was that? Whatever, it was clearly for them.

She opened the door, admitting a rush of air that was even colder than her office. She automatically took the handheld device he gave her. 'Thanks,' she said.

'Just sign there, please.'

'OK.' Elena briefly made eye contact with him. Then she paused.

She'd seen him before.

# CHAPTER THIRTY-TWO

Lexi shut the door to her office, took out her personal laptop and fired up a private internet browser window. She had a free hour now because her patient, Andrea, the young Italian man who reminded her so much of her brother, hadn't turned up for his session. She'd called him, getting through at the third attempt. Normally, it wasn't a good idea to 'chase' a patient too much; they had to be the one choosing to attend and taking responsibility for explaining their absences. But Lexi knew that where Andrea was concerned the rules were a little different. She felt as though, if she could help Andrea, she would've gone some way towards making amends for not being around to help her brother.

Ordinarily, she'd have gone straight to the admin to-do list in the case of a session where the client didn't turn up. But instead of clearing her paperwork, she was getting online again. In the past two weeks since Sophie Wright's death, Lexi had been using more and more of her free time to probe the manosphere for leads on their killer. She didn't want to call him the Throat Ripper, buying into the incel hype that'd now spread to the mainstream media. She had no desire to mythologise a guy who, in all probability, was just a lonely, sad, pathetic man. A man who used extreme violence against women who couldn't fight back because he'd restrained them. A sadist who needed to feel big and powerful. She was reluctant to join in with boosting this guy's obviously fragile ego. And, yet, that's exactly what she had to do.

Despite Dan's discouragement – or perhaps because of it – Lexi was carrying out a kind of extended participant-observer study within this tragic online community. And she had to admit that she found the many and varied expressions of toxic masculinity simultaneously disgusting, enraging and fascinating. She'd created an alias – 'Blake' – and proceeded to engage with a bunch of websites. Today, having logged on to an incel forum as Blake, using the handle everythin_suxx19, she joined a chat thread about the justification for violence against women. One guy had argued that for ninety-nine per cent of human history, women hadn't got to choose who they had sex with, so why should anything change now? Another poster had joked that, these days, women were so promiscuous that the only way to get them to remember you after you'd had sex with them was to punch them in the face. She was considering what Blake should type in support of the idea when there was a knock at her door and a voice came from outside.

'Hi, Lexi.' It was Rob.

She flicked across to YouTube on a different browser window, where she was midway through streaming a panel discussion on PTSD from a psychology conference, recorded in the summer. That was her cover for using the personal laptop: the hospital's firewalls blocked a bunch of big websites to stop staff wasting time.

'Come in,' she said.

He opened the door and entered, holding a mug of tea. It was nice, but he didn't need to do this all the time.

'Here you go.' He placed the mug on her desk. 'Keep you going till lunch.'

'Thanks, Rob.'

He looked across to the laptop, studying the video and its description. 'Ah. I was at that conference,' he said. 'If you're interested, I can run you through the plenary sessions and the keynote speeches. I took a lot of notes.'

'Uh, it's cool,' she replied. 'Thanks. Just wanted to see what was being talked about.' She knew Rob meant well, but she just wanted him to leave so she could get on with her real research.

'Oh, right, OK.' He looked disappointed. 'Well, I'm going to be working on some admin next door. Shout if you need anything.' He retreated towards the door.

'Sure.' Lexi was already turning back towards the laptop. It was a little rude, but she didn't want Rob staying to chat right now.

'Fancy getting some lunch at one o'clock?' he asked casually, hovering in the doorway.

'Uh, jeez, I'd love to but… I can't right now, sorry.' She pulled a face of exaggerated regret and jerked a thumb at her desk.

'Yeah, of course. Right then, see you later,' he mumbled, shuffling out and closing the door behind him.

When she heard the door click shut, she switched the laptop browser window back to the incel forum. What would her alter-ego Blake say? His profile was that of an American frat boy who'd graduated and moved to London for work. Blake was a hard-drinking, computer-gaming nerd who couldn't get dates with women and espoused an aggressive bros before hos attitude.

*We should code a game where you beat the shit out of women you've just fucked*

A flurry of replies to her post came back, lauding Blake's idea, building on it, even offering to help code. It was an awful thing to write but, as far as the target audience went, it was on point. Building Blake's identity and online relationships was a means to an end: infiltrating the manosphere and finding out whatever 'he' could about the killer. Lexi was convinced the guy was on here somewhere, if she just found the right forum.

Half an hour later, she was into an open thread about the murders. Word was that he'd strike again soon. A participant going by the handle BloodCel was particularly vocal, celebrating the Throat Ripper's achievements and talking about him as if they were personally acquainted. Lexi took a breath, then made the step. She messaged BloodCel privately with a simple greeting.

*Sup bro*

Her heart was thumping as she waited for the reply. Nothing came. She was about to close the message window and look elsewhere when the reply pinged.

*red or black?*

It was a test. But Lexi had been immersed in this world for more than a fortnight, and she knew what to say. 'Redpilling' was trying to boost your attractiveness to women through building gym muscles, buying fashionable clothes, getting a cool haircut, learning pickup techniques or anything else that you had some control over. Playing the dating game by women's rules, supposedly. 'Blackpilling' was accepting that the whole system was flawed and rigged against the majority of men, especially those with 'inferior' biological traits, and refusing to participate at all. Those were the dangerous guys. There was only one right answer.

*Blackpill dude. You?*

The reply was quick this time.

*Same*

They went back and forth a little, trading views about women. Then Lexi made her move.

*When's Throat Ripper gonna choke his next bitch?*

*No idea bro*

She waited, staring at the screen. In a therapy session, silence was usually a good way to get someone to open up more. After thirty seconds that seemed like as many minutes, another line appeared.

*Priapus knows the dude tho*

*No way*

Who was Priapus? Lexi thought as she typed.

Then her phone rang. She picked it up and looked at the screen. Shit. It was Dan. After their last exchange, there had to be a good reason for him calling her now.

*Yo, gotta go. Boss breaking my balls at work*

*Laters*

She picked up the phone. 'Hey, Dan.'

'All right, Lexi.'

She knew immediately from his tone that something was wrong. And she could guess what, though she didn't want it to be true.

'What's happened?' she asked, her mouth suddenly dry.

For a moment, Dan didn't speak, and she could hear his breathing. It was like he was gathering himself to give her the news she was already anticipating. When he finally spoke, his voice was clear, his tone firm.

'There's been another murder,' he said.

# CHAPTER THIRTY-THREE

Lockhart rapped on the door and waited.

'Come.'

He entered DCI Porter's office to find his boss standing with his back to the door, hands in his pockets, staring out of the window as rain lashed against the glass. 'Sir?'

'Sit down.'

Lockhart did as instructed. Porter slowly crossed to his desk and took the seat opposite him. 'What do we know so far?'

'Victim was found at approximately 0930 in the offices of a women's rights charity called Hermanas, on the Deptford-Greenwich road. Seemingly murdered in the same way as Kim, Natasha and Sophie. Restrained and choked to death on a metal ball.'

'Terrible.' Porter shook his head.

'We got the call from Lewisham about 1100 hours,' continued Lockhart. 'DI named Zac Boateng from MIT 4 was first senior officer to arrive. He recognised the links to Op Norton straight away and called us in. Colleague ID'd the victim as Elena Fernandez, who runs the charity. Thirty-three years old, Spanish national. She's also a local councillor in Greenwich.'

'Councillor?' Porter raised his eyebrows. 'If we thought this was high profile already, it's going to be even worse now the Throat Ripper's killed an elected official. It could get political.'

*Worse* wasn't exactly the word Lockhart would've chosen. But he hadn't been dealing with the media or Met top brass much; Porter had covered most of that so far, including dampening down tabloid hysteria when the killer's nickname began filtering into mainstream social media. Lockhart's gaze travelled over Porter's desk, alighting on a small foil sheet of pills next to a glass of water. Porter registered his interest and swept the pills away, shoving them in a desk drawer.

'Detective Superintendent Burrows wants me to take over as SIO, you know,' said Porter, leaning back in his chair and linking thick fingers over his stomach.

Lockhart cleared his throat. 'What did you tell her?'

'I told her that I believed in you.' He inclined his head. 'This may be your first case as SIO, but you know it better than anyone. The Super took a bit of convincing, but she relented when I said you'd keep me in the loop on every development. No matter how small.'

'Sir.' It sounded as if Porter had done him a favour, but Lockhart wasn't sure if remaining SIO was better than being demoted to second-in-command on the case. He'd have to run everything past his boss while also taking full responsibility for the results. The sceptic in him wondered whether Porter was deliberately championing him to protect his own untarnished reputation, in case they didn't catch the guy. With each murder, he knew the scrutiny and criticism on the whole police force was growing. And Porter was right: Elena's elected position meant Op Norton was going to get the attention of even more politicians than before. That meant greater pressure without necessarily any extra resources.

'There's a lot of work to do,' said Porter. 'Don't let me down.'

Lockhart tried to retain the impression of calmness and control, but he could feel an ache building behind his eyes. It was a sure sign of tiredness. He'd been out until two o'clock this morning on Dagenham Heathway, not that he had anything to show for that except a dodgy stomach from the kebab he'd bought.

'We'd better get a press conference organised.' Porter checked his watch. 'What are your immediate actions?'

Flicking through his notebook, Lockhart found the list he'd written moments ago. Consulting his notes was the only chance he had of remembering everything although, with three near-identical murders in little over a month, the pattern was becoming painfully familiar. Each step in the wake of a death was a reminder of their failure to find the perpetrator.

'Well, sir, we're tracing Elena's next of kin in Spain. I've contacted Dr Volz about the post-mortem and she's trying to free herself up for tomorrow. DS Smith and DC Khan are visiting Elena's home later today to speak to her housemates. And Lucy Berry's going through Elena's diary and social media over the past couple of months, seeing if there's anything there. Usual phone data, CCTV requisitioning from the area, whatever we can get. Being a main road we might get something off a bus camera. I'm keeping in touch with the Crime Scene Manager for any early leads. Our guy seems to know forensics and doesn't leave a lot behind. But we might get lucky. I'll convene a meeting for the full Op Norton team at 0900 tomorrow.' He didn't mention briefing Lexi Green, for now. Despite his own misgivings about her theories, he felt strangely protective towards her after his team's cynicism so far. 'That's it, at the minute.'

'Good. This is big, Dan.' Porter leant forward and wagged a finger at him. 'Seriously big. It could be the defining case of our careers. The media's going to have a feeding frenzy now there's three confirmed victims. We won't be able to avoid the term "serial killer" any more. Or the inevitable public panic that'll cause.' His boss appeared to have the hint of a smile on his lips. 'But leave that side of it with me. I'll engage the journos and speak to the politicians.'

'I appreciate that, sir.' Lockhart knew that Porter's offer was probably self-serving, but it paid to display gratitude.

'We need to step things up,' continued the DCI. 'I'll make sure you get some more assistance to chase down those leads, plough through every second of CCTV footage that could be relevant. And make sure you go door to door in the area.'

'OK. But it's not really residential premises round there. We might be better off using any additional staff to—'

'The crime scene was an office, you said?'

'Right. Small place, previously a shop unit.'

Porter rubbed his chin. 'So, he's changing his MO, then. The first two were killed in their own homes.'

Lockhart shifted in his seat. 'With respect, sir, I believe his first victim was Kim Hardy, who was murdered in a hotel room. I don't think location is especially significant to him, except for the fact that he needs an environment he can gain control over. Somewhere indoors and isolated gives him the privacy to carry out the murder. He's not a blitz attacker, he takes his time.'

'Hm.'

'And…' Lockhart hesitated, 'on that subject, I'd like to speak to Damon Pagett in prison. As a witness. He might be able to tell us something about Kim Hardy that MIT 12 has overlooked, and which could be relevant to Op Norton.'

'You think so?'

'It's worth a try, sir.'

Porter exhaled loudly through his nostrils. 'DCI Flynn and the rest of Newham MIT aren't going to like it. The guy's in custody charged with Kim's murder and you want to ask him who he thinks killed her?'

Lockhart clenched his fist out of sight. 'You and I both know they've got the wrong guy.'

'They're not going to want to hear that, though, are they? An interview on record could prejudice their case against him.'

'There's no room for ego here, sir. If Pagett knows anything at all about who might've killed Kim, then it's our duty to find out and follow it up. Not to mention the fact that there's probably an innocent man locked up.'

'Pagett's not innocent, Dan. He admitted soliciting for sexual services. That's a crime.'

Lockhart felt his frustration building. 'I meant innocent of murder.' His voice was louder than he'd intended.

Porter scowled and bit his lip. 'You can't meet him,' he said eventually. 'You'd be treading on a lot of toes for something pretty speculative.'

'I don't care about treading on anyone's fucking toes!' He regretted the words as soon as they were out.

For a moment, Porter looked as though he was in shock. Then his eyes narrowed, and he leant forwards, holding up a meaty finger of caution. 'This is not your call, Detective Inspector. Do I need to remind you who's in charge of this team?'

Lockhart had to calm down. He'd already gone too far. He took a deep breath. 'No, sir.'

'Good.'

The silence hung between them. When Lockhart spoke again, he was careful to lower his voice. 'I could just run the meeting with Pagett as an intelligence interview, unrecorded.'

Porter sighed. 'I've already given you my answer,' he replied wearily, taking a document off a pile on his desk. It was his signal the meeting was over. But Lockhart wasn't quite ready to leave.

'Should I ask Superintendent Burrows?'

'No,' barked Porter. 'Leave Pagett alone. That's an order. Now go and do some work.'


Returning downstairs, Lockhart took a few moments to cool off before checking in with his team. The open-plan office was buzzing as MIT 8 went about their assigned actions with renewed energy. He wanted to stay, roll up his sleeves and get stuck in with them, but he had an appointment on the other side of town.

By the time he managed to get back over to south-east London it was late afternoon. He'd called his counterparts in Lewisham's MIT 4 and managed to secure a room to speak to Julia Johnson, the colleague of Elena Fernandez who'd found her body that morning. He was grateful to DI Boateng and DS Connelly – the Irishman who was first to arrive at Natasha Mayston's murder – for setting it up. He'd needed their help. Space wasn't the issue, as in some nicks. Lewisham was the largest police station in Europe and there were plenty of interview suites. What Lockhart required was a place that put someone at ease. In the Met they called them 'bad news rooms': comfortable, non-threatening spaces with sofas and low armchairs, softer lighting and no recording equipment. She was already in there when he arrived.

'Sorry to keep you waiting, Ms Johnson. Can I call you Julia?'

'Everyone calls me JJ.' Julia sounded detached. She stared vacantly through thick glasses, not making eye contact. She was clutching a tote bag with 'Hermanas' printed on it to her front as if it was a shield. Despite the warmth of the room, she hadn't taken off her big woollen jacket and her round cheeks were flushed. A mug of tea sat untouched on the small table beside her.

'OK, JJ. I'm Detective Inspector Dan Lockhart, and it's my job to find out what happened to Elena and catch the person who did it.'

She didn't reply.

'So, I know you've given a statement to my colleagues about discovering Elena this morning,' he continued gently. 'Thank you for doing that. Is it all right if I ask—'

'That's the first time I've ever seen a dead person,' she interjected. 'I mean, my grandad died a couple of years ago, but I didn't see him after, you know... before we buried him.'

Lockhart nodded. It wasn't surprising; in her mid-twenties, there was no reason why Julia would've encountered a cadaver.

He remembered that particular first in his own life, not long after he'd enlisted in the army. The young soldier whose suicide he'd discovered at the barracks. Lockhart could still see the image of him lying there. And what was left of his head.

'She was just so,' she swallowed, 'still.'

'It must've been very upsetting for you to see that.' Lockhart was aware that such a response could sound trivial and insincere, but something he'd learned from Green was that a simple acknowledgment of someone's feelings could go a long way. He'd not really understood that for the first thirty-six years of his life.

Julia blinked, her mouth creasing with the effort of holding back her tears.

'Given what you saw today, JJ, it's completely normal for you to be going through a lot of different reactions. You might have the picture from when you found her popping into your head, you might feel scared or sad, or you might feel nothing at all – just kind of numb.' He paused, letting her absorb that. 'What we tend to see is that those reactions often start to go away with time. If you'd like to talk to a professional about it at any point, though, I can put you in touch with a really good clinical psychologist.' He was sure Green would find time to help JJ after what she'd experienced. Finding the body of someone who'd died of natural causes was traumatic enough. Accidents were often worse because of the shock. But most people couldn't imagine how discovering the corpse of a murder victim could shake your world and make you question everything you thought you knew about humanity.

'OK,' she replied, now turning her head to look at him. 'Do you know what happened, then? Was it that man off the news, the Jack the Ripper guy they've been talking about?'

'The Throat Ripper, they're calling him.'

'Yeah. Was it him?'

'We can't say for sure, yet. But we're already treating Elena's death as the latest in a series of linked incidents where we believe the same perpetrator is likely to be responsible.' The words sounded like one of DCI Porter's media soundbites.

'Why did he kill her?' Julia wiped the back of her hand across her eyes. 'She was such a good person.'

'Right now, we don't know why Elena was attacked. But I was hoping you might be able to give me any information that might help us catch her killer. Is there anyone you know of who would've wanted to hurt her?'

Julia let out a long, slow breath. 'We got some abuse online, a bit of trolling. Mostly just blokes making fun of women's rights, putting stupid memes on social media, that kind of thing. No one threatened to hurt any of us, though. Some of it was personal against Elena because she was more, like, the face of the charity, you know?' Julia's mouth creased up and her voice caught. 'And now she's gone.'

'I'm sorry.' Lockhart gave her a moment. 'I know this must be very difficult, JJ. You're doing really well.'

She sniffed. 'Um, there is one thing I've remembered.'

'Yeah?'

'Well, the woman who was killed in her house about a month ago. Natasha.'

He leant forward. 'Natasha Mayston?'

'That's it. Well, she donated some money to us earlier this year. I don't know if that's important. Quite a few women have made donations, like, a few hundred people, since we started up Hermanas. But I thought, I mean, I wanted to tell you that.'

'Thanks, JJ, that's really useful.' Lockhart made a note. They could check the accounts and confirm the donation. He was already thinking about how the link might advance their search for the killer. Was it someone who knew that Natasha had donated to Hermanas? Were there other financial connections, perhaps between Natasha and Sophie Wright, for instance, that they'd missed? Lockhart had the sense of something they weren't seeing.

'Who else could've known about that donation from Natasha?' he asked.

Julia pushed her lower lip out, thinking. 'It was a private gift, it wasn't on our website or anything. Me, Elena and Milly – she's the other project manager – knew about it, and that's all. It's in our accounts, but we haven't filed them for this financial year, yet. So, just the three of us. I don't know if Natasha told anyone, though.'

Lockhart wasn't sure if this was significant. But he recalled his own mantra, which Khan had quoted back to him in the team meeting after Natasha's death: he didn't like coincidences.

# CHAPTER THIRTY-FOUR

Smith looked up from her desk and scanned the open-plan office of MIT 8. It was nearly 6 p.m. but no one was showing any signs of slowing down, much less leaving. DCI Porter hadn't yet made it clear whether overtime would be reinstated following the latest death, but it didn't matter. The Operation Norton team were taking it personally that they hadn't managed to catch this killer before he'd murdered Elena Fernandez last night. Motivation rekindled, they'd work for as long as they usefully could into the night, go home for a few hours' kip, then start again early tomorrow. And, by morning, the room would be even busier; Lockhart had said that Porter was getting them extra staff to assist with the ramped-up investigation. Smith knew that quantity didn't always mean quality, but she was still grateful. They needed all the help they could get.

Maximum effort was vital in this period. The stats about the first forty-eight hours of a murder didn't lie; you were much more likely to get a result in that window. Eyewitness memories were fresh, CCTV was available before being overwritten, and attrition of forensic evidence from scene, victim and suspect wouldn't yet have occurred. However, they hadn't managed it on the two previous occasions and, following the discovery of Elena's body this morning, Smith felt her frustration with this case building to anger.

In her mind, that anger was now directed at Dean Waters. He'd been out, late last night, and had appeared to be delivering something. Had he used that pretence to gain access to the Hermanas office before choking Elena? Early crime scene observation suggested no forced entry, which would fit. And his moped could've taken him from his home to the Deptford-Greenwich road, where the murder took place, in under twenty minutes. He'd even set off in that direction. But that was as much as Smith knew.

Just a few streets from Waters's home, she'd lost him when she hit a traffic snarl up which he'd easily cruised around on his bike. Her simmering fury was also, therefore, partly towards herself. She now faced the dilemma of whether to report her unauthorised surveillance of Waters last night, as well as his exit from the building around the time Elena was attacked. She hadn't yet told Lockhart and, if she was going to fess up, she'd have to do it pretty soon. Smith had always told her son to be truthful, same as her parents had impressed upon her growing up. Today, however, it was a case of 'do as I say, not as I do' and she felt like a hypocrite, the guilt niggling at her.

'We off soon, then?' Khan's question interrupted her thoughts. She'd been so absorbed, she hadn't even heard him approach. He held his coat in one hand while the other jangled a set of car keys. 'Go and meet these housemates, yeah?'

The visit was important. So far, all of their 'human' information on Elena Fernandez had come from her colleagues at the Hermanas charity. And with the crime scene still being processed, any further intelligence was crucial. Elena had shared a large house in East Dulwich with four others, who might be able to shed some light on her personal life. Then again, in London, it wasn't always a given that you were close to the people you lived with, particularly if you'd found the place on one of those 'spare room' websites and your priority was saving money rather than socialising.

'I'm ready,' she replied, locking her computer screen and grabbing a notebook. 'Let's do it. Do you want to lead, Mo?'

He nodded quickly, eyes widening. 'For sure.'

'Great.' She was something of a mentor to Khan, but today the development opportunity wasn't entirely altruistic. She was too distracted by the Waters business to focus on getting detailed statements from a group of shocked, potentially traumatised individuals – maybe even needing to break the news of Elena's murder to some of them. Since DCI Porter hadn't yet held his press conference, it wasn't clear which of the housemates even knew that Elena had died. They'd obtained the other residents' names from the electoral roll but had only managed to find an office telephone number for one of them. Smith had spoken to that person earlier but didn't know if she'd delivered the news to the others who shared the house. She'd decided that their best option was for her and Khan to visit after 6 p.m. once they were more likely to be back from work. The trip might also buy her a couple more hours to consider what to tell Lockhart, before it was too late and she'd need to keep silent on Waters.

'I reckon we should ask about Elena's dating habits,' continued Khan, oblivious to her inner turmoil. 'You know, cos that was my idea in the beginning, right? That this fella might be targeting his victims off an app or something.'

'Good thinking,' replied Smith vaguely.

'Sweet.' Khan shrugged on his jacket and threw some gum in his mouth. 'I've even managed to get us a pool car,' he added, chewing hard and waggling the keys. 'Are you impressed?' He carried on talking, saying something about rush hour trains and nightmares getting there.

She'd zoned out and was going to ask Khan to repeat himself when Berry's voice carried across the room. 'Max!' she called. 'Come and take a look at this.'

Smith and Khan hustled across to Berry's desk. The analyst sat in front of an array of three widescreen monitors, each of which was crammed with orderly windows of data, webpages and text notes. She directed their attention to the centre screen where a calendar was displayed.

'This is Elena Fernandez's work diary. Her colleagues gave us access to it. As you can see, she was super-busy. There's a hell of a lot in there, but I've been cross-referencing it all afternoon with her social media and the key information from the other three murders.'

'That's great, Luce,' replied Smith. 'But Mo and I are about to head out the door, so—'

'OK.' She dragged a new window across and placed it next to the diary. 'This is Elena's Twitter profile. On the seventeenth of July, she posts about attending a talk at the Southbank Centre on feminism, with the hashtag "feministfutures". The talk was run by the WOW Foundation. Women of the World.'

Smith recognised those terms. She planted her palms on the desk and leant towards the screens, reading the text of Elena's tweet. 'Wasn't that event the one?—'

'Yup.' Berry swivelled in the chair to face her. 'The talk that Sophie Wright attended. It's a confirmed crossover between the victims.' The analyst flashed a smile. 'I'd tell Dan, obviously, but he's not here and I can't reach him on his mobile, so I wanted you to know.'

'Nice job.' Smith was processing it, trying to gauge the significance. It was a concrete lead, certainly. Her theory was still that the killer was attacking strangers; that was why there were so few obvious links between the victims. However, something had to connect the killer with each woman he'd targeted, however random it appeared. If he'd spotted them online, there'd be electronic traces – perhaps on a smartphone app, a dating website, or just on a laptop hidden away somewhere. Even if it was a chance passing in the street, that still associated killer and victim: they were in the same place at the same time. If Sophie and Elena had attended the Feminist Futures theatre talk, had the killer been there too? And how did Natasha Mayston fit in?

'So, what do you want to do, Max?' asked Berry expectantly. Smith realised that Khan and a couple of others were also looking to her. In the absence of Lockhart, and with Porter preparing his press conference, she was the next most senior detective present in the office. She hadn't realised. But now wasn't the time to worry about that; they needed a pragmatic response, and they were against the clock. She took a breath and focussed.

'I think we need to find out everything we can about that talk at the theatre,' she said. 'I know Dan went there and drew a blank, but this changes things. Get whatever you can, Luce. Who's tagged in social media, see if the event had a Facebook page, all that stuff. Don't contact the theatre yet. Brief the gaffer when he gets back from Lewisham. Then in the morning, we'll make a trip to the Southbank Centre and requisition the shit out of their CCTV. Because it's possible that our killer was there on July seventeenth. And, if we're lucky, we might even see him on camera.'

# CHAPTER THIRTY-FIVE

The police press conference had only finished around twenty minutes ago, but social media and the incel chatrooms were already blowing up. He was watching it unfold in real time, savouring every single comment, 'like' and reaction to the death of that ridiculous do-gooding charity worker who thought she was the saviour of womankind. The funny thing was that the bitch's altruism might've gone unnoticed to him had she not insisted on running for the local council.

Hermanas wasn't why he'd killed her; it was just a happy by-product that he'd effectively destroyed the organisation too when he'd rammed a metal ball down her throat. So far, though, the manosphere hadn't appreciated the beautiful symbolism of him murdering her in the office of a women's rights organisation, from where she'd campaigned against violence towards women. Unless they started picking up on that, he'd have to intervene using his Priapus alias and give them a nudge in the right direction. He was optimistic, though. The Throat Ripper was quickly becoming a legend, and surely wasn't far away from sainthood. This was, without question, the greatest achievement of his life. But it posed a dilemma for him.

To be canonised among incels, you not only needed to work your miracles by striking down as many femoids as possible, but people also needed to know your name. What good was it to be elevated above your brothers when you were just a nickname and no one knew who you were? Naturally, he'd pondered that, wondering whether it was almost worth being caught to secure his reputation. Or was it enough merely for his alter-ego, the Throat Ripper, to be immortalised? There was a third option, too. One he'd already been preparing – something the hardcore incels would really enjoy. He'd have to see how that developed…

When the buzz of murdering that barrister slut had worn off, though, he hadn't been able to resist delivering a few insights into the Throat Ripper's mind through his Priapus alias in the chat forums, even claiming that he knew the great man personally. There was a frisson of excitement about doing that, knowing that he was edging closer to exposing his identity. He felt confident he could trust most of the brothers in the private chat – you didn't get in there without someone vouching for you – but even so.

It was less than twenty-four hours since the murder, and he was alarmed by how rapidly the pleasure of it was fading, how quickly his familiar sense of self-loathing was returning. The capacity for hating himself was probably always there at some level, kindled in the impotency of his childhood and the abusive relationship between his mother and father. It was held at bay for years by a thin, fragile layer which had been irreparably shattered by *her*. By her act of betrayal. Once she was no longer around, his self-worth had plummeted to new depths, spiralling out of control and making him question everything he'd ever valued. That was when He had appeared and saved him from himself. With the Guru's guidance, his self-esteem had slowly returned to the point where he was capable of acting on how he felt – how she'd made him feel. That's what the Guru had encouraged him to do, rather than holding it all in. And what a catharsis it'd been.

He had to remind himself, though, that he wasn't simply doing this to repay her treachery. He was doing it for every man out there who was like him. And it wasn't just about the women he was going after; it was a message to every woman who thought she could do whatever she liked. Once it became clear why he was choosing his victims, people would realise his true genius and their respect for the Throat Ripper would reach a whole new level.

No one – not even Lockhart and that whore psychologist who was prostituting her services to him – had been able to discover his pattern. That meant they couldn't fully appreciate his message, yet, but it did at least reduce the chance of anyone stopping him. There was a plan to be followed. He'd made a late change to it after realising that the American bitch was working with Lockhart, but it was certainly better for that addition.

There were two more on his list. Once they'd died, people would connect the dots. And even if the American worked it out then, well, it'd probably be the last thing she ever did.

*

Lockhart gave the screw a final twist with the Phillips head on his Leatherman multi-tool. He gripped the living room shelf and tested the supporting bracket: rock solid.

'There you go, Mum,' he called out. 'It's fixed.'

'Thanks, love,' came the reply. 'D'you want something to eat now?'

'I wouldn't say no.' Lockhart hadn't asked for any food but, having barely stopped all day, a home-cooked meal was an offer he couldn't refuse. Mum had started heating it up almost as soon as he'd come in and the smell of chicken soup had been drifting down the hallway for the past ten minutes while he repaired her wobbly shelf – a task he knew she couldn't manage because her arthritis made holding a screwdriver painful.

He folded away the Phillips head and stuck the Leatherman back in his pocket where he always carried it. He'd acquired the habit in the military and, once he'd shifted to civilian life, he saw no reason to stop carrying the multi-tool. American-made, it was more robust than a Swiss Army knife, although the blade length meant that he had to disable the lock to make it legal to carry.

The device was so useful, it was hard to imagine life without one. He had to admit, too, that when he was feeling a bit jumpy it was reassuring to have it on him. He'd told Green about that; she'd described carrying it as a 'safety behaviour' – possibly another symptom of Post-Traumatic Stress Disorder – and suggested he try to stop taking it around everywhere with him. So far, he'd chosen to ignore that particular suggestion of hers.

In the kitchen, Lockhart found his mum ladling out the chicken soup. He took the bowls across to the tiny table where she'd also piled up slices of buttered toast. The steaming broth was rich and creamy and garlicky. Proper comfort food on a cold, wet autumn night.

'God knows I need some of this,' he said, dipping a corner of toast into the soup and biting it off. It was a much healthier response to the new murder than obeying his craving to go home and drink eight cans of Stella on the sofa without taking his jacket off. Green would be proud of his decision to come here after his twelve-hour shift.

'I saw the news, love.' His mum stirred her own much smaller bowl. 'That poor woman. She was helping so many people.'

'I know.' Lockhart shook his head briefly. 'It's almost like the more good a woman does, the more chance she has of being murdered by this bastard. Sorry.'

'That's what I'd call him too.'

Suddenly, the magnitude of his failure seemed to be pressing down on him, its weight almost physical as the frustration grew and took hold of him. 'I just feel so… powerless,' he growled.

She blew on her soup. 'I'm sure you're doing your best.'

'My *best*?' His nose wrinkled in disgust. 'Like, A for effort?'

'You know what I mean.'

He sighed. 'Whatever my best is, it wasn't good enough to find Jess.' He'd hoped that, if he'd been able to get something concrete on his wife's location, he could lobby his colleagues in the Met to re-open her case, to staff and resource another search. But he understood that without new evidence that was just a dream. In the absence of a solid lead, even he couldn't pretend it was a good use of police time.

'You're still looking.' She tore off a piece of toast and jabbed it at him. 'Just cos you didn't find anything in Dagenham the other night, doesn't mean she's not still out there, somewhere.'

He'd already told Mum how the only thing he had to show for his trip out east was the suggestion of some kebab men that he ask the local 'hookers' up the road. He'd nearly lost it with them before one explained that the sex workers are on the streets 24/7, so they were more likely to have seen his wife if she was in the area. He'd make another visit to follow up when he had the chance. But he could feel his hope slipping away.

'I couldn't protect Jess and I can't protect these women now. What's the point of me being a detective?'

'Hey!' She laid a small, gnarled hand over his fingers. 'That's not my Daniel, is it?'

'I don't know,' he said quietly, staring into the soup.

His mum sat back in her chair and looked at him. 'D'you remember when you were a kid? Ten years old. You used to climb that big fir tree round the corner in Burgess Park.'

'How could I forget? Must've been forty foot tall.'

'And then some. You tried climbing it every day on the way home from school. Used to get a bit higher each time. You'd come in for your tea and tell me which branch you'd got to. Your little face when you got halfway up – you were so proud.'

'Yeah… and then I fell out like a numpty and broke my ankle.'

'That's my point, love.'

He frowned. 'What, that I failed?'

'Nope.' She rubbed his hand. 'The day the hospital took off the cast and gave you the all clear, remember what you did?'

He managed a brief laugh. 'I went straight back up it.'

'There you go.' She nodded at him.

Lockhart stirred his soup. 'Dad said I was crazy.'

'I'd say determined. And you're the same now as you were then, Daniel. You don't know the meaning of give up, do you?'

He swallowed and met her level gaze. Mum's eyes were pale and watery, but he could see she was sincere. She believed in him.

'Guess not,' he replied. 'Just wonder how much time I've got.'

# CHAPTER THIRTY-SIX

From her vantage point in the window seat, Lexi spotted Dan's distinctive figure among the rush-hour crowd as soon as he turned the corner. She recognised the dark North Face jacket that he seemed to live in, a tie knot just visible inside its collar. Dan hated wearing ties; she guessed he had a meeting or something important this morning. Lexi watched as his long, quick strides carried him towards the café.

It couldn't have been more than fifty yards from street corner to door, but she noticed Dan checking around him at least a dozen times. Left and right, front and back, even up and down, always aware of his surroundings. She knew it'd been drilled into him in the military – same as her father – but, as his clinician, she believed it was also a sign of hypervigilance, a key symptom of PTSD. Constant alertness to potential threats in your environment, barely able to relax: that was Dan. And Lexi was sure the stress of solving these murders wasn't improving his mental state.

Approaching the café door, he clocked her and his face lit up briefly as, she guessed, his mind was temporarily on something other than danger. He entered, scanned the interior and took the single stool beside her.

'Hey,' she said, shivering at the blast of cold air he'd brought in, but still giving him a wide smile that she couldn't help.

'Morning.' Dan rubbed his hands together and blew on them.

'Here you go.' She nudged a coffee and a cinnamon bun towards him. 'My treat. Breakfast of champions.'

'Outstanding.' He grinned. 'Cheers.'

Lexi felt a little glow at his boyish enthusiasm. 'You're welcome.'

'Nice spot,' he remarked, craning his neck to see up the stairs behind them.

'Yeah, I made sure to get the window seat, so we're not over-heard. You're always talking about situational awareness.' Maybe some of his security habits were rubbing off on her. She didn't want too many of them.

'I just meant it's a nice café.' He bit into the cinnamon bun.

'Oh, sure.' She took a sip of coffee to hide her embarrassment. '*Blåbär.* It's Swedish for blueberry, apparently. They've got the whole Nordic good-living thing going on. Like *hygge*, you know?'

Dan shook his head, chewing, his eyes vacant.

She gestured around them. 'It's about cosiness, a warm atmosphere, enjoying stuff. Looking after yourself, giving yourself treats and sharing them with others. Being present.'

'Hm.' His scepticism was pretty clear. She imagined Dan didn't do a whole lot of any of that.

'Give it a try.' Lexi smiled and shrugged. 'You might like it.'

'I'm making a start. See?' He swigged from his cup and held up the bun with his other hand. 'When do you need to be at the clinic?'

'Nineish. I'm good for a little while.'

'Sorry I can't stay long.' He took a large bite and spoke with his mouth full. 'Things are crazy at Jubilee House. We've got six new staff joining our team today. And Porter and I are briefing the top brass on Op Norton in twenty minutes. Thanks for making the time, though.'

'No problem,' she replied. 'So, what's new?'

Dan had already given her the headlines yesterday afternoon, disclosing details about the victim ahead of the early evening press conference. That was a sign of his continued faith in her – despite the doubt of his colleagues – and Lexi was determined to reward that trust with some contribution to the case. She'd spent the evening reading extensively about Elena Fernandez and her charity, Hermanas, all the while following the chat forums and reactions online. It was horrible, and there hadn't been any revelations, but her belief that a clue to the killer's identity lay in the manosphere was undiminished.

'We've got a couple of leads,' he said, swallowing hastily. He described some CCTV footage they'd found of a man in black wearing a crash helmet and carrying a box, walking on the road to Elena's office around the time she died. They were trying to work back, see where he came from and if he had a bike they could trace. But that was a big 'if' and the search would take Dan's people a lot of hours. Next, he updated her on the work by Lucy Berry yesterday on the diary and social media. 'Elena and Sophie Wright attended the same theatre talk back in July. Feminist Futures at the Southbank Centre. Smith and Khan are heading there today to follow up.'

'You think the killer was at the talk, and that was how he identified the women?'

'Maybe. Except that Natasha wasn't there. The organisers checked the guest list.'

'Wait.' She paused, coffee cup mid-air. 'Didn't you tell me yesterday that Natasha Mayston donated money to Elena's charity?'

'Yup.' Dan wiped his fingers on a napkin. 'They're definitely linked. I just can't see the big picture.'

Lexi's gaze drifted out of the window, unfocussed. 'Me neither.' She brought her attention back to Dan. 'That's a good lead, though. What's the other one?'

'Scene of crime officers found a bloodstained tissue in Elena's office. We've sent it off for analysis of the blood and any other DNA on it.'

'Fingers crossed.'

He glanced sideways at her. 'You're a scientist. You don't believe in luck, do you?'

'No. Just a figure of speech.'

Silence hung between them for a moment. Lexi knew that Dan would be thinking the same as her: that luck was exactly what they needed if they wanted to stop another murder.

They'd already noted the two-week period between the deaths of Natasha, Sophie and Elena. But it wasn't precisely fourteen days, and they couldn't be sure the killer would stick to that timeframe. In addition, for all their profiling work, they still didn't know who this guy would target next. There were some links between the victims, but they weren't straightforward. So, who should they be warning?

The new forensics might help identify suspects – especially if the theatre talk was significant – but right now, their list was thin. She badly wanted to contribute, but her online research was still a work in progress. Lexi summarised what she'd been investigating with the incel sites and her chats with the guy who went by the name BloodCel. Her account ended with the mention of Priapus, the incel who claimed to know the Throat Ripper. Dan listened, nodding and chewing.

'I think I'm getting somewhere,' she concluded. 'Slowly, but it's there.'

'Really?' He arched his eyebrows and stuffed in the last piece of his bun.

'What? You don't agree?' She snapped back at him before catching herself. She checked her frustration. 'I mean, those murders are like half of what these guys talk about every day. There's got to be relevant material.'

'Not necessarily.' He shook his head. 'Most of them are probably just fantasists.'

'Most isn't all.'

Dan looked at his watch. 'Sorry, Lexi, I have to go.'

'Sure.' She compressed her lips into a thin line.

'If you think of anything else in the profile – victims or killer – call me.'

'You got it.'

He drained the coffee and slapped the cup back in its saucer. 'Thanks for this, by the way.'

'Pleasure,' she replied, without meaning it.

'Talk soon.' Dan stood, took a final scan of the room, and left.

As he marched away from her, Lexi felt deflated. Was he being a douchebag, or had she just let him down, again? OK, she was getting a handle on the psychology of the killer's community, if you could call it that. But Dan was the detective, he'd solved murder cases and experience had taught him where to look. He'd supplied her with data about the new victim and she hadn't been able to offer him anything useful. Not yet, anyway. But she was determined to work on this until she'd found something he couldn't ignore. Until he couldn't ignore *her*.

There was still about a half hour before she needed to be at work. Lexi reached into her bag and took out her laptop. Logging onto the café's Wi-Fi, she opened a web browser. First, she checked out the theatre's website, just to see what Dan was talking about. She ran through recent events at the Olivier Room before reading the staff bios on the 'Our Team' page. There was Will Jacobson, the manager Dan said he'd visited. He had the kind of 'English' look: red cheeks, brown hair, and a hooked nose like the old profile images of Sherlock Holmes. Lexi thought he was cute. Beneath his mini-profile was the operations co-ordinator, Yannis Dimitriou. He had a forgettable face, one you wouldn't look at twice. And, yet, that was exactly what Lexi did. Studying his image, she had the feeling she'd seen him before somewhere. But, unable to place him, she moved on to her main research.

Lexi believed that the victims were connected by something of greater significance than these circumstantial links of attending a talk or charity funding. The Throat Ripper was a planner and a thinker. He was methodical, and she was sure his victim choice fitted a pattern. She'd taken a step inside his head by immersing herself in those misogynist web forums, but she needed to go further. Trying to see it from his perspective was a real test of her empathy skills.

If his campaign of murder was about asserting a kind of masculine, phallic power, then was it possible that the women he attacked had all stood in the way of that power? Rather than being women who helped other women, as she previously thought, were they all women who countered male power, somehow? Lexi felt a little pang of excitement, like she could be on to something. But she needed to know more about theories of phallic power. She had to speak to an expert on the subject. Lexi glanced over her shoulder, angled her screen away from the two women behind the counter, and entered some search terms on Google.

Fifteen minutes and a good number of disturbing images later, she'd found her man. Dr Sam Byers. Lecturer in History and Gender Studies at Birkbeck, University of London. She hesitated. Should she run it by Dan first? No, she reasoned: he was in a briefing right now and, in any case, he didn't really buy her phallic power theory anyway. If she came up with anything useful, she'd let him know.

Lexi logged into her email and began typing a message to Dr Byers. She'd show Dan that she knew what she was doing.

# CHAPTER THIRTY-SEVEN

Smith led the way as she and Khan entered the Southbank Centre. Their destination was the Olivier Room, the theatre that'd hosted the Feminist Futures talk in July. Walking through the front doors by the river, a cavern opened before them. It was only 9 a.m. but already the building thrummed with activity. Two cafés were busy serving customers at opposite ends of a vast atrium flanked by staircases. A dozen staff were setting up a photographic exhibition in the central space, while a hundred voices rose and echoed around them. And this was probably its quiet period.

'Never been here before,' remarked Khan. 'Pretty sick.'

'My fella brought me here for my birthday last year.' Smith gestured towards the main hall. 'We went to a concert of film music. Full orchestra and everything. All the classics.'

'Sweet.'

'Couldn't afford to do it every weekend, though.'

'No shit.'

'All right.' She spotted the signs for the Olivier Room. 'Let's see what this lot can give us.'

They needed anything they could get from the theatre. The pressure on their team for a result was greater than ever, now, and the visit to Elena's housemates last night hadn't yielded much. All they said of note was that Elena had started using a dating app recently, at their suggestion. One of the housemates had immediately concluded that a man from the app must've killed Elena and had started blaming herself. She'd worked herself into a right state, and Smith had needed to go into welfare mode for a bit to calm her down. They'd stayed longer than planned and, by the time they'd crawled through traffic back to Putney, Lockhart had left the office. Smith had texted her boss a quick update but bottled out of calling to tell him about her private surveillance of Dean Waters.

Instead, she'd returned to Waters's apartment block and sat outside in her car, again, but he hadn't appeared and after a couple of hours she'd gone home. She knew that in the absence of Waters's DNA showing up at the crime scenes, DCI Porter had decreed that he was no longer a suspect, and it'd take more than a moped journey to have him reinstated on that list. Still, something didn't sit quite right with her about Waters. Smith tried to push the nagging voice to the back of her mind as she and Khan walked across to the Olivier Room.

At the theatre doors, a couple of young women were arranging posters on display stands while a third photographed them with her mobile. All three were laughing as though it was the funniest thing any of them had ever done. The photographer's knotted T-shirt displayed a slim, toned waist and Smith felt herself experience an absurd stab of envy at the girl's lithe body. At her elegant hands. She glanced sideways at Khan, who'd clearly registered the young woman too. He patted his hair into place as they approached.

'How do I look?' he whispered as they got closer.

'Desperate,' replied Smith, shaking her head. Did he never switch off? She couldn't fault his proactivity, at least. Squaring his shoulders and puffing his chest out slightly, he introduced himself to the woman with the phone and showed her his warrant card. She took a moment to get her giggles under control but, having appraised him and evidently liking what she saw, she abandoned her camerawork and returned his broad smile. Khan explained their business and the young woman cheerfully directed them up a corridor to the manager's office. Moments later, Smith knocked on the door.

'What?' came the reply.

They entered a cramped space that was messier than any squad room she'd seen in twenty years of policework. The place made their MIT office in Putney look as if Marie Kondo herself had organised it. Two men sat back to back. One had a bowl of carefully groomed brown hair, red cheeks and a Roman nose that looked almost like a beak in profile. The other was small, pale, bespectacled and suffering from serious male pattern baldness. She guessed both men were in their early thirties. Neither immediately looked up and she had to cough to get their attention.

'Detective Sergeant Maxine Smith,' she said, loud and clear, holding up her warrant card. 'And this is Detective Constable Mohammed Khan.'

'I'm Will Jacobson.' Roman nose spun his chair towards them. 'I'm the manager of the Olivier. Can I ask what this is about? We've got a hell of a lot on and we spoke to your colleague the other day. What was his name again, Yannis? Dan...'

'Lockhart,' said the smaller guy, who didn't introduce himself. He continued peering at the screen through his glasses, typing and clicking. Smith could see half a dozen tiny white coffee cups piled up behind his mouse mat. Caffeine fiend or lazy slob? Maybe both.

'Dan Lockhart, that's the one.' Jacobson nodded. 'If it's about the murder of that woman, we've already provided him with the details of when she visited the theatre.' He looked from Smith to Khan and back. 'Is there something else?'

'There was another murder two nights ago. You might've seen it on the news yesterday evening or this morning. A young Spanish charity worker and local councillor called Elena Fernandez.' Smith had to force down her anger as the swarthy one carried on typing, and Jacobson just stared at her cleft hand. 'We strongly believe that her death was the latest in a series of linked incidents, which include that of Sophie Wright.' She wanted to say *serial killer*, but without Dr Mary Volz's final verdict, they all had to stick to the ridiculous term *linked incidents* for another day at least.

'Sophie Wright,' she continued, hearing the slight growl creep into her voice, 'attended the Feminist Futures talk here. The WOW Foundation. Remember?'

'Sure,' said Jacobson, breaking his gaze from the gap between Smith's fingers and focussing on her face. 'Yannis checked the guestlist. So, are you here because—'

'Elena Fernandez attended the same event,' interjected Khan. 'She posted on Twitter about it, with a selfie in the talk, so we know she was here.'

'Christ. This is awful.' The theatre manager had lost some of his swagger. Maybe he was realising the implications for his customer base. 'Yannis, get the full guestlist for that talk, now.'

Rotating his seat, the small guy broke away from his computer screen for the first time since they'd arrived, though he kept his hand on the mouse. 'But I haven't finished the ticket price algorithm for the—'

'Just fucking do it!' yelled Jacobson.

As the smaller man clicked and scrolled, Smith wondered if Lockhart had witnessed a similar performance when he came here. The mind boggled at how these two, plus the giggling girls outside, managed to run two or three shows a day for five hundred people, every day, with this chaos around them. Eventually the activity stopped and the swarthy one sat back, satisfied.

'Elena Fernandez was at the talk,' he said as a printer whirred in the corner. He stood and navigated his way across to it, plucking some sheets of paper and slaloming back through the clutter to hand them to Smith. She guessed he was five foot six in his shoes.

Smith scanned the pages. There were hundreds of names, a few of which were repeated on consecutive lines.

'What about the names that appear more than once?' she asked.

'Oh. That's just where one person bought multiple tickets,' said Jacobson. 'Happens a lot. Couples, families, bigger groups of friends. Corporate or organisational guests, too.'

'So, not everyone who attended the talk is actually listed here?'

'No, sorry.'

This was one step forward, another back: it meant that Natasha Mayston could've attended the talk, potentially answering the question of how the killer identified her. It would enable the MIT to home in on new suspects. But it also meant that there were probably twenty or thirty people at the talk whose names they didn't know. And it wasn't just Natasha or the next victim who could be one of them. The killer might be hiding behind those repeated names, too. Smith wondered if Waters was in there, somewhere.

'OK.' She passed the document to Khan. 'We'll need an electronic copy of that as well, please,' she said, handing a card to the smaller man. 'My email's on there. What's your name, please, sir?'

'Yannis,' he said, his arms hanging awkwardly straight at his sides. 'Dimitriou.'

'Thank you, Mr Dimitriou.' She turned back to Jacobson. 'We're also going to need all your CCTV footage for the day of the talk, please.' She didn't need to consult her notes. 'July seventeenth of this year. And I mean all of it.'

She became aware that Jacobson was looking across at Dimitriou, who was shaking his head.

'What?' she asked.

'The CCTV gets overwritten after three months.' Jacobson spread his hands. 'It's a private company that runs the contract and that's what they offer. I remember once before when we couldn't find—'

'Shit!' Smith was unable to hold it in. She knew it was unprofessional, but she felt as if a lead had gone. The list was useful, but the CCTV would've been better.

'Wait, officer.' Jacobson's cheeks flushed red. 'We made our own video of the event. We had a couple of cameras, didn't we?'

'Four,' said Dimitriou. 'Two static, two roving.'

'Yeah.' The manager seemed quite pleased at his own idea. 'The final cut that Yannis did for our YouTube channel is, what, four minutes?'

'Three minutes fifty-one.'

Smith's heart sank.

'But the raw footage should still be on one of these laptops,' added Jacobson. He began shifting stacks of paper and opened a drawer by his desk. 'Yannis, have you got the MacBook?' Jacobson got up and walked across to the spare desk beside Dimitriou. He rifled through a set of drawers.

Dimitriou reached across. 'Er…'

'Here it is!' Jacobson pulled out a sleek metallic laptop and held it out, triumphant. 'Should be about four hours' filming for the event, start to finish. Across each of four cameras.'

'Sixteen hours,' stated Khan. She detected the apprehension in his voice. But it could be worse; she'd had cases where the CCTV had run to hundreds of hours.

'Mo, can you do the paperwork?' They had to document requisitioning the machine.

'Yup.' Khan stepped forward and took the MacBook. 'We'll get this back to you as soon as possible, OK?'

'But we need it for a show,' protested Dimitriou.

'Yannis!' Jacobson's face flushed again. 'It's not up to you. We should have all the key stuff backed up on cloud, anyway.' He shook his head and turned to her. 'If there's any chance of you returning it by next week, that'd be great.'

'We'll see what we can do, Mr Jacobson.' She did her best impression of a smile. 'Will it be easy to find?'

'Should be. There's a "movies" folder on the hard drive with each event labelled.'

'Great.'

The manager was trying to be helpful, and Smith appreciated how he was directing his words to her rather than Khan; she'd lost count of the number of times men had exclusively spoken to the male officer present, no matter how junior they were to her. But that wasn't going to stop her asking her final question.

'By the way, can you tell me where you were two nights ago?' Smith kept her tone casual.

'At home,' said Dimitriou. She hadn't actually directed the question to him.

'Can anyone verify that?' asked Khan, taking out a small notebook.

'Um, no. Well, I got a takeaway delivered.'

'How about you, Mr Jacobson?' she asked.

'Me?' His eyebrows rose. She waited. 'I finished up here about half eight after our show was done, then I went for a few drinks in the pub with a mate.'

'Can I ask which mate that was?' said Khan, jotting a couple of notes.

'Er, yeah. Felix.' He shrugged. 'Felix Campbell.'

'And which pub?'

'The Windmill, on The Cut. By the Young Vic theatre.'

'Right.' Khan clearly didn't know it, but it gave them something to check. Just in case. Smith knew the priority right now was to get the list of talk attendees back to Berry to work her magic on them, while she and Khan copied the footage and got watching.

It was going to be a long day, but Smith finally had the feeling they might be getting somewhere.

# CHAPTER THIRTY-EIGHT

Lockhart shoved in the last of the greasy bacon roll that passed for his dinner and, realising that he didn't have a napkin, wiped his fingers on his trousers. He resolved to get the suit dry-cleaned once this case was over, or if he managed to roster a rest day for himself. At the moment, that was looking unlikely. Operation Norton had gone up a gear and his team were putting in the hours. At times like these, detectives' self-care often took a hit. Sleep, clean clothes and occasionally even showering fell away, while consumption of sugar, fat, caffeine, cigarettes and booze went up in proportion to stress. He didn't need Green to tell him that wasn't sustainable. His sessions with her had given him the awareness that – much as he hated to admit it – even he had limits, and that was OK. But this wasn't the time to let up.

The brass who he'd briefed this morning had given him a couple of extra staff, including a specially trained HOLMES officer to operate the database for cataloguing and cross-referencing information from serial crimes. Given the lack of resources at their disposal, the gesture showed how seriously they were taking the case. Or, at least, how seriously they considered the public opinion about it. They'd made it clear that this was a top priority case. Not *the* top priority for the Met, but one of several that senior officers and government staff from the Home Office were monitoring daily, among operations to counter organised crime and terrorism. Lockhart had to remind himself that, although Op Norton had become his sole focus – even pushing his search for Jess aside – it was just a small proportion of the crime and violence in London. That didn't stop the pressure being piled on them to get a result, though. And he could feel the stress of that expectation growing by the day.

Porter had played the meeting strategically, charming senior officers and their governmental guests. He'd delivered an impressive PowerPoint presentation from his laptop, emphasising his strategic advisory role on Op Norton, while being clear that day-to-day running of the case and decision-making were Lockhart's responsibilities. The big man had positioned himself perfectly to take credit for any success while being able to lay any blame for failure squarely at Lockhart's door. Some detectives would be pissed off about that. But Lockhart didn't give a shit about politics or climbing the ladder. He'd seen enough of that in the army to know how pointless it was, ultimately, when you could lose the things that mattered to you most in an instant. His concern was simply finding their murderer before the guy attacked any more women.

It'd been great to see Green this morning, but he'd been disappointed that she couldn't tell him anything useful about either the killer or his victims. If she wasn't working for free, he'd almost certainly have had to cut her involvement by now. However, thanks to the theatre lead discovered by Berry and developed by Smith and Khan, and the CCTV clip of the man wearing a crash helmet, his team had new, concrete stuff to get stuck into. Lockhart considered those leads to be their best shot and had set most of the MIT to work on it today while he was out. Now, back in the office and crossing to where Khan and Berry sat together, he felt a tremor of anticipation. He hoped they'd got something.

'All right, guys?' Lockhart drained his cardboard cup of black coffee – his eighth or ninth of the day – and tossed it in the bin between Berry and Khan. Both were engrossed in their screens and he was grateful for their obvious effort; Berry especially. She'd asked her husband to pick up the kids from nursery today, then do dinner and bath time without her, so that she could work late. 'Cheers for staying.'

'No probs, guv.' Khan rubbed his eyes and stretched. Lockhart still wasn't used to being called guv, but it came with his rank and he'd have to accept it sooner or later. 'Way it goes sometimes, innit?'

'How was the post-mortem, Dan?' Berry turned to look at him.

Lockhart had spent the middle part of the day with Dr Mary Volz at Greenwich Mortuary before going to another meeting in Newham, where he'd tried again – and failed once more – to persuade DCI Flynn and the rest of MIT 12 to give him access to Damon Pagett, the man charged with Kim Hardy's murder. Porter didn't seem to be backing him on that one.

'Dr Volz did her usual thorough job,' he said. 'But there wasn't much new evidence for us to go on. Elena was restrained in a chair and choked to death on a metal ball. She had the small cuts to her left ring finger. The MO is identical to Natasha's and Sophie's murders, except that Elena was attacked in her office rather than her home. The best piece of evidence from the crime scene was that bloodstained tissue which, I hope, is being fast-tracked at the lab.'

'Do you think the killer panicked and dropped it?' asked Berry. 'I mean, the location was a bit busier and he could've been disturbed before he had a chance to clean up after himself.'

'Don't know.' Lockhart ran a hand across the back of his head. 'He was careful enough not to leave any other clear traces. And I don't expect much else from the scene. Being an office with people coming and going, I reckon we'll just get lots of low-level mixed profile DNA. Let's see what's on that tissue, though.'

'What about the coyote hair that was in Sophie's mouth?' said Khan. 'Any more of that at Elena's murder scene?'

'Not that I know of.' He was aware that the unusual sample – probably from clothing – could prove key, but without a clear source garment to match it to, it'd slipped down the actions list for now. 'What've you two got, then?'

Berry sighed. 'No more on the crash helmet man. We can track him back to a scooter, but you can't see the plates, and then we lose him in traffic. We're hoping to get film from some more cameras tomorrow, see if we can pick him up.'

'Shit. OK, what about the theatre talk?'

'Better.' Khan pointed to the laptop screen where an image of people standing around in a room had been paused. 'We've been going through the video footage.'

'Natasha's there,' interjected Berry. 'She must've been given a ticket by someone else – maybe an organisation she donated to, like Hermanas. And it wasn't marked in her diary.'

'That puts all three of the victims at the talk,' said Khan.

'Three out of four,' noted Lockhart. 'Kim Hardy wasn't there.'

'Right. She was killed two weeks before the talk took place,' said Khan. 'This scene is from a drinks reception after the event. We think we've got Sophie and Elena both there. And we've just seen Natasha.'

'All three of them in the same room?' Lockhart could sense his heart rate quickening, though it might just be the coffee.

'Yup,' Berry nodded. 'So, we've been picking out the men who were at the reception, too.' She rotated one of her screens towards Lockhart. 'These are the three guys we've found talking to at least one of the victims so far.'

Lockhart pointed to the first image. He recognised the aquiline nose and red cheeks immediately. 'That's Will Jacobson, the manager. Who are the other two?'

'That's what I've been trying to find out,' replied Berry. 'Mo and I have been cross-referencing with the guest list. Fortunately, there weren't many men there. Maybe thirty or so – about ten per cent of the total attendees at the talk.'

'OK.' Lockhart took in the two, very different, faces.

'We think this guy is Paul Dixon,' continued Berry, indicating a still that showed a tall, well-built man with shoulder-length hair. He held a drink and was speaking to two women. In the corresponding portrait, he had intense blue eyes, a square jaw and two rows of neat, white teeth. 'He's a personal trainer. Well, more than that. He's a lifestyle coach. His website promises to help women get their perfect body and soul.'

'Soul?' Lockhart frowned.

'Look.' She clicked into her browser and a home page appeared with Dixon stripped to the waist, his hair sleek and shimmering. The wide smile to camera wasn't accompanied by lines around his eyes, suggesting it was fake. He held a kettlebell in one hand and glass of something smoothie-like in the other. The banner underneath read: *Evolve yourself*, but it might as well have been captioned: *God's gift*. Lockhart had to admit Dixon was in decent shape, but he was almost certainly a massive twat.

'He really works the room,' said Khan. 'It's pretty methodical. You can see him giving out his card to about twenty-five women. And his body language is all charm. He might just be trying to get some business, but it looks like he's speed dating.'

'Nice work. You got an address for him?'

'Off the electoral register,' said Berry. 'There's a lot of Paul Dixons, but his personal training business address from Companies House is a residential flat where he's also listed as a voter.'

'Great. I say we go and see him first thing tomorrow,' said Lockhart.

'He's got a job at a gym, too,' she added. 'He might be there if it's working hours.'

'Sure.' Lockhart shifted his attention to the third image. The man had a narrow, gaunt face with wispy goatee beard and his hair was knotted in a man-bun on top of his head. His small, round glasses reflected the light and made it impossible to see his eyes. 'Who's this bloke?'

'We're not a hundred per cent,' said Khan. 'But we think it's Dr Sam Byers. He's an academic.'

Berry clicked into a new tab on her web browser. 'As far as I can tell, it's him.' She nodded at the image. The photo was clearly a few years old and the man's hair was different, shorter and neater, but the face was a match. 'He's on the attendance list.'

Lockhart read off the screen. 'Birkbeck, University of London. Lecturer in History and Gender Studies.' *Gender Studies?* He'd look it up later. 'I reckon we need to go and visit this Dr Byers, too.'

'That's not all, boss.' Khan waggled his fingers as if preparing for a magic trick. 'I've saved the best for last.'

'What?'

'Check this out.' Khan moved some windows around on the laptop and brought up a new image. He zoomed in and re-centred. 'He's not at the drinks reception, or on the guestlist, but you can see him walking past the glass doors every so often, looking in. I might not have spotted it if it wasn't for his carrot-top.'

Lockhart leant in, studying the man in the background and his bright ginger hair. 'Is that?…'

'Yup.' Khan snapped his fingers. 'Natasha's ex-fiancé. Hugh Chadwick.'

# CHAPTER THIRTY-NINE

It'd been a bit like falling in love again. He'd never tell anyone that, obviously. But, when he reflected on what'd happened over the past months, that was the closest thing to which he could liken meeting Him, the Guru. He'd been at rock bottom after her betrayal and departure. Nothing had been able to take the bad feelings away, to fill the void in him that she'd left. He'd drunk and snorted and popped pills time and again until he couldn't remember who he was. He'd even visited a hooker but, well, that'd just ended in flaccid humiliation. He'd scuttled away from the dingy brothel above a Chinese takeaway in Soho, fumbling in his wallet and throwing cash at her for zero services rendered. Must've been the easiest money that slut had ever made. And, for him, the outcome of that particular encounter was nothing new.

When he and his ex were together, in what he'd naively thought were the good days, she'd always reassured him about his inability to perform. Said it was OK. At the end, she'd even told him that it wasn't why she'd cheated on him, but the fact that she specifically mentioned it contradicted that. He knew, deep down, that it was at the centre of things falling apart for them. The problem was that whenever it was time for sex, it was like his body froze and his mind was transported back to his childhood home. To flashbacks of Father slapping Mother, pulling her hair, telling him to *watch and learn*. To the sounds of his mother's whimpering; too scared to ask Father to stop.

As soon as those memories were in his head, he couldn't get hard. He'd been through the embarrassment of that over and over during his teenage years and early twenties before a period of self-imposed celibacy allowed him to avoid it entirely. Then he'd met her. When they'd first got together, she'd been different to the others. Understanding, sympathetic. Interested in his character and what he had to say, not just whether the piece of meat between his legs worked or not. She'd told him there were lots of ways to be intimate, trained him to use his tongue and his hands to pleasure her instead. He'd fallen deeply, obsessively in love. It was his one chance. She was the One. This was it.

But, clearly, that kindness and patience had its limits and, eventually, her true colours had shown. They drifted, talked less, hardly touched at all. She spent more time away from their home with her 'friends'. Then, one day, she dropped the bomb: there was someone else. He'd felt like such a fool. Utterly worthless. Initially, he'd pleaded with her to stay with him, like some pathetic, desperate loser. But she'd just shaken her head and told him that she wanted him to move his stuff out of her place by the weekend.

When binging on chemicals and trying to pay for sex had failed to lift the darkness that'd settled over him, he'd thought long and hard about ending it. A few times, he'd even gathered the stuff together. About a hundred paracetamol and two litres of vodka. Psyching himself up one night – alone, as usual – he'd made a start. He got twenty pills and half a litre into the attempt before losing his nerve and running to throw it all up in the toilet. On his knees in the bathroom, clutching the toilet bowl with trembling fingers, a trail of spit running from his mouth to the porcelain, he'd never hated himself more. He was too weak even to kill himself.

Then he'd discovered the manosphere.

Suddenly, it was as if everything made sense. He wasn't alone. He wasn't the only man to go through such betrayal and failure. It wasn't his fault. Slowly, gradually, he started to feel differently.

He devoured material on the relationships between men and women. Social theories, gender politics, economics, psychology. He'd posted about his experiences and received life-affirming validation from the brothers. For the first time in as long as he cared to remember, he'd felt part of a community. A group united by one thing: the hatred of women. Sure, there were different sub-groups. There were the tough-guy jocks, the pickup artists and the incels; eventually, he'd cleaved to the latter. But one of the recognised heroes for all of them was Him.

The Guru, the Master.

His wisdom was boundless, from debunking myths like the gender pay gap, to explaining the concept of women's sexual market value and how they maximise it to oppress men. It was as if something had dropped from in front of his eyes. Now, he had an explanation for what she'd done. What all the women before her had done. And why Father had acted the way he had for years. He'd followed the Guru on social media, sharing and liking everything he wrote. A couple of times, the Guru even commented back. His self-esteem started to grow. Then, one day, the impossible happened.

The Guru sent him a direct message. He'd never forget the opening line:

*I have a truth for you, young man.*

The truth was a simple one that he already knew, but there was a beautiful clarity to the way the Master expressed it:

*Women do not care about you. They only care about themselves. The sooner you understand that, the better.*

He savoured every word, every keystroke straight from the Guru's fingertips, drinking it in. He'd perform any service required of him for the brothers. And sure enough, there was a task. The message ended with a call to arms which would be the start of everything that'd happened since:

*Now it's time to take that power back.*

*

Lexi grabbed a handful of popcorn and passed the bowl to her right where Liam sat beside her. He did the same and then offered the popcorn to Sarah. The three of them were wedged together on a two-seater sofa, with the lights down and TV on. They were two episodes through *Conversations with a Killer: The Ted Bundy Tapes*. It'd been Lexi's idea to do a Netflix night in, and it'd seemed like a good plan. An evening chilling with her housemates, taking it easy and, crucially, not spending any money. Liam had suggested the documentary, which told the story of one of America's most prolific and terrifying serial murderers. He'd seemed really excited to watch it, pointing out Bundy's charm and good looks to the point where Lexi even wondered if Liam had the hots for him. And, though Lexi didn't mind being pressed up against Liam – their legs, hips and arms touching – the subject matter was anything but relaxing. Especially with what she was involved in right now with Dan and the cops.

She couldn't stop thinking about the so-called Throat Ripper, though she hated that nickname. The killer was out there on the streets of her city, and had already murdered three, probably four women. She couldn't stop thinking about the victims, either. About those four women, roughly her age, who'd opened their doors to a man whom they believed posed no threat. About the way that they died, their windpipes blocked with balls until the air ran out and their brains slowly shut down. It was surely one of the worst ways to go. And she couldn't stop thinking about the victims' families, their loved ones, friends and colleagues. People who'd for ever miss them and wonder why it'd happened, why it'd been their daughter, sister, friend or co-worker who'd been murdered. She thought of the women across London who were living in fear right now, wondering if they would be next. And it frustrated the hell out of her that she couldn't do more to stop that happening.

The other thing that bothered Lexi was Dan's attitude. He'd brought her into the case, shared a whole lot of detail with her. Really sensitive stuff. And, yet, when she'd offered her profile and insights, he'd basically rejected it all. His team had done much the same. What was up with that? Now she thought about it, though, the sequence was basically a replay of their therapy sessions together. He'd opened up to her about his life and his losses, only to stop at the moment where he could take action, where he could make a change. And maybe she wasn't so different. It was all fine and good expecting everyone else to take her advice and change for the better, but could she turn that analysis on herself?

Her rumination was interrupted by her phone buzzing in the pocket of her sweat pants. Liam felt it too and, as she reached down, brushing his leg to take it out, their eyes met briefly. Jeez, she wished he was straight. Lexi glanced at the phone screen. There was an email notification.

'Anyone interesting?' asked Liam. 'New fella?'

'No,' she replied quickly.

'Come on,' said Liam, drawing out the words. 'Is it that fit detective guy you obviously fancy?'

'Screw you,' she replied with a smile. OK, he was right about her liking Dan, but Lexi knew that nothing was going to happen, not with Dan's wife still missing, not to mention the small issue of her being his therapist. She wasn't going to tell Liam any of that, though. So, she just said: 'It's none of your damn business.'

'So, it is a man!' he cried. 'Sarah, d'you know about this?'

'Nope. But I want to,' said Sarah through a mouthful of popcorn.

Lexi stretched out and stood. 'I'm going to the bathroom.'

'Oh, aye?' said Liam suggestively.

Lexi gave him the middle finger and walked out of the living room. She sat on the toilet and checked the email. It was from Dr Sam Byers, the university lecturer. His reply to her message was short.

Hi Lexi,

Thanks for getting in touch.

I'd love to meet up and talk phalluses with you.

When suits?

Sam

She briefly laughed at his turn of phrase. A guy who did gender studies. That was cool. Lexi imagined he was seriously woke. And he had the whole geeky academic thing going on; it was kind of cute. She tapped out and checked her diary. Tomorrow was good. Then she went back into the email app and started typing her reply.

# CHAPTER FORTY

'OK. Everyone know their actions?' Lockhart's question was greeted with a murmur of assent from his assembled team. He clapped his hands. 'Let's get to it, then.'

Lockhart had just finished delivering the morning briefing for what could be a very significant day on Op Norton. Based on the theatre footage, they had three suspects in the frame, each of whom they intended to speak to as persons of interest: lifestyle coach Paul Dixon, academic Dr Sam Byers, and asset manager Hugh Chadwick. The plan was to visit Chadwick at home; he'd called in sick to his office in Canary Wharf, so Lockhart was going to his flat in Chelsea. Smith and Khan were tasked with finding Dixon before going on to see Byers. And one of their team was following up on Jacobson's alibi about being in the pub with his friend the night Elena was attacked; it never hurt to check. The rest of them were putting in the legwork with forensics, CCTV and online inquiries.

The main issue on Lockhart's mind was what to do with their discovery that the feminism talk at the Southbank Centre linked the three recent victims. They hadn't identified all the attendees yet, and the logistics of individually contacting every single person was beyond their stretched team. Not to mention the possibility that, if the killer was among them, it might tip him off to their suspect strategy and allow him to destroy evidence or go to ground. Porter had already advised the public during his press conferences to be vigilant about opening their doors to strangers, and the DCI was reluctant to go for the blanket-contact option. For now, they had to hope the general warning would be enough.

On his way out of the MIT office, Lockhart spotted Superintendent Burrows waiting for the lift. He took his opportunity and jogged over to her.

'Excuse me, ma'am?'

Burrows spun round and smiled. 'Ah, DI Lockhart. Making progress on Norton?'

'Hope so. We've identified some new individuals of interest and we plan to speak to them today.'

'Good, good.' She glanced back to the lift light above the sliding doors. It was one floor away.

'I'd like to ask, ma'am, respectfully…'

Her eyebrows rose. 'Sounds ominous.'

'There's a suspect on remand for the murder of Kim Hardy in July. His name's Damon Pagett. I believe he's innocent and I'd like to speak to him about Norton because I think our killer murdered Kim. And I reckon Pagett can help us.'

'What does DCI Porter say about this?'

Lockhart sighed in frustration. 'He doesn't want to upset Newham MIT, ma'am, so I was hoping we could—'

'And what do Newham MIT say about you seeing him? I assume you've asked them already.'

'They said no.'

'No?'

'To be more accurate, they don't give a toss and they won't admit they might have the wrong man.' Lockhart knew he'd said too much, but he had to tell it like it was. And pray Burrows would understand.

The superintendent shook her head as the doors pinged open. 'I'm sorry, if CPS is moving forward with the prosecution, we can't prejudice the case. We wouldn't want Newham doing that with one of ours, would we?' Without waiting for his reply, she stepped into the lift, briefly acknowledging the two people inside and pressed the button for the sixth floor before checking her watch.

'Like I said, ma'am,' persisted Lockhart, 'I think Pagett's innocent. If I can get a one-to-one with him, just an intelligence interview, then…' He trailed off as the lift doors closed in his face and he stood there a moment, staring at the carpet. Then the doors slid open again. Had Burrows changed her mind?

'I'm sorry, DI Lockhart,' she said, 'I can't intervene. The answer's no.'

As the lift shut once more and glided upwards, Lockhart tried to push down his anger. He needed to think. There had to be another way to speak to Pagett. Porter would be pissed off when he found out that Lockhart had disregarded his order and asked Burrows directly. And that would be nothing compared to the big man's reaction if Lockhart did manage to contact Pagett. A lot of shit would hit a very large fan. But he didn't care. It had to be done. Whatever Porter's reason for not actioning his request earlier, no politics or egos were more important than this case.


The man who opened the door to Lockhart didn't look capable of holding down a successful job in the financial sector. Hugh Chadwick was about five ten and ten stone, Lockhart guessed, but his appearance didn't match the smart city boy that Smith and Khan had described to him. His ginger hair stuck up in unruly tufts and a patchy orange-brown stubble clung to his weak chin and jawline. He wore a white T-shirt with what appeared to be egg stains down the front, and pyjama bottoms with, well, Lockhart didn't want to know what those stains were. The smell that came off him was familiar to Lockhart from years of being around soldiers: stale sweat.

'Hugh Chadwick?' He flashed the warrant card.

'Yes,' groaned the man in front of him. 'I assume the concierge let you in.'

'He did. I'm Detective Inspector Dan Lockhart.'

'And I'm not well.'

'I appreciate that, sir, but I'd just like to ask you a few questions, if that's all right?'

'About what?'

'It's in connection with the murder of Natasha Mayston. We're hoping you can fill in some gaps for us. Do you mind if I come inside?'

Chadwick narrowed his eyes. 'Should I call my lawyer?'

'I don't think that'll be necessary,' replied Lockhart cheerfully. 'Of course, it's your right if you'd like to do so. I'm sure we can find a time for you to come into the station at your earliest convenience and be interviewed under caution. We're not far away. Putney.' He smiled.

'Your colleagues came to my office after Tashy died. I told them everything I know.'

Lockhart just stood there. He couldn't hold the smile much longer.

Chadwick sighed. 'Fine, come in.'

Lockhart stepped through the front door and into an overheated open-plan living room that his whole flat could fit inside twice. Vast canvases of original abstract artworks that he didn't recognise hung from the walls, and high windows gave a view onto the river. He would've described it as palatial, had it not been for the mess. Clothing, newspapers and debris were strewn over the furniture and floor. A low coffee table was covered with unwashed glasses, cups and plates, for which the windowsills seemed to be the overspill. There were pizza boxes, blister packs of unidentifiable pills and clumps of tissue paper dotted around a large Persian rug in front of the sofa.

'Are you all right, Mr Chadwick?' he asked. The scene reminded Lockhart of some of his own low points since Jess went missing, though the soldier in him never let his discipline drop this much.

'Not really,' replied the asset manager, slumping into the sofa and rubbing his eyes with the heels of his hands. 'I'm sick.'

'OK, well, I'll keep it brief.' Lockhart turned to get the measure of his surroundings and spotted a framed photograph on the wall behind him. It depicted a group of floppy-haired young men in dinner jackets and bow ties, each holding a wine glass. Calligraphy on the mount read *Peterhouse Men's Drinking Society 2007*. Something about that rang a bell, but he couldn't immediately place it. Lockhart brought his attention back to Chadwick, crossing and taking a chair across the coffee table. He caught a whiff of the dirty crockery and guessed it'd been there for days.

'You were engaged to Natasha, is that right?'

'Until she decided I wasn't good enough for her.'

'Was that the official reason?'

Chadwick snorted. 'What's that supposed to mean?'

Lockhart softened his tone. 'Had you given her an engagement ring?'

'Of course I bloody had. What do you think I am, some kind of cheapskate? It was my mother's ring, and it'd been her mother's too. I bought if off her for a very generous amount. The thing was antique, one of a kind. Didn't make any difference to Tashy, though.'

'If you don't mind me asking, what happened to the ring after you broke up?'

'She gave it back to me.' Chadwick curled up slightly into the sofa. 'I almost didn't want it. Getting kicked out of her house was humiliating enough without the charity as well. It wasn't as if I needed to sell it. But in the end, I took it. Since it was Mother's, getting it back was better than that bitch keeping it.'

'Bitch?'

'Look,' Chadwick spread small, delicate hands in apology, 'it's just an expression. I'm still hurt, you understand. She didn't deserve me.'

'She didn't deserve to die,' said Lockhart, his frustration returning at this man's arrogance.

'Well, it wasn't me who killed her.' Chadwick folded his arms.

There was a moment's silence before Lockhart spoke. 'Do you have the ring here?'

'I… I don't even know. Maybe. No.' He wagged a finger, smiling. 'I gave it back to Mother.'

Lockhart watched him carefully. 'Where were you three nights ago, sir?'

'Why?'

'Can you tell me where you were?'

Chadwick leant forward. 'Is this about that Spanish woman who was murdered?'

Lockhart couldn't reasonably hide this. 'Yes,' he stated.

'I was here.' Chadwick shrugged. 'Probably asleep. I've been ill recently. Stayed in during the evenings and took the past couple of days off work.'

'I see.' Lockhart knew he could confirm that with the concierge, and there were cameras in the building, too. Khan had checked them when he came here after Natasha's murder.

'Just one further question, sir, then I'll give you some peace and quiet.'

'I doubt that.' Chadwick smirked.

'Sorry?'

'Peace and quiet. I've not had much of that recently.'

'Any particular reason?' asked Lockhart.

'Just… stress. You know?'

'Yeah, I do.' Lockhart paused. Stress was the word men often used when they were having mental health problems. He'd used it enough times himself before he started going to see Dr Green. Part of him wondered if Chadwick needed help rather than investigation, but he reminded himself why he was there.

'On July seventeenth there was an event at the Olivier Room. It's a theatre in the Southbank Centre.'

Chadwick looked blankly at him. 'So?'

He had to be careful what he disclosed about their strategy. 'We have evidence that Natasha Mayston attended that event, a talk on feminism. Did you go there as well?'

'I…' Chadwick's eyes rolled top-left to top-right and back. 'I don't know. I don't think so.'

'You sure about that?'

'Why's it relevant?'

Lockhart was starting to understand why Smith had got pissed off speaking to Chadwick after Natasha's murder. He frequently met questions with questions. Experience suggested people who did that were either curious, anxious, or wanted extra information and time to think because they had something to hide. And Chadwick seemed neither curious nor anxious. So, what was the asset manager hiding? Lockhart knew that they still didn't even have enough to arrest him. For that, they'd need some forensic evidence to turn up linking him to at least one of the other crimes.

'There's a video recording that shows you were in the South-bank Centre too, looking into the event.'

'Maybe.'

'Looking directly at Natasha.'

'If you say so. It was a long time ago.'

It was clear that Chadwick wasn't going to admit to anything. Lockhart had one last gambit. 'We're speaking to a number of individuals who were known to the victims of the recent linked murders. If it's OK with you, sir, I'd like to take a quick cheek swab for DNA profiling, just so we can eliminate you from our inquiries.' He reached into his pocket and produced the buccal swabbing kit.

Chadwick planted his bare, milky white feet on the floor and sat up straight. 'I want you to leave now, please, sergeant.'

'It's detective inspector.' Lockhart knew what Chadwick was doing, but that didn't stop it winding him up. He could feel his limbs tensing and fought back the anger. 'So, you're refusing to give a voluntary DNA sample to us?'

'And they say police officers are stupid.' Chadwick flashed a grin.

Lockhart resisted the urge to punch the over-privileged wanker in the teeth. 'Fine, that's your right to do so. Thanks for your time, Mr Chadwick.' He stood. 'I'm sure we'll speak again.'

'Look forward to it.'

On his way out, Lockhart cast a final glance at the photograph. Downstairs, he stopped at the concierge's desk. The man sitting behind it was portly, his belly straining at a bright red military-style dress jacket with gold braid on the shoulders and cuffs.

'Excuse me,' he asked the concierge, 'does this building have a fire exit?'

'Of course.' The man looked shocked. 'That's the law. Health and safety. We run a tight ship here, sir.'

'Where is it?'

'Through there.' He gestured across the lobby to a smaller door.

'Cheers,' said Lockhart.

The door admitted him to a narrow staircase that clearly ran on the opposite side of the building to the main fancy staircase and lift. He traced the steps all the way up to the third-floor corridor outside Chadwick's apartment and back down again, descending an extra floor to the basement. At the end of a dark corridor on the lower level, a further door led into a small sunken courtyard containing some bins, and an open passage. Lockhart followed it and, after a ninety degree turn and a gate, found himself out in the street that ran behind the building. He returned to the courtyard and scanned the walls up as far as he could see, then went back inside the door and did the same.

There was no CCTV.

# CHAPTER FORTY-ONE

'Should be just up here on the left,' said Smith, checking Google Maps on her phone.

'Not bad round these ends, is it?' Khan nodded his approval as they walked through the centre of Richmond. 'Everything's just, sort of… nice. And clean.'

'Yeah, right. If you think Putney's upmarket, this is one level beyond.'

They'd only needed five minutes on the train to get here from the office, but the wealth of Richmond was obvious as soon as you stepped out of the railway station. One of London's most affluent districts, Richmond was home to a set of millionaire rock stars, Hollywood actors and TV personalities, when they were in town.

'It's a long way from Whitechapel.' Khan shoved his hands in his pockets.

Smith glanced at him. 'Maybe one day you'll move out, eh? Give your mum and dad a break.'

Khan sucked his teeth. 'I'd love to… but after my student debt each month, I ain't got the cash to rent right now. Unless I want to share with, like, eight people. And never go out.'

'It's tough,' acknowledged Smith.

'Plus, my mum makes the best curry in London,' he chuckled. 'I'd be mad to leave that behind.'

'OK, here it is,' said Smith, as they approached a smart-looking, modern building next to a Waitrose supermarket. 'Prime Fitness.'

Khan stopped at the entrance. 'So, basically we're just hoping he'll agree to answer our questions?'

'Yup.'

'And give us a DNA sample to eliminate him from our inquiries?'

'Yup.'

Khan frowned. 'And if he doesn't want to do that?'

'Plan B is we invite him to come to the station for a voluntary interview under caution.'

'All right. Say he refuses that, what's plan C?'

Smith shrugged. 'There isn't one.'

'Shit.'

'We've got no forensics tying him to any of the crime scenes or victims, so we don't yet have sufficient grounds to arrest him.' She grinned. 'We'll just have to work our charm.'

'You got cuffs?' asked Khan. 'Just in case the charm fails.'

'Yeah. Never hurts to have a pair handy. Come on.'

A pleasant receptionist directed them inside, her smile pasted on as she explained that Mr Dixon was with a client. Prime Fitness was as high-end as its location promised. A handful of expensively dressed people exercised gently on shiny, new equipment to dance music that wasn't loud enough to be offensive. Smith noticed they were all yummy mummies; women about her age – forty, give or take – but who spent a lot more time on their appearance than she did. And they probably had that time because they didn't need a job, Smith guessed. She'd never want to be that dependent on a man. Most of them had more make-up on to work out than Smith ever wore; she smiled involuntarily as she thought of her own grunting, sweaty efforts in the clapped-out police gym in the basement of Jubilee House.

On the far side, Paul Dixon was conspicuous as the only man in the room. He wore tapered jogging pants and a tight vest displaying large, smooth muscles in his shoulders and arms, his long hair gathered back in a ponytail. He was standing behind a thin woman in spandex who was holding two tiny dumbbells. Dixon was grasping her waist with both hands and murmuring something to her as she raised the weights out in front of her, breathing heavily.

'Sorry to interrupt you,' said Smith, holding up her warrant card, 'I'm Detective Sergeant Maxine Smith.'

'Detective Constable Mohammed Khan.'

'Paul Dixon?' asked Smith.

'Yeah.' He let go of his client and stood up to his full height. He was about six foot and intimidatingly muscular. 'What do you want?' he grunted, his voice low and rough as sandpaper.

'We'd just like to ask you a couple of questions, please,' she replied. 'Shouldn't take more than a few minutes and then we'll let you get back to work. Would that be OK?'

'I'm busy.' Dixon looked from her to Khan and back, scowling. 'Come back some other time.' He turned and resumed his grip on the woman's tiny waist. 'Just keep that form, yeah?' he whispered to her. 'That's beautiful.'

Khan took a half-step forward and Smith sensed him tensing beside her. She wasn't going to be discouraged.

'We're hoping you can help us with an investigation, sir,' she continued. 'It's important.'

Dixon's jaw set hard. 'Didn't you hear me?' he said, louder. 'Are you deaf as well as dis—'

'It's concerning a series of linked incidents that you might know something about,' persisted Smith. She paused. 'The murders of three young women in London over the past five weeks.'

'What?' Dixon let go of the skinny woman again and moved towards Smith, looming over her, his eyes wide. 'What are you accusing me of, eh?'

Khan immediately stepped in front of Smith, squaring up to Dixon. 'You need to calm down, mate,' said Khan firmly. Those weren't usually the words an angry person wanted to hear. Smith silently cursed his intervention as she moved to one side.

'You fuckin' calm down, *mate*,' growled Dixon, his hands balled.

'Or what?' said Khan. *Red rag to a bull.*

Dixon shoved Khan hard in the chest with both hands, sending him sprawling backwards and crashing to the ground. His female client looked terrified, and everyone else in the gym had stopped what they were doing. Dixon stepped forwards.

'Get out, pig,' he shouted, jabbing a finger at Khan.

But Dixon had forgotten about Smith. Sweeping in from the side, she snapped one cuff down on the wrist of his extended arm, quickly drawing it sideways and clipping the other cuff onto a weights machine.

Dixon spun as if he was about to punch her with his free hand, but Smith moved back out of range.

'Paul Dixon,' she said, 'I'm arresting you for assaulting a police officer.' As she delivered the police caution about his rights, she saw the rage gradually drop from his body as he realised the error of his impulsive action. She took out a phone and called 999, giving her badge number and asking for officers from the nearest station in Kingston to collect him.

She went over to Khan and, offering him a hand, helped him back to his feet. He brushed his jacket down. 'Dickhead,' he spat.

'You OK?' she asked.

'Yeah, fine,' he mumbled. He wasn't hurt but being pushed over by another man in front of a room full of women would've given his ego a bruising. It was his own macho behaviour that'd caused it, though; maybe he'd work that out.

'Look at it this way,' she whispered, 'at least now we don't need his permission to take his DNA.'

Ten minutes later, two uniformed officers from Kingston swept into the gym and, with a great deal of energy and radio communication, set about re-cuffing Dixon to take him away.

'Oi,' said Dixon, quieter now. 'Let me get my jacket before we go outside.'

The uniforms looked to Smith for approval. 'Fine,' she nodded. 'I'll fetch it.'

'It's in my office.' Dixon gestured through the doors to a small room. It was full of paper files and sweaty gym gear. The big winter coat, a parka, was hanging on the back of the door. She noticed it was a Canada Goose; top quality and with a price tag to match. Personal training in Richmond was clearly paying well. As Smith carried it out and they moved towards the patrol car parked outside – its blue lights flashing unnecessarily – something struck her. The hood of Dixon's jacket was lined with thick fur. Suddenly, she became conscious of how she was handling it. Draping the coat carefully over one arm as Dixon was guided into the back of the patrol car, she whipped out her phone and googled 'Canada Goose jacket hood material'. The first page of hits confirmed it: coyote fur.

'Give it here, then,' said Dixon from the back seat. 'I'm freezing my balls off.'

'Sorry,' replied Smith, her pulse quickening. 'I'm afraid we'll need to hold on to this for the time being.'

\*

'Where's Khan?' demanded Lockhart as he strode back into the MIT office.

The nearest person to him, a junior detective, shrugged in ignorance.

'Still in Richmond, I think, guv,' called another from across the room. Lockhart saw Berry look up from her array of monitors.

'He's just arrested Paul Dixon,' she said, a tiny smirk on her face. 'With a big hand from Max, by the sound of it.'

'Arrested?' He crossed towards Berry's desk. 'What for?'

'Assault,' she replied. 'He pushed Khan to the ground when they tried to question him.'

'Right now, I'd probably do the same if I saw him. Or worse.'
She stopped typing. 'What do you mean?'

'I've just been over to Hugh Chadwick's flat in Chelsea, where Khan supposedly checked his alibi for the nights of Natasha's and Sophie's deaths.'

'Right,' said Berry. 'The block's got 24-hour porters and cameras.'

'Not on the fire escape, it hasn't. Goes right out to street level at the back of the building.'

She processed this quickly. 'Chadwick could've gone into the building but left unnoticed. So, his alibi might be fake?'

'Potentially.' Lockhart bit his lip, shaking his head briefly as he tried to hide his anger from the team. 'I can't believe Khan missed that.' He made a mental note to give the young DC a bollocking severe enough to make sure he'd stop and think about so obvious a check next time. He took a breath, tried to calm himself.

'I don't like Chadwick,' resumed Lockhart, when he'd composed himself again. 'He's a slippery bastard.' Taking out his notebook, he checked the latest entry. 'Peterhouse men's drinking society. What can you tell me about that, Luce?'

She googled it and immediately clicked on the top hit. 'Peterhouse. It's one of the colleges that make up Cambridge University,' she stated. Typing again and bringing up Chadwick's LinkedIn page, she scrolled and tapped the screen with a fingertip. 'He was at the college from 2004 to 2008, reading economics, with a master's in management afterwards.'

'Why does that sound familiar to me?'

Berry froze. 'Adam!' She shouted across to the HOLMES officer at one of the far desks. 'Peterhouse. Is it logged on Op Norton? Who went to university there?'

'Hang on.' A flurry of activity as Adam checked the database was followed by him spinning his chair towards them triumphantly. 'Sophie Wright,' he called out.

'Shit.' Lockhart put his hands on his hips. 'What years was she there?'

'2007 to 2010,' replied Adam.

'They overlapped by a year.'

Berry was already back on Google. 'It's the smallest college in the university,' she read off the screen. 'About two hundred and fifty undergraduates. Chances are that Chadwick knew Sophie, then. Or at the very least knew who she was.'

Lockhart nodded, his fury at Khan's mistake receding slightly. 'The circumstantial evidence is stacking up against him.'

'Now we just need some forensics,' said Berry.

'Then Chadwick will have some real explaining to do.'

# CHAPTER FORTY-TWO

'Dr Byers?' Lexi knocked on the open door and leant in. The office was long and narrow. Near the back of it, a man squatted among a pile of books and papers with his back to her. He spun around and his slight shock at being interrupted was rapidly replaced with an awkward smile.

'Oh, hello.' He stood and crossed towards her, extending a hand. He was only slightly taller than her, but Lexi noticed the chunky heels on his shoes. 'You must be Dr Green.'

'Lexi, please,' she said, shaking his hand. It was small, soft and a little damp. She found herself automatically comparing it to Dan's hand: big, strong, warm and dry. Whoa, where had that come from? 'Uh, thank you for making time, Dr Byers.'

'Call me Sam.' He finally let go of her hand and she discreetly wiped it on her jeans.

They stood there a moment looking at one another. 'Have we met?' asked Lexi eventually.

'I don't think so,' he replied. 'I'm sure I'd remember.' He gave a breathy laugh. 'Did you have to come far?'

'Just up on the tube from Tooting.' She'd left the clinic half an hour early to get here for five thirty. Sam had said he was giving a lecture at six on phallic imagery and had invited her to sit in on it after they'd spoken.

'You work at the hospital there, right?'

'Yeah,' she said. 'How did you know?'

'It's online.'

'Oh, right. Yeah, it's a good part of town. I live in that neighbourhood, too.'

'And where are you from?' he asked. 'Originally, I mean.' That old question. The Brits never seemed to get tired of asking it.

'My dad's American, my mom's British. I was born here, grew up over there, and came back here a few years ago,' she said, delivering the familiar lines.

'Fascinating,' he said, holding her gaze a little too long. Then he clapped his hands once. 'Where are my manners? Would you like a coffee? Some tea, perhaps?'

'Sure,' she replied. 'Coffee, please. Just milk, thanks.'

'I'll be right back.' Sam grabbed a couple of mugs off a table, gave them a quick sniff, then hustled out of the room and down the corridor. Lexi was left alone in his office. She looked around, checking out the papers on his desk. There were drafts that he'd written as well as some published papers. Behind the desk, a sheet of mugshots was taped to the wall. There were twenty or so passport-style photos of young women under the title 'MA in History and Gender Studies'. A few had small biro marks next to their names. She turned and wandered down the office towards a bookcase. Most of the shelves were lined with periodicals and textbooks, but one contained objects. Lexi noticed a small picture frame lying face down. Glancing back towards the doorway, she lifted it and peeked at the photo. A woman with short hair smiled at the camera. She carefully put the frame back where she found it and examined a copper-coloured statue beside it. The figurine was male and looked maybe Greek or Roman. She lifted it to test the weight and gasped when the top came away in her hand. Underneath the torso and head of the statue was a giant penis, which now stood erect on the man's legs.

'I see you've found Priapus, then,' came Sam's voice from the doorway.

'Jeez,' she exclaimed, before realising that she was the one poking around his office. 'Sorry, I was just... wait, what did you say?'

'Priapus.' He came over to stand beside her. A little too close for her liking. 'The Greek god.'

'Sure.' Lexi thought of the incel website, of the guy who used that alias, and who claimed he knew the so-called Throat Ripper. She shivered. 'This is him, then?'

'Yeah.' Sam nodded towards the statue. 'Would you like to touch it?'

'No thanks,' replied Lexi. 'I'm good.' She'd started to feel kind of uncomfortable.

'Of course.' He offered her a mug. She hesitated before taking it. 'He's such an interesting mythological character,' added Sam, reaching out to stroke the bronze. He was smiling slightly.

'Right.'

'Although he represents fertility and is typically portrayed with a huge penis, he always lost his erection when the time came to perform,' he giggled, 'so to speak. The goddess Hera had supposedly cursed him with impotence, you see.'

'Poor guy.' She sipped the coffee. It wasn't bad. 'So, he symbolises fertility for some and impotence for others?'

'Exactly.' Sam put the torso back over the penis. 'He's a bit of a contradiction is old Priapus. Later, the Romans took him on as a deity, too. And he's even appeared in early Christian texts as a symbol of health and vigour. Elsewhere, he's a figure of mockery. Sometimes he's a protector, other times a warrior. For some ancient peasants, he was even an avenging killer. But mostly, I think he's misunderstood.' He placed a hand on the statue. 'Aren't you, hm?'

There was a moment's silence before Lexi spoke.

'I don't know whether to feel scared of him or just sorry for him.' She was glad they weren't still looking at a bronze cock while having this conversation.

Sam did the breathy laugh again and pushed his glasses up his nose. 'So, what did you want to talk about? I was intrigued by your email. Come and sit down.'

He took his desk chair while Lexi sat across a small table from him.

'Thanks for making the time.' She'd rehearsed what she wanted to say on the journey over. 'I have a client at the hospital who has some pretty complex issues around his, well, his penis.'

Sam crossed his legs. 'OK.'

'Yeah. So, a little like Priapus, he can't get an erection when he wants to have sex. And he's developed some obsessive thoughts around how that makes him a weak person and women will see him as pathetic. I want to help him build a counter-narrative, where his penis is associated with strength. I thought maybe I could use some theories of phallic power, and I wondered what you could tell me about it? And about the role of women in those theories?'

Sam planted his hands on his knees and exhaled. 'Well, where do I start? The phallus and testes have been associated with fertility in myth and legend for millennia. I mean, the first known penis statue was made nearly thirty thousand years ago. And civilisations have been worshipping the old cock and balls in every imaginable form since then. It's not just about human reproductivity, but about livestock fertility and crops, too. Basically, anything that lives and grows that we depend on.' He described a range of historical examples from ancient Egypt, India and Latin America. 'Humans worshipped representations of the penis as a way of trying to protect life. As you see with Priapus, the Greeks and the Romans were no different. And that laid the basis for our prevailing cultural interpretations of the penis.'

'Most of the time, it's associated with strength, right?'

'Yes.' He nodded. 'The phallus and testes are believed to be powerful, and they've become intertwined with a particular notion of masculinity. That's the concept of the dominant, competitive, emotionally detached male. The hunter, overpowering others and taking what he wants. For this idealised, super-potent male, women are powerless to resist him. Even the mightiest women lose their strength when confronted with his charms. Frankly, it's that kind of myth that's led to our rather penis-centric notion of what it means to be a man, and what sex is about. Toxic masculinity, you might've heard that called in the media.'

'Right.' Lexi had relaxed a little, now. Maybe the Priapus link was just a coincidence; after all, he seemed to be the main phallic god of classical mythology. And Sam was talking a lot of sense. It was making her think about the case, about the signature of the killer…

'So, this guy has a kind of twisted sense of what it means to be a man?' she asked.

'Your patient?' Sam raised his eyebrows.

'Uh, yeah.'

'Mm, I'd say he does. But it's probably not his fault. He's dealing with impotence in a society that – for all our technological advances – still basically worships a big, hard cock. Sorry to put it so crudely.'

'No, it makes sense.' Lexi smiled. 'Thank you.'

Sam glanced at his watch. 'Do you have time to sit in on the lecture?'

'I…' She didn't know what to do. It sounded interesting, but part of her wanted just to go home and get back online, to see if she could make any progress on getting close to the Priapus guy on the website, or develop her profile to share with Dan. Then Sam's desk phone rang.

He snatched up the receiver. 'Yup?'

Sam glanced across at Lexi, swallowed, and said, 'OK, fine. Just ask them to hold for a moment, please.' Clutching the phone, he pushed his glasses up the bridge of his nose and rotated his chair towards her. 'The police are on the line,' he said. 'They want to speak to me.'

'Really?' She was curious. 'Did they say what about?'

'No.' He pressed the handset to his chest. 'But, look, you don't have to leave yet, if you—'

'It's cool. I'll go.' She took her opportunity and stood. 'Thanks again.'

'I'll, er, I'll be in touch,' stammered Sam, his eyes following her to the doorway.

'Sure.' Lexi nodded, then walked back out the way she came. She couldn't say exactly why, but it was somewhat of a relief to get out of that office.

# CHAPTER FORTY-THREE

Smith started the digital recorder and made the introductions. It was just her from the MIT, the only other officer in the room being the large, uniformed police constable from Kingston station standing in the corner. The custody sergeant had insisted on a 'strong male presence' at the interview after Dixon's push on Khan had been followed by a couple of angry outbursts in his cell, with him kicking the door and swearing at custody suite staff.

These flare-ups, along with his lawyer's insistence on a meal break and rest period, had delayed everything. They'd not completed Dixon's DNA swab until mid-afternoon, meaning the lab wouldn't be able to work on it until the morning. Given that tomorrow was Saturday, the analysis might not happen at all until Monday. It was now 8.30 p.m. and Smith had been on the go for twelve hours. She was knackered, but knew she needed to concentrate if she was to get anything out of this interview.

Needless to say, Khan had been left out. As the victim of Dixon's 'common assault', it would've been inappropriate for Khan to conduct the questioning. Instead, he was back in Putney, nursing his pride and carrying out background checks on Dixon.

Across the table from her in the interview room, Dixon leant back in the chair, his arms folded in front of his chest. He'd pulled his hair up into a top knot and he looked quite relaxed. Next to him sat a petite middle-aged woman with immaculate hair and make-up and an expensive-looking trouser suit. His lawyer.

Smith had barely finished listing everyone present when the lawyer cut in.

'Look, detective, we all know why my client is here. A small incident at the gym which got out of hand. But we believe the police share the greater responsibility for what happened earlier today. My client felt threatened by Detective Constable Khan, whose intimidating, aggressive behaviour escalated the questioning – with which my client was entirely happy to engage – into an altercation.'

Smith agreed with the bit about Khan's behaviour, but she couldn't admit that. 'I personally watched you push DC Khan to the ground, Mr Dixon. We'll be recommending a charge of common assault to the Crown Prosecution Service.'

The lawyer shook her head. 'The CPS isn't going to waste its time going after my client for a push, when we have a witness who says your colleague initiated the aggression. We'll be pleading not guilty, if it even gets that far.'

Unfortunately, Smith knew she was right. The CPS didn't have the money to waste on trivial matters like this, particularly when there was an ambiguity over the provocation. They barely had the money to prosecute murder trials. In any case, she wasn't really bothered about the push on Khan; the interview was an opportunity to quiz Dixon about their real matter of interest.

'Mr Dixon, assault on a police officer is a very serious charge and I can assure you that the Met Police will put everything we have behind such a prosecution. But I've spoken to my senior officers and we may be willing to re-examine the charges if you're able to help us with another investigation.'

'What?' said Dixon.

'Paul.' His lawyer scowled at him. 'I wasn't made aware of this,' she said.

Smith ignored her. 'Did you attend a talk on feminism at the Southbank Centre on July seventeenth of this year, Mr Dixon?' she asked.

The lawyer sat forward. 'I don't see how this is relevant to the alleged assault on Detective Constable Khan.'

'Did you?' Smith directed her question to Dixon.

'Maybe,' said Dixon, his arms still folded.

'We've obtained video footage of you at this event, Mr Dixon. Also present at the event were a number of women, including Natasha Mayston, Sophie Wright, and Elena Fernandez.'

'This is not a justified line of questioning, Detective—'

'We also have video footage of you speaking to these women at the drinks reception for the event.'

Dixon tipped his chair up onto its back legs. 'Not a crime, is it?'

Smith wanted to slap his smug face. 'Each of those three women was murdered.' She let that sentence hang in the air. Even the lawyer was momentarily shocked into silence. 'What was the nature of your contact with those women that evening at the talk?'

'No comment.'

'Were you choosing women that you wanted to attack later?'

'No comment.'

Smith could feel her frustration growing. 'Who were you planning to attack next?'

'No comment.' He gave her that wide grin, same as the sleazy photo on his website.

'My client doesn't need to answer these questions, Detective. They aren't related to the case in hand, they're wildly speculative and, given that we have a witness who supports my client's innocence in the alleged assault this morning, he's not under any obligation to assist you with other cases.'

'What were you doing on the nights of October seventh, October twenty-fourth and November twelfth of this year?' Smith laid both hands on the table, jabbing her forefinger with each date. Her breaths were shallower, and she could feel control slipping away from her.

'Detective, listen to me,' said the lawyer firmly, 'unless you have any evidence to link my client to these other cases, you have two choices. You can either charge him with common assault, but I've made our position on that quite clear. Or, you can let him go. If you release him this evening, we will consider not pressing counter charges for wrongful arrest.'

Smith announced that she was stopping the recording and switched the machine off. 'Wrongful arrest? You and I both know that's bullshit.'

'So, this interview is over, then?' asked the lawyer, the satisfaction spreading across her face.

'Sorry I wasn't able to give you a *hand*,' said Dixon, staring at Smith's missing fingers.

'Go fuck yourself,' she replied, sliding her chair back and standing. She marched to the door, grasped the handle and paused. 'We've got your DNA,' she said, turning to look at Dixon, 'and once we've processed it, we'll see where else it's turned up.'

It was nine thirty by the time Smith trudged back into the MIT office in Putney. She was exhausted and pissed off that Dixon and his lawyer had managed to rile her so much. Smith prided herself on being calm in those situations, but her professionalism had gone out of the window. Tiredness had certainly played a part. And Dixon was a creep, no doubt, who could push most people's buttons. But she wondered if her desperation for him to admit something – anything – was also because she wanted him to silence that tiny voice that was still nagging away at her. The one that'd led to her sitting outside Dean Waters's flat when he rode out on the night of Elena's death. Smith still hadn't told anyone about that, because she'd be in deep shit if she did, now. She justified it by reminding herself that Waters wasn't a serious suspect in Op Norton.

Most of the team had already left as she crossed to her desk. Lockhart had pulled up a chair between Berry's and Khan's desks and the three of them were peering at Berry's monitor.

'Max!' Lockhart spun his chair as she approached. 'How was the Dixon interview?'

'Shit,' she replied, grabbing four of the Jaffa Cakes that Berry offered her. 'He properly wound me up and I kind of lost it. Maybe it wasn't the best tactic to ask him about the Norton murders with his lawyer there in an interview about common assault. He just no-commented.'

'We had to try,' said Lockhart. 'If you couldn't get something out of him, Max, none of us lot could.'

'Cheers, guv.' She dropped into the nearest chair, put her feet up on the desk and began eating.

'Anyway, it'll have given him something to think about overnight.' Lockhart reached for a Jaffa Cake and shoved it into his mouth. 'And his DNA won't lie,' he added while munching.

'Wanker,' said Khan, to no one in particular. 'I hope he does time for this.'

'We'll see what the CPS says about the assault, Mo. I'll be on the phone to them tomorrow. Max, are they gonna fast-track his DNA? We'll have to release him at midday if there's no charge.'

She shrugged. 'I'll get onto the lab first thing, but it's Saturday. We'll be lucky if anyone answers the phone.'

'He shouldn't get away with it.' Khan slapped the desk.

'Easy, Mo.' Lockhart laid a hand on the younger man's shoulder. 'He's not going anywhere. He's on our radar now. And don't forget our other people of interest. You've got some follow-up on Hugh Chadwick, haven't you?'

'Yeah. Sorry about that, boss.' Khan looked sheepish. 'I've already started with the CCTV from the streets at the back of Chadwick's building.'

'Nice one,' said Lockhart.

'But Dixon's got form for being a perv, too,' added Khan quickly. He held up a printed report which Smith couldn't read and slapped it. 'I traced his employment history this afternoon and found an allegation of sexual misconduct from last year. A woman in the gym said he touched her inappropriately while she was training and suggested they go someplace private. Dixon denied it, and it was never followed up.'

'Interesting,' acknowledged Smith. 'If unproven.' She imagined there was an unhealthy dose of male ego motivating Khan's search, but now wasn't the time to point that out to him.

'And it's quite a step from groping to serial murder,' said Berry.

'True.' Lockhart took another Jaffa Cake from the rapidly diminishing packet. 'But we've got some good news as well, Max. Right, Luce?'

Berry pointed to a box of compact text on her screen. 'We finally got the Tinder info back from Natasha Mayston's account.'

'They took their time,' said Smith.

'Still quicker than requests we've made to Facebook in the past. I've been comparing it with what we got from Elena's phone – her account wasn't password protected.'

Smith stopped chewing. 'And?'

'There were six guys matched with both accounts.' Berry couldn't supress her smile. 'One of those is known to us.'

'Who?'

'Dr Sam Byers.'

'That's great work, Luce,' said Lockhart. 'It's going to give me something to ask him about when he comes in for his voluntary interview tomorrow.'

# CHAPTER FORTY-FOUR

Despite his late finish last night, Lockhart had risen early this morning, dunked himself in the Thames and swum for half an hour before work. Regular exercise – or phys, as most soldiers called it – had been drilled into him in the military. It always helped him clear his head. And Green had pointed out that, when he was under stress, it was a much better way of coping than drinking eight cans of Stella on his sofa. He'd had a couple of beers last night, just to take the edge off, but he had to admit she was right. Lockhart smiled at the thought of her being impressed with his effort. But, though the freezing water had woken him up, it'd done little to ease the anger he directed at himself for their continued lack of results on Op Norton.

Hugh Chadwick had refused to give a DNA sample, which meant the only way to challenge his alibi for the nights of the murders was through CCTV. Khan and others had been working on that for a day with nothing to show, so far. It appeared Chadwick hadn't left his building via the fire escape route, as Lockhart had found was possible. But they were still searching. Nothing had come from their 'crash helmet' lead, as people in the MIT were calling it, and their efforts were focussed elsewhere, now – mainly on Paul Dixon.

The twenty-four-hour limit to holding Dixon in custody was almost over. Lockhart and Smith had each tried calling the lab today to plead their case for prioritising the analysis of his DNA, but neither of them had got through. DCI Porter had indicated that, because Dixon's arrest was only for common assault, they couldn't realistically seek a duty magistrate's extension to the custody period. The DNA comparison would have to wait.

Listing these dead ends, Lockhart had to bite back his frustration. He could almost hear the clock ticking, not just towards Dixon's release, but to the killer's next attempt on a young woman's life. It was surely just a matter of time. And, when it happened, it'd be on him. He knew that thought wasn't helpful, though. Focus on the present, that's what Green encouraged.

He needed to do that right now. Dr Sam Byers, the only other current person of interest, had agreed to be interviewed this morning. As Lockhart walked into Lavender Hill police station in Clapham, the academic was already sitting in the reception area. He was a good likeness for his photo online. It would've been more convenient to invite him to Jubilee House in Putney and use a meeting room there, but Lockhart preferred to keep anyone in their suspect strategy as far away from the MIT office as possible. His colleagues up the road had obliged by lending him the interview suite.

'Dr Byers?' he asked, crossing to the chairs.

'That's me.' The man leapt to his feet. Byers was smartly dressed in a collared shirt, tweed jacket, dark chinos and brown brogues. His man-bun hairstyle and goatee were just like his picture. Above the sharp cheekbones in his narrow face was a pair of equally sharp eyes behind small round glasses. 'Are you Inspector Lockhart?'

'Yeah.' They shook hands. 'Thanks for coming in on a Saturday.'

'Happy to help.' Byers gave an awkward little laugh. 'So, what is a voluntary interview, then?'

Lockhart wasn't sure what to say. Should he tell Byers that, with a rising threshold for arrest, tighter bail conditions and budget cuts to custody suites, it'd become a default investigative technique for most policework? Should he say that it was often a way of hoping suspects tripped themselves up in the absence of sufficiently solid forensic evidence for an arrest? In the end, he settled for his usual line.

'It means we're hoping you can assist us with our inquiries,' he replied pleasantly. 'I'll explain more once we're inside.'

After ten minutes of setting up, he was opposite Byers in the interview room with audio and video recording rolling. The lecturer had waived his option to have a lawyer present and nodded enthusiastically as Lockhart explained his right to leave at any time and that anything he said could be used in evidence.

'OK, then. Fire away, Inspector.' Byers pushed his glasses up his nose.

Lockhart produced three portrait photographs from a manila file and laid them side by side on the table. 'Natasha Mayston, murdered October seventh of this year. Sophie Wright, murdered October twenty-fourth, and Elena Fernandez, murdered November twelfth.' He tapped each picture in turn. 'Have you ever met any of these women, Dr Byers?'

The academic stared at the pictures. He swallowed and smoothed his hair. 'I… well, yes, I did briefly meet, er, Natasha,' he indicated her photo, 'at a drinks thing a while back. At the theatre.'

'And the other two?'

'Perhaps, I'm not sure. She looks familiar,' he added, touching the portrait of Elena. Lockhart noticed how soft and delicate his hands were, and how he was almost caressing the image.

'Where might you know her from?'

'Er… oh, silly me.' Byers looked up. 'It's Tinder, isn't it?'

'What can you tell me about your contact with any of these women on Tinder, Dr Byers?'

'Sam, please. Well, I think we might've messaged a bit.'

'A bit?'

He did the awkward laugh again. 'I find it easier to, you know, make the first move when it's online.'

Lockhart extracted another sheet of paper. 'After you were matched with Natasha Mayston on Tinder, you sent her a total of twenty-two messages.'

'Mm. I suppose I thought we had a connection after we'd met at the theatre drinks.'

'She sent you one in reply.' Lockhart frowned, reading off the paper. 'Declining your offer of a "hook up".'

'I have been known to get slightly obsessive.' Byers gave a lopsided grin, but he sounded apologetic. 'We matched and I wanted to meet her, but maybe I put her off with my texts, I don't know. Said the wrong thing, probably. I usually do.'

'You then sent fifteen messages to Elena Fernandez without receiving any back, before she unmatched you.'

Byers fidgeted in his seat but kept smiling. 'I have somewhat of a scattergun approach, I have to say, Inspector. My strategy is to swipe right on everyone and, when I get a match, I get stuck into the messaging straight away. But maybe that isn't the best approach.'

'Did you ever see either Natasha or Elena after exchanging messages with them?'

'No.'

'And what about Sophie Wright?'

Byers peered at the photo and shook his head. 'I don't think I've ever met her.'

'If you don't mind me asking, when was the last time you were in a relationship?'

'Um,' Byers coughed. 'I… why do you need to know that?'

Lockhart didn't reply. He was thinking of Green's profile. *Maybe he's lost a woman*, she'd said.

The academic took a deep breath and sighed. 'I did have a long-term partner, but she left London last year to take a job at a college in the US. Unfortunately, the long-distance thing didn't work out for us.'

'Sorry to hear that,' said Lockhart.

'She said I was too needy,' Byers continued, unprompted, staring at his hands on the table. 'I wanted commitment, but she wasn't ready to move to the "next stage".' He made quotation marks for the last two words.

'You proposed to her?'

'Didn't even get that far. I had the ring and everything. But…' he tailed off. 'Never mind.'

In spite of his suspicion, Lockhart found himself feeling some sympathy for Byers. The guy looked genuinely cut up about what'd happened.

'I'm sorry to have to ask you this, Sam, but can you tell me where you were on the nights of October seventh and twenty-fourth, and November twelfth, please? It's just so we can complete our inquiries.'

Byers produced his phone. 'May I?' he asked, holding it up. Lockhart nodded, and Byers proceeded to open the calendar app on screen, scrolling and tapping. 'Yes, lecturing each evening. You can check that with Birkbeck. As our students are all mature and most have jobs, we don't usually start until 6 or 7 p.m. Seminars normally go on until 9 or 10 p.m., depending on the length of discussions.' He shrugged. 'Then I suppose I left and travelled home.'

'Do you live alone?'

'Yes.' Byers picked at his nails. 'I do now.'

'And where's that?'

'Kilburn.' Byers gave the full address and Lockhart noted it down. He did some quick mental mapping. The north-west London neighbourhood was a long way from all four murder scenes. Assuming his alibi was truthful, was it too far for Byers to travel there from home or work before the estimated times of death?

Looking at the man in front of him, with his thin limbs and awkward, downtrodden demeanour, Lockhart had difficulty believing that Byers was capable of murder. Mild stalking, maybe. But, most likely, he was just a lonely, slightly geeky man who didn't know how to do dating. At least Byers was moving on with his life, though, said a small voice in his head. What? Lockhart blinked and tried to stay focussed. Geography and appearance aside, there was one further test that would seal it.

'Thanks very much for your help, Sam. All right, just to wrap things up today, would you mind giving us a quick DNA sample, please? It's so we can properly exclude you from our investigation.' Experience had taught Lockhart that politeness always seemed to increase the chance of a positive response to that question, though it hadn't worked with Hugh Chadwick.

'Yes, of course.' Byers sat up as Lockhart produced the buccal swabbing kit. As the academic rubbed the swab head thoroughly inside his cheek, Lockhart smiled. He wished all persons of interest could make their voluntary interviews this easy.

Emerging from Lavender Hill station into the street where he'd parked, Lockhart saw that he had a couple of missed calls from Smith. He rang her back.

'Guv,' she answered almost immediately.

'What's going on, Max?' he said, unlocking his Defender.

'They've released Paul Dixon.'

'Shit,' he groaned, pausing with his hand on the open car door. He could feel the frustration building quickly inside him, turning to rage. Then he made a fist and smacked it against the roof. 'Fuck!' he yelled, hitting the vehicle again, harder. He realised several passers-by had stopped and were watching him. He had to get his temper under control, it was fraying too easily. What was it Green advised him to do when he felt stressed? Squeeze his hands, count to five, then let the tension go. Breathe. He tried it.

'You OK, guv?'

'Fine,' he growled. 'Tell me more.'

'CPS aren't even pressing charges for common assault,' continued Smith. 'Too minor, they said, and not clear enough that Dixon caused the incident. Without any bodycam footage, it's our word against Dixon and his witness.'

'Wankers. Did you mention anything about a murder charge to CPS?' he asked, clamping the phone between ear and shoulder and climbing up into the driver's seat.

She barked a laugh. 'They wouldn't touch it with a bargepole. All circumstantial, they said, even the coyote fur.' She sighed. 'I don't like Dixon, and I'm pissed off, but they've got a point. Dixon's lawyer would just go and see him on remand, tell him to no comment, and then argue the fibres prove nothing against *him*. We need a better link.'

'You're right,' Lockhart conceded. 'Listen, I'm on my way back now. I'll see you in a bit.'

'All right, guv. Cheers.' Smith rang off and he tossed his phone onto the passenger seat.

As Lockhart coaxed the engine of his old Defender to life, he had the sense that Op Norton was close to something. He just didn't know what the hell it was. And he hoped he didn't snap before they found it. He knew one thing, though: he had to speak to Damon Pagett. Lockhart couldn't take no for an answer, whatever Porter, Burrows and Newham MIT told him. Pagett was the X factor that might blow the case open, if only Lockhart could get face to face with him. And Smith's mention of the lawyer had just given him an idea of how to do it.

# CHAPTER FORTY-FIVE

Coco Adams applied the final touches to her selfie, upping the contrast so her eyes looked even more striking, her hair even blonder. She'd already made her cheeks a little thinner, her lips a little bigger, and added a diamond tiara on her head. Perfect. Coco's followers loved her daily selfie shot; the reactions didn't lie. She'd often get a thousand likes and a hundred comments just for one of them. And it was important to grow her following and keep them engaged. That was her job.

Her Instagram had over fifty thousand followers for her frequent #lifestyle posts, while her legendary weekly vlogs on YouTube had racked up nearly twenty-five thousand subscribers. OK, so she'd paid for some of them, and a few were bots… but most were real people who wanted her to tell them what to buy. Now, when the brands contacted her, she'd dangle that massive audience in front of them with one hand while holding out the other hand for their cash. Two hundred pounds for an Instagram post. Five hundred for a ten-minute YouTube video. And the money just rolled in. Oh yeah.

Ten years ago, when Coco was still at school, the job of being an influencer didn't exist. Some people said it wasn't a *real* job, that she didn't help people like nurses or teachers or social workers. Or they said she didn't *make* anything, like a builder or a chef or an artist. They tried to make her feel bad because she hadn't been to university and done a degree. But those people were idiots. She'd bet she was earning more than any of them. She was definitely earning more than any of her schoolfriends.

In the hours between her posts, emailing with brands and trying on all the free clothes and make-up she'd been sent, Coco had plenty of time to check up on those old schoolfriends. The ones who weren't really friends. Who'd bullied her mercilessly from thirteen to sixteen when she left and went off to college to study hair and beauty. What were those bitches doing now? One of them worked on a supermarket till, another was a receptionist in an office services building… and none of them had a fit boyfriend. But Coco did.

She was in a relationship with *gorgeous* DeAndre. He was an influencer who lived in California. OK, so she didn't see him loads. They Skyped, and he was talking about coming to London next summer when the weather was better. She would've gone out to LA to see him, obviously, if she wasn't scared of flying. He understood that. It was cool. They were together. And he was soooo fit.

The point was that Coco had made a success of her life. She'd worked super-hard to get where she was. There'd been a time when she didn't think that was going to happen. When her self-esteem was, like, on the floor. #Broken. In her teenage years, whenever she looked in the mirror, all she saw was a big, fat, disgusting monster with a hairy, spotty face, bad teeth and mousy brown hair. People told her she was beautiful. Her mum, her cousin, some of the boys. But she never believed them.

It was only once she properly learned how to do hair and make-up, set about transforming her body in the gym, went full-blonde and mastered the Instagram filters that her body image began to change. She could make herself look how *she* wanted to look. And she started to actually like the result. So did others. Fifty thousand of them. She'd once had three hundred and eighty-six comments about how hot she looked in one of her daily selfies. The girls from school probably didn't even know three hundred and eighty-six people between them.

There were times when she felt lonely, sure. When the only people she met in real life were the guys who delivered the brands' packages to her flat or the trainer at the gym who helped her with a booty workout. She called her mum and her cousin most days and messaged DeAndre loads, too. But it was harder to go out and make friends. That was funny, cos she lived in Shoreditch which was full of boys and girls like her – twentysomethings whose fashion sense was on point – but she never seemed to speak to any of them. She didn't need to go out dating, cos she had DeAndre. She felt nervous about talking to her neighbours, cos she didn't know any of them. And she didn't want to risk chatting to a random person in a coffee shop or something, cos that'd just be *weird*.

So, most of Coco's time was spent alone, in her flat, planning her posts, testing out new emoji combinations and engaging with her followers. She'd made the right choices. She was a successful young entrepreneur. But she wasn't going to lie. Some days, she was desperate for the doorbell to go. Just so she could exchange a few words with a real human being.

*

He scrolled through her Instagram feed again. Though its content physically repulsed him, he forced himself to do it. It was research, after all. Time spent in reconnaissance and all that. He couldn't believe how much of her day this insane bitch appeared to spend on social media. It was as if she lived her entire life through a set of fake photos and meaningless hashtags. Almost as if she didn't have a job. Oh wait, this was her job. The thought made his lips twist into a smile of contempt.

How stupid was that? Spending all day holding your phone at a ridiculous angle somewhere above your head, tilting your chin down at an equally ridiculous angle – presumably in a forlorn attempt to make yourself look thin – pouting, snapping and plastering the results all over the internet for strangers to ogle? What had society come to, that you could make a living from being an *influencer*? Perhaps he had it the wrong way round, though. Maybe it was the consumers who were the morons and the influencers were the clever ones for financially exploiting their stupidity. Clearly, there was decent money to be made sitting in your flat all day and posting about yourself. Decent enough for a nice pad, at least, in a fashionable part of town. He'd travelled there and taken a good look at where she lived, surrounded by overpriced boutique places and revoltingly attractive people. He loathed her apparent success. He hated her because he envied her.

All his life, he could only dream about having the power this woman wielded. She was twenty-three and, as far as he could tell, had done nothing in her time except photograph and film herself. But, now, she was paid to do that, and when she posted something, tens of thousands of people saw it. Hundreds, sometimes thousands, reacted positively to it. After years of having his ego repeatedly stamped on by his father, his co-workers, and later – worst of all – *her*, he could scarcely believe that such influence over others was possible. Perhaps the Throat Ripper could achieve that status, or even go beyond.

Of course, her entire life was a chimera, a myth. Men had created the technology that enabled her ludicrous existence. Men developed the web, the smartphones, the platforms and the apps. She was simply a vacuous automaton at the end of that system pressing buttons. And her followers probably cleaved into two groups: cretinous women who – like most of their kind – just wanted to be told what to wear, and men with nothing better to masturbate over.

Well, she was going to regret drawing so much attention to herself. She had a new follower now. And, when the time was right, all the sheep who hung off her every post were going to see a totally new kind of selfie from her. One that could go viral.

#Choking.

# CHAPTER FORTY-SIX

Waiting and paperwork. Two things that Lockhart hated, but which constituted the majority of time spent in a major investigation. In this instance, the waiting was for the lab to get back to him on the recent DNA samples. He'd even dropped the Byers swab off himself on Saturday afternoon, hoping the personal touch would speed things up. But there was only one technician working and a backlog of priority cases to get through. They'd half-promised him a result by midday Monday, at least. Probably just to get him to leave them alone.

Since he'd arrived at Jubilee House shortly after 8 a.m., Lockhart had been checking his watch frequently, gauging when the earliest acceptable call to the lab would be. He reckoned 10 a.m., immediately before their team meeting. He glanced at the Suunto display: 9:47. Following his idea on Saturday, he'd already gone into the files to find the contact details of Damon Pagett's lawyer and fired off a message to her. Now, he was trying to distract himself for a few more minutes with the essential but tedious tasks of that other investigative pillar: paperwork.

Most people outside the police didn't appreciate how bureaucratic the whole business had become. The extra accountability was probably for the best, given the corruption and malpractice of past decades – especially in London – but all the form filling still pissed him off. In a complex investigation like Op Norton, every choice he made had to be recorded and justified, every evidential detail sorted and filed, every hour of staff time rostered and approved.

Fortunately, DCI Porter was more easy-going than most brass on that stuff. But it didn't feel like he was supporting them much of late. Lockhart had been unable to reach the DCI all weekend. That wasn't unusual; Porter often went out of town for a break. Lockhart also knew from the grapevine that his boss's marriage had broken up earlier this year, meaning he had a lot of personal stuff to deal with. But even so, with a triple – quadruple – murder case in progress, he'd expected more from Porter.

Lockhart scrutinised the team roster for the coming week, making sure everyone who'd worked over the weekend had at least one rest day. He clicked into the spreadsheet and was about to make a change when he thought of Green. They hadn't spoken in a few days. Lockhart was suddenly keenly aware of her absence and his desire to contact her, then immediately felt guilty. He told himself it was a strictly professional interest in whether she was still following up her internet lead on the killer. He was wondering if he could call her before the team meeting when his phone rang. The screen just said: 'Lab'.

He snatched it up. 'DI Lockhart.'

'Morning, Dan, this is Petra. How are you doing?'

'Fine, thanks.' The suspense was killing him. He didn't ask how she was.

'So, we've got the results on those DNA profiles.'

'Yeah?'

'First off, the blood on the tissue found at the Elena Fernandez murder scene belonged to Elena.'

'OK.' That's what they'd guessed. 'Anything else on the tissue?'

'Yes, there was. We ran an amylase test for saliva and found a sample on it. The DNA profile of that saliva was different to the blood, meaning it came from another person.'

'Who?'

'Well, no one on the existing database. But the saliva was a match for one of the two new samples you brought to us. Let me just check…'

Lockhart wanted to scream 'who?' at her down the phone.

'Yes, here we are,' said the technician, eventually. 'Paul Dixon.'

'Dixon.' Lockhart gripped his mobile harder.

'That's right. It's his saliva on the tissue that also has Elena's blood on it.'

He was already standing and scanning the MIT office, seeing who was in. 'Thanks, Petra.' He hung up and pocketed the phone. This could be the breakthrough they'd been waiting for. He could see Khan across the room. On Friday, he could've punched the young DC for his sloppy work on checking Hugh Chadwick's alibi. Today, he wanted to give him a hug. If Dixon hadn't pushed Khan, they wouldn't have arrested him and made this connection. Sometimes it was a chance event like that which blew a case wide open. A direct forensic link between victim and suspect could be enough for a murder charge against Dixon. The only problem was that they'd already released him.

Lockhart clapped his hands. 'All right, listen up everyone,' he shouted across the room. 'Stop what you're doing. We've got an arrest to make.'

Fifteen minutes later, with the flash and wail of blues and twos, they sped towards Paul Dixon's flat. Lockhart was in the passenger seat, gripping the handle above the door to steady himself. One of the uniformed officers from the MIT drove, his jaw clenched and knuckles white on the steering wheel. Smith, Khan and another uniformed PC had deployed in a second car to Prime Fitness, the gym in Richmond where Dixon worked. Lockhart and his crew had a longer journey, heading further south-west to Twickenham, a residential area on the outskirts of London.

'Bring him on,' said Andy, the tall and well-built detective constable Lockhart had asked to come along, from the back seat. 'I'm ready for him.'

'Me too,' growled the uniform. 'We're gonna nail that bastard.'

'Easy, lads,' replied Lockhart. 'We have to find him first.' Operational tours in the military had taught him the value of remaining calm ahead of a potential 'contact' with the enemy. Excitement and emotion didn't do anyone any favours. If Smith and Khan's experience on Friday was anything to go by, Dixon wasn't going to come without a fight. Lockhart would deal with that as and when it happened but charging in with fists and batons flying wasn't his preferred tactic. Dixon's apartment could be a treasure trove of evidence against him, which Lockhart didn't want contaminated or destroyed. And he definitely didn't want to be facing counter charges from Dixon's lawyer for police brutality.

'The scumbag's gotta pay for what he's done, guv,' said Andy, behind him. 'Simple as that.'

Lockhart was about to respond when his phone vibrated in his coat pocket before the ringtone sounded. He grabbed it. Smith.

'He's not at the gym, guv,' she blurted, breathless. 'Receptionist says he's off this week.'

'OK. Is he travelling?'

'He's taken leave, but they don't know where he is. No one's seen him since his arrest. And he didn't mention specific plans to any of his colleagues here. Then again, he wouldn't, would he? If he was gonna run off and hide like a fucking coward.'

Lockhart could hear the anger in her voice, same as with the two guys in the car with him. It was the sum of six weeks of solid graft by all of them with almost no result. Six weeks of dead ends and dead young women whose murders they'd failed to prevent. The rage was understandable; he felt it too, maybe worse than his team did. He just hid it more than most.

'Nice one, Max,' he replied. 'Call Berry and get Dixon put on a ports watchlist. Then gather up any other evidence from the gym that you think might be useful and keep in touch.'

'Got it.'

'We're nearly in Twickenham. Talk soon.' He rang off.

Lockhart signalled the uniform to cut the lights and sirens, and after a couple more turnings, they arrived outside Dixon's building. It was a five-storey mansion block, near the river, much like Lockhart's own flat in Hammersmith. Unlike Hugh Chadwick's building, however, there was no concierge to open the main door. The fifth buzzer they pressed answered and admitted them.

Climbing four flights of steps to Dixon's landing, Lockhart felt his pulse quicken. He slowed the other two men down and positioned them either side of the door outside number 37, Dixon's flat. He took a breath. Then he knocked on the door.

Nothing.

'Mr Dixon, this is the police. Open up.'

Silence.

'If you don't open the door, we will break it down.'

Lockhart glanced at the men flanking him. Then he stepped back and aimed a hard kick at the door lock. The wood splintered as it burst open and he glimpsed the interior. Dark.

He motioned the others to left and right and stepped inside ahead of them. Lockhart didn't expect Dixon to have a serious weapon, but he was suddenly aware of being unarmed.

The hallway of the apartment was dark and silent. They crept down it, checking the kitchen and a bathroom to the sides. A large open living space appeared empty, but Lockhart noticed the final door was shut. Probably Dixon's bedroom. He paused outside, listening. A slight sound came from within, barely audible. The rustle of fabric, maybe?

Lockhart reached slowly for the door handle and, taking a firm grip, twisted and threw it open.

He felt the whip of air before he saw the spark of movement to his right. His eyes were still adjusting to the gloom when he heard the noise.

*Meow.*

Clutching Dixon's bedsheets, its claws out and teeth bared, was a large, fluffy cat.

Lockhart exhaled and stepped inside. Quick searches showed nothing under the bed or in the wardrobe.

'Have a final check around, you two,' he said, taking out his phone and calling Smith. She picked up straight away. 'He's not here, Max.'

'Bollocks.'

'I know. Let's get the paperwork going for an arrest warrant. We want it signed off and circulated ASAP.'

'Guv.'

Lockhart stood in Dixon's bedroom, hands on hips, staring at the cat. He could feel the fury rising quickly and cursed himself for missing their chance when Dixon was in custody. And he wondered whether they were already too late to stop him killing again. He shut his eyes. It wasn't even midday, but Lockhart could already feel the urge to crack open a Stella and drink it in one go. Then another, and another, until his fridge was dry and he could forget about his failure for a few hours, at least.

# PART FOUR

# CHAPTER FORTY-SEVEN

At six thirty on a late November evening, the South-West London Trauma Clinic had closed for the day, but Lexi was still in her office, absorbed in her laptop screen. She'd joined an incel web forum using her 'Blake' alias and was participating in a thread entitled 'Female empowerment is bullshit'. The usual names were online, including BlackPillll97 and BloodCel, with whom she'd been cultivating a relationship ever since their first private chat. Her aim was to get BloodCel to introduce her to Priapus; apparently, he was the one who knew the killer. She'd just replied enthusiastically to a thread where someone had posted:

*Isn't it about time the dudes took some power back?*

In response, she'd typed:

*female power is an oxymoron.*

She hated the kind of stuff she had to write on here but kept reminding herself there was a purpose to it. She was winning their trust, slowly but surely.

Lexi stretched and rubbed her eyes. She was alone in the building. Rob Edwards had left a little early today, saying he wasn't feeling great. She didn't want to tell him that he looked like shit, but he did: pale and shaky. She asked if he needed help, but he just rattled a box of pills in his hand and forced a smile, saying he'd 'man up' and get through it. Maureen and her other colleagues had already gone home, and it was time she left, too.

But there was a good incentive to stay: despite its inadequate heating, her office was the most private place to continue her online research. It didn't matter that Dan's team had their prime suspect. For Lexi, the task was still urgent. More than a fortnight had passed since the murder of Elena Fernandez, but the MIT hadn't yet caught this guy Paul Dixon, the personal trainer whose DNA had turned up at Elena's murder scene. She still wanted to help Dan, even if he wasn't keeping her in the loop like before.

There was an unspoken sense of failure for them both; for Dan, locating their prime suspect, and for her, making the contribution that would help him achieve that. Perhaps that's what was keeping them apart. The feeling of unfinished business was what drove Lexi to put in the hours online every day, now. She was fully aware that the killer was still at large and, if he was determined to continue his pattern of a murder every fortnight or so, then another attack could be imminent.

But there was more than that, and she knew it. She and Dan had barely talked in the past couple weeks and Lexi had to admit that, well, she missed him. She'd wondered more than once in that time about her interest in Dan. Had it gone beyond the professional? Was that what she wanted? Lexi didn't know any more. Right now, Dan was totally focussed on finding Dixon, understandably. And Lexi had plenty of her own work to do.

Her phone buzzed on the desk and, glancing at the screen, she saw it was a text from Sam Byers. He'd been messaging her a lot over the last two weeks. At first, he'd been desperate to explain that the business with the police was nothing serious, just a misunderstanding because he'd been at the same feminism event as the victims. Pretty quickly, he'd moved to telling her how attractive she was and suggesting they go for a drink. His text-flirting had all the subtlety of a sledgehammer, totally the opposite of how he'd been in person. She didn't object to directness in a man, but Sam was a little full-on for her liking. Besides, she wasn't interested in him romantically.

Lexi thought back to her conversation with Sam in his office at the university. What was it he'd said? Something about the phallus and testes representing power and masculinity… an idealised man, a hunter… *women are powerless to resist him… even the mightiest women lose their strength…* She looked back to the incel web forum. The chat thread about taking back power. Something clicked in her mind. Then it hit her.

She knew the killer's pattern.

She needed to call Dan right away.

Grabbing her phone and ignoring Sam's text, she stabbed the screen and rang Dan's mobile.

It went straight to voicemail.

*

Tonight. He was going to do it tonight. He looked in the small mirror he'd hung off a nail on the wall. The transformation was starting to take place. He was no longer the weak, pathetic loser who usually stared back at him with dead eyes. The fool who'd been lied to, cuckolded and abandoned by a bitch he should've known better than to trust. He was becoming the Throat Ripper, the one who was wresting power from the sluts who thought they had it now. How wrong they were. His hand slid down to his groin and, holding his own gaze, he began to stimulate himself. He didn't need to worry about being disturbed. Not here.

This was where the transformation occurred. Not an office or a bedroom, but a secret place. His own place. He stored everything here: his choking equipment, his clothes, his transport. It was out of the way, a Batcave that nobody knew about. He'd rented it in a false name from a guy who didn't even ask for any documentation, just cash. There were no cameras around, no nosy neighbours.

In the six months he'd been using it, he'd only seen a handful of other people coming and going. It was perfect. And it'd kindled a fantasy that wouldn't let go of him.

He wanted to bring a bitch here. To strap her in to the chair he'd bought and modified, to watch the fear in her eyes as she realised her fate. Realised that no one was coming to save her. That no one could even hear her scream. To take his time with her, make it last. He shivered at the thought. Maybe he'd do that with the last one. A special ending. But it wouldn't be tonight.

Tonight, he was making a home visit.

# CHAPTER FORTY-EIGHT

It was late, and Lockhart was knackered, but he had to concentrate. He didn't want to squander this opportunity. After days of waiting, numerous phone calls and even a visit to her office, he'd managed to convince Damon Pagett's lawyer that he believed Pagett was innocent. Not only that, but that Pagett could assist the inquiry into who had killed Kim Hardy as well as the recent London victims. The lawyer had taken some convincing, but eventually she'd agreed to take Lockhart to visit Pagett in Pentonville prison in north London. Lockhart was attending in a personal capacity, badged as an assistant of the lawyer who was exercising the right to meet her client.

The meeting would be off-record, meaning nothing Pagett said could be used in evidence, but that was fine by Lockhart. He just wanted to talk, to hear Pagett's side of what happened the night Kim Hardy was murdered; something which everyone else seemed determined to stop him from doing. Lockhart knew he could be in serious trouble if Porter, Burrows, Flynn or Newham MIT found out – maybe facing disciplinary charges – but he didn't care. He wasn't about to let it go just because that lot were obstructing him. Porter was the one he'd expected to fight his corner, but the DCI had refused to budge. Was he that concerned by politics? Lockhart didn't really get it; in his mind, Op Norton won out every time. Four victims – probably more if they didn't act – versus some Met Police politics? It was no contest.

And that was without considering the impact on the man who'd just been brought into the tiny prison meeting room and seated opposite him and the lawyer. Damon Pagett. A man who was, most likely, innocent of murder. Lockhart took in his chubby, solid physique and vacant eyes, set far apart in a doughy face. If Pagett had cared about his appearance outside prison, he certainly wasn't looking after himself inside. Several days' patchy stubble darkened his cheeks and throat, while clumps of hair stuck up randomly from his head. A faint body odour wafted across the table from his stained T-shirt.

'Damon, this is Dan Lockhart,' said the lawyer. 'He's interested in our case, and he'd like to chat to you about the night that Kim died. He thinks you might be able to help the police work out what really happened.'

Pagett scratched his face and yawned. 'OK.'

'But if I'm not happy with any of his questions,' she added, glancing at Lockhart, 'then I'll advise you not to answer.'

'Thanks for seeing me, Damon. My name's Dan. I'm a Detective Inspector in the Met. I work on serious crimes, down in south-west London.'

'What's serious crimes?' Pagett's voice was incongruously high-pitched.

'Things like murder,' replied Lockhart.

'Like what they said I did?'

Lockhart nodded. 'That's what some of my colleagues think. But I'm not sure they're right. What do you say, Damon?'

Pagett shook his head, cheeks wobbling. 'I loved Kim. I didn't kill her. I'd never do that.'

Lockhart clasped his hands on the table. 'But people think you did it.'

The lawyer leant forward, and Lockhart wondered if he'd pushed too far, too soon, but before she could intervene, Pagett spoke.

'They said I did and I said no and then they kept telling me I did and now, I'm just confused about it.' He massaged his scalp hard, producing new tufts of hair. 'I'm not sure what I did any more.'

Lockhart turned to the lawyer and waited for her to give a small nod before he continued. 'What can you tell me about the night that Kim died?'

Pagett's lower lip curled down and his eyes darted side to side. 'I went to see her as usual. We did sex, but we also did cuddles. That's what I call it.' He smiled briefly. 'Sometimes I just liked that best.'

'What happened after the, er, cuddles?'

'I went home, and I made some cheese on toast. Then I watched football on TV. The Women's World Cup semi-final was on.'

Lockhart pictured the photographs of the hotel room where Kim had been murdered. He tried to visualise Pagett's journey from the room, down the stairs, through the entrance hall and out into the street.

'Did you see anyone else on your way out of the hotel?'

Pagett rubbed at a mark on the table, his tongue protruding in concentration. 'There was the hotel reception guy. He was always there. I don't like him.'

'Why's that?'

'I think he's jealous of me, getting to do sex with Kim.'

Lockhart nodded. 'Anyone else?'

Pagett screwed his eyes shut. 'Um, there was a man at the front. On a scooter. But I didn't see his face cos he had a helmet on.'

'OK.' There was no mention of that in the eyewitness accounts. 'Do you remember anything more about the guy on the scooter?'

'Just… it was all black. Everything was black. His clothes, his hands, the bike, the box on the back of it. Black.'

'Do you know if this person went into the hotel?' asked Lockhart.

'No.' Pagett made a fist, the knuckles dimpled with fat. 'I miss her,' he said.

'Yeah. I knew Kim, too.'

'Really?'

Lockhart nodded. 'She'd helped me once. That's why I want to catch the person who killed her.'

'Well, you should ask her friend, then.'

'What friend?' Lockhart turned to the lawyer, who looked back at him blankly. Evidently, she'd not heard of this person either. 'What friend, Damon?'

'Her friend. Suzy. They were together a lot.'

'Suzy? Who's she?' Lockhart couldn't recall reading about this in the case notes on Kim's death. No friend had been interviewed by Newham MIT. 'What's her last name?'

'Dunno. She's like Kim was. You pay her if you want sex. But I didn't.'

'OK. So, this Suzy, she knew Kim well?'

'They were like best mates,' replied Pagett quickly. 'And they looked after each other, too.'

'How?'

'Well, whenever anyone went to see them – you know, for sex – they'd do a quick photo of the man on their phones and send it to each other.'

'Really?'

'Yeah. Kim told me it was in case the men did anything bad. Insurance, she used to say.' Pagett wrinkled his nose. 'It was a bit embarrassing, cos I don't like having my picture taken. But I always sat up straight and tried to smile. Kim told me she couldn't do that with most men though. They didn't want people to know they'd been to see her. Maybe they're married or they've got girlfriends and it's a secret.'

Lockhart tried to process this. 'So, what did Kim do if a guy didn't want to have his picture taken?' He imagined that applied to ninety-nine per cent of her clients.

'Oh, she'd just pretend to be on her phone while they got undressed or whatever and then she'd do a quick photo of them when they weren't looking.' He mimed the action.

'Did you tell the other detectives this?' asked Lockhart.

'Nope.' Pagett shrugged. 'I would of done but they just kept saying I killed her and then my head went all fuzzy and I forgot.'

'Shit,' blurted Lockhart. This changed everything. It meant there could be a picture of their killer. He knew no phone was retrieved from Kim's murder scene. 'Do you know where I could find Suzy?'

Pagett bit his lip, closed his eyes.

'Damon?'

'I'm thinking.'

Lockhart waited.

Suddenly, Pagett opened his eyes. 'I remember where Kim told me Suzy works a lot.'

'Where?'

'Dagenham. You know, up the Heathway.'

'Yeah.' Lockhart swallowed. 'I know it.'

'We need to take action on this,' said the lawyer.

'We have to find Suzy, first,' replied Lockhart. As they sat in silence, he wondered if there could be any connection to the sighting of his wife. Surely not. It wasn't possible… was it?

Pagett stared at the table top before looking up. 'The detectives from Newham told me I'm going to stay in prison for the rest of my life,' he said.

Lockhart met his gaze. 'Did they?'

Pagett nodded. 'Is it true? Will I?'

Lockhart flicked his eyes to the lawyer and back to Pagett. 'Not if I can help it.'


Emerging from the interview, Lockhart thanked the lawyer for her help and promised to be in touch as soon as he found Suzy. Then he retrieved his mobile phone from the reception and checked it as he walked out and across the car park. There were six missed calls from Lexi Green in the past hour. What was going on? She'd also sent him a text, thirty minutes ago. He clicked into it. The message was simple.

*Am at your office. Get here soon as you can. I have something.*

# CHAPTER FORTY-NINE

The street lamps of Newham strobed through his tinted visor. He was a few miles away, at most, and closing in. He tried to focus, to control his breathing and slow his palpitating heart. The beta-blocker pills didn't seem to have taken effect fully, yet. He hoped they'd kick in by the time he arrived. Which wasn't long, now. The anticipation was killing him. Ironic, really.

It was tempting to throttle the engine harder, but he kept his speed steady. The last thing he wanted was to get pulled over by the cops, with what he was carrying in the top box behind him. Inside his crash helmet, he smirked involuntarily, imagining the look on a police officer's face as he lifted the lid. The penny dropping as he connected the contents: plastic cable ties, washing line cord, a mouth gag, a bag of metal balls, the thick steel spanner that forced them down, and a Taser. He chuckled at the thought of them finding an engagement ring tucked incongruously in his pocket. There was no explaining it away. It'd be game over.

So, as usual, he took care. No speeding, no bus lane violations, no running red lights. He'd painstakingly mapped a route through the back streets, westward from his private lock-up garage to the doorstep of a converted factory where that ridiculous slag lived. Staying off the main roads, there was less chance of being caught on traffic cameras or the police's Automatic Number Plate Recognition system. Not that it mattered too much; he used a different, fake plate on his scooter for each mission.

One thing that was making him more nervous than usual, however, was the location. Zone 1. There was CCTV all over the inner part of London. He couldn't avoid it, and he knew he'd be captured on film near the bitch's apartment. He'd have to keep his helmet on until the last possible moment. Hopefully, it wouldn't be enough for Lockhart and his minions to join the dots. And there were advantages to being central. Constant bustle, noise and movement. No suburban curtain-twitchers or neighbourhood watch schemes. And plenty of delivery riders for him to blend in among.

With any luck, there'd be one of those warehouse parties going on nearby. Thumping music, open doors and screeching, intoxicated partygoers. No one would notice a guy on a scooter. No one would remember anything unusual.

And no one would hear a scream.

*

'I'm telling you, Dan, this is it!' Lexi was unable to hide the exasperation in her voice. She jabbed her Montblanc pen against the sheet of paper on Lucy Berry's desk. She'd drawn it out, plain and simple. And still he wasn't convinced.

'She's got a point, Dan,' said Lucy.

Lexi was so glad Lucy Berry was here. When she'd failed to get through to Dan, she called his office. It was Lucy who'd picked up. She was about to go home but, when Lexi explained the theory to her, she promised to stay until Lexi got there and work on it with her. When she'd arrived, Lucy was already getting into the profiling, having arranged for her husband to take care of their kids solo tonight. Lexi didn't think she would've gotten the same response from DS Maxine Smith.

Lockhart folded his arms, peered at her writing and frowned. 'Run it by me one more time.'

'OK. It's an old theory from sociology called the five bases of power. By two guys called French and Raven. They developed it in the fifties as a way of modelling different forms of social power. The victims so far correspond to those types of power, in the order they appear in the theory.' Lexi spread her hands. 'It's obvious.'

'Reward power?'

'Yeah. That's number one on the list, and Dixon's first victim in the sequence, Natasha Mayston. She was rich, she invested, she distributed money.' Lexi was speaking quickly. 'Natasha had power to reward in bucket-loads. Her murder is symbolic of taking that power back from her and the women she helped.'

Dan didn't say anything. He just bit his lip.

'The second kind of power is coercive. The power to punish.' She hit her pen on the desk, making Lucy flinch. 'That's Sophie Wright, the barrister. Her career was dedicated to punishing men who abused women. She used the law as a weapon against those men. Dixon kills her, and he removes the threat she represents towards violent men.'

'Makes sense,' acknowledged Dan, staring at the paper.

Lexi tapped her pen against the third item on the list. 'Next up in the theory is legitimate power. That's power you hold in office or an organisation or whatever. Elena Fernandez was head of a women's rights charity and she was an elected local councillor. She symbolised the power of, like, official structures.'

'Hm.'

'All of these women attended the Feminist Futures talk at the theatre. Dixon meets them there, he finds out who they are and what they do, and he chooses the victims to represent different kinds of power which women have today. Power that we didn't have in the past.' Lexi's frustration was rising; why couldn't Dan see it?

He shook his head, blinked. 'It's a bit vague, though, isn't it?'

'It's not vague at all, dammit!' Lexi hadn't meant to raise her voice. 'Sorry.'

'All right. Suppose Dixon is following this old theory, French and…'

'Raven.'

'Right. You've got Natasha, Sophie and Elena. What about Kim Hardy?'

Lexi inclined her head. 'She's not part of the sequence. I think she was his first, kind of a trial run.' The words sounded awful, but she couldn't think how else to express it. 'She was vulnerable. He paid her for sex, he got her alone in a room. Maybe she was on drugs at the time. He subdued her in that shitty little hotel. And he tested out this horrible MO on her.' Lexi shut her eyes briefly at the thought of it. Strapped to the chair, unable to move. The gag forcing your mouth wide open against your will.

'Once he knew the choking method worked, then he went to the talk two weeks later and started to choose the victims for his killing campaign, based on this theory of power,' added Lexi.

'It's there in the video, Dan,' said Lucy. 'Dixon's talking to all the women.'

Lexi knew what Lucy was referring to; they'd watched some of the raw footage from the event together and Lucy had shown her all the main people of interest. In addition to Dixon, she'd recognised Will Jacobson and Yannis Dimitriou from the theatre's website, and Dr Sam Byers. There were glimpses of the red-headed asset manager, Hugh Chadwick, too.

'He takes his time planning it all out,' added Lexi. 'That's why there's a three-month gap between Kim's and Natasha's murders.'

'It just seems so… complex.' Dan reached for the list, picked it up and sat back in his chair.

'Dixon is a misogynist,' continued Lexi. 'He's wrapped up in his own little world. He hates the way women are starting to get what we want these days, and he's making a statement about it. It's convoluted, sure, but when you try and see it from his point of view, it's kinda logical. His behaviour fits the profile I gave you,' she said, aware that she sounded a little defensive. 'Except that I thought it was about male power. It's not. It's about *female* power.'

Lexi watched as Dan's eyes scanned the page, left to right, top to bottom and back up again.

'Type four, referent power,' he read. 'And five, expert power.'

'Sure,' said Lexi. 'Expert's the last one, someone who has power through their knowledge or skills in some area. But the next one in the sequence is referent. What we're looking for is a woman who attended the feminist talk with referent power.'

'Which is what, exactly?' Dan handed the list back to her.

'It's power to influence. By making something desirable, making people wanna join your group, emulate what you do, basically be like you. Think of it as advertising, setting a trend. It's the power of people listening to your opinion and following it.'

'So, it's a woman in advertising?' asked Dan. 'That's his next victim?'

'Maybe,' said Lucy. She gestured to her screen. 'We've found a couple of women at the talk who work at a public relations company. That's pretty close.'

'You call them?'

'Lucy called their office,' replied Lexi. 'They were both there.'

'We've advised them to be careful and not to open their doors to anyone,' said Lucy. 'They have a security guard at the office block. And they both live with family or partners.'

'Nice one.' Dan planted his hands on his knees, scanning the monitor. 'All right, who else from the talk might fit the profile?'

Lucy clicked her mouse and displayed the attendance list. She highlighted a name, then brought up a web browser with Instagram. A pouting, heavily made-up young woman.

'She's a social media influencer,' said Lexi. 'I guess it's one of the main kinds of referent power today.'

'There's no phone number, but we've got an address for her,' added Lucy. 'From the electoral register.'

Lexi slipped the pen back in her trouser pocket and leant forward. 'I think we need to act fast.'

Dan turned to her and she held his gaze, her jaw clenched. He seemed to be weighing something up. Something in her eyes.

Eventually, he nodded. 'OK.'

*

Coco Adams was bored. A few hours ago, she'd finished recording a short video of a 'haul', where she'd tried on a bunch of different tops that'd been sent to her by an online fashion retailer, giving her opinion on each one in turn. She'd edited two versions: one which cut between tops, and another which showed her in a push-up bra as she changed clothes in real time. She'd uploaded the second one and the reactions so far had been *amazing*. She had almost forty new subscribers already, and she guessed a few of them were probably guys. It was pretty straightforward: the less she wore, the more people watched. But she had to find the balance. Too much skin and some prude would tag the content as 'inappropriate'. Then you had to sign in to see it and there was no way that was going viral.

Now, as people were going to bed and the views were slowing down, she had nothing else to do. Settled on the sofa, she'd thought about re-watching *Game of Thrones*. But then she'd got caught up checking the social media accounts of other influencers on her iPad. She'd started out with the good intention of making a list, ranking her rivals by followers to compare her success to theirs. But she'd just ended up stuck on the Insta feed of a prettier girl and now she was feeling #ugly as well as bored. It was at times like this that she felt loneliest, though she'd never tell anyone that.

Tearing herself away from the screen, Coco picked up her iPhone and decided to WhatsApp DeAndre. It was the afternoon in California and if DeAndre wasn't getting buff in the gym, he might be up for some sexting. Just as she unlocked her handset, the doorbell went.

'Who is it?' called Coco, checking the time on her phone. It was kind of late.

'Delivery,' came the reply.

More clothes? Or was it the make-up that beauty firm said they were sending her? It didn't really matter. She'd barely spoken to anyone all day long and this was a chance for a little chat. She jumped up from the sofa.

'Coming,' she called, as she slipped into a pair of heels.

Coco checked herself in the hallway mirror, zhuzhed up her hair a bit, cocked her hip and then opened the door.

There was a guy standing there, all in black. She recognised some couriers, the ones who came regularly. But she didn't think she'd seen this man before.

He was holding a big box.

He was smiling.

# CHAPTER FIFTY

This was it. It was happening here and now. He tried to stay in the moment, not to let his thoughts run away with him, imagining what would happen tomorrow when the world found out.

He'd already given her a couple of bursts with the Taser and she'd got the message pretty fast. She screamed, but after he'd told her to shut up or be electrocuted again, she'd kept quiet. Whimpering and sobbing, mascara running down her cheeks, she'd sat there like a rag doll while he fixed her wrists and ankles to the chair. He'd seen that chair in her videos, knew it'd be perfect for strapping her in nice and tight. No escape.

He tucked the Taser into his belt at the back as he straddled her. That left both hands free to apply the dental gag. He was wearing gloves to avoid leaving prints and touch DNA, and as protection in case she thought biting him was a good idea. But she hadn't tried that. It was as if she was just accepting her fate. And her meekness only added to his dominance. It was taking him over, now. His hands tingled as he wedged her mouth open and buckled the leather straps tightly at the back of her head.

'Do you know who I am?' he asked. He didn't even need to whisper; the music that'd been playing in her flat when he entered was loud enough to mask all their noise.

*Gah*, she replied, her tongue working behind the metal O-ring of the gag. Some dribble leaked down her lower lip.

'Do you?' He lowered his face level with hers. Up close, she wasn't half as pretty as she looked online.

She blinked away tears and did a disgusting, juicy sniff. Then she made a noise that sounded like *I think so*.

'That's right.' He let his grin form slowly. 'I'm the Throat Ripper.'

*

Coco didn't know what the hell was happening. One minute, the delivery guy was saying something about a parcel and the next her whole body was on fire, frying with pain. She must've blacked out. Now she was strapped to a chair, her teeth scraping on the metal thing in her mouth, the sound making her shiver. Her lungs and heart were pumping hard and she was scared.

So scared she felt sick.

This was like some horror movie. She didn't understand what was going on. She'd heard of the Throat Ripper in the news. Who hadn't? But why was he here? Why was he attacking her? What had she done to him? None of it made any sense. And the worst thing of all was that she didn't know what the fuck to do. She was just panicking and trying not to make a noise because then he'd make that pain go through her again. All she could think about was avoiding the pain.

He'd got up off her now, thank God, and she didn't have to smell his sweat and his breath right in her face. He fiddled with a little box, whispering something like he was telling her a story, but she couldn't make out the words over the Iggy Azalea song playing on her speakers. He produced a ring, which he held up to her.

It looked like a vintage engagement ring.

Now he was trying to put it on her left ring finger, muttering to himself about women and betrayal and ownership. Instinctively, her fingers curled inwards, but he grabbed the third one and yanked it back out and up, shoving the ring on. It was tight, and the pain was horrible, stabby and angry over her knuckle, breaking the skin. She willed herself not to scream. As she watched a streak of her own blood spread around the metal band, Coco had a sudden realisation.

There would be no more videos, no more selfies. No more posts, no more likes.

Because she was going to die.

OMFG.

She was going to die.

*

Lockhart drove east in his Defender, making decent progress but stopping short of whacking on the portable blues and twos and driving at twice the speed limit. That was fine. It wasn't an emergency, just a routine house call to make sure the woman who fitted Lexi's profile for the next victim was OK. As such, he'd opted to do it himself rather than call up a local unit.

Weird as it was, he had to admit that the academic theory Lexi had identified fitted the pattern of the Op Norton murders. He couldn't claim to get inside Paul Dixon's head like she could, but he knew that offenders with deviant personalities could create all kinds of elaborate fantasies and rituals around their crimes. And if Dixon had experienced some loss or trauma – as Lexi had suggested – then Lockhart was well aware of the effect that could have on a person.

It was probably the most complex victim profile he'd ever encountered, but Lexi had seemed so certain of herself that he had to follow up. There was that hope in her eyes that he craved, that he clung to and couldn't ignore, however wacky her ideas seemed. Was it hope just for the case, or for him, too? He couldn't say.

Despite Lexi's confidence, though, something still nagged at him. Would Dixon, having gone to ground, continue to rigidly follow his pattern of one victim every two weeks or so? Would he, having been confronted by Smith about the feminism talk in his custody interview, continue to choose victims that he'd met there?

Lockhart couldn't say. But, if Lexi's intricate psychosocial model or whatever it was helped them find the next victim before Dixon got there, then he swore never to doubt her again.

Nearing his destination, Lockhart was already thinking beyond the check on the social media influencer. He was wondering if he should continue east afterwards, back to Dagenham Heathway, in search of Kim Hardy's friend Suzy. And, he acknowledged with sudden sadness and guilt, in search of his wife, Jess.

*

In it went. He loved that moment when the metal ball popped through the O-ring on the dental gag and entered their mouths. When they began making frantic efforts to stave off the inevitable. He enjoyed the fight they put up; any normal human being's reaction to having a foreign object in your mouth. But, whether pushing back with their tongues or trying to move their heads, it was futile. They weren't strong enough to resist the force of the long ring spanner and, sooner or later, they yielded and stopped breathing. He could sense it – now – as her body went rigid.

He waited.

Then she tipped her head back and, somehow, swallowed the ball down.

Damn. She must have a wider throat than the last one. He guessed from her spasms and groans that it was stuck somewhere in her oesophagus. She was breathing again, now, sucking in lungfuls of air.

Cursing, annoyed with himself for misjudging it, he got up off her and returned to his box. He stooped and selected a fractionally larger ball. Just a quarter of an inch. That should do the trick. As he stood, a siren whooped outside, audible over her autotuned pop music.

He froze, then glanced at her. She was twisting her neck to look out of the window towards the sound, but there was nothing to see. He'd closed the blinds long ago. Surely, there was no way she or anyone else had called the cops. And, even if by some miracle they arrived, no one could stop the Throat Ripper. Not now.

Clutching the new ball, he walked slowly, deliberately back towards her.

*

Lockhart scanned the buzzers outside the building. He pressed the one for the influencer's flat and waited.

No response.

He tried again, with the same result.

After pressing five more doorbells, he was admitted to the entrance hall.

Striding up the stairs, he found apartment number 8. Checked his notes to be sure. This was the one. He knocked.

No answer.

Leaning towards the door, he listened. He could make out some noises inside, including something like singing.

He knocked again, harder and louder. 'This is the police,' he called out.

Nothing.

Lockhart put his ear up close, strained his hearing. The singing had stopped.

Should he break in? He tried to assess the risk – did he really believe there was a life at stake? Perhaps he could use the Leatherman tool in his pocket to slip the lock instead…

A few quick footsteps came from within before the door flew open.

A young woman with dark hair stood on the threshold in a bathrobe, towelling her wet hair.

'Can I help you?' she said.

'Er, yeah.' Lockhart produced his warrant card and introduced himself. 'Melissa Roberts?'

'Yes,' she replied cautiously.

'Just a check to make sure you're safe and well,' he began. Now he was here, and there was clearly nothing amiss, he wasn't quite sure what else to tell her. He felt slightly awkward. Had Lexi got it wrong?

Lockhart started to explain his visit. But he was already thinking about driving on to Dagenham. And wondering how many Stellas he'd need to get to sleep tonight.

# CHAPTER FIFTY-ONE

Lexi spun in her office chair, checking the wall clock as she rotated – 9.05 a.m. – and spun some more. She was waiting for Maureen to call through and let her know that her first client of the day had arrived. She wanted to take her mind off the serial murders, but she kept thinking about last night. She felt a little embarrassed at pressuring Dan to cross town right away to make sure the influencer was OK. He'd texted her late to say the woman was fine and that Lexi shouldn't worry. She didn't know if that meant success or failure. Her theory *had* to be correct. It was so clear. Wasn't it?

On the desk, her phone beeped. Sighing, she picked it up and unlocked the screen. The new message was from Sarah. Her cryptic text read:

*Have you seen Insta? #ThroatRipper*

It ended with one of those open-mouthed emojis of shock or fear. Dread creeping through her belly, Lexi opened Instagram and searched on the hashtag. She almost dropped the phone.

#ThroatRipper was all over it. She swallowed hard, pressed her lips together tightly and felt them trembling as she tracked back to the original post. At exactly 9 a.m., an account called @CocoAdamsLifestyle had put up a single photograph. Lexi could feel the tears pricking her eyeballs as she stared down at it, her mouth dry.

A young blonde woman sat, strapped to a chair, her head bowed. It wasn't immediately obvious that she was dead, and Lexi briefly let herself imagine it was just a sick hoax. But the images from the previous crime scenes were seared into her brain. And she recognised those white plastic ties at the wrists and ankles. The orange cord around the chest, just below the woman's breasts. Details she knew hadn't been made public.

Below the picture, the caption read:

*Do you get the message now? #ThroatRipper #choking*

There were already hundreds of reactions. Lexi couldn't believe it. Who was Coco Adams? She didn't remember the name on the attendance list from the talk… but then she recalled that Natasha Mayston hadn't been on the list, either. Her head was swimming and she couldn't think straight. This was her fault. She unleashed an involuntary cry and slapped her hand on the desk.

Lexi heard the door on the other side of the wall open and seconds later, Rob was in the room.

'Are you all right, Lexi?' he asked, concern wrinkling his face. He looked drawn and haggard, but there was a kind of manic energy in his expression. 'I heard a noise, and—'

'Go away, Rob!' she yelled, hiding the phone from him.

'Yes, of course, my bad, sorry,' he said, shrinking and putting up his hands as if she was going to hit him. He sloped out of her office, mumbling apologies as he went.

'Jesus Christ,' she moaned, before shouting, 'God fucking dammit!'

Gathering herself, Lexi took a few deep breaths. This wasn't the time to beat herself up or lose her shit. It was time to act. She picked up her laptop, brought it to life and began logging in on the manosphere websites she'd gotten so familiar with. There had to be something on there, some clue to Dixon's location.

While the chat pages loaded, she grabbed her phone and scrolled to Dan's name in her contacts. She could already imagine what his colleagues were saying about her 'psychobabble', but she had to face up to that and talk to him right now if she wanted to help.

She took a deep breath and called him.

\*

Lockhart had been in the Jubilee House canteen, fuelling up with a breakfast of eggs on toast, when Green had called. He'd barely been able to believe what he was hearing from her. They'd had the right profile, even the right time, but the wrong victim. His mind was racing to work it out. After breaking the news Green had said something about continuing her internet profiling strategy, but Lockhart hadn't been listening properly. Ending the call abruptly, he'd run upstairs to the MIT office, leaving the eggs half-finished, and gone straight to Lucy Berry.

A minute later, everyone in the room was gathered round Berry's set of screens, stunned into silence. Some guys had started getting worked up, kicking furniture and threatening to choke Paul Dixon themselves when they found him. One had even thrown a chair. Lockhart wanted to do the same but, as SIO, he had to keep his head and rise above it. The next thing he'd done was call it through to the Met's communications centre. He'd been informed that local units from Tower Hamlets borough were already attending.

Since DCI Porter wasn't in the office yet, Lockhart's next call was to him. But Porter didn't pick up. So, for the second time in as many weeks, he'd gone over his boss's head to Superintendent Burrows. She'd ensure that the Homicide Assessment Team on the scene knew it was very likely to be the latest Op Norton murder and, therefore, Lockhart's case.

*Latest.* Like it was just a normal thing that the so-called Throat Ripper had killed again. Lockhart was furious at himself. This was his fault. He'd failed to catch Dixon and now another young woman had died. The pain and the hate and the hopelessness were building inside him, taking over. He balled his fist tight to help him stay grounded. Squeeze, hold, release, breathe, repeat.

Now, half an hour later, he'd had a chance to sit and think. To calm down and plan. Rather than charge off to the scene immediately, he wanted to set up a strategy with his team here, then go to Shoreditch. That was why he'd called the emergency meeting. There was no tea and biscuits today, no gallows humour. Just fifteen officers and two civilians waiting for their SIO to tell them what to do.

Shirtsleeves rolled up and hands on hips, Lockhart took a deep breath and scanned their faces. 'Listen up everyone. About an hour ago, the image of a young woman, who appeared to be dead, was posted on a social media account belonging to a Colette Adams, also known as Coco, age twenty-three. The caption on the post included the phrase "Throat Ripper". We believe the young woman to be Coco, and officers who broke into her flat at approximately 9.20 have confirmed that she is deceased, almost certainly murdered.

'Now,' he continued, 'we have the first crime scene pictures through. Thanks, Mo.' Lockhart paused as, alongside him, Khan pinned up the hastily printed photographs. 'Officers on the scene have reported that what looks like a metal ball is visible at the back of her throat. We can consider Coco our perpetrator's fifth victim.'

Lockhart felt his head drop, the guilt consuming him. He forced himself to straighten up.

'It appears that Coco had not attended the theatre talk on feminism which connected the previous three victims: Natasha, Sophie and Elena. We need to confirm that. Max?'

He glanced to his right and saw Smith on her phone. It was unusual for her attention to be divided in a briefing. 'Sorry,' she said.

'Can you get back to the theatre and check their records to see if Coco ever went there?'

'Guv.'

'Mo, I want you to go through the interviews and meeting notes of anyone connected with Op Norton and see who knew about our victim strategy. Who was aware of the link to the feminism talk?'

'Got it, boss.'

'Andy,' he pointed to the large DS at the back, 'I need you, Priya and Sam to get as much CCTV as you can from around Coco's flat. Lucy will give you the address. Next up, we want—'

The footsteps behind Lockhart were loud enough to make him turn. Porter stood there, his eyes bulging, broad chest heaving. If he hadn't been wearing a suit, Lockhart would've said he'd come straight from the gym. Maybe he had.

'Dan, what's happening?' he boomed, striding across to the whiteboards.

'Sir, I tried to call you, but—'

'I was busy. What's the latest?'

Lockhart began filling his boss in. Rather than expressing shock, Porter was already talking about an early press conference and telling him to send what they had to the media office right away. As Lockhart retorted that they first establish the crime scene facts, he was distracted by Smith whispering on her phone in his peripheral vision. He stopped talking to Porter and turned to her.

'Max?'

She covered her mouth and spoke some more.

'Max!'

She ended the call. 'Apologies, guv. That was Kingston police station.'

'OK.' Lockhart shook his head. Why was she taking a call now? 'And?'

'It's Paul Dixon,' she said. 'They've just arrested him.'

# CHAPTER FIFTY-TWO

After the usual booking in, medical check, rest period, meal break and legal consultation, it was mid-afternoon by the time Smith was able to interview Paul Dixon. It was almost an exact replication of two weeks ago: Dixon across the table from her, smug and nonchalant. His lawyer alongside him, confident and slightly hostile. Khan in the next room, watching via video link. A large police officer behind Smith, in case Dixon kicked off. But something in the personal trainer's manner told her that was unlikely.

Something had changed.

Smith did the usual introductions for the digital recording and cautioned Dixon that the interview was evidential material. He shrugged and said, 'Whatever.' After recapping his arrest that morning – the receptionist at his gym having called the police – she asked where he was last night.

Dixon glanced at his lawyer, who nodded once. 'Staying with a friend,' he replied.

'What's the name of your friend?'

'Ahmed Hamza. Do you want his address and stuff?'

'Yes.' Smith took down the details. 'Can you account for your whereabouts over the last two weeks, Mr Dixon?'

'Just...' He smirked. 'Staying with friends.'

'Were you aware of the warrant for your arrest?'

'Nope.'

Dixon was relaxed, but Smith could see that he didn't look well. His skin was pale, the lines and cracks around his mouth, eyes and forehead more visible. He appeared exhausted.

'We'll need the details of those friends you were staying with.'

'OK. But I don't know all of them. I can't remember everything.'

'You don't know who you were staying with?' Smith was sceptical. 'Why not?'

Dixon's lawyer laid a delicate hand on his arm, then whispered something to him that Smith couldn't catch.

'No comment,' said Dixon.

Smith decided to change tack. She opened a folder she'd brought with her and extracted a photograph of a white tissue partially stained with blood.

'This paper tissue,' she began, 'was recovered from the scene of Elena Fernandez's murder in Deptford, which took place on November twelfth. The blood on the tissue was matched to Elena. Our lab also found saliva on the tissue. Who do you think the saliva belonged to, Mr Dixon?'

'Haven't got a clue,' he said, folding his arms.

'It belonged to you.' Smith rotated the picture and slid it towards him. 'Do you want to tell me how a tissue with your saliva on it ended up covered in Elena Fernandez's blood?'

He shrugged. 'No comment.'

'Is it because you murdered her on the night of November twelfth?'

'No.'

'Last time we arrested you, Mr Dixon, we weren't in possession of this evidence and I wasn't able to ask you about it. Now we are, and you're telling me you have no explanation for it?'

'Right.'

'This tissue is a direct link between you and a murder victim. We have video footage which shows you talking to Elena three months earlier, on July seventeenth, at the Southbank Centre. I've already spoken to the CPS and advised them that we'll be seeking to charge you with murder. Do you understand how serious this is, Mr Dixon?'

He didn't reply.

'If there's anything you'd like to tell me,' said Smith, 'now would be the time.'

Dixon's broad shoulders dropped. He seemed to be thinking. He leant across to his lawyer and they exchanged a few whispers. Then he took a deep breath and made eye contact with Smith.

'I met Elena at the feminism talk. I met a lot of women there. It was part of my business development work. I like a bit of a flirt.' He smiled, looking away. 'My clients like it too. I was there to offer my coaching services. But I didn't kill that woman, or anyone else. I swear.'

Smith could see he was struggling with something. 'That's not what this evidence suggests,' she said, tapping her finger on the photo in front of him.

'Look, on the twelfth of November, I was in north London. With…' He swallowed. 'With some men.'

'Can you elaborate on that, please?' asked Smith.

Dixon blinked, and when he spoke again, his voice was low and quiet. 'I was at a chemsex party.'

'What?'

'I… I went to a flat in Kentish Town. There were twenty or so guys there. We took some G.'

'GHB?' Smith knew the drug was popular on the gay party scene, though it'd also been used as a date-rape narcotic in numerous sexual assaults.

'Yeah. And some crystal meth. And we fucked each other. All night. Which is pretty much what I've been doing for the past two weeks as well. Happy now?'

'So, you were at a sex party for gay men?'

'I'm not gay,' replied Dixon. 'I'm MSM. A man who has sex with men.'

Dixon's lawyer cleared her throat. 'So, as you've heard, detective, my client could not have been responsible for this crime and, by extension, any of the linked events. He can provide addresses and some names of witnesses to his presence at this, er… chemsex party, and his mobile phone data will corroborate his location, miles away from the murder of Elena Fernandez. You'll find he was engaged in similar activity when your other victims were attacked, should we need to respond to associated charges. My client has informed me that, in one instance, there's even a video of said activity.'

Smith was stunned. For the past two weeks, Op Norton had been focussed almost exclusively on finding Paul Dixon. The tissue had made him their prime suspect. It was concrete, physical evidence you could rely on, not the vague predictions of Lockhart's psychologist friend Dr Green, whose crystal ball gazing sounded like something off a horoscope. And, now, Dixon was offering what appeared to be solid proof of his innocence.

'The tissue,' she began. 'You have to explain why—'

'Coincidence,' replied the lawyer. 'My client wipes his mouth at the theatre talk. The victim pockets the tissue, perhaps not realising it's been used, and it sits in her clothing for three months until the night of her murder. Your tissue doesn't even prove my client was in Deptford, let alone that he murdered Elena Fernandez.' The lawyer forced a small, tight laugh. 'I'm sure we all have tissues in our pockets which have been there for weeks, especially if they're items we don't wear often. It's not enough for a murder charge. And you know that, Detective.'

Smith hated to admit it, but the lawyer was right. Obviously, they'd need to go through Dixon's alibis and check everything in detail. But an uneasy feeling was growing in her that, for the last fortnight or more, they'd been after the wrong man. And worse, perhaps, that their error had enabled the Throat Ripper to kill again.

She tried to concentrate on wrapping up the interview, on the next procedural steps.

But all Smith could think about was her earlier suspicion, before they'd identified Paul Dixon. Her gut instinct.

The man with form for choking women, who'd been out on his scooter the night Elena had died. The man she'd failed to follow and not told Lockhart about.

Dean Waters.

∗

Lexi was wrapped in a bathrobe, sitting in bed with her laptop open. A hard CrossFit session after work had helped clear her head, although she'd walked home with frequent glances around her. Dan would've been proud of her situational awareness, but it wasn't really a conscious effort to be safer. It was the product of deep suspicion that had spread its tentacles around her, making her look twice at every man she passed in the street, even men she knew. Wondering if any one of them was responsible for cold, deadly violence against a woman. Choking her to death. And doing it again, and again, and again. It was terrorism; exactly the kind of fear this serial murderer wanted to cause. Lexi's empathy told her that she wouldn't be the only woman feeling that way in London right now.

The anxiety might've started to wane, if Paul Dixon was going to be charged with the Op Norton murders. But she knew that wasn't happening. Half an hour ago, Dan told her that he now thought someone else was responsible and Dixon would probably be released in the morning. The news made Lexi feel like a fraud. She'd delivered her theory on victim choice as if it was about Dixon. She'd fitted the facts to that assumption. It was a basic error of science, and she should've known better, but she'd done it anyway.

Still, she believed her principle was correct. And if the killer was still out there, it meant he had one more victim in mind for his campaign. Expert power: a woman whose knowledge and skills gave her power. That could be a whole lot of women.

So, she was back online, posing as 'Blake' and currently in a private chat with the guy who called himself BloodCel. They'd traded some views about Coco's murder, BloodCel openly gleeful about it. Lexi had to fight her conscience, but she knew she was close. BloodCel had already brought her into the invite-only threads, but she needed to go further. Finally, she made her move and typed:

*So, when u gonna introduce me to Priapus? I need to learn from that dude*

There was nothing for a while, then BloodCel replied:

*OK. What u wanna learn bro?*

Lexi's pulse quickened, and she could see her fingertips trembling above the keys.

*Got plans of my own, u know?*

*Sure :)*

Just as she was working out what else to put, a new private message window popped up. It was Priapus. His opening line was simple:

*You wanted to speak to me?*

Lexi closed her eyes. There was no going back from here. She typed, carefully:

*I wanna be like the Throat Ripper. I'll do whatever it takes.*

Before Priapus could reply, there was a knock on her door. It opened and Liam came into her room. He was holding his laptop.

'Y'all right, hen?'

She closed the chat window on her screen, cursing inwardly.

'Hey, Liam,' she smiled. 'What's up?'

He shook his head. 'Nay good men out there, eh?' He perched next to her and showed her the screen. It was a dating website.

'Jeez, tell me about it. So… your thing the other week didn't work out, huh?'

'What thing?' He frowned.

'The thing… uh, I thought there was a guy you'd hooked up with?'

He stared blankly for a moment before something clicked. 'Oh, aye. A hook up. Nay more than that.'

'My bad.' He was so close she could smell him, a musky, male smell.

'Did I tell you about the time I got dumped?' he said.

Lexi put her laptop to one side. 'No,' she replied, intrigued. 'Who was the dumbass guy that did that?'

'Girl. Dumbass *girl*.'

'What?'

'Yeah. I wasn't always into men. We were together quite a while. Then she dropped me, pretty much overnight. For a friend of mine.'

'Holy shit!'

'Yeah. Can you believe that?'

'Hell, no. That sucks.' She paused. 'You wanna talk about it?' She shuffled over on the bed to make room for him and he wriggled in.

'It's a sad wee story,' he said.

Lexi met his gaze. 'I'm listening.'

# CHAPTER FIFTY-THREE

Lockhart felt as if they were back to square one. Smith had updated him on the Paul Dixon interview at Kingston police station, and on Dixon's apparently solid alibi for at least two of the murders. It had shaken Lockhart's confidence that he'd pushed their suspect strategy so hard on one guy, almost entirely on the basis of DNA, and it'd turned out to be wrong. Could he trust his own judgement? And would his colleagues trust him? He needed their belief and effort more than ever, now. Far from what they'd all thought that morning, this wasn't over.

Before leaving Jubilee House, Lockhart had sent most of his team home with instructions to rest and come back early tomorrow. A few with pressing actions had remained: Smith was writing up her interview and Khan was making calls to follow-up on Dixon's alibis. Two other detectives were still working on CCTV from the vicinity of Coco's murder in Shoreditch last night, having obtained some promising film from a traffic camera. The recording showed a scooter rider, much like the one near Elena Fernandez's office, approaching and leaving the street where Coco lived around the estimated time of death.

It was after 9 p.m., now, and Lockhart's final task of the day was to conduct the check he'd assigned to Smith that morning: had Coco been to the feminism talk? No one in his team had seen her in the video footage, and she wasn't on the attendance list. He didn't expect to find anything at the theatre. He wanted to do the visit and drive home, grab a Stella or two – just to help him relax – and get his head down. But, after failing to locate Kim Hardy's friend Suzy last night, Lockhart knew he should probably go on to Dagenham and keep searching. If what Pagett had told him was accurate, Suzy could be the key. And there was always the chance of finding something on Jess out there, too.

The fact that he wasn't focussing on his wife made Lockhart feel uneasy. Guilty, even. Jess was still the most important part of his life; nothing had changed about that. But he knew that the lead on her was thin and the pressure on him from top brass, media, colleagues and himself to catch this killer was starting to push her aside in his mind. He had to fight that. As Green reminded him, there was always hope.

He'd called ahead to check Will Jacobson was still at the Southbank Centre. Inside the building, he found the theatre manager ensconced in his office, surrounded by the usual chaos.

'How do you find anything in here?' asked Lockhart.

Jacobson moved some papers and gave a lopsided grin. 'I sort of know where most stuff is.' He shrugged. 'Yannis and I get by, just about.'

Lockhart had forgotten about the assistant. 'Where's Mr Dimitriou?' He gestured to the computer whizz's empty desk, which was piled with debris, including a stack of coffee cups.

'At home, sick,' replied Jacobson. 'It's been a nightmare, to be honest. I might do most of the talking, but it's Yannis that keeps this place running. You really notice when he's not here.'

'What's wrong with him? Anything serious?'

'Don't think so.' Jacobson sighed. 'He says flu, but I reckon he's just a bit run-down. Stressed.'

'Yeah, I know the feeling,' said Lockhart, glancing at the monitor. 'Did you have a chance to do those searches yet?'

'Just finishing them off now.' Jacobson rotated the screen slightly towards him. 'No luck so far, though. Seems like Coco

Adams didn't come here. I checked under Colette, too.' He passed over some print-outs.

Lockhart flicked through them, noting the system search queries and lack of hits. 'How far back?'

'Six months. I can do a year, if you like?'

Lockhart suspected that wouldn't get them much further, but it was worth doing. 'That'd be great, cheers.'

'No worries.' Jacobson nodded and began typing. 'We've got time, our shows are done for the night.'

'Appreciate it.'

Lockhart was already starting to shift his opinion. The feminism talk may have been where the killer selected his initial victims, but he seemed to have moved on, now. And that meant his next target – someone with 'expert power', if Green was right – could be almost anyone. He'd spoken to her twice by phone today, each skirting around the guilt and frustration at their mistake, profiling the wrong influencer. She was still obsessed with her internet-based lead, but Lockhart didn't hold out much hope for that. He was foolish to rely on Green for optimism. She wasn't his saviour. He thought about that while an hourglass rotated interminably on the computer screen.

'Nope, sorry. Nothing.' Jacobson displayed the results. 'You're welcome to have a play with it, if you want? I know it's probably not in line with data protection or whatever, but I won't tell.'

'Thanks. Don't worry about it, though. I think I'm done.'

Lockhart left the building and stepped into the freezing night air. Watching the lights from the opposite bank sparkle and shimmer on the black Thames water, self-doubt began creeping over him. Staring at the river's undulating surface, opaque and slick as oil, he knew he was failing. Failing to do the one thing he'd promised Jess, promised himself: protect the people of London. A heaviness grew in his limbs. Maybe he should just forget Dagenham and go straight home. He hadn't found anything on his previous visits east. And there was beer in his fridge…

Then his phone rang, snapping him out of it. It was Smith.

'Sorry to bother you, guv.'

'It's fine. This about Dixon?'

'No.'

'OK.'

There was a pause on the other end.

'Max?' He couldn't tell if she was still there.

'I've got something to tell you, guv,' said Smith. 'I should've said it before, but I didn't. And now I know I've screwed up.'

'Go on.'

'It's about Dean Waters.'

*

It'd been a stroke of genius to use that bitch's phone to schedule a post of her own body on Instagram. The brothers had clearly enjoyed that and their jubilation had lifted him, briefly. Like a drug, though, the effects were increasingly short-lived and his euphoria had given way to self-loathing again. He tried to motivate himself by focussing on the inspiration he was providing to his fellow meninists to reclaim male power. They were writing online about the confidence his campaign was giving them to take their own action. That was something to be proud of.

One incel from the forum had seemed particularly ready. His handle online was everythin_suxx19 and he went by the name Blake. Using his Priapus alias, they'd made contact earlier that evening. Blake seemed like a fanatic. Almost too eager, in some ways. A small alarm bell rang in his head, but not enough to withdraw. Blake's praise for the Throat Ripper was life-affirming. He'd just need to do his homework on the young man.

It also made him realise that he hadn't thought about the Guru so much, lately. That was significant. Coupled with the adulation of others and Blake wanting to learn from the Throat Ripper, with Priapus as the go-between, his status was changing. He was becoming independent.

Maybe he was even becoming a guru to others, now. He imagined how much more damage he could do with that kind of influence. Calling brothers to take up arms, to fight. To kill. All over the world, perhaps.

The thought excited him. Slowly, he slid a hand between his thighs and began massaging. It felt nice and he closed his eyes for a moment.

But he couldn't get ahead of himself. He had a plan to complete, first. Returning to the web browser, he opened a new private window and entered his search terms:

*Dr Lexi Green, psychologist, London.*

# CHAPTER FIFTY-FOUR

Driving towards the docklands of east London, Smith felt as if she was getting a second chance. She'd fessed up to Lockhart last night about her unauthorised surveillance of Dean Waters, and how she'd seen him leave home on a black scooter with a top box shortly before Elena Fernandez died. The guvnor had been pretty good about it, all things considered. He'd given her a ticking off but thanked her for the honesty. There was no mention of reporting it, for the minute; Lockhart just wanted to concentrate on what they should do next. With Paul Dixon apparently in the clear, the obvious step was to visit Dean Waters again and find out what he was doing two nights ago when Coco Adams was murdered.

Smith had told Lockhart she felt awful about it, but he'd reassured her that Waters wasn't a clear suspect. He had no forensic links to the crimes – although his scooter would now be the subject of investigation – and, when they'd shown his photograph to Michael Litman in Hatton Garden, the jeweller hadn't picked him out from the pack of six mugshots. Then again, Litman hadn't picked out any of their people of interest. He'd also reminded them that neither his eyesight at distance, nor the lighting in his workshop, were particularly good. They might as well have shown him a six-pack of characters from *The Muppet Show* or their own MIT.

Outside Westland House, Khan brought the unmarked car to a stop. Smith gestured across the street below the tower block where a battered, cheap-looking scooter rested on its kickstand.

'That's the bike registered to Waters,' she said. 'It's not the same plate as in the CCTV from Shoreditch…'

'But he could've used fake ones.'

'Exactly. And Damon Pagett told the boss he'd seen a man on a black scooter outside the hotel just before Kim Hardy was murdered.'

Khan nodded, his jaws working hard on a piece of gum.

'Right.' Smith took a breath. 'Let's go and see if Mr Waters's alibi is any better than last time.'

They photographed his scooter and entered the building, taking the lift to the tenth floor. When they reached flat number 52, Smith was surprised to find the door ajar.

'Mr Waters?' she called through the gap. 'It's the police.'

There was no answer.

'Mr Waters, are you there?'

After a few seconds' silence, Khan raised his eyebrows. 'Quick look?'

Smith knew she'd already broken the rules once on Op Norton. But this was too important. Time for a tried-and-tested trick. 'I'm sure I heard something from inside,' she said.

'Me too,' said Khan, nudging the door wide open with a knuckle and peering in.

The hallway was dark, but lights were on in the living room at the end. They moved carefully towards it, checking left and right. The other rooms were dark and there was no sign of Waters. But he'd clearly been here very recently.

'Check this out, Max.' Khan pointed to the small folding table in the cramped living room. On it sat a laptop, some electrical components, a scattering of tools and an open beer can. It was much like she'd glimpsed over Waters's shoulder when they'd visited a month ago. But what she hadn't seen from the doorway was the clear plastic bag. Nestled among the spanners, pliers and screwdrivers, it contained a set of white cable ties. Just like the ones used to lash the victims' ankles and wrists to the chairs in which they died.

Smith extracted a pen from her jacket pocket and used the tip of it to press the laptop's space bar. The screen came to life. The webpage it displayed looked like a chatroom. She scanned the text. Then she read it again, slowly, to make sure she wasn't imagining it.

'Jesus Christ.'

It was a conversation about rape. Waters appeared to have posted some enthusiastic messages of support, claiming *the slags want it*, before encouraging others to *have a go* and *be in control*. There was mention of using drugs like GHB to incapacitate the women.

'You horrible little bastard,' whispered Smith.

'I think he's our guy, Max.' Khan's voice was low and steady, but his fists were clenched at his side. He turned towards a set of shelves against the wall. 'Let's see what else is here.'

'Be careful what you touch,' she said. 'The cable ties alone could be enough for an arrest. Then we can come back and do this properly. I'll stick my nose in the kitchen before we go. You have a glance in the bedroom when you're done in here.'

She returned up the narrow hallway and stepped into the tiny room. Despite the lack of light, she could make out half a dozen cans of strong beer piled beside the sink. They were open, crushed and, therefore, empty. She was crossing to a cork board with scraps of paper pinned to it when a voice made her freeze.

'What the fuck are you doing?'

Smith recognised the high-pitched tone: Waters. She edged towards the kitchen doorway as footsteps pounded down the hall.

'What you doin' in my house, eh?' The words were slurred, confirming who'd drunk those beers.

'Your door was open,' she heard Khan reply.

'You're on my computer and all?' yelled Waters. 'You've got no right to be 'ere. Get out!'

Smith stepped into the hallway and approached the living room. She could see Waters was agitated, pacing around. Then he squared up to Khan. That usually didn't end well for anyone.

'Mr Waters,' she said gently.

He turned around.

'We saw the door open and were concerned for your safety,' she continued. 'We'd just like to ask you a few more routine questions, please.'

'No way!' he cried, shaking his head. 'No fuckin' way.' He spat on the carpet.

Then he ran at her.

Smith put her hands up to defend herself as Waters charged forwards, shoving her against the wall before he barrelled past her and out through the front door.

'Oi, stop!' she shouted.

'You OK?' Khan was next to her.

'Yeah.' Smith picked herself up. 'Come on. You take the stairs, I'll get the lift down, we nick him halfway.'

Khan was already running.

Smith followed him along the walkway, jabbing the button to summon the elevator as Khan descended via the open stairwell. Ten seconds later, it appeared. She hit 'G' and then '>|<' to close the doors, willing the numbers to drop faster. At 'G', the doors pinged open and she dived out.

No sign of Waters.

She headed for the stairs, taking them two at a time as she climbed. Reaching the second floor, she heard footsteps and, just before the third floor, she saw Waters. He clocked her and broke left along the walkway. He was trapped.

'It's OK, Mr Waters,' she said, advancing towards him, palms up in the no-threat stance. He was wild-eyed, panting like a dog.

'I'm not going back to prison,' he said. 'Never again.'

'We just want to talk to you,' she replied calmly, though her heart was hammering against her ribcage.

Waters closed his eyes and emitted a howl of anguish.

Then he began to climb over the walkway.

Smith bolted towards him. 'No, stop!'

He lowered himself down as she reached him. He was clinging to the concrete with his hands alone.

'There's nowhere to go.' Smith was unable to keep the urgency from her voice. Khan arrived alongside her.

'Let us help you back up, Mr Waters.' She held out her right hand. Her strongest hand. Khan was offering his too. Smith leant over and saw his legs flailing below. She got a stab of vertigo. It was a long way down.

Waters shot out a hand and grabbed her sleeve. He was gasping, frantic. Khan reached forward for Waters's wrist. Then his grasp on Smith's jacket slipped and, before Khan could hold him, he was gone.

The piercing scream was followed by a dull crump.

# PART FIVE

# CHAPTER FIFTY-FIVE

'Waters is still in a medically induced coma.' Lockhart flicked through a pile of papers on his desk and extracted the one he was looking for. 'Both legs broken, massive spinal injuries, internal organ damage. Medic says that even if he lives, he'll never walk again.'

Green produced her fancy Montblanc pen from her jeans pocket, where it seemed to live, and tapped on the desk slowly. She was always doing something with that bloody pen. Tapping, clicking, twirling it in her fingers. He was about to reach across the desk and grab the damned thing when, as though she'd read his mind, she stopped.

'I'm not sure how I feel about that,' she said.

'Meaning?'

'Well, it's, like, really sad what happened to Waters.' She shrugged. 'But the guy was a grade-A asshole.'

'Is that your professional diagnosis, Doctor?'

'Just my personal opinion.'

'Right.' Lockhart offered the report to Green. 'I agree with you on the arsehole bit.'

'Thanks.' She took it and he watched her begin skimming the front page.

'Not into karma, then?' he asked.

'I don't know if anyone *deserves* to fall three storeys onto concrete.' She puffed out her cheeks, exhaled slowly and thumbed to the second page. 'Even if he *is* a killer.'

Lockhart jerked his head across the room to the desks where his team sat. 'Some of our lot wouldn't see it that way. Despite the fact our job's about using the law to get justice, there are plenty of coppers who wouldn't mind dishing out their own bit of revenge every now and then.'

'That's not cool,' said Green without looking up from the page. 'Judge, jury and executioner?'

'Don't get me wrong,' he replied. 'I'm a detective, not a vigilante. I believe in the law. And justice. I'm not pleased that Dean Waters has been in a coma for ten days. I'm not pleased that two of my best officers are confined to desk duties while the investigation into their conduct takes place. And I'm not pleased the media's been all over us, talking about "Watersgate" and the rest. All I care about is whether or not Waters is the Throat Ripper and, if he is, can we prove it in court?'

'I hate that name.' She shivered and lifted her eyes to meet his. 'So, there's no clear evidence against him?'

'Not yet. I'll spare you the details.'

Since Dean Waters had dropped from the balcony of his tower block, MIT 8 had been focussing their attention on him as a suspect. There was enough circumstantial material to warrant serious investigation: his record of alleged violence against women, including choking; his scooter with its top box, like in the CCTV; uncertainty over his alibis for the murders; the plastic cable ties in his flat; and his extensive activity on misogynistic websites. But, so far, they hadn't got him.

They were just lucky he wasn't going anywhere. And, after they'd screwed up with Dixon, Lockhart was keeping an open mind on Waters's guilt. That hadn't stopped several of his team deciding the ex-con was definitely their man. But, if it was Waters, he must've had access to some other place where he kept the tools of his attacks; crime scene investigators had found nothing more in his home.

'I wanted to show you this, though.' Lockhart pointed at the document. 'Full technical report from our computer forensics team. There's content from the chatrooms he was in, stuff he'd downloaded, contact lists.'

She flipped a few more pages. 'It's seriously thorough.'

Lockhart cleared his throat. 'I thought, you know, since you were looking at internet-based leads, maybe there'd be something on there you'd recognise.'

Green tilted her head. 'Didn't you say my online profiling project was a waste of time?'

'I don't think those were my exact words. Anyway, the facts have changed, now. You can see how important this menisphere is to Waters.'

'Manosphere.'

'Whatever it's called.'

'I'll take a look at it,' she said. 'I'm guessing I can't take it home?'

'Nope. But you can read it here as much as you like.'

'OK.' She waved the pen. 'Can I write on it?'

'Yeah.'

'Cool.' She carried on reading and Lockhart returned his attention to the paperwork on his desk. They worked in silence for a few minutes before Green sat up straight.

'Oh my god,' she blurted. 'Did you see the Hugh Chadwick article this morning?'

Lockhart snorted. 'Couldn't miss it. "My love life with Throat Ripper's victim". I thought Chadwick was bereaved. Why would he do that?'

'Money?' suggested Green. 'I know your tabloids would pay a hell of a lot for a story like that. There's so much interest in this case right now.'

'The guy's loaded.' Lockhart shook his head. 'He doesn't need their cash.'

'Attention, then? Narcissistic personality?'

'Maybe.' He leant back in his chair. 'It's totally insensitive. I can't imagine what Natasha's family think of it.'

'It's horrible.'

They worked on, Green reading the computer report and Lockhart preparing his briefing notes. He and Porter were meeting the top brass that afternoon for an update on Op Norton. They'd have some serious questions to answer, and Lockhart had no doubt that his boss would take pleasure in passing the hardest ones to him.

Porter had been steadily upping the pressure on Lockhart since discovering – via an explosive call from Newham MIT – that he'd secured access to Damon Pagett. There'd been one almighty bollocking where Lockhart had been summoned to Porter's office and shouted at with such force that people on the floors above and below had heard it. Burrows was considering major disciplinary proceedings. Now, Porter was demanding twice-daily updates on Norton while making it clear that, because of his disobedience, any mistakes were squarely on Lockhart's shoulders. It might mean his time as SIO or in the MIT generally would be short, but if that was the price he had to pay for following his instincts then so be it. Whatever the personal consequence, he'd bypass them all again to get the job done, if necessary.

The previous week, in one of their briefings, Porter had asked to meet Green, *to see where their money was going*, he'd said. Lockhart had reminded him that the psychologist was working for free, but the DCI still wanted to speak to her. Lockhart couldn't quite explain it, but something made him feel slightly protective of Green. It was ridiculous, he knew that. But he couldn't help it. It was the same way he'd felt about Jess.

After another hour, Lockhart glanced at his watch. 'Do you want to get some lunch?' he asked her. 'My shout.'

'Sure, thanks.' Her face lit up with a smile whose attractiveness took him by surprise. He immediately felt guilty and looked away.

'Least I can do when you're giving up your Saturday morning,' mumbled Lockhart, grabbing his North Face jacket. 'Come on, then.'

She put the report down, stood and pocketed her pen.

'I'm still in contact with Priapus, you know,' said Green as they took the stairs down.

'Who?'

'The guy on the incel web forum. The one who says he knows the Throat Ripper.'

'You think he's legit?'

'No reason he's not. He's been a little quiet lately, but I wanted to try meeting him.'

Lockhart paused on the stairs, turned to her. '*Meeting* him? But he thinks you're a bloke.'

'Yeah, there is that.' She shrugged and continued down the steps. 'I'll come up with something, if it happens.'

He snorted a laugh. 'What, like a false moustache?'

Green clicked her fingers. 'Hey! I have an idea. Do you wanna meet him? You could be Blake. I mean, you're a little old, but…'

'I'm not *old*.'

'Older than my character Blake.'

'Fair enough.'

'How about it?'

'I haven't got time,' he replied.

'OK, fine. I'll meet Priapus, then.'

Lockhart realised she was serious. 'That's a bad idea, Lexi.'

'No, it's not. I think it's the best way to find out about him, put a face to an alias. If he's telling the truth, there could be a link to Waters… or someone else,' she added. 'It could form part of the evidential case against the killer.'

Lockhart shook his head. 'It's too risky to just go off and meet some man who you know is a misogynist with violent ideas. And if he doesn't know anything about the killer, it's totally pointless as well. Don't do it.'

'But we have to meet him to find out,' she protested. 'In any case, it probably won't be me that gets face to face with him. How about someone like DC Khan?'

'No chance. He's basically not allowed out of this building at the moment.' They paused by the door at the bottom of the stairs. 'My advice is let it go, Lexi. You've found out about this sad little community and that was really useful. It helped your profiling, and it gives you the tools to analyse Waters's online activity now. But that's probably where it should end. And if it doesn't end, then you've got to be honest: are you doing this for the case, or for yourself?'

'That isn't fair.' She gripped the handle and yanked the heavy door open. 'I think there's something there. I know there is. I'll find a way to meet him.'

'I'm telling you, don't.' He could hear his voice rising.

Green stopped and fixed him with a stare. 'You don't get to tell me what to do.'

'If you do this,' he said firmly, 'I can't guarantee your safety.'

She tilted her chin up. 'I don't need you to protect me, Dan. I'll look after myself.'

Lockhart saw the determination in her face. He wasn't talking her out of it. He let out a deep sigh and held up his hands. 'All right, well, you've been warned.'

'Appreciate it.' She turned and went through the door.

'Fuck's sake,' he muttered, following her.

They emerged into the reception area of Jubilee House and, as Lockhart made his reflex check of the room, he did a double-take. Sitting across the lobby was Dr Sam Byers, a newspaper folded on his lap. The academic stood as soon as he spotted Lockhart but seemed to hesitate when he noticed Green.

'Dr Byers,' said Lockhart.

'Oh, um, hello.' Byers scratched his head. 'Hi, Lexi.'

'Hey, Sam.'

There was a moment's silence.

'Did you get my texts?' Byers asked Green, his voice almost a whisper.

'Uh, yeah, but… I've been, like, so busy.'

'Of course, of course.' Byers shook his head quickly.

Lockhart looked from him to Green and back. Again, his protective instinct kicked in, in a way that he couldn't quite explain. 'You two know each other?'

'Yes,' Byers said.

'No.' Green spoke at the same time as him.

Lockhart gave her a look that said: *you can explain later.* He zipped up his jacket. 'Can we help you, Dr Byers?'

'Sam, please.'

'Sam.'

'Well, er…' He brandished the newspaper, unfolding it clumsily to display the double-page spread of Hugh Chadwick's tasteless kiss-and-tell article about Natasha Mayston. 'I saw this piece this morning.'

Lockhart shoved his hands in his pockets and rocked on his heels. 'So did we.'

'I'm sure. The thing is, you see, when I saw it, it must've triggered off something in my memory. Subconscious or whatever. Lexi would probably have a name for it.' He gave a breathy laugh that died when he realised that neither Lockhart nor Green were smiling.

'OK.'

'And, I remembered that I'd seen this man before. When I came in for my interview, you asked me about meeting the women who'd died. I talked about the theatre, but I didn't remember seeing the second woman. Sophie.'

Lockhart coughed.

'So, anyway, when I read that piece this morning, I recognised the man. Chadwick.' He pointed unnecessarily at the red-headed banker, posing thoughtfully in an open-necked shirt below the

Facebook photo of him and Natasha on their Swiss skiing holiday. 'And I knew that I'd seen him before. It was at the theatre talk. He was hanging around at the drinks event afterwards.'

'OK,' Lockhart said again. They already knew that. He had to acknowledge, for the last few weeks, Hugh Chadwick had been nothing more than a peripheral figure in their suspect strategy.

'He was there,' said Byers.

'All right, well, thanks very much for your time, Sam. We're actually just heading out now, but we'll call you if anything—'

'No, you don't understand,' said Byers. 'Sorry, I haven't finished. This Chadwick guy was there. And after the drinks, as people were heading off, he was watching Sophie.'

'Hang on. Sophie Wright?'

'Yes.'

'Not Natasha?'

'No. I'm sure of it. I had seen her, I just forgot.'

Lockhart recalled that Sophie and Chadwick had been at university together. He was thinking, now. 'Then what?'

'And then he followed her out of the Southbank Centre.'

Unzipping his jacket, Lockhart took out his wallet and held out twenty pounds to Green.

'Lexi, would you mind grabbing us some lunch, please? Anything's good. I just need to get the statement from Sam about this and then we'll catch up in a bit. Sorry, is that OK?'

Green clenched her jaw as she studied the note in silence for a moment. 'You know what?' she replied, 'you can get your own lunch.' Then she spun on her heels and marched out of the building.

# CHAPTER FIFTY-SIX

After their disagreement over her internet lead, followed by him ditching her for Sam Byers in the office, Lexi and Dan hadn't spoken for a few days. She was still mad at him for ignoring her effort, for undermining her profiling. Well, if he didn't need her, then she didn't need him. She was determined to prove that there was a genuine link to the killer online. And, now, she had the chance. It'd taken weeks of work since she first heard about him but, finally, Priapus had agreed to meet this evening. Screw what Dan thought; she was going to blow this case wide open. It was on.

'Remind me where we're off to, again?' said Liam, as they rattled east on the underground train.

'Barking.'

He lowered his voice, though there were few people in the carriage now it was late. 'And I'm supposed to be this guy, Blake, am I?' He made quotation marks with his fingers for her alias.

'Yeah. You were an actor in college, right?'

'Aye,' he nodded.

'So, pretend to hate women.'

'Hm.'

'You could just imagine you're talking about your ex.'

Liam froze, blinking. Lexi knew she'd said the wrong thing.

She laid a hand on his arm. 'Jeez. Sorry, that wasn't what I meant, I just—'

'It's OK.' He flashed a smile. 'Really.'

'Can you do an American accent?' she asked.

Liam shifted in his seat and licked his lips. 'You want me to talk like an American?' he said, perfectly impersonating one of her compatriots. Not a distinctive accent of the West Coast, Deep South or northeast cities, but more like a generic movie or TV character. Definitely passable to a Brit.

'There you go!' Lexi nudged him. 'That was awesome.' She was psyched that Liam had agreed to help her. Apart from the benefit to the case, she hoped this would bring them closer together. They were showing trust in each other. And, Lexi had to admit, after discovering that Liam used to be in a relationship with a woman, she was showing a little more interest in him than previously. It was cool that they were doing this like a team. It was an adventure, and she was ready: phone, pen and notebook in her pockets. She'd borrowed Sarah's digital camera with its zoom lens. Her plan was to observe the encounter, maybe get a photo or two of Priapus, if she could.

'And where did this lad want to meet?' Liam had reverted to his usual strong Scottish voice.

'By the canal in the park.'

'At night?' He arched his eyebrows. 'Bit sketchy, isn't it?'

'His choice.' She shrugged. 'I guess he didn't want it to be anywhere too public. I mean, he's obviously security conscious. Which tells me he's worth meeting. I'll be watching from across the way.'

'It's going to be bloody freezing out there.' Liam folded his arms. 'Lucky I've got my winter woollies on, eh?'

'Me too.' Lexi punched the quilting of her down jacket.

'And you want me to find out about the Throat Ripper?' He turned to her, wide-eyed, trilling the Rs in the name. 'Like, personal details and stuff?'

'Yeah, if you get the chance. You wanna go through it one more time?'

'No need, hen. I'm all over it. I know Blake's story.' He sucked his teeth. 'And I know what his plans are, too.'

'OK, perfect.' Lexi sat back in her seat and checked the map opposite. They were over halfway there, now. And she had no intention of turning back.

*

Having left Smith and Khan in the office, crunching data on a late shift, Lockhart was driving east in his Defender. His destination was the same as it had been for six other evenings over the past fortnight: Dagenham. The district which nestled north of the river between Barking and Romford was the place he still hoped to find Suzy, Kim Hardy's friend. Night after night, he'd spoken to sex workers on the streets, as well as people in bars and late-night fast-food restaurants, all with no result.

He knew that, much like the possibility of finding his wife there, it was a long shot. But if he just kept going, sooner or later they'd find one piece of evidence that'd nail the Throat Ripper – whether that was Waters or someone else. The killer had led a charmed life so far, but his luck couldn't go on for ever. And, when it ran out, Lockhart would be there.

Apart from his cold weather clothes, he had minimal equipment: his phone, Leatherman multi-tool, and a couple of photographs. One picture was of Kim Hardy, to jog people's memories about Suzy, and the other was of Jess. Just in case. He knew the image of his wife so well he could conjure every detail of it in his mind without taking it out of his pocket. Her wide, beautiful smile still made his heart ache. He could never forget it. And he could never lose hope.

Common sense told him to give up, go home, rest. Drink Stella. But his mum's words echoed in his mind. He could see her kindly expression, the lines around her eyes, as she reminded him what'd happened when he fell out of the tree as a kid.

*You don't know the meaning of give up, do you?*

*

It'd worked out better than he could've planned. He'd suspected from their first, dubious exchange online that there was something odd about 'Blake'. At first, he'd thought it was just enthusiasm for the cause. But the passion didn't seem to be fuelled by pain, like it was for most of the brothers. Blake was too upbeat. Then there were his turns of phrase. Blake was American, sure. But some of his meninist expressions were a bit off. Slightly wrong. Not by much, but enough for him to investigate.

Fortunately, he knew a thing or two about computers, so it wasn't hard. And what he'd found had angered and excited him in equal measure. It turned out that Blake and Dr Lexi Green had a hell of a lot in common. Obviously, they were both American expats in London. But they also appeared to be online at the same time, using the same IP address. At first, he'd wondered if Blake was merely a colleague of the American bitch. But when his digging revealed that they were co-located in a hospital, a residential road in Tooting, and a third spot around the corner from Lockhart's office, there could be no doubt. The same time and place, over and over again, could only mean one thing.

Blake was Lexi Green, and Lexi Green was Blake.

He'd known that she was involved with Lockhart and his minions, ever since the televised press conference over a month ago. But he hadn't realised quite how devious the little slut was being. Trying to wheedle her way to the Throat Ripper by deceiving the brothers. It was typical of a woman to lie and cheat to get what she wanted. Well, she was about to get a whole lot more than she wanted.

He'd parked a rented van beside his chosen meeting location: an isolated spot with no cameras that he knew of, not too far from his private place. His Taser was charged and ready. He had that tingling feeling, like he'd experienced the first time the Guru had sent him a personal message. It was the same feeling you got before a first date. In some ways, that's what this was: a first date.

And, if all went according to plan, she'd be coming back to his tonight.

# CHAPTER FIFTY-SEVEN

Lockhart moved systematically north up the Heathway, stomping east and west along its side streets. He'd asked in three pubs, two fried chicken shops and a bookmaker. Nothing. Since it was so cold, there weren't many sex workers out in the open air. So, he was also keeping an eye out for the 'massage' adverts that could lead him to a brothel where he might find Suzy, or someone who knew how to find her.

After nearly an hour without success, he started to get that familiar feeling of failure. Then he rounded a corner and saw the woman. Lockhart stopped in his tracks. He hadn't seen her before.

She stood alone, clutching her handbag to her stomach. Not dressed for winter. She was shivering slightly. He watched her, his breath clouding in the night air. They were the only two people in the quiet road off the main strip. Somewhat reluctantly, she met his eyes and then looked away. But she didn't move.

He held up his warrant card as he approached her.

'Go fuck yourself,' she hissed, turning and marching in the opposite direction.

'Wait!' he called after her. 'I just want to ask you a question.'

She picked up her pace, stiletto heels click-clacking on the pavement.

'It's about Kim Hardy.'

She froze.

'I need to find her friend Suzy,' he said.

There was a moment's silence before the woman turned. 'That's me.'

*

Standing behind some trees, Lexi squinted through the camera's zoom lens. There wasn't a whole lot of light around the canal, but she could still make out Liam. He was some way off, sitting on a bench, waiting. They'd been there nearly a half hour, with no sign of Priapus yet. The cold was making Lexi's ears sting and she pulled her woolly hat down tighter on her head.

She watched as Liam stamped his feet, then stood and started rubbing his hands. She scanned the towpath beside the canal up one way, back past Liam, and down the other way. There was no one around. She sighed, swinging the lens back to the bench. But Liam was gone.

Dammit! Where was he? Shit. She swept the lens across the path one more time. What the hell was he doing? Now wasn't the time to just randomly go off someplace. She needed him there, otherwise Priapus might get spooked. Then she'd lose the chance to photograph him and find out who he really was. She told herself to relax. Liam was probably just taking a pee in the bushes. She heard some movement a way off, and a noise that sounded like a car door, but there was nothing more. Just silence and the occasional sound of a fox or distant vehicle.

After waiting a little to see if Liam came back, Lexi decided to call him. She stuffed the camera into one pocket and, with a frozen hand, fumbled in the other pocket for her phone. She ripped off a glove and hastily tapped the PIN. Got it wrong because she'd lost sensation in her fingertips. Swearing under her breath, she keyed it in again.

That was when something hit the back of her leg.

A sharp, stabbing pain, like cat claws. Digging right into her flesh.

Then a crackle and she was falling forward, unable to catch herself, unable to move.

Lexi smacked into the hard ground. Agony rippled through her limbs and skin as if her body was burning. She screamed but the noise was distorted, inhuman. She willed the pain to stop, knowing even as she did so that she had no control over it.

Her vision blurred, and the last thing she felt was a gloved hand covering her nose and mouth.

*

Inside the all-night café, Lockhart handed the steaming polystyrene cup of tea over to Suzy and sat down opposite her at the quiet corner table. He watched as she stirred in three sugars and slurped a mouthful, gasping at the heat, before warming her hands on the cup.

'I never believed Damon killed Kim,' she whispered. 'He was one of the nice ones.'

Lockhart had explained on the way to the café that he'd known Kim, that she'd helped him on a case. That she'd had the courage to act as a witness. That he'd liked her.

'I spoke to Damon in prison,' he said. 'He's on remand for Kim's murder.'

'Yeah, I know.'

'He said that you guys used to look out for each other. Send photos of clients, you know…'

'In case any of 'em got nasty. That's right. Like a bit of insurance or whatever.'

Lockhart blew on his own tea and took a sip. 'What about the night Kim died? She send you anything?'

Suzy shook her head. 'I tried to tell your lot about it. But did they listen? Did they fuck. They didn't even take a statement from me. No point, they said. *Unreliable.* Dickheads.'

That explained why the first he'd heard of Kim's friend was when he'd spoken to Damon. Newham MIT simply hadn't bothered to do their homework. Suzy hadn't featured in their witness strategy because they hadn't given her any credibility. Probably because of her job.

'Listen,' he said, looking her in the eye, 'I'm sorry about that. But those weren't my guys. That was a different team, and they've clearly missed something important.'

Suzy's gaze lost focus and she shook her head. 'Kim said that Damon was always gentle with her.'

'Did she send you anything that night? After Damon had left.'

'Yeah, she did. A photo. Not the clearest, but still…'

'Where is it?'

She fished in her bag and pulled out one phone. A cheap, pay-as-you-go handset. 'Not that,' she mumbled, dropping it back in and pulling out a second one. 'I think it's on here, somewhere. If it ain't been deleted. Hang on.' She unlocked the device and began searching. 'I have to change phones quite often, you know, what with work and that…'

Lockhart could feel his pulse quickening. Was it possible that, after all his efforts to find her, she'd had an image, and then lost it?

'Can you remember anything she said about the guy that visited her after Damon? Any texts or anything?'

'Er… let me think.' She stopped scrolling and covered her forehead with a hand. Lockhart waited. Twenty long seconds passed before she spoke again. 'Yeah, that's right. He'd come to her once before. She said they didn't do nothing that time, he just asked about prices and places they could go and that. What she'd do for what money. She always asked their names and probably most of 'em told her the first thing what come into their heads. John Smith or Tom Jones or whatever. But I remember him, cos she said he had a funny name. Mr Proplus, Mr Prepuss, something like that…'

'Priapus?'

Her face lit up. 'That's it. Priapus. I remember thinking, he must be foreign.'

He reached for his own phone. 'Keep looking for that photo, please, Suzy,' he said, selecting Smith's number and tapping the 'call' icon. He hoped she was still in the office.

*

As the ringtone sounded, Smith saw Lockhart's name on the screen and picked up.

'What's going on, boss? Are you still in Dagenham?'

'Priapus,' he said.

'What?' She glanced across at Khan, who'd stopped peering at a spreadsheet and was now looking at her.

'I want you to check our records of the equipment purchases for anything like Priapus, as a name.' He spelled it out to her.

'I'll start with the dental gags,' she said. 'That's the shortest list. Mo can check our metal balls list. Wait a sec.' She clamped the phone between ear and shoulder as she passed the instructions to Khan and they both began opening files, typing, clicking.

'Pri-a-pu—' She froze. 'It's here. Where did you get that name, boss?'

'Kim's friend,' replied Lockhart. 'What does it say about him?'

Khan had slid his chair next to her. 'Mr Priapus,' he read off the screen, 'ordered a dental gag online, from one of the Amazon marketplace suppliers, back in June.'

'It's got the name,' said Smith. 'And there's an address. Unit 12—' she gave him the rest. 'I'll text it to you.'

Scooting back to his computer, Khan was already keying in the details. 'It's a lock-up garage,' he stated.

'Did you get that, guv?' she told Lockhart. 'Looks like the place is a lock-up garage.'

'Listen,' replied her boss, 'I need to stay here a bit longer. Can you and Mo get over to the address and take a look, please?'

'Now?'

'Yeah.'

Smith glanced at Khan, who mouthed 'What?' at her. 'Er, Superintendent Burrows restricted us to desk duties, remember?' she said. 'Until the internal—'

'Just get over there. I've got your back.'

'Guv.'

Lockhart said, 'I should've listened to Lexi.' Then he hung up.

\*

Lockhart was onto his second cup of tea and had ordered bacon sandwiches for him and Suzy. He sat, waiting for her to locate the photograph – assuming she still had it – and trying not to let his impatience show. He'd called Green to ask her about the Priapus guy she'd mentioned. But she hadn't picked up, so he sent a text asking her to ring him back.

He stared out of the window, watching the late-night life of east London passing by. Two drunken pubgoers trying to find a cab. A street sweeper picking up trash around a homeless person bedded down in a shop doorway. A wandering man in a ragged suit, waving a Bible and shouting something about judgement on the wicked. A blacked-out 4 x 4 idling at traffic lights, the bass of its sound system making the café windows vibrate. A snapshot of the city he'd grown up in, his city. The place that'd sucked in thousands of people from all over the world for hundreds of years with the promise of a better life. How many of them did that dream work out for? And how many wished they'd—

'Got it.' Suzy's words broke his train of thought. 'This is the bloke what called himself Mr Priapus.'

Lockhart slammed his tea on the table, half of it slopping out. 'Show me.'

Suzy rotated the phone and held it out to him.

He zoomed in on the figure. The image quality was poor, the lighting low. But there was no mistaking its subject. This was Mr Priapus. The man who, in all likelihood, had murdered Kim, Natasha, Sophie, Elena and Coco.

Lockhart recognised him. And he knew Green would recognise him too.

Then it clicked: *expert power*.

# CHAPTER FIFTY-EIGHT

Lockhart remembered that Green had talked about trying to meet Priapus. She believed the man who used that alias was an associate of the killer, someone who knew the Throat Ripper personally. But, from what Suzy had told him, and from the name on the dental gag purchase, Lockhart suspected that Priapus *was* the Throat Ripper. Now, thanks to Suzy finding Kim's photo, he knew who that really was.

Last Saturday, Green had told him about her idea of getting a man to meet Priapus, pretending to be the Blake character she used online. But she'd also threatened to meet him herself. There was no doubt in Lockhart's mind that Green was at risk. Particularly as the next victim in the sequence – a woman representing 'expert power' – could easily be Green herself. And, given that she knew the man Lockhart had just identified, that risk was all too real. Real enough to make Lockhart act immediately.

He had to get hold of Green, firstly to check she was all right and warn her about their discovery, and secondly to see what else she could tell him about Priapus. He cursed himself for dismissing her lead earlier. He should've had more faith in her ability to understand the killer's mindset.

He should've had more faith in *her*.

Lockhart dialled her number again, willing her to pick up. This time, the call went straight to voicemail, as if the phone was switched off. He didn't like it at all. His threat assessment had just gone up a notch.

It was too late for Green to still be at work, but he googled a number for the hospital switchboard and called it anyway. He gave his name, rank and badge number to the operator, who put Lockhart on hold. He stood, pacing in the café while he waited for what felt like half an hour but was probably two minutes. Then she came back on the line to confirm that Dr Lexi Green was not on the premises. Lockhart asked for her 'next of kin' and was given the number for a friend called Sarah Tomkins, a social worker who lived with Green. He dialled the mobile straight away.

'Hello?'

'This is Detective Inspector Dan Lockhart from the Met Police,' he said, speaking quickly but clearly. 'I'm in one of the Major Investigation Teams.'

'OK. Is this about a client?'

'No, it's nothing to do with your work, Sarah. Your flatmate, Lexi Green, has been helping us on a murder case and—'

'Oh my god. The Throat Ripper?'

'Yes. I'm trying to get hold of Lexi, urgently. But she's not picking up her phone.'

'Hang on.' There was a pause and Lockhart heard some shuffling before Sarah called out Green's name a few times, with no audible response. 'She went out a couple of hours ago,' said Sarah, 'with our other flatmate, Liam. They were off somewhere in east London, Liam told me. Guess they haven't come back yet. Lexi!' she shouted again. 'Nope, she's not here. Sorry.'

'She's with Liam?' confirmed Lockhart.

'Yeah,' she replied. 'Is that important?'

'Listen, I have to—'

'Is everything OK?' Sarah asked. 'I mean, is Lexi all right?'

'I hope so. Thanks for your help.'

Lockhart ended the call. His heart was pounding, his mouth dry.

The waitress brought two bacon sandwiches over to their table. Lockhart gave Suzy his card with a mobile number for her to forward the photo of Mr Priapus. As she sent it to him, he slid his own plate towards her.

'You might as well have this one, too,' he said. 'I've got to go.'

Opening Smith's text with the address of the lock-up garage in Barking, he copied it into Google Maps, noticing the slight tremor in his fingers. The app told him it was a seventeen-minute car journey. Lockhart checked his watch. He reckoned he could make it in ten. He put a twenty-pound note on the tabletop for their bill and said goodbye to Suzy, promising her an update.

Then he was gone.

*

He had to pinch himself. It was almost too good to be true. He'd dreamt of this possibility from the first moment he laid eyes on her. Dr Lexi Green, clinical psychologist. A perfect female symbol of expert power. The fifth and final part of his masterplan. And here she was, strapped to the chair in his private place, ready to die. It was time to savour this moment.

His gaze travelled over the cable ties at her wrists and ankles, the washing line cord strapping her torso to the chair. Her little whore mouth forced open by his dental gag. The same gag that'd propped open the mouths of those other bitches. The Taser probes, embedded in her stomach, ready to shock her into total submission if she tried to resist. She'd screamed, of course, but after realising that no one could hear her, and no one was coming to save her, she'd stopped. Now, he could take his time.

This was going to be special.

He had his back to the door, which he'd shut and locked from the inside. Behind her, in the opposite wall, was a window. He'd covered it with a blackout blind for extra privacy, although no one ever really came around here. That was why he'd chosen this location in the first place. All he could hear was distant traffic.

And even that was half-drowned out by the noise of his breathing as his excitement rose.

He plucked a small box off the side table and opened it. Within, nestled in the black velvet, the engagement ring glinted under the bare lightbulbs suspended overhead.

He stepped forward in front of the lamp he had pointed in her face.

She looked up at him, incredulous, tears streaming down her cheeks.

'We're engaged, now,' he told her, placing the ring on her finger.

She shook her head, eyes pleading with him. 'Why?' she asked, the word barely discernible through the gag in her mouth. Seeing her reduced to this, he felt a nanosecond of empathy. After all, he knew her well.

But there was no room for mercy.

The *Throat Ripper* couldn't stop now.

# CHAPTER FIFTY-NINE

The engine of Lockhart's Defender roared as he put his foot down and overtook a car. He just had time to swerve back in as a motorbike sped towards him. Working the steering wheel hard right and then left, he slalomed between a pair of tightly parked vehicles in the residential street. On a straight stretch, he tapped out of Maps, selected Smith's number and called her.

'We're on our way, guv,' she said immediately.

'How long?'

'Ten minutes, maybe,' replied Smith.

'I'll be there in five,' he stated.

'Received.'

'You driving?'

'Yeah.'

'OK. Tell Mo to call in some backup. Local units, on the hurry up. And get a paramedic on standby.'

'Guv.'

'One more thing,' said Lockhart. Then he told her who they expected to find at the address.

'Jesus Christ,' she exclaimed.

He rang off and went back into Maps to check his route. Up ahead, he could see the traffic was stalled. He craned his neck. It looked like roadworks. Shit.

Lockhart braked hard, then threw the Defender in reverse and, turning in his seat, backed up to the sound of blaring horns as cars stopped and skidded to a halt behind him. He spun the wheel and his tyres screamed as he took the side street to box around the blockage.

His pulse was thumping in his neck as he accelerated again, moving up through the gears.

He wasn't going to let this bastard murder another woman.

And he damned well wasn't going to lose Lexi Green.

\*

Lexi was trying to relax, trying to use her brain. But it wasn't working. At all. After everything she'd read, seen and heard about this killer, she couldn't process the fact that she was here with him now. It was as if her mind had been overwhelmed with the physical pain of electrocution and her body had just shut down. She must've blacked out, because the last thing she remembered was the cat claws in her leg, the vibration scorching through her body, and falling. Then nothing, until she woke up here. She couldn't see her abductor, because a lamp was shining right in her face, but she could hear him moving behind it.

From what little she could see, she was in a dirty room that looked like a garage, strapped to a chair. She'd tried wriggling and shifting every part of her body, but it was useless. Her wrists and ankles were bound hard by sharp plastic that cut into her skin when she moved. She'd also been tied to the chair with a tight cord that dug into her ribs, barely giving her room to breathe. The chair itself was rock solid, like it'd been bolted to the concrete floor. Two wires ran from her belly to the ground and into the darkness behind the lamp. She knew what they were.

Then there was the pain in her face. It felt as if a fist-sized piece of metal had been stuffed between her teeth, rendering her all but speechless. Not that there was much point making noise. After Lexi had come to, she'd screamed, like a reflex. But Priapus – or whoever he was – had obviously planned for that, and there was no one around to hear her. Instead, she'd gotten another jolt of electricity through those wires and, going by the wetness and smell, she'd peed in her pants.

People always told her she was smart. But right now, Lexi couldn't have felt dumber. The meeting was a set-up and she'd taken it too lightly. What'd happened to Liam? Was he OK? Worst of all, she hadn't told Dan or anyone else where they were going. No one knew she was here. The hopelessness of her situation enveloped her, and she started to cry.

That was when the guy stepped in front of the light, partially blocking it. Blinking away tears as her eyes adjusted, she knew exactly who he was. She couldn't quite believe it. But, as she tried to make sense of it, she realised he was holding something out to her. It was a ring. The ring whose damage she'd seen in a bunch of crime scene photos.

Grabbing the third finger of her left hand, he jammed the ring on, twisting and pushing until the skin was cut and she felt blood ooze beneath it.

'We're engaged, now,' he said with a smile.

Lexi knew what came next. She felt the terror rising from her belly and taking over her body. It seemed as if there was no point even resisting. One part of her brain told her just to get it over with, a quick end.

Then another part of her mind kicked in. A self-preservation instinct. *Come on, Lexi.* She had to do something, try to stall him and maybe think of an escape strategy. Anything. She wasn't going out like this. Hell, no. She had to get him talking.

'Where's Liam?' she managed to ask.

'What?'

'Liam. My friend. Where is he?' Every word was an effort through the dental gag.

'Oh.' He smirked. 'Don't worry about him.'

'Did you hurt him?'

'He tried to stop me getting to you.'

'No!' Lexi couldn't bear it. If anything had happened to Liam because of her, she wouldn't be able to live with herself. 'What did you… do to him, you piece of shit?'

'Hey! Watch how you talk to me.' The man gazed at the ring on her finger. 'You liked him, didn't you?' he said eventually. 'Although maybe not as much as you like that detective.'

*Liked.* Not like. Did that mean what Lexi thought it meant? Was Liam dead? Dear God, please no. She started to cry again but, once more, her survival instinct took over. Whatever he'd done to Liam, there was nothing Lexi could change about that now. The best thing she could do was buy herself time to find a way out of here. *Keep talking.*

'Why?' She sniffed, eyes wet. 'Why all of this?'

He stood still. He seemed to be thinking. She saw something like anger flash across his features, just for a second.

'Why?' he repeated. 'But, surely you already know that, Doctor?'

'I know… I'm expert power.' The words were barely coherent.

'Clever girl.' He smirked. 'Very good.'

'I want you to… tell me,' she gasped, 'your story.'

'*My* story, hm.' He cocked his head, studying her. Then he held up a finger. 'I've got an idea. Why don't you tell me why I'm like this? Why I do this. Since you have all the answers.'

'I can't…' She glanced down. 'With—'

Walking over to her, he reached around the back of her head and roughly loosened the gag, leaving it hanging at her neck. She tried to work the numbness out of her lips and jaws, closing her eyes briefly as the sensation started to return.

'You've got two minutes to give me your professional opinion,' he said flatly, walking back behind the lamp. He moved something, and she heard the clinking of metal on metal. 'I want to know what's wrong with me. Deep down.'

'Uh, OK, sure,' she said, trying to stay calm. She had two more minutes to live. But her fight-or-flight response had kicked in as soon as she'd woken up again and the adrenalin was still well and truly in control of her system. Her mind was racing and, despite all her theories and time spent studying this man, she didn't know what to say.

'One minute fifty,' he whispered.

# CHAPTER SIXTY

Lockhart killed the lights as he turned into the side road. It snaked around two corners before he spotted the lock-up units, about a hundred yards further on. A row of large, square metal doors beneath a long, flat roof. He pulled up and switched off the engine. He could see a plain white van parked by the garages, but there were no other signs of life. Another burst of adrenalin shot through him, rippling from his stomach to his limbs.

Stepping down from the Defender, Lockhart put his phone on silent. He might miss a call from Smith or Khan, but he couldn't risk a ringtone giving him away. They'd just have to find him when they got here. He ran lightly over to the garages, trying to make as little sound as possible. Numbers were painted on the doors and when he found the one marked 12 – as Smith had told him – he paused outside, listening. At first, all he could hear was the blood throbbing in his temples. He slowed his breathing, tried to focus.

Then he heard her.

There was no mistaking Lexi Green's accent and intonation, coming from behind the door. Her voice was somehow soothing, and it reminded Lockhart of their therapy sessions. She sounded calm, but he knew she'd be fighting the panic. And every second she could keep the killer talking was another second for him to get inside. He assessed the door; it was one that swung up and slid in parallel to the ceiling.

Crouching, he carefully tried the handle close to the ground. Locked.

He thought about taking out his Leatherman multi-tool and trying to pick or jimmy the mechanism, but it risked alerting Green's captor. He needed surprise on his side. And he knew he didn't have much time.

Lockhart crept back a few paces to take in the whole structure. Behind it, he noticed some trees. Their trunks were set back from the rear wall, which meant there was a stand-off. And, therefore, possibly another way in.

*

'It isn't your fault,' said Lexi, mustering every ounce of empathy, though she didn't really believe what she was saying. 'It's the way the world has treated you.'

He came towards her slowly, and the lamplight glinted off the metal ball in his hand. 'You've got one minute left.'

For the first thirty seconds or more, she'd just babbled about trauma while thoughts of Liam and Dan popped into her mind. But now she was getting into her stride, hoping some of her words would hit home and give her more time.

'Maybe you suffered when you were growing up,' she continued, recalling her profile. 'You might've witnessed some violence… perhaps even at home?'

He blinked. 'Go on.'

'That's really tough for a young person. It normalises acting that way towards others, makes it seem easy or OK. And, when you're young, you can't do a whole lot to stop an adult. So, using violence later on becomes a way to restore how you see yourself, as a strong person.'

'I *am* strong.'

'I know you are. But those experiences can leave a trace on anyone for a long time. Your personality grows and develops around all that like a hard shell, to protect you.' Lexi paused. 'Maybe you even think there's something bad inside you. But there isn't.' She tried to make eye contact with him, but it was as if he was looking through her.

'It's not your fault,' she said again.

'It's *her* fault.' His voice caught slightly. 'I was OK until she came along.'

'I know you suddenly lost someone you loved a lot,' she went on, trying to decode his body language. He seemed to be relaxing slightly, though his fist was tight around the metal ball he still held.

Lexi briefly thought of her brother, Shep. If she moved her hips slightly, she could feel Shep's pen in her pocket, where she always kept it. Carrying a memory of him with her.

'And I know what that's like,' she added.

'Do you?' Something flared in his eyes and Lexi thought maybe she'd gone too far. 'Are you talking about your flatmate?'

'No, not Liam.' Lexi pushed away the thought of what'd happened to him. 'My brother killed himself. OK, maybe it's not what happened to you. But I do know about loss, and I know it hurts. You feel angry, you wanna attack someone, anyone who was responsible. Or who you think represents… her.'

'All of you are like her. You bitches are all the same,' he growled.

'I can see how you could think that,' she said gently. 'But we're not. I promise.'

'You're lying.'

'I swear.' Lexi swallowed, searching his face. 'You don't have to believe what those guys tell you on the websites.'

His shoulders tensed. 'Those men are my brothers.'

'It might seem that way, but they're not. They're just full of hate. Life doesn't have to be like that,' she said quickly. 'Whatever they want you to do, you can choose not to do it.'

His eyes narrowed. 'You're trying to trick me, aren't you? Like you tried to trick me online.' He stuffed the ball into his pocket and took two strides towards her. 'Slut!'

'No, wait!' she yelled. 'Please!'

But he was already grabbing the mouth gag. She tried to twist her head, clamp her teeth shut. He drew his fist back and delivered one punch to her solar plexus. The air went from her lungs and she gasped. Then the gag was back in her mouth, pressing hard against her teeth. And he was on top of her, pulling the buckle tight behind her neck. He stood up and backed away.

She knew what was coming, now. She'd seen the crime scene photos, imagined the victims' final moments over and over. Her breathing became quick and shallow as she saw him pick something up from the side table. He marched towards her, a thick spanner in one hand, steel ball in the other.

And Lexi knew there was no escape.

*

'We must be close.' Smith checked her mirrors. 'Where next?'

'Left up here, then the road goes right and left again,' said Khan, holding the phone in front of him. 'Looks like the garages are at the end.'

Smith took the turn. They'd switched off the blues and twos a minute ago to avoid signalling their arrival. The radio bleeped and crackled to say their backup was five minutes away. Smith acknowledged the message and brought the car gradually to a halt as the lock-ups came into view. Khan turned the radio down.

She could see Lockhart's old, dark green Land Rover parked nearby – apparently empty – and a white van up ahead.

'Where's the boss?' asked Khan.

'No idea.' Smith squinted into the darkness ahead. She took out her mobile and tried calling Lockhart, but he didn't pick up. She swore and pocketed the phone.

Khan turned to her. 'What do we do, Max?'

Smith undid her seatbelt. 'We go in.'

# CHAPTER SIXTY-ONE

Lockhart followed the path around the garages and discovered a narrow strip of concrete running behind them. There was no lighting at the back, but he could make out a window in the rear wall of each unit, about four feet off the ground. Probably a fire escape requirement, since they were big enough for a person to get out, although several of the garages had their windows boarded up.

He counted along until he reached the right one. The window was blacked out. He stopped next to it and held his breath, checking for confirmation from inside, but there was only silence. He counted the units again. This was definitely the one.

Without warning, a memory came to him of standing outside another building whose windows were covered. For a moment, he froze, the panic building in his chest as he felt the hot, dry desert air on his skin, tasted its sand and grit in his mouth once more. He wrenched his mind back to the present. It was time to get inside.

Lockhart took off his jacket and wrapped it around his left forearm.

Then, holding the Leatherman in his right fist, he took aim and smashed it into the middle of the window. The glass shattered, and large pieces of it dropped in. He punched at the rest of it, throwing his jacket over the shards that lay in the wooden frame and hauling himself up and inside. He fell through, his shoulder smacking into the floor as he landed on broken glass. Ignoring the pain, Lockhart scrambled to his feet as he heard the garage door sliding up.

In front of him, facing the door, Green was tied to a chair, her body bucking and spasming. She was completely silent.

Choking.

Beyond her, lifting the garage door, stood a figure. Though he was in the shadows behind a lamp, Lockhart recognised him. Just as he'd done when Suzy showed him the photograph of Mr Priapus from the night that Kim Hardy had been murdered. There was no mistaking the ruddy cheeks and aquiline nose of theatre manager Will Jacobson.

He spun to face Lockhart. He was breathing hard, but there was a malevolent grin on his face.

'You've got to choose, Dan,' said Jacobson. 'Me or her.' Then he sprinted out into the night.

It was no contest. Lockhart ran to Green and knelt beside her. Her skin had a blueish tinge. She briefly focussed on him, then her eyes glazed over again. He needed to act fast. But he had to stop her moving, calm her as much as he could. He wrapped his arms around her and, just for a few seconds, held her close.

'It's alright, Lexi,' he whispered. 'I'm here.'

Then he drew back and pulled the lamp across to see inside her mouth. He could just make out the metal at the top of her throat. He remembered Dr Volz's words at Natasha's post-mortem: *she would've required surgery to get it out.* He thought of his battlefield medical training. Then the idea came to him. He'd heard about the emergency operation being done successfully, in Afghanistan, once. It was risky, but there was no other option if he wanted to save Green's life. He had to open her windpipe.

Outside, an engine caught and revved hard.

Lockhart folded the knife blade out from his Leatherman.

Green looked at him, but he registered nothing in her face. She was losing consciousness, her skin already bluer than a moment ago. He knew her oxygen levels were running out and, if he couldn't get some air into her lungs, she'd be dead in less than a minute. There wasn't enough time to cut her bindings and lay her on the ground. He had to go straight for her neck.

'Keep your head back,' he told her. 'This is going to hurt a bit. Hold still, OK?'

*

When the garage door had slid up, Smith and Khan began running. Will Jacobson had reached his white van and started the engine by the time they got to him. Smith sprinted to the driver's side as the white reversing lights came on and Jacobson threw the van backwards, hitting Khan and knocking him sideways. She saw him spin and drop.

Fury spiked within her and, as Jacobson shifted gear to drive away, Smith grabbed the handle of his door and yanked it open. She just had time to grip the internal handle with her right hand as Jacobson pulled away hard, dragging her with him as he drove with the door open.

Her legs were scraping along the tarmac, burning, but she clung on. Jacobson tried to kick at her, but as he lifted his foot off the accelerator the van slowed. Smith took the chance to throw her left arm out, grabbing the leather belt around his waist. She held tight to it with her two fingers and thumb, pain coursing through her hands and feet. The image of Dean Waters falling flashed into her mind. She wasn't letting Jacobson get away from her.

He hit the gas again and Smith knew she couldn't hold on much longer.

Gritting her teeth, she flung her right hand out and caught a fistful of Jacobson's jacket as she fell backwards from the door, pulling him out of the van. Smith howled at the impact as he landed on top of her and the momentum took them rolling across the tarmac. He tried to stand but she wrapped her legs around his and twisted her hips, forcing him back down.

Then Khan was beside her, locking Jacobson's arms and, together, they pinned him to the ground. When Jacobson was cuffed, face down, Khan controlling him with a knee to his back, Smith stood. She was shaking. The endorphins were stopping her feeling the pain she knew would come later. Walking across to where the van had ploughed into the undergrowth beside the track and come to rest, she popped the rear doors and peered in.

There was a man in the back.

He wasn't moving.

*

Lexi was losing it. She knew that much. The panic had gone, now, and her vision was darkening. It'd be easy to let go and just slip into oblivion. No more pain. Patients she'd worked with – old people or those with severe, chronic pain – had sometimes talked about death as a relief, but she never thought she'd feel that way. She'd never truly understood what they meant, until now. Lexi could see the end, and part of her wanted to reach out to it, to embrace it and go where Shep had gone. Liam was probably dead and that was her fault. Maybe she deserved to join them both in that beautiful calmness on the other side...

She was dimly aware of Dan kneeling beside her, of his instruction to keep her head up. She wanted to do that, but it was so hard. She had no energy left.

Lexi felt his hand pat her left leg near her waist, then the right. He worked his fingers inside the right pocket of her jeans and pulled out her pen. The one Shep had given her.

Shep.

A picture flashed into her mind of the two of them as kids. They were sitting next to each other on an aeroplane, holding hands as they took off to return to the States from England. Both a little scared, but there for each other.

Lexi knew she couldn't give up. She owed it to Shep to keep fighting for her life. She owed it to Liam. And she owed it to Dan, who was trying to save her, right here, right now.

Her head felt as heavy as a kettlebell. But she strained with every fibre to hold it high.

*

Lockhart took the Montblanc pen he'd extracted from Green's pocket, unscrewed the top and pulled out the ink cartridge to leave the barrel of the pen empty. A hollow, rigid tube about three inches long. Clamping it between his teeth, he picked up the Leatherman, its knife blade extended, and held it in his right hand.

The fingertips of his left hand worked up Green's throat, feeling for the notch on her windpipe that he knew was the cricoid cartilage. Just above that, under her skin, was a tissue called the cricoid membrane. It was the only place where the trachea wasn't covered with solid bone or cartilage. That was where he needed to make the incision. There was no room for error. He drew the blade lightly across as a practice run. Remembered how calm Green had been in the hospital reception two months ago when she had the knife to her neck. She was just as still now.

Outside, there was a squeal of tyres and shouting. Lockhart stayed focussed on Green. He took a breath. Then, slow and steady, he made the first cut, followed by another just behind it. A second later, the blood began to run.

Green was virtually passed out and the pain must've been unbearable for her. Somehow, she was still managing to keep her head back. Lockhart used his left hand to keep the skin open while he took the pen barrel out from between his teeth and pushed it gently through the incision, into her trachea.

There was a moment's silence.

Then he heard the sound of air being sucked in and saw her chest rise as her lungs filled. She took quick, shallow breaths and he could feel the air being blown out of the barrel. He stayed kneeling next to her, holding the barrel in her throat, keeping her chin up and watching her skin gradually return to its normal colour as the oxygen flowed through her system and her breathing slowed to a regular rate. He pressed his fingers to the wound to stem the blood; it looked bad, but he knew it was only minor blood vessels that would soon clot. If they could get her to the emergency ward soon, she'd make it.

Green blinked rapidly, her eyes rolling. She looked at him, expressionless. He nodded.

'You're going to be OK,' he said.

The wail of a siren rose in the distance, getting nearer.

As Lockhart held her, she shut her eyes and began to shake silently. Tears of relief ran down her cheeks.

And she breathed.

# CHAPTER SIXTY-TWO

Lexi opened her eyes. At first, she thought she was still asleep, and that the hospital ward was part of a dream. But, a second later, she remembered why she was here. At least she didn't have that intubation tube down her throat any more. The doctors had put it there to make sure she could breathe properly with all the swelling in her neck. Now, three days later, the inflammation had reduced, and they'd taken the tube out.

She reached up to her throat and touched the wiry stitches closing the wound that'd saved her life. Picturing the knife going in, even feeling it again, she grimaced and screwed her eyes shut. It was going to take a little while to get over that. The physical pain would be gone pretty soon. Her memory of the garage, on the other hand, would stay with her much longer.

She had survived that night, but Liam hadn't been so lucky. Lexi held herself responsible for his death; against Dan's advice, she was the one who had dragged Liam out to meet Priapus. Now Liam was gone. It was almost all she'd thought about since she'd been here. That, and how Dan had saved her.

At the sound of footsteps, she opened her eyes again. Dan was walking across the ward, holding a cardboard cup. The sight of him made her feel a little less awful.

'Hey,' she croaked, shuffling to be more upright in the bed.

'You're awake,' he said. 'I would've got you a coffee if I'd known.' He raised the cup. 'But I don't think they'd let you have it. I mean, I could try pouring it in the tube if you want…'

'No thanks,' she just about managed a smile. Dan had done a great job of trying to keep her spirits up the past couple days. Gallows humour, they called it. Lexi was starting to see why it was necessary in his line of work. 'Should only be a couple more days until I get to have hot food and drinks,' she added.

Dan took a sip and pulled a face. 'You're not missing much, to be honest.' He shifted a chair next to her bed and sat down. 'Nurses just said you'll probably be able to go home tomorrow,' he told her.

'Really?'

'Yup. But they don't know how much longer your voice is going to sound like Darth Vader. It could be permanent.'

She breathed a laugh and felt a stab of pain in her throat. 'Ah, jeez,' she winced.

'Has Sarah come by again today?' asked Dan.

'Yeah, this morning,' Lexi replied. 'She was trying to cheer me up. But she's totally broken herself, and that's my fault, too.'

'No, it's not.' Dan stared into his coffee. 'I'm so sorry about Liam. But you didn't kill him.' He paused, looked up at her. 'We got the pathologist's report earlier from Dr Volz. Liam died from cardiac arrest after Jacobson tasered him in the chest. It's rare, but it happens. He would've passed away while unconscious.'

'That doesn't make it any easier. I mean, he shouldn't even have been there. If only I'd listened—'

'Hey. You can't go down that road. You of all people should understand that. No "shoulds" or "if onlys" or "what ifs".' He placed his hand in hers, and she squeezed it. They stayed like that for a few moments before letting go of one another.

Dan took another swig of coffee, scanning the room. Apparently satisfied that no one was too close to them, he lowered his voice a little. 'Crown Prosecution Service says we've got a strong case to charge Jacobson with at least one murder, as well as attempted murder, and a count of manslaughter.'

'That's good, I guess.'

'Damned right it is, because he'll get what he deserves. And, most importantly, he's not out there, trying to kill anyone else. In fact, he's talking to us. Seems like he's even enjoying the recognition.'

'The guy's a narcissist,' replied Lexi. 'He wanted everyone to know what he'd done, to be a hero to those douchebags on the misogynist websites.' She'd had plenty of time to consider this, lying here in hospital. 'It was a way of restoring his ego after the trauma of his break up. But he couldn't take credit for it without revealing his identity. That's why he hid behind the name Priapus and claimed he knew the killer.'

'You were right about the alias,' he said. 'I should've paid more attention to your profile earlier. It was bang on. So was your idea of going online. If I'd taken it seriously, maybe got some surveillance, then we could've…' he tailed off, glancing at her neck.

'What did you just tell me?' Lexi coughed and swallowed painfully. 'No "shoulds" or "ifs", right?'

'Yeah,' he sighed. She knew this case had taken its toll on him, too. 'Guess we can't help it.' Dan shrugged.

'That's normal.' She touched the stiches on her neck again and met his eyes. 'Thank you. I wouldn't be here without you.'

He acknowledged her with a tiny nod. 'The evidence against Jacobson is so solid, his lawyer may just advise him to plead guilty,' he continued. 'We've got the photo from Kim Hardy's friend, Suzy. That means we can put Jacobson in the hotel room with Kim just before she died. Max Smith also has a picture of the hotel guest book, and we've matched Jacobson's handwriting to an entry on the night of her murder. No matter how much DCI Flynn and Newham MIT hate me now, even they couldn't ignore that. They've released Damon Pagett.'

'Awesome.'

'Then there's Jacobson's attempt to frame Paul Dixon.'

'He probably hated Dixon because of what he represented,' offered Lexi. 'The alpha male physique, the machismo.'

'Reckon so. He hasn't admitted it yet, but we can see how he could've taken the fibre sample from Dixon's jacket at the theatre talk, as well as the tissue Dixon used. Giving himself evidence to plant at the crime scenes later. A jury would see that as premeditation.'

Lexi held up her left hand and inspected it. There were still some small scabbed-over cuts and bruises to her third finger. 'What about the ring?' she asked.

'We showed the jeweller, Michael Litman, the images of it. He's confident he modified it himself, but he didn't recognise the photo of Jacobson when we showed him previously. Turns out Jacobson had got his assistant, Yannis Dimitriou, to get the ring done for him. Dimitriou told us that Jacobson said he wanted to give the ring to his mum instead, but he was too embarrassed to take it to Litman after his girlfriend broke up with him.'

'More premeditation,' said Lexi.

'Exactly. He'd thought the whole thing through carefully. He only made a couple of mistakes. One was that he used the alias Mr Priapus when he was buying his restraining equipment online. Thanks to your online research, we identified his lock-up garage through the name. The other was leaving his DNA at the scene of Sophie Wright's murder. He usually cleaned up after his attacks, but he missed that. Jacobson got away with that at the time, though, because we were focussed elsewhere. And, when his alibi checked out, we never got the DNA swab from him. Now we have it, we've confirmed it's his.' Dan shook his head. 'I should've pushed it more.'

'No "shoulds".'

'Sorry.'

'Guess you can't investigate everything, huh?'

He sighed. 'True.'

Lexi frowned. 'What do you mean, Jacobson's alibi checked out?'

'It was for Elena's murder. He claimed he was in the pub with a friend. And it was true. Except the drink was a set-up. Jacobson's friend was cheating on his wife and arranged "drinks" with Jacobson as an alibi of his own whenever he was seeing his lover. They'd have one in the pub and then both leave. Bar staff confirmed they were there.'

Lexi processed this. 'So, Jacobson made use of the same alibi, knowing his friend would always back him up. And he chose one of those nights to murder Elena.'

'Right. The fact is, Jacobson was barely even a person of interest in our case. He was there, the whole time. I just didn't see it.'

'You got him, though.'

'*We* got him.'

Lexi sat up and poured herself a cup of water from the jug by her bed. They sat drinking in silence for a moment.

'There was no sign of my wife, either,' Dan said, eventually. He was twisting the wedding band on his finger.

'Oh. I'm sorry.'

'Yeah. Suzy hadn't seen her, and no one else had, either. I thought it was just a mistake. But, when the computer guys got Jacobson's laptop, they found it was him who'd posted about the sighting of her.'

'He was screwing with you?'

'Looks like it. He'd probably done his research, knew that Kim had been a witness on one of my cases. She and I were both named in the papers at the time. And there's stuff online from years ago about Jess going missing that quotes me as her husband, appealing for help.'

'Jeez, that's horrible. What an asshole. Sorry.'

Dan looked at her, his eyes wet. 'Why would he do that?'

She thought about it. 'I don't know. Maybe he was trying to distract you from investigating her death. Or maybe you just represent the hero figure he wished he was but could never be.'

'Hero?'

'Uh, yeah.' She said the word as if it was obvious.

They fell into silence again for a while.

'I was thinking,' said Dan.

'Yeah?'

'Maybe we shouldn't go on with the therapy.'

'Oh, OK.' Lexi felt suddenly deflated. If there was one thing she'd been looking forward to, it was resuming her sessions with Dan. But her disappointment now made her question the reason for that anticipation. Was it really about the treatment? Or did she just want to keep seeing *him*? Again, Lexi found herself unable to answer.

'I mean, I want to,' he continued. 'And I need it. But... after everything that's happened.'

She tilted her head. 'It might be a little weird. I know what you mean.'

'Is that all right?' he asked.

'Sure. I can recommend another therapist.'

'As long as it's not Rob Edwards.' He grinned.

She chuckled and got a bolt of pain in her neck. 'Dammit. I can't even laugh.'

'You will. Soon enough.' Dan met her gaze and she felt the warmth in his expression. And something else, too. Hope.

He checked his watch. 'I need to get back to Putney,' he said. 'You wouldn't believe how much paperwork there is on a case like this.'

'If it's half as bad as hospital bureaucracy, you have my sympathy.'

He paused. 'One thing I never asked you, though.'

'What's that?'

'That day, a couple of months ago. When I came into the clinic and the old guy had a knife at your neck.'

'Oh, that.' She closed her eyes again, briefly.

'How did you know how to take the blade off him?'

She shrugged. 'I took a few self-defence classes a while back. After…' she swallowed, 'a man…' What should she tell him? 'Attacked me.'

'My god.' Dan's eyes widened. 'Were you OK?'

'Just about. But, after that, I wanted to be able to protect myself.' She shook her head. 'For all the good it did me the other night.'

He stood to leave. 'You kept yourself alive in there.'

'I just felt so powerless.' She could feel her lip curling, her eyes moistening. 'So weak.'

'You're not weak, Lexi.' Dan took her hand and held it. 'You're one of the strongest people I know.' He let go gently and smiled. 'I'll see you soon.'

\*

Lockhart knew it was time to leave the office. He was alone in the MIT 8 room, the dent in his admin task list barely noticeable after a whole day slogging away at it. His back ached and his eyes hurt, and his legs were stiff from sitting. A pile of handwritten documents and files lay to one side of the computer whose monitor displayed the latest electronic note he'd logged. There was a ton of evidence to collate ahead of presenting their case to the CPS for Jacobson's prosecution. Putting it together would be weeks of work. Enough for one day, he concluded, stretching and yawning loudly. Time for a Stella.

As he shut down the Met's record system, he automatically refreshed the missing persons website he had running in parallel, as usual. Force of habit, he supposed. Finger resting on the mouse button, cursor hovering over the cross top-right ready to close it, he glanced at the screen. Stopped. Blinked. Scrolled up and down to check he was on the right page, then read it again, his heart racing.

A new message had just been posted on the thread he'd started three months ago, about Jess.

*I recognise your wife. And I think I've seen her.*

# EPILOGUE

Robert James Williams, better known as RJ to the few people who gave a shit about him, stared at the laptop screen. He could barely believe what'd just happened. A direct message had landed in his Twitter inbox. And it was from a guy who, over the last couple months – since his girlfriend had broken up with him – had become like a brother. No, not a brother. More like a *father*. A father who was actually there for him.

RJ had read everything this man had written, watched all his videos on YouTube, liked and commented on every one of his social media posts. This was a dude who had *answers*. Who understood what life was all about. RJ wished he could literally just download this guy's knowledge into his own brain. Right now, he was trying to absorb every little piece of wisdom. And it was helping him get his confidence back.

The confidence she'd destroyed.

He'd thought Melissa was the one. He was ready to commit. He'd secretly bought the two of them plane tickets to go travelling together in Europe over spring break. Then, just before Thanksgiving, she'd come over to his college dorm room and ended it. In front of his roommate. RJ wasn't only heartbroken. He was humiliated.

Everyone had talked about it on campus for weeks, saying what a loser he must be. A rumour had started about him having a really small dick. Other girls didn't want to date him. It was like he'd been ostracised. He didn't even know what he'd done to cause it, where it'd gone wrong. A week later, Melissa was already dating some dude from the basketball team who was six foot six and ripped.

The whole thing had left RJ depressed. He missed classes, spending more and more time in his room, online. Feeding the anger that blazed inside him like a Californian wildfire. Looking for salvation, inspiration. Anything that'd help him feel better. And, in this man's philosophy, he'd found it. Now, a direct message from the guy was validation of his loyalty.

With trembling fingers, RJ clicked into the message. Blinking, he read the opening line:

*I have a truth for you, young man.*

This was incredible. It'd been written to him and him alone. A *private* message. Personal. He read on:

*Women do not care about you. They only care about themselves. The sooner you understand that, the better.*

He understood that, all right. He'd read the guy's book. There was science behind it. It was biological, evolutionary. RJ didn't want to be a passive victim of natural selection. He'd learned that the system was now run by women, ever since they could choose who they mated with. He was sick of it. And he wanted to do something about it. As he read the next line, he knew that he had the chance. He'd been chosen.

RJ shivered with excitement as he re-read the call to action:

*Now it's time to take that power back.*

# A LETTER FROM CHRIS

Dear Reader,

First and foremost, thank you for buying *Knock Knock*, the first book in the Lockhart and Green series. I hope you enjoyed it. If you did, please leave a rating and review.

If you're interested to know more about the books, please join my mailing list. Your email address will never be shared, and you can unsubscribe from the updates at any time.

*www.bookouture.com/chris-merritt*

For anyone who has read my Detective Zac Boateng series, the switch of setting from Lewisham to Dan Lockhart's office in Putney might seem a short journey across London. But creating *Knock Knock* was quite a change from the guns, organised crime and police corruption of Zac Boateng's world.

Writing a serial killer thriller was a challenge. It's been done so many times before (both well and badly) that it would be easy to slip into cliché. However, when I happened to read an article about online misogyny in late 2018, in a newspaper someone had left on a train, an idea started to form for an original take on the traditional plot.

I read extensively about online misogynists and the subculture of incels. While the movement started out as a virtual community for people to share experiences of dating failures and loneliness, it quickly became overtaken by a violent, vitriolic kind of hate speech against women. Some incels maintain the early ethos of frustrated romantic aspirations, but they seem to be a minority. Hiding behind aliases and avatars, the majority discuss every conceivable way to denigrate, manipulate and attack women. The topics Lexi Green finds on the web forums are all genuine. And the mass murders by incels mentioned in the book are, unfortunately, real.

Hearing stories about the radicalisation of romantically disillusioned men and seeing the growing influence of prominent misogynists, masquerading as life coaches and self-help gurus, made me want to explore these issues in a novel. Through the prisms of Dan Lockhart's policework and Lexi Green's psychological profiling, I attempted to break down the mindset of someone who would carry out an act of violence against women in the name of 'men'.

Clearly, there are people out there who need help, including the kind of therapy that Lexi Green could offer. Hopefully, reading about the subject will highlight how someone could be drawn into this sad, angry world, as well as the devastating effect its violence can have on victims and their loved ones. The more educated we are about this problem, the better we can act to address it.

Thanks again for your support. If you'd like to get in touch, please drop me a line on Twitter or via my website. The sequel to *Knock Knock*, also featuring Dan Lockhart and Lexi Green, is released in July 2020.

Best wishes,
Chris

@DrCJMerritt

www.cjmerritt.co.uk

# ACKNOWLEDGEMENTS

Firstly, I'd like to thank my agent, Charlie Viney, and my editor at Bookouture, Helen Jenner, for their advice in helping to develop and shape this new series. Helen's editorial input greatly enhanced the story, as did the contributions of Janette Currie and Natasha Hodgson, who spotted all the mistakes I'd deliberately inserted to keep them on their toes. Others in the Bookouture team did a fantastic job as usual: Peta Nightingale, Noelle Holten, Kim Nash, Alex Crow and Emily Gowers.

For the plot details, I owe huge thanks to those people who gave their time and expertise to explain things to me. DC Ellie Lawrence told me what it's like to be a detective, while Amy Gorman again described the work of a police analyst to me. Lynn von Koch-Liebert, Stacy Kangisser and Shelby Fields all shared their experiences of being an American in London, which helped round out the character of Dr Lexi Green. Jerry Kraus gave some tips on the CrossFit training Lexi would be doing, while Matt Buckley's account of open water swimming was enough to put me off trying it… for the winter, at least.

'The Major' supplied some details on military terminology and Dan Lockhart's old army unit. Clinical psychologist Dr Clair Killikelly at University of Zurich informed me about Prolonged Grief Disorder, the condition which Lockhart is suffering alongside his other traumatic stress symptoms. Criminal barrister Kieran Moroney explained the custody system over more than one pint at the Brockley Brewery. Drs Becky Dudill and Charlotte Trainer dispensed the unpleasant but essential medical knowledge about what happens to a person's body when they're choked; any inaccuracies in physical symptoms are mine.

Frank Tallis, Mark Billingham and Charles Cumming generously offered advice and informal mentoring on building a writing career and starting a new series, which was very much appreciated as I embarked on the Lockhart and Green project towards the end of 2018.

Finally, I want to thank my family and friends for their support to my books. It means so much to know you're there.

# FURTHER READING

For those interested in the realities of a murder investigation, I would thoroughly recommend *Manhunt* by retired DCI Colin Sutton. The story tracks his team's meticulous and, fortunately, successful pursuit of serial killer Levi Bellfield from crime scene to courtroom. Equally captivating is *On the Line* by Alice Vinten, a brilliant collection of human stories from everyday policing in London. These two books provided plenty of background detail on the Met, which I hope I've been able to capture in Dan Lockhart's world.

Two academic papers were crucial in devising the emergency medical operation which takes place at the end of the story. The first is by David Owens et al. (2009), who conducted an admirably niche study of which pen is most effective for creating a temporary tracheostomy tube. In the second, Christian Braun et al. (2017) ran a somewhat grizzly experiment in which volunteers were asked to use a knife, a pen and a real corpse to perform the surgery that Dan carries out to save Lexi's life (known as a cricothyroidotomy or 'crick'). Unbelievably, one person in their study managed it successfully with a Montblanc pen in ninety seconds. I like to imagine Dan could do it even faster.

Printed in Great Britain
by Amazon